Fireworks in the morning

J M HALL

ISBN 978-0-9568705-0-6

Cover design by Clare Brayshaw

Prepared and printed by:

York Publishing Services Ltd
64 Hallfield Road
Layerthorpe
York
YO31 7ZQ

Tel: 01904 431213

www.yps-publishing.co.uk

For Alex

Acknowledgements

First, my sincere thanks to my Catalan friend, artist and writer, Gonçal Sobrer, for his generous advice. Any mistakes are my own.

Also, to Peter Hartas (MBA) for his help with the mysteries of my computer.

And my husband, Ray for his patience and encouragement.

Chapter 1

Barcelona 1938

The sudden silence was eerie, but short-lived. The gunfire started again, echoing between the tall buildings, mingling with the screams of a terrified child and the excited yapping of a dog. Elizabeth hurried through the pale wintry shadows, darting across the uneven setts of the road to take refuge in the entrance of an empty hotel, its cracked windows plastered with gaudy political posters, the marble floor littered with paper and broken glass. But as she became more accustomed to the continual rattle of gunfire, there came a strange new sound and it was a moment before she recognised the clatter of galloping hooves. Fearing who the rider may be, she drew back, pressing herself against the boarded up door.

A rider-less horse came into view, with reins and stirrup irons flapping wildly. Crashing and slithering on the hard paving, it veered round a tree but lost its footing and fell heavily to the ground. For a moment it lay still, and then with flailing hooves it struggled to get back to its feet, flanks heaving as it fought for breath.

With a cry of consternation she immediately ran toward the steaming animal, careful to avoid the frantic thrust of hooves as it rolled and struggled on the ground. Having grown up with horses she felt no fear and quickly spotted the reason for its difficulties. The sudden fall had thrown the loose rein over its head, entangling its foreleg and also, caught up in the rein was the carbine that had become dislodged from the leather holster by the saddle. Staying close to its head, she made soothing sounds and stroked its neck until it calmed a little, allowing her to fondle its muzzle as the snorting grew less. Sliding her hand along its sweating, foam-flecked neck and over the withers, she reached towards the ensnared leg and managed to undo the buckle in the heavy leather strap. After further calming the animal she was able to slide the rein free and coax it to its feet where it stood trembling at her side.

Soon the horse's ears pricked, the wild look fading from its eyes when it turned its head towards her, nodding vigorously as if in appreciation. Relieved to find it showed no sign of injury, she re-buckled the strap and ran up the stirrups, making the tack secure. But as she hugged its neck there came a loud slap from behind, sending the startled animal galloping down the *Rambla* in the direction of the port.

Concerned for its safety she swung round to admonish whoever had caused the horse to bolt, but shocked to find herself confronted by the leering features of an unshaven, middle-aged man, she held her tongue. In an attempt to appear unafraid, she averted her eyes and went to move past but his hand shot out, pulling her into his arms. With a cry of alarm she struggled to free herself from his crushing embrace but, stocky and muscular, he easily overpowered her. And when his wet lips sought hers she caught the nauseating smell of drink on his breath. Desperate to avoid his kiss she turned her head away and screamed, but his grip tightened and his cajoling tones were suddenly harsh although she couldn't understand what he was saying.

"No! Please, no!" she cried but he merely grinned and grabbed her hair, drawing her towards him to silence her protesting mouth as his other hand fumbled beneath her coat.

Terrified, she made a frantic attempt to push him away, her cries muffled as she dragged her head aside and kicked wildly at his shins. But this seemed to arouse him further. His hands closed round her neck, pulling her roughly against him so that she feared for her life as he spat out a stream of curses.

Suddenly, he was jerked away so violently that she almost fell to the ground and saw her assailant being dragged across the road by another, much younger man. Unsure of the newcomer's intentions, for safety's sake she picked up the gun that had fallen from the saddle when the horse went down. She had never before held a gun, its unfamiliar weight difficult to balance in one hand as she dashed to the cover of the hotel doorway to rest it against the woodwork.

Drained of energy, she closed her eyes and leaned back against the door, tears streaming down her cheeks as the shock of the assault and the predicament of the horse washed over her afresh.

The gunfire had abated to more distant sporadic volleys, but just how long she stood there, trying to erase the distressing events from her mind, she had no idea. As the racking sobs quietened in her breast she drew a deep, wavering breath and opened her eyes. It gave her quite a jolt to find she had been observed in this emotional state when she met the concerned gaze of the tall young man who had dragged her assailant away.

"*Bon dia, senyoreta,*" the man greeted her softly in Catalan, and continuing in his own tongue asked, "*S'ha perdut?*"

Not being familiar with the Catalan language, she gave him a puzzled look and shook her head.

"*Vostè, és francesa?*" he asked, his dark brows raised.

"No, er...*soy inglés,*" she replied warily in halting Spanish, the gentleness of his concern dispelling her initial alarm.

"Ah, English!" he exclaimed with a smile, extending his hand to continue in an attractively accented voice, "Good afternoon! I am *Maurici Bachs i Serra*. I may know your name, please?"

Somehow, she managed to suppress a threat of hysterical laughter. Such a ludicrous situation; formal introductions made, not in the comfortable drawing room of an English country house, but the incongruous surroundings of shattered buildings, gunfire, and the pungent smell of cordite. Apprehensively, she met his dark, watchful eyes; the litter swirling round her ankles as it was snatched up by the draught eddying in the doorway. Brushing back a stray lock of hair, she took courage and accepted his proffered hand to respond with an uncertain smile, "My name is Elizabeth Purcell, and I am extremely grateful for your intervention."

He gave a slight shrug and nodding towards the gun leaning against the woodwork he queried, "You are with the International Brigade – the wife of a soldier, perhaps – yes?"

Relieved by the normality of his manner, she confided, "No, I'm with my parents, my father is a journalist."

Gesturing along the tree-lined avenue, he asked, "But why you wait here, alone in *la Rambla?*"

Slightly taken aback by his abrupt question, she paused to brush the dust from her coat before explaining guardedly, "I am not waiting, *señor*. I was on my way to the hospital when the firing started. I thought it best to shelter... and then that man..."

"Very wise," he put in, stepping forward to take possession of the gun. With a slight inclination of his dark head he offered, "Allow me to escort you, *senyoreta*. It is not safe for a young lady alone, and the tramcar is not passing for some time."

Assured by his courteous manner, she thanked him, welcoming his company in the gathering dusk through unfamiliar streets.

"I must confess the journey here took longer than I anticipated," she admitted, falling into step beside him as they approached Plaça de Catalunya where laughing children unconcernedly rolled clay marbles into small holes gouged out in the expanse of dry, dusty earth.

"But why you are so far from the hospital, I may ask?"

Unwilling to divulge her reason, she said, "I wanted to see the famous *Canaletes* fountain," and caught a flicker of amusement on his wide mouth.

Crossing the vast square, they entered a narrower street, an entirely different route from the one she had used earlier. And, although his manner toward her remained pleasant, there were moments when she wondered if it had been wise to accept his offer as escort. But once she recognised the grim building ahead she realised it had taken considerably less time to reach the hospital than expected. He explained, as a *Barceloní*, he knew every alley and short cut in the area.

At the hospital entrance he gave a brief, formal bow and said in polite but halting English, "Good day to you, *senyoreta* Purcell. I am pleased to make your acquaintance."

"Goodbye, and thank you, *señor* Maurici..."

She couldn't recall his full name, but as she entered the cool, dimly lit hospital corridor his warm smile stayed in her thoughts. He had eased the terror she suffered from being confronted by the man on the Rambla. Feeling better able to cope, she hurried along to the ward where her mother would be helping to serve the meagre rations of food to the sick.

* *

At Woodington Hall in England, a country house situated in a sleepy village bordering the Vale of York, Elizabeth's grandparents, Jane and William Cussons were taking afternoon tea in the upstairs sitting room.

William sighed, his expression reflective as he gazed through the rain-splashed window to the dismal scene of leafless trees and waterlogged lawns outside. He missed the company of his daughter who always seemed to cheer him on a day such as this, but now Molly was away there was no one to brighten his gloom. He glanced across to his wife who was engrossed in brushing crumbs of cake from the long, grey cashmere cardigan she was wearing.

"I wonder what the weather is like with Molly," he ventured, dabbing a linen napkin on his greying moustache.

Jane compressed her thin lips. "I expect it will be uncomfortably hot and dusty," she said, adding acidly, "but it was her choice."

William's heart sank. "It is not hot all the time," he insisted gently. "Barcelona is further north than you realise."

Closing her eyes, Jane clasped her sinewy hands and shuddered delicately. "Wherever it is, she can't possibly be as comfortable as it is here. Spain always was a backward country – I can't understand why Molly chose to go..."

"To be by her husband's side, of course," William replied, a challenging expression entering his faded blue eyes. "She was determined they should not be parted and as James' paper chose to send him there she accepted it."

"But I don't consider it a suitable place to take a child."

"One can hardly describe Elizabeth as a child," he said with a placatory smile, "she's almost nineteen. Many young ladies travel these days, she'll learn from the experience."

"Young ladies of our class take a cruise, or holiday in Switzerland, not gallivant around the poorer areas of southern Europe," she returned and snatched up the newspaper, her attention on the front page.

William lay back in his chair, his thoughts returning to his daughter whom he hoped with all his heart was safe. Had he been a younger man he would have volunteered to join the International Brigade himself and, in opposition to his wife's views, fight alongside the Republican army.

Anything in preference to the dull life he led. He envied James' freedom, risky though it may be, he craved a little excitement yet declined to ride with the hunt. He looked from beneath the hooded lids of his half-closed eyes to where his wife was seated. He was aware that she thought him cowardly, she readily rode to hounds whenever the opportunity arose which repulsed him increasingly as each year passed. He wondered why he had married her, a woman so embittered, reminding him continuously of his father's business failures which meant he had inherited very much less than she had expected. They shared few of life's pleasures yet, he reflected, she was once so beautiful, so desirable, he had been infatuated by her gay charm. And then there was Molly, a daughter he dearly loved; if little else, he had Jane to thank for bringing her into the world.

He uttered a soft sigh, screwing up his eyes as he glanced over to the newspaper Jane held before her, hoping to spot any headlines of foreign news in the local press.

"Any news from Spain?" he queried. "It's a while since we had word from Molly."

She tossed the paper in his direction. "Yes, it's time we heard something, she's been gone almost a month,"

"She did telephone soon after they arrived. Of course, there could be difficulties with the postal service, or perhaps they didn't receive our letter."

She shot him a hard glance. "Even so, she can write to us! It was just the same in nineteen-seventeen, when she was at that London hospital, she hardly ever corresponded with us then."

"I know, dear, but she was very young, and casualties were coming in by the hundred..." William broke off as an item of news caught his eye. "Good Lord, they're having a dreadful time off the coast of Ireland! Gales, heavy seas..."

"Our own coasts are being affected by fierce gales," she returned coldly, "and now the thaw has set in the river is well over its banks. Consider the damage it will do to our lawns instead of worrying about the Irish."

"But we're not starving, dear, whereas they're getting no supplies..."

Jane flashed him a derisive glance. "Well, James appears to relish such conditions."

"James was raised in a very respectable Dublin family," he countered with a thrust of his jaw. "I like the man – most agreeable – and don't forget, he is Molly's husband."

"Forget!" she cried bitterly. "Why my daughter chose to marry a foreigner, I will never know. Working in London was her downfall." She paused, smoothing down the pleats in her tweed skirt. "Yes, Miles Grant would have been a much better choice."

William lowered his newspaper in despair. "Dash it all, Jane, she and James have been married twenty years," he said heatedly, the sagging flesh of his cheeks turning a dull red, "so why bring Grant's name into it!"

Jane rose to her feet. "It may be too late for Molly," she conceded, "but I have plans for Elizabeth."

William's greying brows drew together. "Plans?" he queried cautiously, laying the paper aside. "What, exactly, have you in mind?"

"I would have thought it obvious," she returned with a smug smile. "Miles Grant would be an excellent choice of husband for Elizabeth."

"I must assume you are joking!" William exclaimed, startled. "Miles Grant is twice her age! And if he resembles his father in any way, he most certainly would not be my choice of marriage partner for Elizabeth."

"I doubt he could be more ill-bred than James," she bridled as she swept across the faded Aubusson carpet towards the carved stone fireplace.

"James is a perfect gentleman..." William began but, realising his wife was goading him to argue, continued more mildly, "Molly adores him..."

"To return to a more important subject," she interposed, pressing the bell to summon a servant. "Any further news of the cliff fall along the Filey coast?"

With a heavy sigh, William merely shook his head. Jane was determined to belittle James at every opportunity. He ought to have known better than to suggest his son-in-law possessed attributes greater than those of Miles Grant.

"Ah, there you are, Pincott," Jane said as the butler entered the room. "Add more wood to the fire will you. It is decidedly chilly in here."

* *

Granted a day's compassionate leave from his field hospital duties, Maurici had been making for home when he heard the distressed cries of the young English girl on the Rambla d' Canaletes. And when he saw a man indecently accosting her he went immediately to her aid. His unexpected intervention gave him the upper hand and he was able to frog march her assailant away before returning to discover her sobbing in the doorway of a dilapidated hotel. At first she had seemed unaware of his presence, then she'd looked up, her startled eyes the colour of sapphires. She had appeared so young and vulnerable yet, although she loitered in an area sometimes frequented by women of easy virtue, he had sensed a difference in her bearing. Once recovered from her distress, her guarded response to his questions told him he was not mistaken.

Now, as he waited by the port for his colleague to transport him the few kilometres to his home in Sant Adria del Besos, he transferred his thoughts from Elizabeth to the welcome he was likely to receive. He'd had news of his father's illness, a chronic bronchial condition aggravated by a poisoned wound from a pitchfork wielded by a peasant of an opposing party for which his mother held him responsible because of his absence from home. She'd brushed aside his attempts to explain his need to join the medical team in the field hospital, tending those wounded in their struggle to free Catalunya of its oppressors. It would take four more years to complete his medical training, meanwhile, he intended to devote his time to caring for the injured, regardless of their political or religious leanings. He had saved many a life in the ragged hospital tent where suffering men begged to be relieved of their pain. If only she could understand his predicament: torn between loyalty to his family and the maintaining of life amongst the fighting men.

A motorcycle drew alongside, bringing him back to the present. Slinging the gun across his shoulders, he seated himself on the metal carrier and clung to the man in front as the engine roared into life, speeding them away over the uneven surface of the road. In a short time they were travelling through countryside where fields of almond and cherry trees were beginning to burst into blossom, soft clouds of pink and white, still visible in the fading light. Soon they passed the boundary of his father's land with its neatly planted rows of vines, a sign that he was almost home.

His mother, *Senyora Carmen Bachs*, was standing in the doorway when the motorcycle came to a halt on the drive. "*Ai, Maurici!* Here at last!" she cried as he went to place his lips on her plump cheeks.

Replying in the language familiar to them, he said, "Only until this evening, *mama*, then I must return."

"So soon?" She shook her head, the silver pendant earrings swinging weightily from the lobes of her ears, then spying the gun she clicked her tongue. "I never thought I would see the day when a son of mine arrives home carrying a gun."

"I took charge of it purely for safety's sake," he assured her, stowing the gun in the long case clock which stood in the dark, tiled hall. "Has father's doctor called today?"

"Yes, but now you are here all will be well."

"But he has more experience with *papa's* condition, and being too old for the army he has more time for his patients."

"But you are his son," she pointed out, tucking a strand of dark, greying hair into the loose coil at her nape. "You are needed here!"

At the foot of the wide staircase he turned to her with a sigh of impatience. "Please, *mama*, not again," he pleaded. "Today I spoke to an English lady and discovered that both she and her mother are helping out at the hospital..."

"Are you suggesting I should do that, with all my extra work here?" she intervened sharply. "Has it not occurred to you that most of our servants have gone to the army?"

"Of course not, *mama*, you have work enough," he broke in with a smile of contrition. "What I mean is, if the English can help with our sick and wounded, so should I."

"English!" she snorted. "What do they know of our way of life? If one can believe the newspapers, they soon may have troubles of their own."

"Let us hope not," he murmured as they reached the landing above.

"But why do they choose to work here, unless they are religious – maybe nuns? Though as things stand at present theirs can be a hazardous calling."

He looked down on his elderly mother and shook his head. "No, it was not a religious order which brought them here. They volunteered to help the nuns so we shouldn't criticize.

Actually, the young lady's father is a journalist for a London newspaper."

She shot him a shrewd glance. "Ah, now I understand. It is the girl who interests you, my boy, not solely your admiration for the work they are doing."

With an indulgent smile she brushed him aside and opened the door to the sickroom, preceding him to her husband's bedside.

Maurici looked down on his father, lying against a stack of pillows, and saw the laboured heaving of his chest. He appeared to be sleeping but, as if sensing a newcomer, he stirred and opened his eyes.

"*Quina sorpresa!*" Josep Bachs exclaimed, extending a wavering hand.

"*Si*, a surprise indeed," agreed Maurici," clasping the work-worn hand to his chest. "You look much better, *papa*.

What does the doctor have to say?"

"He says I am much improved," replied *senyor* Bachs with a weak, rattling cough.

"That is good news!" Content, Maurici drew up a chair and the conversation continued, slow and laboured on the part of his father as he voiced his concern for the continuing success of his celler.

"Your cousin, Lluis, is working hard to ensure the quality is maintained," Josep told him. "Now we have only women in the vineyard he has much to do."

"Have all the men gone to war?" he asked, realising it had been a while since he visited.

"All but the older ones..."

"They have more sense!" the *senyora* interjected as she fussed with the bed-cover, ensuring the fringe lay even.

"*Mama!*" Maurici reproached. "Do you not want to see *Catalunya* free?"

"*Ach* – politics!" she cried, raising her hands in despair. "What do I know about politics?"

The older man looked from one to the other. "Should I be younger I would join the fight for freedom!" he declared, his voice growing surprisingly strong.

The *senyora* shot her son a sharp glance. "Maurici! Don't encourage your father. Lluis does not speak this way, he is not interested in this war of yours."

Maurici rolled his eyes to the ceiling. "You know my interest in the war goes no further than treating the injured but, considering our opposing views, it is fortunate Lluis lives here and not I."

"War is the work of the devil!" she retaliated, but he merely smiled.

By mid evening Maurici made ready to leave for Barcelona, knowing he must prepare for a return to the front the following morning. To avoid his mother's inevitable protestations, he promised to visit later in the week when he expected to bring back another group of casualties, and to prevent her worrying he had convinced her that a friend would be transporting him back to barracks. In reality, he set off on foot confident a vehicle would be passing his way.

Looking up at the clouded February sky which hung heavily over the vine-filled precincts of his home, he thought it strangely quiet. The silence was weird; his breathing sounding unnaturally loud, his booted feet clattering on the rutted road. He paused and held his breath, anticipating goodness knows what... perhaps it would have been wiser to carry the gun.

He had walked almost two kilometres before the welcome sound of a vehicle came from behind. As the noise of the engine drew near he turned to see a lorry looming through the darkness with only a pinprick of light to guide it. Hopeful of a lift he raised his hand, but because of its speed it passed by almost twenty metres before it slithered to a screeching halt.

He ran forward to see the passenger window open when a voice demanded in rough Castilian, "You from *casa Bachs*?"

"*Si, si!* Are you heading to the city?" he called, advancing towards the cab. But the unexpected glint of a gun barrel sliding through the window brought him to a sudden stop.

He turned to run, but before he could get out of the firing line he heard the word *"Capitalist!"* and felt a tremendous blow to his thigh, sending him off his feet. He heard laughter, then a second bullet struck. Expecting more he kept his head low, but the lorry moved off, its tarpaulin cover flapping noisily as it accelerated away.

"Ui! Fill de puta!" he cursed, endeavouring to pull himself onto the verge. Striving to remain conscious, he felt the warmth of his blood as it oozed from his thigh, yet the only pain he was aware of was the intense stinging sensation along his right index finger, and the hard ridge of earth at the roadside pressing against his ribs. He knew that to attempt to crawl back home was impossible and prayed the occupants of the next vehicle coming in his direction would offer more goodwill.

As he lay in the grassy rut at the roadside, he fancied he heard the sound of an engine but it seemed never to arrive. *"Déu* – help me!" he gasped as a curiously light-headed sensation overcame him and the engine sounds continued to drone in his ears.

Chapter 2

Molly Purcell was washing her hands when her daughter rushed to the cloakroom to say, "Sister Teresa is looking for you."

"Oh dear, I was about to leave," Molly said tiredly, drying her hands on the rough towel.

"We can't leave now," protested Elizabeth. "Another wounded man has been admitted. Sister asked if we'd stay until she knows the extent of his injuries."

Molly gave a weary smile. "Very well, but do remember to call her nurse or you may put her in grave danger," she advised, fastening a clean apron round her trim waist to return to the ward.

By the light of an oil lamp placed near the foot of the narrow iron bed, the nun was already tending her new patient, busily cutting along his trouser leg.

"Thanks be to God you had not left," she whispered. "This young medical student once worked with us here."

"What would you like me to do?" Molly asked, while Elizabeth's distressed gaze strayed to a portly, middle-aged man who appeared to be administering the last rites to a dying soldier. Like the nun, the priest wore no garment as a sign of his calling, but she spotted the small, round box containing the bottle of holy oils and saw his covert glance as he returned it to his pocket.

"Perhaps the *senyoreta* will bathe his face whilst you and I remove his clothing," the nun directed, folding back the trouser leg to reveal a blood-soaked dressing. "I want him ready for when the doctor arrives."

Catching Elizabeth's attention, Molly sent her to fill a bowl from the pan of water simmering on a stove in the vast kitchen. By now the new patient was regaining consciousness, moaning softly in the shadowy gloom as he tried to push the nun's hand away from the wound in his thigh.

As she wrung out the cloth Elizabeth glanced along the bed, horrified by the sight of the exposed wound. Returning her attention to the patient she attempted to bathe the blood-caked abrasions on his brow as he tossed his head in semi-conscious protest. But when the nun moved up from the foot of the bed, allowing the lamp-light to fall on his face, she uttered a gasp of surprise.

"I know this man..." she whispered, pausing as he half opened his eyes, "but he didn't say he was a medical student."

Molly glanced at the young man's partly washed face. "Well, continue," she said briskly. "I'm sure he'll be pleased to see a familiar face."

Once he became fully conscious Elizabeth found her task made easier, though he didn't appear to recognise her in the dim light of the ward. She had just finished bathing the slightly stubbly area around his chin when the doctor arrived and she stood aside as Molly drew a rickety screen along one side of the bed.

She was cleaning sediment from the bowl when Molly came in to dispose of the blood-stained clothing.

"We managed to change him just in time," Molly remarked. Then noting Elizabeth's distress explained, "If we remove soiled dressings and clean the wound the doctor can assess the injuries without wasting precious minutes."

"Oh, for a moment I thought you meant he'd died," Elizabeth said with unconcealed relief. "That wound looked dreadful. I almost fainted."

"But you didn't," Molly shot her a comforting smile. "He may lose part of one finger, the first joint was shattered, but he's strong, his leg should heal well."

"I do hope so. He's the man who escorted me here this afternoon. He was so polite, spoke almost fluent English."

Molly smiled as she unpinned the bib of her soiled apron. Pushing up the sleeves of the shapeless dress beneath, she turned on the gleaming brass tap. As she washed, a nun came by on her way to the ward where she was to spend the night, her severe nurse's uniform reaching almost to her ankles.

"Your husband is in the vestibule," the nun paused to remark. "You are blessed, he is a patient man."

Molly nodded. "I'll not keep him waiting. We will return in the morning."

"May God go with you," whispered the nun, a flicker of a smile on her serene features as she adjusted her white cap, pulling it over her roughly shorn locks.

The unmistakable figure of James Purcell came into view immediately they reached the long corridor. Standing tall and lean in his dark overcoat, Molly hurried towards him after her particularly stressful shift.

James' handsome features broke into a smile. "Here you are, my darlings! I've been concerned for your safety after hearing about the street battles today."

"No need, James, we were fine... well, Elizabeth encountered trouble on the Rambla."

"God save us!" he exclaimed, his tone unusually sharp as he turned to his daughter to demand, "Whatever possessed you to go there?"

"I'd heard cigarettes were being sold near the Metro."

"You must remember, it is an offence to purchase black market goods."

"I'm sorry, Daddy, but the men in the hospital are without supplies."

"They wouldn't expect you to endanger your life for them, Elizabeth. People are being shot for lesser offences," he said gravely, his deep blue eyes troubled as he replaced his Trilby and stepped out into the cool, night air.

The streets were very quiet as the three made their way back to their hotel to find they were the only diners there. "Perhaps it's the menu!" James joked as plates of boiled lentils dotted with tiny pieces of what he suspected were horse meat were set before them.

Molly smiled at his attempt at cheerfulness yet sensed a curious air of foreboding. Barcelona seemed strangely quiet but, like James, she chose not to discuss her fears in the presence of their daughter.

"Elizabeth, tell Daddy about the young man you were in conversation with earlier," she prompted, hoping to maintain a relaxed air throughout dinner.

Reluctant to mention the man who had accosted her on la Rambla, Elizabeth related the episode of the horse and her meeting with the young Catalan. "He's a student doctor with impeccable manners, but I didn't mention anything about politics."

James nodded thoughtfully. "Sounds like an educated man. Even so, you were right to heed my advice."

"Which could account for his knowledge of English," Molly supplied. "He was admitted this evening, badly wounded, even I found it a most gruesome injury."

James expression was grave. "Many died, or suffered dreadful injuries today. As I came into the city I noticed makeshift ambulances everywhere."

"We had an extremely harrowing day," Molly put in. "I expect my father will be anxious when he reads the news, I really ought to write home."

James had resigned himself to the fact it was unlikely they would be served with dessert, so he gaped in surprise when the old waiter placed a bowl of oranges on the table.

"*Esplèndid!*" he cried, pressing a generous tip into the waiter's ready hand before he passed round the fruit, now so scarce.

After their meal, feeling reasonably content, he suggested they should retire to their rooms. He was looking forward to a small glass of local brandy and one of the dark cigars he'd managed to purchase on his way into the city. He smiled to himself as they took the strange antiquated lift to the second floor where he kissed Elizabeth good night. Slipping his arm around Molly's waist, he drew her into their adjoining room; they would share the brandy, she'd appreciate that; he hoped her day at the hospital had not proved too tiring.

In the next room, Elizabeth put down her book, smiling to herself as she stared up at the crystal chandelier with its heavy, chipped pendants. She could hear faint laughter coming from her parent's room, a comforting sound after the trauma of the day. In her sleepy state she could picture her father's smiling face, but his handsome features kept fading to be replaced by the agonized expression of the injured young man in the hospital. This new image distressed her and she had to concentrate her thoughts on their earlier meeting when his face had been unblemished. He didn't have her father's striking blue eyes and pale complexion, but a light tan, together with the broad forehead and slightly hooked nose, features said to be typically Catalan. And although she anticipated the morning with a degree of unease, it was with this pleasant memory she drifted into sleep.

The following morning Elizabeth accompanied Molly down the long corridor leading to the ward where they were met by the appalling sound of men in pain. During the journey she had experienced a certain amount of trepidation, and these disturbing moans, together with the strong smell of disinfectant and the crash of bowls and buckets coming from the wash room, served only to increase her nervousness. What would she find? Vacant beds? The priest in attendance? She had a fear of death, and the line of still, sheeted bodies in the anti-room never failed to distress her and she dreaded what this morning may reveal.

"It is God's will," the priest had declared. But those silent bodies, once vibrant with life, were not those a good God would take, were they? She hesitated in silent prayer. Please, God, don't let Maurici die...

"Come along, Elizabeth," Molly prompted as she removed her hat and slipped off her fashionable hip-length coat. Then, spotting her daughters ashen face, advised, "If you wish you may stay in the visitors room until we have made everyone comfortable."

"No, I'll need to help with washing and breakfast," she insisted, and immediately they entered the ward her eyes went to the empty bed the young medical student had occupied the previous evening; something she had anticipated with dread.

"I see the young man you met is in the third bed," her mother whispered, pointing across the crowded ward.

Relief flooded Elizabeth. She longed to approach the bed yet knew she must wait until instructed to do so. When the nun suggested she assist with washing the patients, she was delighted to be allotted a section of the ward where his bed was now situated.

"You know what to do," Molly said as they went to the wash room. "Face, hands, teeth, and hair. Nurse and I shall be giving bed baths later."

Elizabeth filled an enamel bowl with warm water ready for her first patient, though she longed to approach the bed in which Maurici lay.

When it came to filling the third bowl she realised it would be strange to wash someone with whom she was acquainted instead of the nameless row of wounded men. As she approached he turned his head, his dark, pain-filled eyes fixed upon her as she drew near. At first, his bruised appearance shocked her but she managed a nervous greeting.

"Good morning, *señor*... I'm sorry, I don't remember your name."

A hint of recognition entered his dark eyes. "I think I am dreaming," he murmured. "Last night, you are here, yes?"

"Yes, I told you yesterday. My mother is a volunteer nurse, we come here every day," she said with a shy smile. "It was extremely busy last evening so we stayed to help, otherwise I wouldn't have known you were here."

"I thought my eyes deceive me, I am not realising it is the same hospital."

"You were only semi-conscious when you arrived, she explained softly, but now I'm here to help you wash."

"Ah, *senyoreta,* you are an angel."

Elizabeth turned to the bowl on the side-table, dunking the cloth in the water more times than was necessary until the colour had faded from her cheeks. Then, emulating her mother's efficient manner, she gently wiped the perspiration from his brow as she enquired, "How are you feeling today?"

"Last night the surgeon performs the operations," he said, raising his heavily bandaged right hand, "but now the anaesthetic has left my body, I have problems with the pain."

"Perhaps nurse can give you something to ease it," she suggested, carefully drying his face, "I'll ask for you."

"You are very kind, *senyoreta* Elizabeth. I am permitted to use your name?"

Avoiding his gaze, she pushed up the sleeve of the theatre gown he was still wearing and applied the cloth to the long fingers of his sound hand.

His soapy fingers tightened around hers. "*Senyoreta,* I cause you offence?"

"Of course not," she denied, disengaging her hand. "But if sister overhears..." She broke off, flustered by her mistake, but he appeared not to have noticed.

"If she comes, I shall call you *senyoreta* Purcell."

Surprised he remembered her name, she continued with her ministrations. "Your name is too long to remember."

"*Bachs i Serra*," he replied, taking the comb with his sound hand, proceeding to run it through his thick, dark hair.

"A hyphenated name, is it?"

"*Bachs* is the family name of my father, and *Serra* my mother, it is the custom here."

She laughed softly. "I think Mister *Bachs* is quite enough for me."

"Your laughter is music..." he murmured, wincing a little as she reached across to straighten the sheet.

Blushing again, Elizabeth darted a nervous glance over her shoulder to see her mother advancing her way.

"You haven't made much progress," Molly remarked with a faintly reproachful glance at her daughter's flushed cheeks.

"I was talking to this gentleman," she explained, picking up her bowl.

"It is good practice to speak to your patient," Molly said once they were in the washroom, "providing you don't neglect others."

"But he's the only one I'm acquainted with," Elizabeth complained.

"Come, come, darling, you know enough Spanish. A pleasant greeting is all you need."

"Actually, I believe he speaks Catalan."

"Maybe you are not aware the Catalan language is frowned upon by some, although many choose to use it, there could be consequences. Almost everyone can speak Castilian which is safer. A friendly word is valuable to the patient," Molly went on to approve, "but not when directed solely to that young man."

With the remainder of the ward comfortable and each smoothly sheeted bed in line, the time had come for breakfast to be served. Food was becoming less plentiful – to Elizabeth's eyes unappetising – accompanied by insipid looking coffee, served without milk or sugar.

"Will you give this drink to the patient over there?" the nun said, glancing to where Maurici lay. "He has no problem drinking, whereas the poor soul in the next bed requires your mother's expert care."

Elizabeth felt proud of the way her mother ministered to the dying man; a man uttering none of the terrible moaning sounds of many in the ward. And now, as she neared Maurici's bed she noticed the patient her mother attended appeared to be smiling, and she was struck by a dreadful thought. Maurici didn't voice his pain, he also appeared tranquil as he took the cup from her trembling fingers. Was he going to be all right?

"I hear the Republicans and Nationalists are fighting in Teruel," he said, anxiously. "Do you know this is true?"

"I'll ask my father this evening," she offered, plumping up his hard pillow.

"Thank you, Elizabeth. I welcome news from all parts of Spain."

Immediately he spoke her name, she shot an anxious glance towards the next bed. But her mother was too preoccupied to notice. She was sliding the pillow from beneath the head of the man lying there, and gently closing the lids over his now sightless eyes. Uttering a horrified gasp, Elizabeth quickly averted her head. But the sudden pressure of a hand on her wrist prevented her from rushing away, and she turned to see Maurici's sympathetic gaze.

"He is now at peace, *senyoreta*," he assured her softly. "He feels no pain."

Elizabeth felt her throat constrict and could only nod as she withdrew her hand from his grasp to return to where the nun was busily serving breakfast.

Whilst Molly drew a screen around the bed of her dead patient, the nun called in the doctor, adding a whispered message for him to bring along the priest. Elizabeth found it hard to believe death could be so dignified and quiet. She had always envisaged it to be accompanied by bustle and hysteria but the serene ministrations of her mother and the nun were helping to assuage her horror. As Maurici had explained, the man now feels no pain, and in that quick glimpse she had seen only an expression of peace on the patient's face.

"It has been a difficult day for you, I know," Molly said later as they walked along the dark corridor, "but I noticed the young medical student helped you a little."

"He was very kind," Elizabeth disclosed, quietly. "Do you think he'll be all right?"

"Yes, I'm sure he will. If we can avoid infection his wounds should heal well."

Elizabeth's sigh of relief was inaudible, but the release from anxiety brought back the sparkle to her eyes.

* *

At Woodington Hall, Molly's father, William experienced a surge of pleasure as he caught sight of the buff envelope on the silver tray.

"Ah! I see we have word from Molly and James," he said, screwing up his eyes as he moved closer to the window. "Tell me; what is the date, Pincott? March the, er..."

"The fifth of March, sir. It is Saturday," Pincott replied, rolling his eyes to the ceiling.

"No need to be quite so damned precise, I do know what day it is!" William snapped, trying to discern the date on the blurred print over the Spanish stamp. "February ninth, thirty-eight," he muttered then cried incredulously, "Good Lord! It has taken almost four weeks to reach us!"

"Madam will be pleased to have news," Pincott remarked in his usual ingratiating manner before going on to enquire, "May I ask, how is Miss Elizabeth bearing up in such difficult circumstances? Madam is most anxious."

"And so am I," William reminded his servant, and as he turned in the direction of the breakfast room he felt the hair on his neck prickle. Pincott always had this effect upon him. There was something about the shifty-eyed butler with his glass-smooth hair he didn't quite like, but Jane considered that he displayed a dignity befitting Woodington Hall.

He started guiltily as Jane joined him, fearing he may have spoken his thoughts aloud. Avoiding her tight-lipped expression of disapproval, he gathered courage to counter her stare as he held up the letter.

"What have you there?" she demanded, shaking out her linen napkin.

"A letter from Spain," he replied, taking up his table-knife to slit open the envelope.

She clicked her tongue. "It is Pincott's place to bring in the post. At least he knows which is a stationery knife."

"I was much too impatient," he explained and offered as atonement, "Would you like to read it first?"

She ran a critical eye over the immaculate tablecloth. "After breakfast, and I do wish you would stop behaving like a servant."

"It really doesn't matter, dear..."

"Of course it does! One has to keep up appearances in the presence of one's servants."

As he withdrew the letter from the envelope she uttered a hiss of derision. "Can't you wait until breakfast is over!"

William felt his stomach muscles contract but continued to unfold the letter.

"Well, now you have it open, you may as well read out the contents."

As he read aloud, William tried to relax, but already the gnawing discomfort had started and his stomach felt like a ball of fire. He'd begun to realise it was happening more frequently and usually when Jane was in similar mood. He'd always considered himself to be of a tolerant nature, but now he was experiencing bouts of rising anger which he found hard to suppress, particularly when the pain nagged his guts.

"Apparently, they are quite well," he related. "Molly and Elizabeth still help in the hospital, although there are more casualties than it can accommodate."

"It is hardly the kind of work for ladies of their position. Dirty, smelly soldiers, the majority from lower ranks, I imagine... ugh!"

"I admire Molly's courage, and Elizabeth's. It can't be easy for one so young. James says their hotel is quite comfortable," he continued, "though most foods are in short supply." He leaned back in his chair to murmur thoughtfully, "It's very sad."

"Sad?" she repeated, carefully buttering her toast. "The shortage of food, do you mean?"

His eyes held a faraway look as he shook his head. "No, I mean the war," he said gravely. "It's a terrible situation when men fight their own countrymen, on their own soil. The worst kind of war."

Biting sharply into her toast, she remarked, "Actually, I consider them stupid and ignorant, nowhere nearly as cultured as we British."

William's eyes narrowed. "Spain has bred men of various professions who are held in extremely high regard in this world," he countered, striking the table with the handle of his knife. "James tells me he enjoys their company, and their culture..."

"He would!" she interrupted viciously. "They're two of a kind, the Irish and the Spanish."

William uttered a groan of exasperation and flung down his napkin. The pain in his insides was growing worse; he'd ask cook to mix him a dose of bicarbonate, it usually helped.

"You're extremely rude this morning!" he heard as he left the dining room. But he was in too much pain to retaliate. Grimacing, he hurried across the stone floor towards the kitchen, promising himself a visit from Doctor Wilson as soon as it could be arranged.

Chapter 3

Rising from the chair beside his patients high, four-poster bed with its fading brocade drapes, Doctor Alexander Wilson folded his stethoscope and dropped it into his case. "Lost a bit of weight, I see," he remarked, drawing the linen sheet over Williams exposed chest. "Eating well, are we?"

"Not really," William complained. "A dose of bicarb helps, but the past few days have been absolute purgatory!"

The young doctor nodded. "And your diet, can you manage a normal meal?"

"Is that all you can say?" he returned irritably. "It's these damned pains I want attended to, not my diet." Heaving himself into a sitting position, he grimaced, and with a derisive snort, added, "My wife claims it's because I'm too highly strung. Like that young stallion of hers, you know, excitable."

Alex smiled to himself over the comparison but encouraged him to continue.

"There again, one is bound to suffer to some extent when the news is so depressing. Hitler's troops marching into Austria... Shocking business."

"A sad state of affairs, I agree, but your wife could be right, your blood pressure is a trifle too high."

Buttoning the jacket of his flannelette pyjamas, William uttered a ragged sigh. "I expect you're going to advise me to rest, though how anyone can rest in this household..." He broke off, conscious of threatening tears, and fingered his moustache in an attempt to hide the tremble of his lips.

"Tell me what troubles you," the doctor urged, noting William's increasing emotional state. "Is the pain so unbearable... or, is there something else?"

"Well, it's a dashed awful pain," he admitted, once composed. "And, like most people, I have my worries. But we must keep going..." he ended with a thrust of his unshaven chin.

Alex strolled across to the window to gaze out over the windswept lawns. "I expect you worry about Molly,"

"Had a letter a few days ago, before this started." William indicated the tender area below his ribs. "Molly's fine, tells me she's doing voluntary hospital work. Elizabeth, too."

Alex smiled. "Very commendable. But your wife, is she able to cope with the anxiety?"

William gave a sudden shout of laughter, a harsh note that caught the doctor's attention. "I assume she is less enthusiastic," he pursued and saw the pulse on Williams temple flicker.

"Afraid so," he agreed, his expression one of utter dejection. "Personally, I consider it a great experience. Risky I know, but Jane thinks it foolhardy of James to take them with him." He heaved a long sigh. "She will not let the matter rest, yet he's a splendid fellow, most agreeable."

The doctor nodded and withdrew his watch from the pocket of his waistcoat. "I'll have a tactful word with your wife on my way out, and should you not feel easier by tomorrow I'll ask her to give me a call."

William felt comforted. But, watching the younger man button the jacket of his dark suit, he hoped he hadn't indicated too strongly how Jane felt. On reflection, his newly found ease began to fade; how tactful would Alex be?

The doctor found Jane by the stable, engaged in conversation with her groom.

"Good morning," he said pleasantly, turning up the collar of his overcoat against the biting March wind. "You may like to know how I find your husband today."

"I expect you found little ails him," she said, dismissing her groom. "He's only sixty-seven, you know, whereas my father was active into his eighties. Wouldn't have allowed a little indigestion to get him down!"

Wilson's jaw tightened. "Hardly a little indigestion, I'm afraid. It is my opinion your husband could be suffering an ulcerated stomach, and his blood pressure is rather too high."

Her eyes narrowed. "Which means?"

"It means he should rest for at least a week, take a bland diet, no alcohol. I'll write a prescription to be delivered to the house which should help reduce the pain. I know I can rely upon you to ensure he is free of all anxiety," he ended, favouring her with his most charming smile as he walked beside her along the gravel path.

The smile he received in return matched the chill of the day, and he made a decision to visit his patient the following morning without waiting to be called.

"Your father would have prescribed fresh air and exercise," she said, drawing her tweed jacket tightly round her narrow body. "One of the old school, didn't agree with these modern ideas, good huntsman, too!"

Stifling his anger, Alex responded, "So I believe. And how is your daughter, and the family?"

Jane turned an unbelieving gaze in his direction. "I'm surprised he hasn't mentioned them, although it is a subject upon which we strongly disagree."

"Then, perhaps it would be advisable to keep the subject out of conversation," the doctor suggested mildly and, with a secret feeling of devilment, ended, "I take it your husband is not in agreement with their visit to Spain."

"Quite the reverse, I am the one who opposed it."

"You do surprise me. I'd have thought a lady with your spirit would have encouraged the adventure. My own father was extremely adventurous, one of the old school."

She ignored his sarcasm and went on to berate the qualities of her son-in-law. "He's quite irresponsible!" she said viciously. "It's the Irish in him, no breeding."

"My father was a Dubliner," he remarked as they reached the house, pity they couldn't have met." Raising his hat he ended smoothly, "Good day to you, madam."

"Impertinent young brat!" Jane muttered, entering the house by way of the stone hall where the dull winters light filtered in through mullioned windows. She remained in bad humour all the way up the massive oak staircase to William's room. "Pity old Doctor Wilson retired, she complained, he would have had you up and about in no time."

"I must say I feel more comfortable in bed," William ventured, laying aside a newspaper from the previous day. "And I'd be greatly obliged if you would ask Pincott to bring an extra copy of the Press. Bit of a luxury, I know…"

His request only increased Jane's cantankerous mood. He lay back on the pillow, eyes closed to block out the sight of her bitter expression.

"Speaking of luxuries, perhaps you overlooked the matter of your medical expenses. Wilson presented his bill for two guineas! Furthermore, consider the cost of your present treatment," she continued. "I've a mind to call in a doctor from Malton, make Wilson take stock of himself!"

William's expression grew more strained. "No, my dear, Alex wouldn't overcharge me."

"Well, it won't do for you to call him too often, particularly now when we need a new car."

His eyes brightened. "Ah yes, that reminds me," he began, opening up the paper. "There's a new Humber sixteen on the market. A nice machine, frightfully expensive, three hundred and thirty pounds, or thereabouts."

Jane glanced at the advertisement, her expression softening. "Oh, I wouldn't say that, dear, it would be an improvement on our present car." She clasped her hands, her eyes on the ceiling as she enthused, "Just think what an impression we would make, driving into Malton in a Humber!"

"I was thinking of the engine, she'll purr along," he said, the tension easing from his body when he saw the enthusiasm on his wife's face.

"Then why don't we place an order?" she suggested, patting her fine, windswept hair into place. "When the weather improves we could drive to the coast. I haven't visited Scarborough in years!"

"That would be a most pleasant journey," William agreed, experiencing a tingle of excitement, "particularly when the double track road has been completed. Construction work is already well on the way."

"So, you must agree, this is the right time to buy."

"It would take a sizeable sum from my bank balance," he put in doubtfully.

"You can afford it," she encouraged, giving his cold hand a brief squeeze.

"Mm, yes, I'll telephone right away," he volunteered, pushing aside the covers.

But before his feet touched the worn Indian carpet she put out a restraining hand. "No, dear, I'll make the call. I want you well again to enjoy the new car.

William found the excitement quite exhausting and sank back, eyes closed, drifting into a light doze when visions of her benevolent expression floated before his eyes. His lips twitched. This was the Jane he had loved, he reflected sleepily, so unlike the bitter, ageing woman she had become. He didn't wish for a submissive wife, had once admired her strong spirit, but now there was no gentleness, no affection. He'd never forced his attentions upon her, but a mere kiss, the feel of her arms about him was all he longed for. He felt cheated...

He groaned softly. Fully awake now, he became aware of the beginnings of the tearing pains which so frequently invaded his guts. Jane would have her new car, but for how long would the smile remain on her lips?

* *

Because of the increasing numbers of injured, Maurici had volunteered his hospital bed to a more needy patient. It was growing dark, but still warm when he alighted from the lorry to walk the last kilometre to his home. He had covered barely half the distance when, even after almost five weeks of treatment, the thigh wound began to cause him pain. Cursing, he searched the roadside, and with his sound hand dragged a length of wood free of the undergrowth to aid his progress.

Needing to rest, he made for the low stone bridge where the click-clicking of insects came from the undergrowth. Looking down on the clothes he was wearing, he smiled over his good fortune. *Senyora* Purcell had realised that he possessed little to wear, and as soon as he was on his feet had brought him a pair of grey flannels and a double-breasted jacket from her husband's wardrobe. These, and his own freshly laundered shirt had enabled him to leave the hospital smartly attired. His thoughts drifted back to the ward and Elizabeth's shy smile as she left that afternoon. Over the weeks he'd grown fond of the pretty young volunteer and wondered if she would miss him when she came on duty in the morning.

Absorbed in his thoughts, he was not immediately aware of the faint smell of wood smoke mingling with that of sodden weeds rising from the flooded riverbed as a result of the recent storm. Attributing the smell to a soldiers camp-fire somewhere in the vicinity he looked warily around, but as the reek of burning wood grew stronger he caught sight of clouds of smoke billowing over an orange glow that stood out against the dark backcloth of the hills beyond. His heart jolted when he saw a sudden burst of sparks which he quickly realised came from the direction of his home! His eyes narrowed and his heartbeats quickened; had his home fallen foul of the opposition?

Fear gripped him as he got to his feet, limping along as best he could in the direction of the flickering glow. Darkness had fallen swiftly and a fire at the masia was something he hadn't foreseen. Praying he would find his parents unharmed he pressed on without regard for his own suffering, but as he drew nearer his spirits sank. Occasional flames sprang from the smouldering skeleton of the *celler* which stood beyond the house, and a flurry of sparks rose like a freshly-lit firework each time a charred piece fell. With relief he saw his home still standing, darkly outlined against the glow, and angry tears coursed freely down his cheeks as he struggled towards it...

"Identify yourself!"

The powerful command from the open front door brought him to a sudden halt on the drive. Was he being challenged by an armed marauder? Seeking cover, he dived into the shadow of a carob tree, freezing at the splatter of stones beside him together with the crack of a rifle.

"*Bachs!*" he yelled, "I have no quarrel with you..."

"Maurici!" came the choked response he instantly recognised, and he saw the gleaming barrel of the gun his father carried as he emerged from the house.

"*Gràcies a Déu!*" Maurici exclaimed as he hurried forward with awkward gait. "Where is *mama?*"

Josep Bachs gathered his son in a close embrace. "She is safe," he replied shakily. "It is terrible, we tried to contact you, they destroyed everything..."

"Who did?" Maurici demanded, urging his father back into the house. "I see the *celler* is almost burnt to the ground."

Josep nodded, but further debate was curtailed when his mother appeared in the doorway, sobbing and shrieking as she rushed forward to take Maurici in her arms.

"At last!" she wailed, clutching him to her breast as she berated him over his absence in her time of crisis.

Feeling as though the air was being crushed from his body, he eased her away. "*Mama,* why are we standing here? It is safer indoors."

With his arm about her heaving shoulders he led her in to the shuttered sala as she wept afresh over his injuries. "They are healing well," he lied consolingly, patting her warm, fleshy shoulder. "Now, tell me what happened here."

Speechless with emotion, she could only shake her head, her ample bosom quivering beneath the silky bodice of her dress as her sobbing continued. But once Josep had secured the outer door and re-lit the oil lamp she calmed a little, casting Maurici an anguished glance as her husband took up the story.

"You see what they have done?" he began, gesturing around him as the flame in the lamp rose. "They have destroyed my *celler,* our possessions..."

In the increasing light, Maurici began to realise exactly what his father meant. He saw the glass-fronted bookcase was shattered, its contents strewn on the floor. Even the family bible had been torn apart, its wispy pages cascading over the arm of the settee where tufts of horsehair protruded through a heavy tapestry cover.

"We were taking our *sesta* when they came," continued his father, adding with a shrug, "The doors were open, as you'd expect, unlike the city we never need to lock them ..."

"*Si,*" Maurici interrupted with a gesture of impatience. "Did they ransack every room?"

Josep nodded and gestured round him with a work-worn hand. "Down here, yes."

"Were either of you harmed?"

"They entered my bedchamber!" his mother interjected shrilly. "Filthy, uncouth men, jeering as I lay there only partly clothed..." Overcome by emotion, she paused to press a handkerchief to her eyes.

Containing his anger, Maurici drew her close. "Hush now, it's over. I doubt they will return. The *celler* matters little compared with your lives."

"*Capitalists*, they called us!" she declared brokenly. "Yet, we've worked hard for what we have..."

"Carmen, please, calm yourself," Josep pleaded, and from a wall cupboard he brought out a bottle and glass *porró*. "Let us take wine to fortify ourselves."

"*Bravo!*" cried Maurici, admiring his father's composure, yet noticing the tremor of his hand as he poured the wine; a glassful for Carmen, then into the *porró* which he raised and tilted, delivering a thin ruby-red stream from its tapered spout into his partly open mouth.

"*Exquisit!*" Josep sucked in his lips. Lowering the vessel he passed it to Maurici who directed it towards his own mouth with similar expertise, extending his arm until the spout was almost thirty centimetres away.

A rejuvenating warmth spread through Maurici's aching body, but his dismay over the destruction of his father's business remained and he pressed him to continue.

"The *celler* must have been well alight before they entered the house," Josep related, "though, had we been awake I doubt we could have saved it. The solid timbers have burned for hours, buckets of water were useless, now there's nothing left to save. I considered it wiser for us to remain indoors as it occurred to me they may return. Thank God, we found your gun in the clock!"

Maurici shot him a wry smile. "Had you much stock?" he enquired, looking through the rear window to where the wine store smouldered.

"Fortunately, I sold the bulk of it the previous week, though had I listened to Lluis and waited for a better price it would have exploded with the rest."

"Where is my cousin? I expected to find him here."

The old man pursed his lips. "Lluis went home, ill from the smoke, I understand."

"Could he not have brought pumps? The river is in flood."

"Lluis had taken the wagon to the city to distribute food amongst the orphans. It was well alight when he returned."

"Pity, *papa*, otherwise he may have been able to douse the flames before they got a hold on the building."

"I doubt it," the older man sighed. "From the smell I reckoned paraffin had been poured around the store. It was well ablaze, too late to save anything."

Wringing her hands Carmen wailed, "We are reduced to paupers, no business, no money…"

"We have money," Josep told her. "There's money from the wine sale."

"And you still have a home," Maurici put in, in an effort to placate her. "Some have lost everything."

She raised her hands and cried, "You call this a home! Look at it, things I've had for years, all destroyed…"

"They can be replaced, whereas you and *papa* cannot."

Josep was defiant. "He is right, Carmen. Give me time, I shall rebuild the *celler*. All I have lost is my sympathy for the Communists!"

"They never had mine!" Carmen countered savagely. "Perhaps now you realise why!"

"Let's leave politics out of it, *mama*. In the morning

we'll discuss a safer place to live until this wretched war is over."

"Safe, until this war is over!" she echoed shrilly. "Such youthful optimism! Tell me, son, when will that be?"

"It can't go on much longer, there have been too many casualties. Of course, you could stay with Lluis' family, near Sitges. They have plenty of room."

"For your mother, yes, Josep agreed, but I have much work here."

"But you can't rebuild until the mess out there is cleared up. Why not let Lluis do that while you relax by the sea?"

Josep shook his head and drew a thin roll of dark tobacco from the pocket of his blackened shirt. "And this season's crop?"

"You'll never have another *celler* ready in time, *papa*, however hard you work. Have a word with your friend in Vilafranca, his vineyard is only half the size it used to be, you could take the fruit there for pressing."

"I'll consider it," Josep said without enthusiasm as he lit his cigar from the lamp, backing away with a curse as the flame singed his moustache.

"Then you'd better consider it quickly," Maurici advised. "As things are now, I can't guarantee your safety here."

"But if we go to Sitges where will you be?" asked his mother. "I worry about you with those awful injuries."

"I'm to spend four weeks recuperating before I return to my Course. The hospitals are crowded, there's a desperate shortage of beds, so I have to find somewhere. What better place than Sitges?" he said with a smile. "Now, *mama*, what you need is a sound night's sleep. I intend to stay down here with the gun at my side."

It had turned midnight before Maurici retired. After taking a final look around the smouldering ruins of the *celler* he had stretched out on the settee, watchful and alert. He dozed only occasionally throughout the night yet, at half past six in the morning, he felt surprisingly fit, his leg no longer causing him pain.

Taking the rifle with him, he went out in the early light to check on the *celler*, bringing back wood to add to the kitchen fire he'd lit earlier, his movements clumsy, hindered by the protective dressing on his hand. Reaching a heavy pan from the rack, he filled it with water and set it on the stove to boil. He saw the hams which usually hung from the ceiling were missing and recalled his mother complaining the intruders had taken their food, but he discovered one under a mesh cover in the cupboard, most of its dry, sweet flesh already cut away. Cursing the unknown thieves, he cut off a slice, giving an agonized gasp when he put pressure on his stump of finger.

"Maurici!" Carmen cried as she bustled in, clicking her tongue when she spotted greasy marks on the well-scrubbed table. Nudging him aside she insisted, "Let me do it, it is not man's work," and indicating the wooden rack above the sink, directed, "Reach me a plate."

"I intended to make breakfast before you rose but there doesn't appear to be any bread in the house."

"Then I shall make some," she said, her dark eyes flashing.

"Make some?" he echoed in amazement. "Not today, were moving out."

"Why not?" she retaliated. "We must eat!"

Realising she would be better employed with her chores rather than allow her thoughts to rekindle the events of the previous day, he capitulated with a grin, "Have you the ingredients?"

"They may have taken my bread but I still have a few kilos of flour," she chuckled, rummaging in the cupboard and sieving some into a bowl.

Maurici left her kneading the dough and found his father upstairs putting clothes and blankets into a heavy trunk. For a few moments he watched from the doorway, observing the deep lines on his ageing fathers face.

"I'm glad you agreed to leave, *papa*. This place is too isolated; you'll be safer in Sitges."

The old man gave a ragged sigh. "So many farms have been abandoned, but your mother refuses to go without me."

"I'll feel easier knowing you are with relatives; let Lluis make a start on repairing the damage here."

Josep returned his attention to the blankets he was folding. "Let us hope it won't be long before it is over," he said wearily, dropping them into the trunk.

"*Papa*, why are you packing blankets? Are there not sufficient in your brother's house?"

"He tells me the spare blankets went missing – has no idea where they are."

"Strange," Maurici agreed, dragging the trunk to the head of the stairs where an aroma of freshly baking bread invaded his nostrils. "Come, let's get this downstairs."

Encouraged by his son's enthusiasm, Josep helped carry the trunk, but the increased pressure on his leg made Maurici wince as they left the house to slide it into the van. With a groan of relief he sat down to breakfast, the pain soon diminishing as he sank his teeth into the hot, flat bread and ate with gusto.

It was approaching midday when they finished loading and prepared to start out. Making the house secure, they took a last look around, gazing sadly upon the ashes of what had once been a thriving business. Carmen's eyes were brimming with tears.

"Think of it as a holiday," Maurici said as the van pulled away. "Like old times."

"*Si*, we've had many happy times in Sitges," she agreed brokenly.

"I recall having ice-creams at the cafe in the square but I doubt such luxuries exist today."

"When the business is re-established we will have a real holiday," Josep put in, shooting his wife a glance. "How about a cruise to Mallorca?"

"Such dreams..." she sighed recovering from her tears, her eyes averted from the shuttered farmhouses and deserted vineyards along the way.

Saddened to leave his freshly pruned vines, Josep fixed his eyes on the road ahead, away from the coast in a south-westerly direction. "I thought it wiser to avoid the city," he said as with a grating of gears he turned the van in the direction of Vilafranca del Penedés. "Too much political violence, we'll take the safer route."

Maurici nodded. "There's less chance of meeting trouble on country roads." But as he spoke he reflected upon the night he was shot on such a road as this. However, all was well and their detour towards the coast once more, was uneventful. And the tension further eased when the bell-towers of the church of Sant Pere de Ribes came in sight and they drove into the empty village streets.

"Poor Lluis must be suffering still," Carmen remarked, then nudged her husband. "You have told the girls there is no work for them now?"

"*Si*, I went to the village after breakfast to pay what I owed in wages, said we would contact them on our return."

She settled down again when the calm, blue waters of the Mediterranean came into view. Soon they were drawing up at the home of Josep's brother, situated on a hill overlooking the small seaside town of Sitges, a kilometre or so away.

Alighting from his cramped position in the rear of the van, Maurici eased his stiff limbs. "I'm surprised cousin Lluis hasn't come out to greet us," he commented, helping his mother alight, but then his aunt appeared in the doorway, her hands outstretched in welcome.

It was almost ten o'clock and very dark when Maurici decided to take a stroll before bed. As he lit a small, black cigar he pondered over why Lluis had retired so early. Had he not recovered from inhaling smoke and fumes? Yet he had refused Maurici's offer to examine his chest and throat and appeared quite taken aback when told he and his parents were to be staying for a while.

He had just reached the point of the hill beyond the house when he thought he heard a distant rumble of thunder, only realising it was the droning of an areoplane as he came to a halt. Holding his breath he listened, soon to discover not only one plane, but many, flying over the sea, going north in the direction of Barcelona.

Inhaling thoughtfully on his cigar, he watched them move into the distance, appearing to decrease height as they flew on towards the city. Then, as he watched and waited, he heard another sound, deep, not unlike that of an explosion, closely followed by another, then another, and fancied he saw a faint glow of light coming from the same direction.

With a gasp of horror, he threw down his cigar and limped hurriedly back to the house. Barcelona was under attack, bombed by the planes he had seen pass overhead.

Chapter 4

Elizabeth had just dropped off to sleep when she was jolted back to consciousness. Unable to discern the cause, she assumed it was just another violent storm and snuggled down. Seconds later came the wail of a siren, a flash of light penetrated the slatted shutters and the windows vibrated as a series of heavy thuds sounded somewhere near. Suddenly, as the room was plunged into darkness, she heard an urgent knocking and her father's voice.

Struggling into her dressing gown she unlocked the door. "An air-raid, darling," he said, "we're going down to the cellars."

In the beam of a lamp he ushered her from the room to join her mother at the top of the stairs. "I thought it was another storm," she gasped, flinching as each explosion sounded closer than the one before.

It seemed as though the hotel was being shaken to its foundations when showers of plaster fell from the ceiling to clatter down the stairwell ahead of them. People were converging on the staircase, their voices fearful in the near darkness. But James kept going, along the panelled corridor to another flight of steps leading down to the cellar. Urging them towards the barrels he put out his lamp to conserve energy. Molly remained calm, but as the sound of bombing increased Elizabeth trembled and hid her face against her father's chest, her thoughts with Maurici, praying he would be safe.

People in varying states of dress were sitting or standing in the flickering light of a candle. A baby screamed in protest over being disturbed, the sound reverberating round the dingy walls and James gave up his place to the grateful mother who rocked the child in her arms until it quietened. A bottle crashed to the floor, the contents forming a dark red pool, releasing a tantalising aroma. Someone gave a nervous laugh, suggesting they drink the remaining bottles stored there to reinforce themselves against what was to come. But the response was weak, and for what seemed an age they huddled together, listening to the odd word of conversation and the anxious cries which rose each time the building shook.

It was early the following morning when the all clear came. For a moment everyone fell silent, looking from one to the other for an indication of what the next move should be. Then someone made a start towards the door and others followed, shoving their way up the narrow staircase in their eagerness to reach the freedom of the street.

James held Molly and Elizabeth back. "No need to rush," he advised in his soft, authoritative voice and stretched out his long legs with a groan of relief. "We'll wait until the majority have gone, otherwise someone may get hurt." With a chuckle he suggested, "I think we should celebrate with a nip of brandy. After all, it's Saint Patrick's Day!"

In Elizabeth's room, they discovered the blanket was

missing from her bed. "Imagine, having to steal a blanket," she sighed. "How sad."

"That's what this war has done to people," said James. "Blankets are scarce. Never mind, I'll fetch you one of ours."

Once settled in her bed, Elizabeth was soon drowsy and, although she'd hated every sip of the fiery brandy, she was thankful for its soothing effect. Maurici had been constantly in her thoughts and she prayed he had escaped the bombing as she drifted into sleep.

Only a few hours later she awoke to the sound of another air raid. This time it was her mother who called and they reached the cellar to find it less crowded. "Your father has left, his paper will expect a report," Molly explained, "but I'm sure he will be back for breakfast."

It was mid morning when James returned, his overcoat and Trilby covered in dust, his expression grim as he related what he had seen. "The city is a complete shambles!" he exclaimed as he took a grateful sip of coffee. "Dense clouds of smoke rising over the centre, buildings torn apart, and hundreds of homeless people carrying their bedding on their backs." He shook his head. "Everyone is devastated. One bomb dropped only yards from the British Club, and I believe the golf course got a battering, too." With an ironic smile he added, "Doesn't look as though I'll get a game of golf until all this is over."

"Any news of the hospital?" Molly asked.

"That side of the city escaped the worst, but they're bound to admit many casualties. The first aid centre was overflowing after the early morning raid."

Her brow furrowed. "We weren't needed on the ward yesterday but this will change everything. I must go."

"But, darling, there could be another raid..."

"I know, James, but we have cellars."

"I could go, too," Elizabeth broke in, relieved to hear the hospital had escaped the bombs.

"It may upset you," Molly said and saw the immediate disappointment on her face."

James observed his daughter with an indulgent smile. "So, I'll come with you. I can write my report later as I may get a good account from one of the patients. Firsthand experience is worth a lot."

Molly touched his stubbly cheek. "Darling, you must be dreadfully tired."

"I'm fine," he insisted. "If you wait here a moment, I'll arrange transport."

Shortly, James was back to say a car was waiting. A colleague and photographer, Enric Puig, soon had them away in his old Renault, dented by falling masonry only that morning.

Barcelona seemed strangely different, Elizabeth noticed, trams had ceased running, yet a continuous stream of ambulances and vehicles of all shapes and sizes drove through the streets. Then, as they turned into a road strewn with rubble, she noticed blood splattered on a wall, dark and sickening amid clouds of dust, forcing them to draw to a halt. Men worked amongst the debris, heaving aside broken masonry, whilst others lugged corpses to a stationary lorry just ahead. She uttered a horrified gasp, realising some were tiny lifeless bodies of children, their sparse clothing hanging in tatters as they were slid onto the bare boards. A pall of smoke hung over the buildings, and across the street an old woman emitted a continual wail as she scrambled amongst the rubble, clawing at it furiously with her bare hands. A lean-bellied dog stood by, watching her every movement, its tail between its legs.

With some streets closed, their route to the hospital was slow, with further diversions when fresh falls of stonework crashed down in their path. On arrival, they were met by scenes of overcrowding far greater than anticipated. The long corridor leading to the ward where Molly and Elizabeth usually worked was packed with those with less severe wounds; men, women, and children, their faces gaunt as they waited for medical attention, their expressionless eyes following them as they made their way through.

"Dear God, what a terrible mess!" James exclaimed softly.

Molly nodded and slipped off her jacket. "I'll let nurse know we've arrived then leave you to it, James."

Relieved to see the building had withstood the raid, Elizabeth was impatient to reach the ward. But when she and her mother had donned an apron and been issued with a list of duties, it took time to find their appointed places. Areas where doctors and nurses were treating minor injuries non-stop were roughly screened off, and makeshift beds filled every corner. In addition to their injuries, many were in poor health, suffering pellagra and scurvy as a result of their inadequate diet.

Aghast at what she saw, Elizabeth reflected on her stolen blanket, hoping it was being put to good use. But as her eyes flitted over each bed in the ward she turned an anguished face to her mother. "Maurici – he's not here!"

"He's reasonably ambulant now and may have been transferred to another ward," Molly suggested. "Be patient, I'll ask."

Elizabeth found that her duties were much harder because of the overcrowding, made worse by a further short raid. There was a lack of bowls and towels, and the food was hardly sufficient for the number of patients in their care. And when a young doctor called her over to assist him with the undressing of a wounded child, its trusting smile brought a lump to her throat. Just then Molly brought news of Maurici, quelling her fear he had been killed in the raid. "Nurse tells me the doctor was satisfied with his progress so he went home the evening before last," she related, adding with a chuckle, "Fortunately, I'd brought in some of your father's spare clothes."

"It must have been after we left," Elizabeth murmured, pleased for Maurici, but wondering if ever she would see him again.

Molly worked extremely hard throughout that afternoon tending injuries resulting from the third bombing raid, while Elizabeth was kept busy painting angry circles of ringworm with iodine, disposing of used dressings, and cleaning bloodstains from the floor.

It was turned six o'clock when a grim-faced James arrived to take them to their hotel, his expression of foreboding one that Molly dreaded. "The port has suffered more bombing, and there are fears of further raids," he said. "People are fleeing the city, and it's rumoured that the British may be advised to leave."

"Leave!" Molly gasped. "You mean, the three of us?"

James gave a helpless shrug. "Obviously, I shall be expected to stay. It's my duty..."

"I can't possibly leave without you."

"But we must consider Elizabeth... you promised."

"Oh, James, surely it can't be that serious," she said, glancing to his colleague for confirmation.

"Darling, the situation here is dangerous – you must leave..."

"I'm not leaving Barcelona," Elizabeth interjected, coming to a halt beside them. "I want to stay and help the people here."

James raised his hands and turned to the slightly younger man. "Didn't I tell you now!" he exclaimed and returned his attention to Molly. "I do have an alternative suggestion, but I'll brook no argument from either of you."

Molly raised her eyebrows. "It rather depends upon what it is."

"Can you be packed and ready to leave within the hour?" he asked, indicating the man beside him to explain, "Enric, here, has offered us accommodation in Sitges."

Molly turned towards James' stocky colleague. "Oh, how kind!" she exclaimed. "But what of your family, *senyor* – will they not object?"

"I have no family, *senyora*," Enric told her, his eyes downcast as he explained, "My mother is killed in street fightings here three weeks ago."

Filled with contrition, Molly took his hand. "I'm so sorry, James did mention it, but I had no idea it was your mother he spoke of. What a dreadful shock."

Managing a quivering smile, Enric indicated it was time to move on, and in less than an hour James had settled his hotel account, telegraphed his paper with a forwarding address, and arranged for a porter to carry suitcases out to the car. With their luggage aboard and sirens wailing in the distance, they pulled away from the hotel. Suffering an ache of almost unbearable sadness, Elizabeth huddled quietly in the dark interior of the car as it left the city to travel the coast road leading to Sitges, thirty seven kilometres south. A tear slid down her cheek as she stared out unseeingly, convinced she would never meet Maurici again.

It was her mother's exclamation of delight that brought her from her sad reverie. They were driving on a narrow road that clung to the tortuous cliff-side above a calm sea sparkling in the moonlight.

"We are almost home," Enric announced as the church of San Bartolome came into view, silhouetted against the clear night sky, its foundations bathed by the sea.

"How picturesque," said Molly as they entered the narrow streets of Sitges. "It's like being on holiday."

Elizabeth could not share her mother's joy, but as they drove along she began to take notice and wound down the window. Here, the pattern of life appeared tranquil with open shops and families strolling peacefully along with no sign of conflict, or sound of gunfire.

Enric brought the car to a halt beside a small whitewashed house, one of the buildings extending from the church, facing the sea. "My home," he announced, alighting from the car. "Please, be welcome."

"Thanks be to God you brought us here," James murmured with a gentle shake of his head. "Otherwise there would have been no alternative but for them to leave."

Enric shrugged off James' gratitude and drew him aside to say, "It is reported a ship is coming into Barcelona to take foreigners away from the city, also more bombings in the port, they are safer here." And as he opened the boot he pointed a stubby finger along the coast to continue in reminiscent tones, "I remember, here in Sitges, after the beginning of the war, a ship came by that point to take off English tourists. But the Republicans, they think is a Nationalist ship, and I plead with them not to fire on the boats sent to take tourists away."

"You've seen quite a lot of action, one way or another," James commented as he helped unload the tightly packed boot.

Enric lifted his broad shoulders. "Gives plenty work, *si*?"

"But there's been an increase in censorship," reminded James. "I don't relish the thought of being expelled – or even worse – if there's anything amiss in my dispatches."

Once inside the house, Enric lit the lamps before going to help James with the remaining luggage. In the flickering light, Molly and Elizabeth took in their surroundings, their eyes travelling up from the traditional patterns of the floor tiles to the ceramics and paintings displayed on each white wall and the ceiling arched between each beam in Catalan style.

Setting down another case, Enric gestured round the room. "Sorry, *senyora*, is not the big house you are having in England."

Molly turned and smiled. "Please, don't apologise, it is charming. And must we be so formal, Enric? Please, call me Molly."

The house consisted of two downstairs rooms and two bedrooms, the latter of which Enric insisted they take. And with complete disregard of their objections, he chose to sleep on the huge settee in the smaller downstairs room.

"It's damned generous of you, Enric," said James, his hand on his colleague's shoulder, "but I insist we give a hand with the chores."

Enric raised his hand. "No, I have a lady who is coming three times in the week – she is cleaning and washing – but cooking, no." His dark eyes travelled hopefully to Molly. "Maybe you are good with the cooking – yes?"

Molly smiled to herself. "Well, I don't have much experience, but I'm sure we can concoct something."

"Excellent! But today I make the omelette," he announced, and producing a round loaf from the cloth bag he brought from the car he laughed as he held it aloft. "Also the good Catalan bread, is exchange for my ration of sugar."

With their appetites whetted, Molly and Elizabeth went upstairs to unpack their clothing, storing it away in the huge carved wardrobe.

"My mother would be horrified," Molly chuckled as they emptied the cases, "yet I'm quite enjoying myself."

"At least we shall know where everything is," Elizabeth approved. "I can't find a thing after Mrs Dowkes unpacks."

"Your father always says it does no harm to learn how to look after ones-self, and he's most independent."

"Yes, Grandpa told me I'd learn more about life here than ever I would in twenty years at Woodington."

With a neatly folded pile of clothing in her arms, Molly paused. Placing the clothing in a drawer she gave a rueful smile, "There will be times when he'll be very lonely. I must write to him soon."

"I'm glad you're not like grandmother," Elizabeth remarked as she tidied away the rest of her things, "and I know she doesn't like Daddy."

"I'd rather you didn't speak of your grandmother that way," Molly admonished gently. "There are times when adults have conflicting opinions but it doesn't mean anything."

"She once referred to him as a common Irish newsvendor!" Elizabeth pursued heatedly. "I overheard her myself."

"Oh, darling, she wouldn't mean it. She can be irritable at times, I know, but we should make allowances..."

"I don't care, she shouldn't say awful things about Daddy," Elizabeth returned petulantly.

"Elizabeth, please!" Molly cried in dismay. "Now, finish your unpacking, there's a dear."

Downstairs they found Enric had pulled the bare wooden table into the centre of the larger room, and James was busily setting out cutlery. "Enric keeps apologising for everything," James told them, "but I've insisted we'll be very happy here."

"Come," said Enric, placing a huge omelette on the table. "*Bon profit!*"

Elizabeth thought this one of the best meals she had tasted for some time, and the glass of wine her father allowed helped to relax the tension she was feeling. Whilst the others raised their glasses to a speedy end to war, she added a silent toast to Maurici and prayed that her wish would be realised. Sadly, she knew this was a forlorn hope.

* *

"Pincott!" William bellowed down the wide staircase. "You haven't changed the accumulator – my wireless is dead!"

"I'm sorry, sir, I understood madam to say you wouldn't need it," the butler explained, hurrying up the steps.

"Why the hell not?" William exploded, his face purple.

"Madam considers the news far too distressing, sir," replied Pincott, his voice almost a whimper.

"It's more damned distressing not to know what's going on," William roared. "Attend to it, immediately!"

"As you wish, sir," the servant conceded, descending the stairs at a less dignified pace.

Seething, William returned to the drawing room, bringing his fist down on the Bakelite wireless when he yelped from pain. Why the devil did Jane give orders contrary to his wishes? He needed to hear every snippet of news from Spain, however insignificant it may seem to her. It had shaken him to read Barcelona had been a victim of repeated bomb attacks by Italian planes. He couldn't rest until he heard the report confirmed on the news.

Expecting to see Pincott, when the drawing room door opened, he turned from the wireless to find Jane in the room, her lips compressed in a thin line.

"Pincott appears quite distressed," she remarked. "What have you been saying?"

"I simply wish to hear the news on the wireless so I directed him to attend to it," William stated as evenly as he could. "I do wish you wouldn't countermand my orders."

"It was entirely for your own good..."

He smacked his fist into the palm of his other hand to exclaim passionately, "But, damn it all, Jane, they're not bombing only military targets in Barcelona as one would expect. I must know the family are safe!"

"Do you think it doesn't affect me? Molly is also my daughter, you know."

"I know, dear, but quite frankly, I'd rather be there than waiting here worrying about them."

"In your state of health, William, quite impossible!"

"You're right, of course." Suddenly, a note of excitement crept into his voice as he decided, "I have a mind to telephone them, just to be sure they are safe."

Down in the draughty hall, with the earpiece held tightly to his ear, William requested an international trunk call. But his hopeful expression was quickly replaced by one of extreme disappointment when he was informed lines to Barcelona were not available, suggesting he try again the following day. Utterly dejected, he returned to the drawing room, going to the mahogany cupboard to pour a large brandy.

"I expect the lines are down," he said. "I'll leave it until the morning."

"I don't suppose you'll learn anything if you do," she said, nodding towards the glass he held to comment coldly, "Drink plenty of that and you'll probably forget all about it."

"I think I'll retire early," he announced, bewildered by her lack of emotion. "I'm rather tired."

"What about dinner?"

"I'm really not hungry," he declined, and picking up the brandy balloon he left for his room.

William had barely time to undress before the pain started, an agonizing, burning sensation below his ribs. However much he tried to relax as he lay between the cold linen sheets, the pain gnawed relentlessly at his stomach.

He took a large dose of the chalky mixture Doctor Wilson had prescribed and was beginning to feel some ease when came a tap on the door and Pincott sought permission to enter.

"Yes, what is it, Pincott?" he called irritably.

"Excuse the interruption, sir," said Pincott, his head appearing round the door. "Madam asked me to tell you there has been a telephone call from London."

William sat bolt upright. "A telephone call, from London?"

"Yes, from Mr Purcell's newspaper office..."

"Well, go on, man!" William snapped. "What do they say?"

"They have received a telegraph from Spain and wish to inform you your family is safe."

A harsh sob escaped William's lips. "Thank God!" he gasped, sinking back on his pillows. But in seconds he was again upright, vomiting a marbled mixture of brandy and magnesia onto the carpet.

Chapter 5

"Any news, uncle?" Maurici asked, taking his place at the table.

"I've heard nothing," replied Miquel and glanced in his son's direction to ask, "You been to Barcelona, Lluis?"

"Too dangerous," Lluis mumbled, without raising his head.

Noting this, Maurici pondered over Lluis's frequent absences from home and thought it strange that he hadn't learned anything on his travels.

"I wonder how they are coping with the shortages of meat and bread," Carmen said, seating herself beside her nephew.

Lluis shot her a sullen sideways glance and reached for a piece of bread. "I'll bet the Capitalists don't go short!" he said with unexpected ferocity as he tore the crust apart.

"No-one should go without, regardless of their beliefs," his father contradicted mildly. "The majority of us are hard-working people who don't give a fig for politics."

Lluis glanced up. "Then you should, father, otherwise the Capitalists will totally suppress the working classes while they feed off the fat of the land..."

"We're not suppressed," his mother interjected, ladling the thin vegetable soup. "We have sufficient food."

"Indeed," Josep concurred politely. "We have eaten well during the past three days, one would never think we're in the midst of a war."

To draw the conversation away from politics Maurici remarked, "How quiet it is today – no sign of planes."

Josep scratched his head. "You're right, for the last three days and nights we heard little else. God only knows what dangers they face in the city."

Talk of danger had transported Maurici's thoughts to Elizabeth for the umpteenth time; he now felt compelled to check on her well-being for himself.

The afternoon was incredibly warm, the air buzzing with insects and Maurici caught the sweet smell of wild rosemary through the open window of the van as he drove. Drawing to a halt he took out his penknife to cut a bunch of the aromatic herb mixed with some of the golden blooms which were growing in abundance at the roadside. Perhaps it would bring a breath of country air to the drab ward.

It was almost five o'clock when he reached the city where the scene of devastation caused him to slow to walking pace. He knew there had been many planes and much gunfire, but the scene of the destruction horrified him; a truly heartbreaking sight of homeless people wandering aimlessly through the streets, laden with what possessions they could salvage.

Cursing the futility of war, he drove on past sandbagged cinema doorways, between lines of trees, their branches trailing grotesquely in the rubble beneath. He saw a row of apartment blocks with ragged curtains hanging behind glassless windows, another with its outer wall completely blasted away to reveal the dusty furnished interior, almost like a film set. Many shop windows had been boarded up, others abandoned as the blast had left them with shards of glass protruding from the frames, and window dressing scattered on the pavement. Looters had been at work, shops containing anything edible were totally cleared. With great relief he found the hospital had lost only a few panes of glass, whereas apartments only streets away had suffered considerably. Finding a shady parking place, he took the flowers and his walking stick from the van to enter the hospital.

Scanning the quiet ward, he saw Sister Teresa, her expression serene until his shadow fell beside her when he met her quick, apprehensive glance. Not wishing to disturb her dozing patients, he held out the flowers to enquire softly, "How are you managing to care for so many? You must be totally exhausted."

"Sadly, many of those admitted during the first raid passed away," she told him, "it was so unexpected they had no time to reach shelter. And although we transferred children requiring surgery, there is still a shortage of beds."

"And staff?" he queried casually. "These past days must have stretched your endurance to the limit."

"We manage," she said on a sigh. "It is truly amazing what the human body is capable of in times of crisis."

"But you have the volunteers," he said with a supposed air of indifference.

"One only. The English ladies are no longer with us."

Maurici's spirits dropped, but rose again when she went on to add, "After that first terrible night of bombing, senyor Purcell decided his family would be safer elsewhere."

"You mean England?" he pressed. "Assuming they survived."

"Yes, they survived, but they haven't left for England. They are with a colleague of *senyor* Purcell, in Sitges."

His spirits lifted. "What a coincidence! My parents are with relatives only a kilometre or so from there."

"I do miss them," she went on, warmed by his expression, "but the shortage of petrol makes travelling difficult."

"Difficult indeed, but at least they are safe."

"The *senyora* is devoted to nursing so I suggested the colony for orphaned children in Sitges would welcome her."

"*Bé,* they will be grateful for her assistance," he agreed softly.

"And you must not neglect your studies."

"I will do my best," he promised.

"May God go with you," she whispered as he bid her a polite, "*Adéu,*" and limped away.

His spirits soared as he drove off, singing an aria from Tosca, and barely fifty minutes later he was touring the streets of Sitges, hoping to see the Purcell family taking an evening stroll. He had no idea where they were staying and finally drew the van to a halt by the deserted beach, alighting to gaze thoughtfully out to sea. Shading his eyes he turned, his gaze travelling over the row of fisherman's houses, to the hotel at the end of the promenade on one side, then along towards the church on his right. But he saw no sign of Elizabeth as he lingered there until his injured leg began to throb. Deciding to resume his search in the morning, he drove out of Sitges back to his uncle Miquel's home.

* *

William felt as though a load had been lifted from his shoulders as he replaced the earpiece following a telephone call from Molly. News of the bombing had almost driven him insane, but to be assured that the family was a safe distance from the war-torn city was good news indeed. Smiling to himself, he climbed the stairs and went along to the oak-panelled library to run his eye along the shelves in search of an atlas. Sitges, Molly had said, and she'd spelt it out so that he could check its position on the map. With hands that trembled he held a magnifying glass over the appropriate page and traced his finger down the north-east coast of Spain. Coming to Barcelona he paused and uttered a sigh of pleasure when, in the smallest print, a little further south, he found Sitges.

Taking the atlas into the drawing room with the intention of showing his discovery to Jane, he remembered that she was out riding. He frowned; she seemed always to be missing when he had some item of interest to impart. Yet, because of her absence he'd had the duration of Molly's call to himself. She had sounded exuberant, assuring him the move suited them well; James could work on his assignment, whilst she and Elizabeth enjoyed the sea air which was bringing colour to their cheeks.

Leaving the atlas on the table he went to the white-tiled bathroom where he studied his own complexion in the mirror. His once wavy, golden hair had rapidly faded to grey, and there was more than ample room to run his finger around the inside of his stiff, white collar where folds of crêpey flesh shrank beneath. Tightening his tie, he returned to the drawing room where he poured himself a glass of sherry to celebrate the call.

He sank contentedly into a chair, his glass clasped between his hands. He could rely upon James to protect them, he mused comfortingly as he succumbed to waves of tiredness resulting from his sleepless nights.

It was the thud of a door that roused William when, suddenly, he became embarrassingly aware of a curious wetness seeping between his thighs. Fully awake now, he got to his feet, sending the empty sherry glass bouncing over the carpet. Once realising the reason for the sensation he took out his handkerchief to wipe the front of his trousers just as Jane entered the room.

"What on earth are you doing?" she asked, spotting the stain on his beige suit.

"Only sherry, dear, I must have dozed off."

"Little wonder you can't sleep at night."

"Molly telephoned a short time ago," he glanced at his pocket watch, "twenty minutes to be precise." His expression became almost dreamy as he continued, "It was wonderful to hear her voice – unbelievably clear for such a distance..."

"Maybe so, but is she coming home?"

"She didn't say, dear," he said, retrieving his empty glass, "but it seems they moved out of the city to a place further south."

"And into more trouble, I expect! James has no right to put their lives in jeopardy – they should be here, at home."

"But he has to be there, it's his assignment..."

"I'm not suggesting he returns with them. If he wants to risk his life, that's his concern."

"That's hardly fair, dear," he reproached gently, beckoning her towards the open atlas. "Come and look, I've found the place where they're staying."

Taking only a brief glance at the spot he indicated, she crossed over to ring the bell. "After so much bombing, I expect the war is almost at an end," she remarked, sliding off her riding jacket. "And if the Republicans haven't realised the futility of their efforts by now, they never will."

"I doubt they will submit without putting up a fight. Molly tells me the bombing continued until the eighteenth, but there's no talk of surrender."

With a shrug of indifference, she commented, "Our Prime Minister's birthday – sixty-nine, I believe – yet he appears in excellent health, which reminds me of an item I read in the paper. Doctors now advocate we should drink hot water to combat that sluggish feeling in the mornings."

William shot her a despairing glance.

"It also helps prevent middle-age spread," she went on waspishly. "You should try it, far better for you than sherry."

"Knowing Molly is safe is a sufficient tonic for me."

She gave a derisive snort. "I suppose Alex Wilson put that idea into your head, but I don't hold with any of his modern ideas. In my opinion, you drink too much, and the amount of rice pudding you eat is disgusting!"

"But I never put on weight," he protested, patting his belly which sagged beneath the waistband of his trousers. "In fact, I've lost pounds!" He was cut short by the arrival of the housemaid.

"Mr Pincott has stepped out for a moment," Elsie explained nervously when she saw her mistress' enquiring frown.

"Has stepped out for a moment, what?" Jane bit out. Behind her, William cringed.

"For a moment, madam," Elsie corrected herself, her colour rising.

"Don't let me have to remind you again!" Jane insisted sharply. "And tell cook we shall dine out this evening."

Elsie bobbed a curtsey. "Yes, madam."

Jane dismissed her and saw William's expression of surprise.

"I hadn't realised we were dining out tonight."

"Grant issued the invitation when I rode with him earlier."

"I'm not sure I ought to, dear, I find their meals too rich for my digestion."

"For goodness' sake, William, I accepted. It is your place to accompany me."

"B-but, you've only just told me I eat too much," he protested, "and I've such a delicate constitution."

"Oh do stop making excuses," she said wearily. "All you ever want to do is listen to that old wireless. It will do you good to leave the house for a while."

"Very well," he submitted with a sigh, "though I do find these occasions rather tiresome. Grant is hardly the most stimulating of conversationalists."

"If you only discuss cars or golf, what do you expect?" she shot back. "Our social life is fast diminishing; we did little at Easter which meant I missed the showing of Private Lives at York Rep."

"I'm sorry, I wasn't up to going anywhere over the Easter week-end."

"But you're well enough to dine with the Grant's this evening, particularly if you don't overdo things at lunch."

Snatching up her jacket she swept from the room. William watched her go, noting that for a woman of sixty-three years she still retained her slim figure and grace of movement. He smiled, Jane's bitterness slipping away as Molly's telephone call returned to mind. But before going down to lunch he made his way to the tiny oratory adjoining the guest room where he lowered himself to his knees and thanked God for sparing his daughter from the violence of war.

Dinner at the Grant's proved to be a less tedious occasion than William had anticipated. He'd not felt so well for some time and found himself seated next to a younger man who shared his enthusiasm for motor cars and entertained him with his adventures when taking part in a hill climb at Garrowby. He could sense the other man's elation as he recounted the speeds he'd travelled and longed for such an experience in his own dreary life. He'd taken an extra glass of port when the ladies withdrew, and enjoyed a cigar without Jane's nostrils twitching in distaste.

"I hope you haven't drunk too much," she said as they drove back to the Hall, buffeted by a strong March wind.

"Not too much," he said mildly, and to satisfy a devilish urge added, "Not nearly as much as Grant, or his father."

She drew her fur wrap tightly around her. "That remark was uncalled for. Young Miles Grant is a perfect gentleman."

He laughed. "Young Miles? He's well into his forties!"

"Forty-one, actually, and in extremely good health."

"Prime of life, I suppose," William granted. "I recall saying to James..."

"Ah yes, which reminds me – Miles was enquiring after Elizabeth, asked when she was expected home. I told him, he will be the first to know," she said, adding with a sideways glance, "I want to cultivate his interest in her."

"He's more than twice her age!" cried William, momentarily losing control. The car veered, narrowly missing the stone pillar at the entrance to the drive.

"For goodness sake, you'll have us both killed!" she shrieked, her beaded evening bag slipping from her lap.

He steered back onto the pebbled drive. "I'm sorry, but when you speak of Grant in such terms it worries me."

"Elizabeth needs a mature partner," she pressed, regaining her composure, "and Miles would make an ideal husband."

Fetching the Humber to a skidding halt, William brought his hands down on the wheel with a forceful smack. "So, not only do we disagree over James, but Miles Grant as well!"

* *

During the days following their arrival, Molly and Elizabeth acquainted themselves with Sitges whilst James and Enric travelled into Barcelona to report on the state of things there. Each afternoon, while the locals dined or slept, they had taken to strolling through the narrow streets, admiring the ancient buildings crowded behind the church, or meandering along the beach where the fine golden sand almost reached the row of fishermen's cottages. A little further along they lingered beneath the palms, watching men make barrels to be filled with local wine; all older men they noticed, assuming the younger men had gone to war. On warm days they would sit in the shade of a parasol, watching the gentle waves lap the beach beyond the *casamata*, a curious object, like a concrete hayrick, set there in defence of the town.

One particularly warm day as they relaxed in the sun, Molly expressed something that had been playing on her mind. "It's lovely sitting here in the sun but I really need to be occupied, do something useful. I recall sister mentioning the local orphanage. Perhaps I could help out there. Enric is bound to know where it is."

"I'd like to go, too, especially to be with children."

"Why not volunteer for the afternoons? I can manage the cooking." Molly smiled. "I mentioned it to your grandpa when I telephoned, he thought it most amusing."

Elizabeth laughed. "If grandmother saw you wearing an apron, she'd faint!"

* *

Following his visit to the hospital, Maurici positioned his van near the orphanage after touring the narrow streets. But after another futile wait he began to think the sister had misunderstood the Purcell's destination. Unable to bear the continued frustration he decided to visit the hotel in Barcelona, the one Elizabeth had mentioned.

Coming to a halt outside the hotel, he discovered the building had suffered minor damage, though business continued inside. But when he enquired if the Purcell's had left a forwarding address, the receptionist merely shook his head.

"Actually, I wish they had – they owe money," the man told him. "But our register was destroyed during the last night of bombing,"

Maurici frowned. "That does surprise me."

The receptionist took an envelope from one of the key slots and slapped it on the desk. "This came two days ago, a photograph of the *senyoreta*. Considering the charge, it's not a professional job. Look for yourself."

With eager fingers Maurici withdrew the photograph which showed an image of Elizabeth standing beside the Canaletes fountain. A photograph of poor quality, he had to agree, but clear enough to make his heartbeat quicken. "I'll pay," he offered. "How much?"

"But how are you going to deliver it without an address?"

"I have a friend who knows exactly where they'll be staying," Maurici lied, reaching for his wallet.

"You know them well?" the receptionist queried, his eye on the wallet.

"Very well," Maurici assured him, handing over coins exceeding the amount owing. "It is only due to the bombing that we lost touch."

The receptionist's expression brightened. He handed over the photograph and pocketed the money. Returning the picture to the envelope, Maurici smiled to himself; he would willingly have paid double that ammount for it, or even more.

On Wednesday morning, with the photograph of Elizabeth in his breast pocket, Maurici drove into Sitges to where the post office was situated. His hopes of tracing her had risen, along with the desire to renew her acquaintance. He had been attracted to her from the moment they met; not only her fine features and startling blue eyes, but also the sweetness of her nature.

Deep in reverie, he almost bumped into a postman setting out, his leather bag bulging weightily from the strap over his shoulder.

"Ah, just the man I seek!" he cried, producing the photograph. "I need to contact an English family here but, unfortunately, during the bombing, I lost their address. This young lady is their daughter."

The postman shook his head then, as an afterthought, asked, "Are they with the Internationals?"

"Her father works for an English newspaper."

Spotting a colleague leaving the office, the postman called him over. Taking the photograph, the second man studied it for a moment then nodded. "*Sí*, I have seen the *senyoreta*," he said, then casting Maurici a cautious glance, queried, "What is the reason for your enquiry?"

Assuring him he had only the most honourable of reasons, he went on to say he had promised to deliver something from their hotel in Barcelona. To this, the first man grinned, suggesting he would gladly deliver something to the pretty *senyoreta* himself.

"Ah, *sí*," the second man said, "at the end of the narrow street leading to the *taverna*," and he added the owner's name, *Enric Puig*.

"*Moltes gràcies!*" Maurici slid back into the driving seat to steer the van in the direction of the address given, careering through the square, past the barricade of stone and sandbags, at such a ridiculous speed even the Civil Guard standing there enjoying a cigarette turned to gaze after him in amazement. Down a narrow street leading to the sea-front he braked noisily and turned towards a row of whitewashed houses.

Spotting an old lady mending fishing nets, he enquired for the house of Puig. But she merely shrugged, waving a scrawny arm towards a house slightly larger than those occupied by the fishermen. There he saw a woman on her knees, scrubbing the tiled entrance.

When he drew up she rose awkwardly to her feet. "What is it, *senyor?*" she challenged, drying her hands on her hessian apron. "Who are you?"

"I am acquainted with an English family residing with *senyor* Puig. I must contact them."

She came up to the van to peer inside. "You from the authorities?"

"No, no," Maurici assured her, "I was acquainted with them in Barcelona. I have an important letter to deliver."

She straightened and looked back to the house. "This is *senyor* Puig's residence but there is no-one here."

"Thank you, *senyora*. When do you expect them to return?"

She blew out her cheeks and shrugged. "Maybe noon, maybe later." Reaching through the open window she offered, "Give me the letter, I will put it on the bureau." Seeing him hesitate, she confirmed, "Don't worry, they trust old Rosa. It will be quite safe."

"Very well, *senyora*, but first I'll add a message." He wrote a few words on the envelope, adding his present address, before the woman tucked the letter into her apron pocket and returned to her chores, leaving Maurici feeling a trifle defeated. Would Elizabeth respond to the delivery of a mere photograph? Would she connect it with the day when they met amidst the terror of gunfire and death in Barcelona?

Chapter 6

"I believe this is intended for you," said James, passing an envelope to his daughter.

Elizabeth's lips parted in delight as she read the short message on the outside. 'This arrives at hotel in Barcelona – you may wish to receive,' it said, followed by Maurici's name and the address of a house near Sitges.

"Oh, that is kind!" she exclaimed, taking out the photograph. "I wonder how it came into his possession."

"According to your mother it was delivered by the young man you both nursed."

"It was taken on the Rambla the day we met," she said, passing it to her father.

James' brows rose as he studied his daughter's likeness. "I suspect he is hoping to renew your acquaintance."

"Do you really think so?" she murmured, blushing as she looked up to meet her father's striking blue eyes. "I wish I'd been here when he called."

James' smile faded. "Perhaps not. After all, you hardly know the man."

"But I should thank him for his trouble, it would be only polite."

"Indeed, maybe a brief note," he agreed. "Actually, I'm travelling that way tomorrow, I'll deliver it if you wish."

That evening Elizabeth wrote a letter in her most careful handwriting. "You're keeping it brief, I hope," Molly remarked with a glimpse over her daughter's shoulder. "Do add my good wishes for his recovery."

"Yes, Mother," she conceded stiffly. "Don't worry, I'll not include anything indiscreet."

Mother? With a pang of sadness Molly realised her daughter was growing up. James was right; there was something quite different about Elizabeth's interest in this young man. Her high spirits since she'd received word from him betrayed her desire.

* *

With Elizabeth's letter in his hand, James slid into the car beside Enric. "Would you mind stopping to deliver this?" he asked, indicating the address on the envelope.

"Ah yes, it is the Bachs family home," Enric commented warmly.

James glanced round with interest. "You know them?"

"Of course, my father and old Bachs were school friends," Enric chuckled. "They were a shrewd pair."

"Something you have inherited," James grinned. "I've seen you strike many a bargain with your ration card."

They laughed and drove away in companionable silence until Enric turned off the narrow main road to travel along a rutted track leading to a house standing amidst fruit trees, their branches enveloped in a haze of blossom.

"Is this Maurici fellow the son?" James queried as they drew to a halt.

Enric shook his head. "No, they do have a son but his name is Lluis."

James alighted and walked towards the house when a tall young man who looked to be in his early twenties, came limping from between the trees to call out a greeting.

"*Bon dia!*" James responded in his basic Catalan, continuing haltingly, "I have a letter for this house."

"You are English, sir?" the young man queried.

"Ah, you speak English!" he said with relief. "I expect you also speak Castilion which I can manage slightly better."

The other gave a faint smile. "Only if necessary, sir."

"Either way, perhaps you can help me. I have a letter for *senyor* Maurici Bachs. I believe he resides at this address?"

"I am Maurici Bachs," the younger man told him, extending his left hand. "This is the home of my uncle, Miquel Bachs and, since the bombing, also my temporary home."

Slightly on his guard, James took the proffered hand. "So you are the gentleman who was hospitalised in Barcelona," he said spotting the dressing on Maurici's other hand. "I understand you met my wife and daughter there."

"Indeed, they help my recovery," Maurici acknowledged. "I have admiration for them."

Gratified by the other's manner, James found himself agreeing unashamedly. "Yes, they insisted on going to the hospital, even when the bombing started..." He hesitated. Meeting this young fellow seemed to release the tension which had built up the previous evening.

Suddenly aware of the look of expectancy on Maurici's face, he murmured awkwardly, "My apologies, *senyor* Bachs, I must not take up your time."

Maurici smiled. "They are your family, it is natural for you to commend them."

"Good of you to agree," James nodded, and handed over the letter. "Thank you once again, it was most kind of you to deliver my daughter's photograph."

"A moment, sir," said Maurici as James made to move away. "Have I your permission to call on the ladies, to thank them?"

James paused. "I expect that would be in order," he managed, meeting the other's hopeful expression, "though it's hardly my place to invite you. Not my house, you see, but perhaps a short visit one Sunday."

Maurici inclined his dark head. "Thank you, sir. My regards to the ladies."

With a rather curt farewell, James returned to the car to exclaim, "I must be out of my mind! I've actually agreed to the fellow calling, and without your consent."

Enric grinned. "Is all right – is your home also – your friends are welcome."

"B-but he's not my friend!" James spluttered. "And he had the cheek to ask if he could visit the girls – well, obviously, it's Elizabeth he means."

"You must be admiring his nerves," Enric grinned.

"Admire his nerve," James corrected, and with a hiss of impatience continued, "But damn it all, I don't know if I should encourage such a friendship – we hardly know the man." James turned to his colleague, brows raised. "You do see my situation?"

"He would be contriving the way to meet her," Enric responded shrewdly. "We Catalans are a determined breed."

James shot his colleague a faintly disapproving glance. "Determined or not, I don't like Elizabeth associating with just anyone. Not that I have anything against your countrymen," he added quickly. "I mean anyone – British, Irish, Catalan – whatever their nationality."

Enric suppressed a smile. "But he is an educated man – a student – different from the son, Lluis."

"Why do you say that?"

Enric shrugged. "He is, as you say, the black sheep, never mixing with local boys." Pointing ahead he said, "Ah, there, with the motorcycle, that is Lluis Bachs."

James looked in the direction Enric indicated to see a solidly built young man who glanced up from his machine to fasten his cold, dark stare on them as they drove by. "Arrogant looking young devil," he remarked as they left the bumpy track to return to the main road.

"According to the gossip, he is mixing with the young Communists of Barcelona – not like the man you speak with."

"Oh, I see," James responded vaguely. "Then, you don't object to him calling?"

Enric's brows rose. "Who? The son?"

"No, this Maurici fellow. I have to admit, he was uncommonly civil."

"Possessive father, eh?" his colleague chuckled. "But, James, it is good for Elizabeth to have the company of someone her ages. You agree?"

"Well, maybe," James admitted reluctantly, "but only if we're at home."

Still clutching the unopened letter, Maurici watched as the car drove away and turned towards Vilafranca. He couldn't believe his good fortune, or that he'd had the audacity to seek the permission of *senyor* Purcell to visit his wife and daughter. Yet, although he admired the *senyora*, it was Elizabeth he so desperately wanted to meet, and for one awful moment he'd thought her father was about to refuse. A Sunday, he'd suggested. A short visit. The whole family could be present, but even that was preferable to a refusal.

Seeing Lluis approaching he slipped the letter into his pocket even though he was aching to read its contents.

"Who was that?" cousin Lluis demanded.

"Someone I knew in Barcelona. No-one you know."

"What did they want?" Lluis persisted sullenly, wiping his oily hands on the seat of his corduroy trousers.

"They merely enquired after my health," Maurici supplied and saw Lluis' smirk.

Knowing there would be little privacy indoors, Maurici strolled away through the trees and along the ridge of the steep slopes overlooking Sitges where he seated himself on the stump of a pine. Opening the envelope with the utmost care, he withdrew the single sheet of notepaper and read, 'Sitges. 25th of March, 1938. Dear Mister Bachs. Thank you so much for delivering my photograph. As I have no idea how you came by it, I would be most obliged if you could let me know to whom I owe payment. I do hope you are making progress and join my mother in sending good wishes for your recovery.' The letter was signed, 'Elizabeth J Purcell'.

He read it once more then gazed into space. A polite little note of thanks but, unaware he would seek permission to visit, had she included the question of payment in the hope of receiving a reply? Smiling to himself he returned the letter to his pocket. He would call on her this coming Sunday. Two more days which, for him, couldn't pass quickly enough.

* *

William was gazing through the rain-splashed window when Jane returned from her Sunday morning ride. Looking down, he saw Pincott hurrying out to meet her, taking her under the shelter of a large, black umbrella as she handed him her hat and crop. Turning from the scene he sighed, hoping she was in better humour than when she left. What was it that drew her away from the comfort of the house on such a day? He enjoyed the occasional ride over the estate but never ventured out in the pouring rain.

"More rain," Jane complained, joining him by the fire, "and it could be worse next week when April comes in."

"But good for the garden," he murmured evenly.

"Turning her palms to the crackling logs, she related, "I've just heard of the accident at the Bedale point-to-point races yesterday. Miles tells me the horses came down like nine-pins, throwing the riders under the hooves of those behind."

"Oh dear. Many hurt?"

"Quite a number. Evidently the ground was extremely hard."

"This rain will ease it," he said, helping her out of her jacket. "Was Grant competing?"

"Sorry to disappoint you, he was merely a spectator and quite unscathed."

William gave a guilty start. "That was fortunate," he said, adding under his breath, "for Grant, anyway."

She cast him a sharp glance. "Did anyone call whilst I was out?"

"Only Alex on his return from church, just a social call. I do wish I'd asked him to pick me up on his way there, it's simply ages since I attended a service."

"You can go with me this evening."

"I never feel well later in the day," he complained. "I'm much brighter in the mornings."

She gave a dismissive snort. "And what else did Wilson have to say?"

"Actually, he was telling me about the Spanish refugee children staying in Scarborough. They're from the Basque area, needing homes until the war in Spain is over. I recall a meeting concerning them being held in York."

"I hope he wasn't expecting to place any with us?"

He hesitated. "Well, it had crossed his mind," he said at last. "We have the room, and it would be wonderful for those poor, unfortunate children..."

"You can put that idea out of your head right away! Foreigners here, at Woodington? Whatever next!"

"Dash it all, they're only children," he began, when she spun round to face him, a spot of high colour on each cheek.

"There are no spare rooms in this house!" she declared savagely. "Any space we have is for the use of Molly and Elizabeth, and I intend writing to James' superiors to insist they are brought back, immediately!"

Sunday dawned with a clear sky; a perfect day for visiting the Purcells. Maurici shaved with a freshly honed razor, adding an extra splash of cologne saved for special occasions before donning a crisp white shirt.

Combing his short, dark hair into place, he drove down to Sitges to go in search of a newspaper and flowers. It was only a quarter to eleven. To pass the time he parked on the promenade and read the newspaper, occasionally glancing across the beach to where a group of children dug holes in the sand. It warmed his heart to hear their laughter, their complete unawareness of the problems around them.

Checking his pocket watch with the church clock, he alighted from the van and reached for the bunch of budding Ginesta. His heartbeat quickened as he drew near to the house where *senyora* Purcell and two men, whom he recognised as Elizabeth's father and his colleague, were engrossed in newspapers spread out on a table between them.

Molly glanced up, her crimson lips parting in surprise. "*Senyor* Bachs – how lovely to see you!" she said, smoothing down the pleats of her dress as she rose to meet him.

This was the first time Maurici had seen the *senyora* out of uniform and he was greatly impressed, responding with an equally warm greeting as he presented the flowers.

"Come, join us," she invited, sending him a wide, beautiful smile.

Both men had risen, James introducing Enric who invited him to be seated, while Molly went indoors to fetch out more refreshment; pieces of fruit in a jug of red wine.

Accepting a glassful, Maurici glanced up to see Elizabeth hesitate in the shadow of the doorway, her smile faintly tremulous, before coming out to join them. He rose instantly, his pulses racing, and could only stare in speechless admiration. This morning she appeared particularly beautiful; her dark, shoulder length hair gleamed in the sunlight, and the simple lines of her blue dress revealed a hint of her shapely figure. He took her hand almost too eagerly, murmuring a breathless greeting as their eyes met.

Enveloped in silent wonderment, he suddenly realised they had become the centre of attention, until her father pulled up another chair, its metal legs screeching on the paving, breaking the spell.

"Who is going to propose the toast?" Molly asked as she filled a glass for her daughter."

"Health and happiness," proposed Enric, "and this war to end. *Salut!*"

With a glance in Elizabeth's direction, Maurici added, "To a peaceful future."

"Tell me, *senyor* Bachs," Molly began once they'd settled, "how are you progressing?"

"Thank you, I am now very well," he said, taking great care with his English. "I hope soon to return to my work."

"What exactly is your work, *senyor?*" asked Enric.

"I am a student doctor in my third year," Maurici replied, and indicating his part missing finger, added, "Before this happened, I was assisting in a field hospital near Barcelona."

"Admirable work!" James commended, relieving Maurici of his anxiety when at first he thought the man appeared as if he would remain silently aloof from the conversation.

James went on to enquire, "Have you met up with any British medical workers in the vicinity of Barcelona?"

"No, sir, because of my accident I have not been in the field for almost two months."

"*Senyor* Bachs also suffered a severe injury to his thigh," Molly put in, and to Maurici added, "You were in a shocking state when we admitted you."

He gave a wry smile. "I remember nothing of that moment, *senyora,* but I am grateful to you all for saving my life."

"By what my wife tells me, you're lucky to be alive," James remarked as he refilled the glasses. "Fracture, dreadful wounds, most unfortunate."

"I think you were extremely brave," Elizabeth murmured, directing him an admiring gaze.

"No, *senyoreta,* many were in a worse situation than I," he said modestly, "especially those who were bedridden during the bombing."

"Indeed," Molly agreed, "particularly when the ward was so crowded. Regretably, we had to leave after the first attack, since then I hear people are almost living in the shelters. Did you come to Sitges immediately you were discharged from hospital?"

"No, *senyora*, I went to the house of my parents near Sant Adria," Maurici replied, going on to relate events that followed, and their decision to move away.

"Who you think is responsible?" Enric asked, his eyes narrowing thoughtfully as he went on to remark, "I hear of many businesses like that of your father, destroyed by the Communists, and with support of the unions."

"Quite possibly, *senyor*," he agreed. "But my parents are not politically inclined, they are simply hardworking people wishing to earn an honest living."

"Yes, both sides have a great deal to answer for," James commented, "but unlike some of my countrymen, the Irish, I can't entirely agree with Nationalist policies. On the other hand, the opposing parties appear to have been at loggerheads." He pursed his lips before going on to add, "But now, after well over a thousand lost their lives in the recent bombing, I believe they have realised the need to pull together if they are to defeat their oppressors."

Maurici nodded. "My feelings also. We must have democracy, but with Germany and Italy on the side of the Nationalists, what hope do we have?"

"It is my opinion the Germans are testing their military strength in this country with some future hope of ruling Europe," James forecast, his expression grave. "And may God save us if ever it happens."

"Have you news regarding Nationalist progress?" asked Maurici, "I am anxious to know."

James leaned back in his chair and sighed. "The last we heard, they are closely approaching Llerida, only a matter of a few kilometres away."

"I am hearing this city is hidden with clouds of smoke after they are exploding petroleum tanks two days ago," Enric included with a worried shake of his head.

While this conversation continued, Maurici noticed the *senyora* rise and go into the house leaving the chair beside him vacant, and it wasn't long before Elizabeth slid across to the empty seat to tell him about her plans to do voluntary work at the local orphanage.

"I'm starting tomorrow afternoon, actually, and Mummy is doing a morning shift whilst I do the shopping."

"They will be happy for the help," Enric put in. "The colony is more work than the nuns are able for doing."

Maurici smiled. "I admire these brave Christian women who work in the orphanages and hospitals, but I would never speak of this to the authorities."

"Is wrong priests must go in prison, they should not be political," sighed Enric, shrugging his brawny shoulders.

Clearing away the newspapers and glasses, James turned to his colleague to say, "Molly is making preparations for lunch and suggests we may like to dine out here. What do you think, old chap?" Gazing up at the clear, blue sky he remarked, "It's so different from when we first arrived, I would never have believed it could be so damned cold!"

"We had the very bad winter," Enric agreed, "now is hot."

"Maybe, but I pity those poor devils crossing the Pyrenees into France, particularly the women and children," James put in. "It will be damned cold for them up there."

"An extremely arduous journey," said Maurici, rising as he took the mention of lunch as a signal for him to leave.

But, to his delight, Enric insisted he dine with them, adding a teasing remark about the English style menu which would be served at an earlier than usual time.

Caring little about the time, the menu, or of what it consisted, Maurici accepted. He was almost beside himself with joy. He would be grateful for a crust if it meant spending more time with Elizabeth. But when the meal was served he studied the piece of what looked like well-risen brown omelette with a curious eye, and caught the expression of amusement on Molly's face when she offered him a jug of sauce she called gravy to pour over it.

Finding the dish more tasty than he thought possible, he was interested to learn it was a typical dish from Northern England and, by tradition, eaten with this hot gravy before the meat course. Even the ersatz coffee served after the meal seemed to take on a more mellow flavour, and when James insisted he accept one of his small cigars, Maurici began to relax.

At first he'd sensed a flicker of resentment in the tall Irishman's manner, though it had faded as the meal progressed. Had the *senyor* been wary of his political views, he wondered, or had he sensed his affection for Elizabeth?

Chapter 7

Over breakfast the following morning, James mentioned their visitor of the previous day. "Seems a decent fellow," he commented.

"Yes, we got to know him quite well during his stay in hospital," Molly agreed. "His knowledge of English helped."

"But I noticed he'd lost touch with the situation regarding the war."

"I was relieved you didn't dwell on the subject and spoil what turned out to be a most pleasant day."

"I was surprised he wasn't aware the Nationalist troops are advancing on Llerida, a place of considerable importance," he persisted, "or the bombing of nearby Fraga. Over a hundred planes were involved. In fact, it looks as though Barcelona will be cut off from the rest of Republican Spain."

Draining his coffee, he continued, "Of course we're fortunate, we have the advantage of being in touch with other areas from where we receive a first-hand account on the progress of the war."

"Fortunate!" she cried. "I think I'd rather remain in ignorance."

"I hope you're not regretting your decision to forego the opportunity to sail on the Penelope? That is, assuming she got away."

She reached to plant a kiss on his cheek. "No, darling. Anyway, what on earth would I do in Marseilles without you?"

"Imagining you in the arms of a young French matelot would drive me wild with jealousy," he winked, shrugging on his overcoat.

Upstairs, Elizabeth was deep in happy reverie, her thoughts on the previous day. She'd had little opportunity to speak with Maurici alone, but to be away from the confines of the hospital ward, wearing something she considered more flattering had made it a memorable occasion. He had appeared even more attractive than when she'd last seen him, his English almost perfect, and she had the feeling her father had been suitably impressed.

"Dear Maurici," she murmured, recapturing his smiling expression until Rosa's raucous cry from below prompted her to finish dressing.

During the morning she went shopping, hoping to catch sight of Maurici as she visited the small family businesses in the town. After purchasing a supply of fresh vegetables, she dawdled in the square, but all she met were the curious stares of the townsfolk as they went about their business. Soon due at the orphanage, she hurried back to change into something serviceable.

Molly was returning from her duties as Elizabeth left the house, and after a word of encouragement from her mother she approached her new venture with less apprehension. Reaching the old residence housing the orphaned children, she found the heavy wooden door in the impressive entrance stood open to reveal a traditionally tiled vestibule where the sharp sound of young voices echoed from deep within.

With a slight feeling of trepidation she rang the brass-mounted bell and heard the pad of footsteps before a short figure in heavy robes appeared in the doorway, a stiff white wimple framing her gently smiling countenance.

"*Buenas tardes,*" said Elizabeth, giving her name and purpose in halting Spanish.

Beckoning her inside, the nun informed her of the number of children residing there as she led the way into the dining room where only one voice spoke in prayer. After the response the scraping of spoons commenced, then a pause as seventeen pairs of curious dark eyes fastened on Elizabeth. All had lost their parents in the war and it caused her a pang of distress to see so many children deprived of the comforts she herself had known. And yet they seemed unaware of their deprivation as they tucked into dishes of lentil soup and pieces of greyish bread, giggling and nudging each other as they ate. The boys, she noticed, had near shaven heads, and the girls locks were nowhere near the length of the present style. Their clothing appeared to be a rag-bag selection of cotton dresses and trousers, smocks and shirts, and worn, ill-fitting shoes. Managing to overcome her initial sadness, she set to work in a remarkably tranquil atmosphere, ensuring that the younger ones washed before they settled down to rest in a sparsely furnished upstairs room.

Lowering the slatted blinds, Elizabeth left them to return to the day room where one of the older girls attempted to sew on buttons and mend shirt collars ragged with wear.

Needlework had always been one of her favourite pastimes so she was delighted when the nun agreed to her helping with the repairs. She could recall the stitches Mrs Dowkes used when repairing the linen at Woodington Hall, and had spent many hours watching the housekeeper replacing hooks and eyes on grandmother's corsets, or turning the frayed collars of Grandpa's shirts.

The girl proved quite able with needle and thread, but her eyes filled with tears when the time came for Elizabeth to leave, her smile only returning when she promised to call again.

On her way back to the house Elizabeth paused, deciding to enjoy the warmth of the late afternoon sun by taking a stroll by the sea. She was about to cross to the beach when she sensed someone behind and glanced round to find Maurici standing there.

"Maurici!" she gasped, a delicate flush rising to her cheeks. "I didn't expect to see you."

His brown eyes twinkled as he said softly, "I wait here because I cannot help myself."

Her eyes widened. "Is something wrong?"

He smiled and shook his head. "No, no, I only wish to speak with you, to ask if you will drive out with me on Wednesday?"

Almost speechless with delight she gave him a wide smile. "Thank you, I'd like that – that is, assuming my parents will allow it."

"You think they will object?"

"No, I think they like you."

"I will arrive at half past ten if that is suitable for you, but I will avoid Barcelona if you are nervous."

"How considerate. I'm not exactly nervous, but I found the sights there quite upsetting."

"I also suffer when I see so much destruction, and for what reason? The Catalan people will never submit to Fascism, whatever Franco threatens." He gave a rueful smile. "Sorry, I should not speak of these matters."

"It's quite understandable, we all feel a loyalty to our region. I'm always ready to defend dear old Yorkshire."

He smiled. "That is your region, Elizabeth, yes?"

"Yes, England's largest county, with beautiful countryside, wild moorland..."

"Ah yes, this is what the lady, Bronte, is writing about."

Elizabeth's eyes widened. "I'd not realised you were familiar with our writers."

"Shakespeare, Dickens, Bronte, I enjoy them all. Also, many notable authors from the country of your father."

"Daddy would be delighted to hear you say that!"

"You will tell him I wish to take you for a drive on Wednesday? I hope he will not find reason to object."

"I'll be ready when you call," she promised, feeling the gentle strength of his injured hand as it lingered round hers.

"Until Wednesday, Elizabeth. *Adéu!*"

Her intention to walk along the beach forgotten, she hurried back to the house, apprehension rising over the thought of seeking her father's permission to go driving with Maurici. However, she found he and Enric had not yet returned so perhaps she could enlist her mother's help.

"Providing you promise to behave sensibly," was Molly's reply to her appeal. "I think you know what I mean."

Elizabeth's cheeks grew warm. "Of course I do, but he's not like that, he reads Bronte and Shakespeare."

Molly smiled to herself as she stirred the thin meatless stew simmering on the stove. "Even so, at twenty four he's a mature man. He will possess all the natural desires of any male being." Tapping the wooden spoon on the edge of the pan she turned to gaze fondly at her daughter. "So, it will be entirely up to you, darling," she said gently, touching Elizabeth's soft, pink cheek.

* *

On Wednesday morning Maurici drove down to Sitges wishing he could offer Elizabeth something more comfortable in which to travel. Yet, however shaky the old family vehicle, it was fortunate it had not been commandeered for military use.

Drawing up in the narrow street, he spotted her leaving the house. "Would you like to visit my home?" he asked, the faint whiff of her perfume tantalising his nostrils as he held open the passenger door.

She nodded, and with her mother's advice clear in her mind, she smoothed down the pleated skirt of her silky lemon dress and took her seat.

Elizabeth had seen little of the countryside inland and as they drove away from Sitges her interest in the terrain increased as areas planted with vines and fruit trees came into view. The route took them via Sant Pere de Ribes and Vilafranca, skirting the city to arrive at the village of Sant Adria without mishap.

"Welcome to Can Bachs!" he said and heard her soft exclamation of surprise as she looked at the mellow stonework of his shuttered home. Inserting a key in the lock, he pushed open the heavy wooden door and ushered her into the dark hall, suggesting she wait whilst he opened the shutters of the downstairs rooms.

Going first into the sitting room to let in the sunlight, he turned from the window and frowned, realising there was something amiss in the room. The atmosphere smelled strongly of stale tobacco, and on the settee lay a heap of rumpled blankets in an unfamiliar colour. He picked one up and caught the odour of unwashed bodies, but when Elizabeth came in he made no comment and let it slip to the floor.

Noting his grave expression, she asked, "Is this the room that was ransacked?"

"One of them," he replied with a quick smile. "We did not have time to make everything clean before we left. The kitchen may be better."

But the kitchen was in a worse state than he anticipated, the stale smell of cooking and smoke, and the sight of unwashed dishes making him curl his lip in distaste. "*Déu!*" he exclaimed. "What happens here?"

He strode across the littered floor, muttering in Catalan as he unbolted the rear door.

"Someone lives here without permission!" he said furiously, his accent more pronounced, as he went to investigate the upstairs rooms.

Going from room to room, he was relieved to find nothing amiss, but on his return to the lower floor he met her enquiring eyes. "Perhaps it is only my cousin, Lluis," he explained. "I will ask him to make it clean."

With that, he swept the litter aside, except for one piece of printed paper which he slipped into his pocket. Planning to confront Lluis later in the day he stifled his annoyance and suggested that they move on. The sun shone warmly as they drove back into the countryside, stopping to refresh themselves in the village of San Sadurni d'Anoya with local sparkling wine, olives, and tiny morsels of fish and ham on dry bread.

Content, they drove on, leaving the looming pinnacles of Montserrat behind, their conversation interspersed with laughter as he related his experiences during training.

"But the war interrupted my training," he said, "and now I must wait for my leg to recover before I return to duty."

"Does it trouble you very much?"

"Sometimes, when I am walking far, so until it is better I will go to teach soldiers in the barracks in Barcelona."

She shot him a puzzled look. "Do you mean first aid?"

"No, not medical. I will help them with reading and writing."

"Reading and writing!" she echoed in disbelief.

"Yes, many never had the opportunity to learn, particularly older ones."

She uttered a small sigh. "I suppose there are illiterate people in England, too, especially amongst the poorer classes."

"I believe no-one is poor in your country."

"Well, things are improving. Daddy says the Trades Unions are hoping to secure holidays with pay for the workers."

About to reply, he hesitated, hearing the sound of a plane, and peered closer to the windscreen. "Is a Nationalist plane!" he cried, spotting the markings on its wings.

Elizabeth followed his pointing finger and caught the sun glinting on its fuselage as it appeared to decrease in height. And she heard his sharp intake of breath when, with engines screaming, it swooped towards them, fountains of dust rising from the road ahead as it passed over.

Bringing the van to a shuddering halt, he flung open the door. "Elizabeth! Quickly!" he yelled and slid from the van, limping round to the passenger side to drag her out almost before she had gathered her wits.

"The areoplane, it is shooting!" he gasped, hurrying her across the grass to pull her down into the ditch beneath a tree, shielding her from the horror he predicted.

And, sure enough, only moments passed before they heard the sound of the plane coming towards them from the opposite direction. Pressing himself against her, he covered her ears with his hands, feeling her body tremble beneath him as the war machine roared overhead. Again, blasts of dust and gravel spouted up from the road, scattering over Maurici, followed by a shower of twigs and leaves as bullets seared the branches above.

"Be still," he urged as she gasped in fright. Certain his olive green clothing was scarcely visible from the air, he ensured the skirt of her yellow dress was tucked beneath him.

Again the areoplane shrieked low overhead, then rose in height and continued on its way over the mountain. Still protecting Elizabeth, he lifted his head to watch as it faded from sight, his heart beating madly. And it was only when it lessened its wild pounding that he became aware of her firm breasts pressed against him and the warm curve of her thigh beneath his groin. He felt his body respond to the contact and let out a shuddering sigh. Turning her face to his he pressed his mouth against hers in an urgent need to assuage the heat within him. He felt her struggle, heightening his need of her until he came to his senses and raised himself to look down into her startled sapphire eyes.

"I did not wish to frighten you," he murmured huskily, "but you look so tempting, I cannot help myself..."

Elizabeth's lips trembled, she closed her eyes, and he could only admire her beautiful features as she lay beneath him. Taking courage, he kissed her lightly on the lips and said softly, "I think the areoplane will not return."

"I hope not," she responded in a small, wavering voice, her eyes remaining closed, "it was horrible..."

He grinned. "I assume you mean the strafing."

Detecting the humour in his voice, she opened her eyes. "It was very frightening, and so close!" she exclaimed tremulously. "I didn't realise the plane was hostile."

"Its white wing tips and the black cross on its rudder told me it was a Nationalist plane."

"Oh, Maurici," she gasped, "you saved my life!"

Rolling onto his side in the narrow gully, he raised himself on one elbow and took her hand. "We were fortunate, the pilot did not see us."

"And you were so quick," she said, pulling herself up to a sitting position.

"And you look so beautiful," he murmured, leaning towards her. When she didn't shrink away, he took her in his arms and kissed her again, his lips lingering, savouring her sweetness.

It was Elizabeth who drew away. "Someone may come," she said breathlessly, brushing bits of grass from her dress.

"I doubt it," he replied with a twinge of disappointment and shook the dust from his hair. Her flushed cheeks and bright eyes had been a clear indication of the pleasure she felt, but now he had brought his ardour under control he didn't want to rush her into something she may regret.

He rose to his feet, his arms outstretched to bring her up beside him, flicking bits of undergrowth from her back before he limped away to inspect the van.

Fortunately, the van had escaped the strafing though what they would have done should it have received a direct hit and gone up in flames had not occurred to him during this moment of passion.

"Why did the plane fire at us, Maurici? We're not enemy."

He shrugged. "Maybe he is practicing, or he thinks this is a Republican vehicle containing ammunition to fight the Nationalists."

"Really?" she responded, wide-eyed.

Taking her hands he drew her towards him. "Unexpected things happen in war," he said, a faint smile forming as he dropped a light kiss on her mouth. "But I would do everything it is possible to protect you."

She sighed. "Oh, Maurici, you're so brave..."

He drew a quick breath. "No, Elizabeth, not brave... I say this because I love you."

* *

"I wonder what poor Elizabeth is doing," Jane said absently as she poured tea into delicate china cups. "I don't expect she will be enjoying afternoon tea."

"I believe they drink mainly coffee in Spain," William supplied as he reached for the sugar tongs, and with a small contented smile, continued, "Elizabeth always liked coffee so she should be all right."

"But how will she pass the time? She'll not have friends – well, not English friends."

"From her letter she seems content, and both she and Molly are taking up voluntary work at the local orphanage. Should suit her admirably, she loves children."

"Speaking of letters," she began, meeting William's gaze with a ready defiance, "Pincott has posted mine to James' paper with regard to bringing Molly and Elizabeth home."

William's head shot up. "But it is up to James to decide what is best for his family – you had no right..."

"No right! Even you must realise he's totally irresponsible, otherwise he wouldn't put them at risk."

"But it's not our place to tell him what to do!" he retaliated. "He'll tell you to mind your own business!"

"He wouldn't dare!" she cried. "Once it's made clear to him just where his responsibilities lie, even he must see we are right."

William's brows shot up. "We are?" he repeated. "Don't include me, I would never interfere."

"You're weak," she accused, crashing her cup down on the saucer.

He gave a weary sigh. She was obsessed with this James business and he didn't know how to deal with it; should he simply close his ears to her ranting?

His anxious thoughts increased when Jane stated that she would not allow James back into the house. "And with all those Austrian refugees flooding in, we shall be outnumbered by foreigners," she concluded agitatedly.

"I'm not so sure," he said, regaining some control. "I understand the Austrians have brought a great deal of wealth into this country."

"Hmm, well, a better class of people, I suppose, but foreigners just the same."

Unable to contain himself, William struck the arm of his chair and yelled, "My God, woman, you're nothing but a damned Fascist! You ought to join Mosley's lot – they'd welcome you with open arms!"

Chapter 8

Since the previous afternoon, Elizabeth had been in carefree mood. Maurici's declaration of love had far outweighed the terror of the strafing; had the pilot been on target she would have died fearlessly in his arms.

Her father had been bewildered to find she was taking the matter so lightly when he learned she had been only inches from certain death, and praised Maurici's quick decision to abandon the van. And, although he made it clear he wasn't opposing their friendship, he asked for her promise not to go out of Sitges whilst there was a likelihood of further attacks. But, providing Rosa was about, he didn't object to him paying a visit to the house.

This had pleased Elizabeth, but that evening her father seemed uncommonly thoughtful throughout dinner with little to offer the conversation. More than once she noticed her mother dart him a curious glance. Enric appeared oblivious to his colleagues strained manner, and after the meal he made an unexpected suggestion.

"Elizabeth? You like to go out for the coffee, yes?"

"Good idea," James put in encouragingly. "We are rather tired."

"Very well," she agreed, puzzling over the invitation as she put on her coat.

"The air will be good for us," Enric said, "and I will tell the history of Sitges as we walk."

Elizabeth conceded willingly; there was a possibility Maurici may be about.

James waited until the door closed behind them, then beckoned Molly to sit beside him.

"Are you unwell, darling?" she asked worriedly.

"No, Molly, I'm fine. I asked Enric to take Elizabeth out because there's a matter I must discuss with you."

"I suspected something was wrong when you arrived home."

"Yes, but I needed a little time to compose myself," he said, pouring a measure of brandy.

"For goodness' sake, James, don't keep me in suspense!"

He took a satisfying sip, then announced, "I had a telegraph today, from my paper. When I finally managed to get through I learned that Jane has demanded they bring us back to England. Well, you and Elizabeth, naturally I wasn't included." He gave a short laugh. "She considers it much too dangerous for you here and accuses the paper of supporting my irresponsible attitude towards my family's safety."

Molly's expression was one of complete incredulity as she set down her glass. "Good Lord, how embarrassing."

"It was, rather," he confessed, "but then I realised the British newspapers may cause her anxiety – reports can be alarming, it's understandable."

"It's good of you to see it that way, but she should realise I want to be here with you?"

James pursed his lips thoughtfully. "I wonder why she persists with the mistaken idea that I don't care about the possible dangers you face," he said at last, and sliding his arm under Molly's shoulders he drew her towards him to murmur, "I do care, darling, truly. In fact, there are times when I do wonder if it's wise to keep you both here."

She let her head fall against his shoulder. "Don't say that, I couldn't bear to be parted."

"I know," he murmured, hugging her close, "but it doesn't stop me worrying. Only today there were fears of further raids. Actually, Barcelona escaped, but I hear five people were killed during an attack on the neighbouring town of Mataro." James uttered a tired sigh. "I don't wish to alarm you, but it doesn't look good. We now hear of bombing on Tortosa further down the coast, plus a school in Tarragona, and one communiqué claims the insurgent pressure on Llerida is being held, whereas other reports maintain the city is completely surrounded. It's all very confusing."

"So that's why I can never find a newspaper," Molly complained. "I must confess those heart-rending reports of mothers trying to identify the bodies of their children in the mortuaries stayed in my mind." She paused to add chokingly, "I feel so helpless..."

"What concerns me is the possibility of a raid on this area which, after Elizabeth's experience, seems quite probable," he surmised anxiously. "In the past few days hundreds of Republican militiamen, in addition to the women and children, have crossed the Pyrenees into France."

"You would prefer me to go home?" she queried, holding his gaze.

"Darling, of course I want you with me, but…"

"But you'd feel happier knowing I was safely away from this war?"

He shrugged to express his helplessness. "Yes, but I didn't want to alarm Elizabeth." Brushing his cheek against her hair, he continued, "The situation here is not improving. Franco's troops are determined to conquer Catalonia and I have an awful feeling it may be sooner than we realise."

"And should this happen you would be expected to stay?"

"I'm afraid so, but promise me you will take Elizabeth home if conditions here deteriorate further. I love you too much to risk endangering your lives," he ended softly and kissed her.

"Only if it becomes risky for Elizabeth," she murmured. "Meanwhile, I shall write a strong letter to Mother – remind her not to interfere."

With the beginnings of a smile flickering round his mouth he said, "Now relations between Ireland and Britain are well on the way to a settlement with regard to the economic war, she may well begin to see me in a different light."

Enric considered Elizabeth a most delightful companion, albeit rather shy and naive for her nineteen years. Yet, almost overnight she had matured into a most desirable young lady with an air of confidence he hadn't realised she possessed. She was twenty years his junior, yet he felt curiously proud to be seen escorting her.

Together they walked the narrow streets, past the rather grand residences which Enric told her had been built late in the last century by Catalans returning home after making their fortunes in Cuba. She gazed in fascination over the colonial style architecture, remarking on the beautifully tiled entrances, lofty, arched windows, and the tiny elegant balconies beneath. Pleased by her show of interest, he gave a thoughtful sideways glance, seeing her perfect features, flawless complexion, and the shine of anticipation in her eyes.

He tucked her hand in the curve of his arm, feeling strangely protective towards her, almost fatherly, he fancied. He could appreciate James' anxiety over his decision to bring his daughter to Spain. Earlier in the day, as they had studied reports on the progress of Nationalist troops, he'd agreed with his colleague; the war was closing in on them, her safety could be in jeopardy.

Suddenly, he was aware of her eyes upon him, questioning his thoughts, but he merely indicated they turn towards the town square where they entered the busy cafe. Ensuring she was comfortable in one of the cane-seated chairs he took one opposite, noting her interested gaze travelling the room whose walls were barely visible behind the display of paintings and ceramics. Then she turned back to face him, her slightly flushed cheeks betraying her awareness of the interested stares of the clientele.

Again he experienced a surge of pride, and as he signalled to the busy waiter he glanced across the room, his gaze coming to rest on the sullen face of Lluis Bachs.

"Ah, I see the cousin of Maurici is here!" he said, indicating the man with a nod of his head, and saw Elizabeth's quick glance, her eyes bright with expectancy. "The man with a little moustache." he told her, raising his hand to acknowledge Lluis' dark stare. But, before he could continue, he saw Lluis' scowl deepen and he retreated, ignoring Enric completely.

"You mean the man who just left?" she asked on a note of disappointment.

Enric nodded. "Maybe he is not recognising me," he said with a careless shrug. "Is not important."

"He's not in the least like Maurici," she remarked a short time later. "Was he alone?"

"I think so, yes," he agreed, her few moments of silence a clear indication her interest in the student doctor was far greater than she would have him know and sensed she had been affronted by his cousin's hostile stare. Yet, in contrast with Lluis, however presentable a young man Maurici appeared to be, Enric found himself fighting a twinge of jealousy each time his name was mentioned. And although their conversation was light and friendly, as they drank the bitter coffee he found himself avoiding Maurici's name and introduced the subject of her home in England.

It was late when she and Enric returned. Relieved to see her father appeared more relaxed, she didn't spot the surreptitious smile he gave Enric.

* *

"Damned good of you to take Elizabeth out last evening," James said as he and Enric drove through the city. "Didn't have the opportunity to thank you."

"It was a pleasure for me," Enric responded truthfully as they motored through the bomb damaged streets towards the busy Plaça de Catalunya. With a sideways glance at his colleague, he asked, "You and Molly were speaking about the problem of leaving?"

"Yes, we spoke," James replied on a sighing breath. "But she won't leave unless it becomes too risky for Elizabeth..." he continued vaguely, his attention caught by a banner-waving group on the corner.

"What's happening over there, Enric? Can you pull over?"

"Better not, James, looks like a political meeting, they are angry."

"Communist group, I think." said James, and as they drew closer he exclaimed, "Good God! Isn't that young Bachs, the relative of Elizabeth's friend?"

"*Sí*, is Lluis Bachs," Enric confirmed, accelerating the car. "I told you he has interest for the Communists."

"Young fools!" James snarled as they drove past the jeering mob. "They'll never get together with the rest of Republican Spain if they can't agree amongst themselves."

* *

Since his visit to Sant Adria, Maurici spent restless nights reliving the memorable moments in the ditch with Elizabeth, and puzzling over the signs of disturbance at his home. In the privacy of his room, he read the printed sheet he had discovered in the kitchen, finding it to be Communist party propaganda. At first he had intended to confront Lluis with his discovery, demand an explanation, but as his initial anger began to wane he realised he needed more proof. It was possible his cousin had no knowledge of intruders to Can Bachs. Even so, should Lluis prove innocent of any involvement with the Communist cause, the fact remained he had not checked the place was secure before he left for home.

By morning he had reached a decision; until he had an opportunity to visit his home he would not disclose his discovery to anyone, including Elizabeth whom he had arranged to meet in the square at midday. Knowing he would shortly be considered fit enough to return to his duties, he intended to make the most of his remaining sick leave by seeing her as often as possible. Never before had he experienced such a yearning; just thinking of her brought an ache of longing to his body. He was confident she was inexperienced yet, during that short time in the ditch, he'd been pleasantly conscious of her response to the enforced contact with his body. He smiled to himself, reflecting upon his own initiation to intimacy. Was it two, or maybe three years ago when a Barcelona prostitute had welcomed him to her bed? By her experience, the excitement she aroused within him soon dispelled any shyness he'd felt. But with Elizabeth it was different, however strong his desire he must be gentle.

Shaking off the arousing distraction he returned to the task of dressing, at the same time checking the site of the injury to his thigh. Satisfied the flesh was now well healed, with no sign of the infection which had invaded it, he marvelled at the skill of the surgeon who had done a remarkably neat job of closing the wound considering the acute shortage of medical equipment and drugs. In time the scar would fade and diminish in size. He drew in his flat belly and flexed his biceps, regarding his lean, muscled reflection in the age-flecked mirror with a certain smug satisfaction.

Completing his dressing he went downstairs, his limp barely visible as he went out to the orchard where a thick carpet of faded blossom beneath the almond and fruit trees bore promise of a good harvest. Taking a rake he joined his father and uncle who were busily clearing the ground. But where was Lluis? He suppressed the urge to drive to Sant Adria knowing he must conserve the little petrol he had for his visits to Sitges, and Elizabeth.

* *

Elizabeth had been distressed to overhear her father relating the movements of Maurici's cousin to her mother that afternoon. He spoke of seeing Lluis with a Communist group, a chanting, banner-waving mob bent on violent confrontation with anyone who opposed the policies of their Party. Yet Maurici displayed none of the aggression of his cousin and was courteous and gentle when they met, his kisses discreet. When the plane had sent them hurtling into the ditch she'd enjoyed his closeness, but something told her to repeat such a close embrace could lead to desires beyond their control.

Deep in thought, she was suddenly aware her mother had returned to the kitchen and hurriedly slotted the last of the plates in the rack to drain.

Molly laughed. "Darling, you were miles away!"

"I was just considering what to wear, it's very warm."

"Ah yes, you're meeting Maurici this afternoon so why not wear that pretty little pink dress with the cape sleeves?"

Elizabeth pulled a face. "It's rather childish, don't you think? I prefer the yellow."

Wearing her freshly laundered dress, Elizabeth waited for Maurici to arrive. She'd hoped Enric would invite him to lunch again, but this way they could spend more time alone. And when the van drew up outside she rushed to the door, only slowing to a more dignified pace as she left the house.

"We will not drive very far," he said, concerned over the level of petrol in the tank as he put the vehicle into gear. "We can sit by the sea and talk. I have with me a blanket, so your dress will not get dirty this time."

"You remembered, I wore this the last time!" she exclaimed unbelievingly.

"I remember everything about you," he said, giving her hand an affectionate squeeze before turning his attention to the drive out of Sitges on the narrow, unfenced road.

Feeling she would burst with happiness, Elizabeth relaxed, admiring Maurici's tanned, muscular forearms with their covering of fine dark hair. Lifting her gaze, she cast him a covert glance and thought him the most handsome man she'd ever known.

They drove only a few kilometres before he turned onto a rough track which ran steeply down towards the sea, drawing to a crunching halt on a ridge of pebbles by the beach. "It will be cooler here," he said, spreading a blanket in the shade of the van, "and I have wine if you are thirsty."

Carefully smoothing down the skirt of her dress, she seated herself beside him, and running her hand over the coarsely woven fabric, remarked, "This is almost like the blanket that was stolen from my room on the night of the bombing."

"Are you suggesting I stole it?" he teased.

She laughed. "Of course not, but Daddy says many people in Barcelona are without bedding so I didn't mind."

"I imagine the thief would sell it, or..." he began when a fresh thought struck him. Had the blankets on the settee at Sant Adria come from the home of Lluis? His uncle was at a loss to know where they had gone.

"Or what?" she prompted, regaining his attention.

He smiled. "I would not steal your blanket, I would get into the bed to keep you warm."

"Maurici!" she cried, laughing, "Would you really?"

"Nothing would I like more," he murmured, holding her gaze as he edged closer to enfold her in his arms.

Aware of her vulnerability, she held her breath, but the sensuous feel of his lips as they trailed across her cheek made her utter a faint gasp until they found hers to kiss.

"I love you, Elizabeth," he whispered as their lips drew slowly apart, and she sighed contentedly as he lowered her to the blanket to kiss her again.

Elizabeth had never known such ecstasy, could feel the warmth of Maurici's caress through the thin fabric of her dress. As his searching fingers came to rest on the contour of her breast, her lips parted in response to his kiss until she felt his hand move down to slide beneath her skirt.

"Maurici, no!" she gasped, struggling to escape the captivity of his embrace. "We shouldn't..."

"Please, for me. I love you," he persisted, his breathing growing harsh as he drew her closer to his hard body.

The pleasure Elizabeth had felt turned swiftly to alarm as she realised the extent of his desire. As she pleaded with him to let her go, he sat up, his face set in harsh lines of self-control as he begged her forgiveness.

"For me, you are very desirable," he said huskily, brushing his forearm across his perspiring brow, "but I will not force you to take me."

"I just don't want to do anything I shouldn't – you know," she said, turning away as she smoothed back her hair.

His eyes filled with emotion as he brought her back to face him. "Please stay, I will not frighten you again."

With a slightly nervous smile she remained seated beside him staring out to sea. After an uncomfortable silence, when the rasping sound of his breathing had subsided, she managed to ask, "Will you go back to medical school soon?"

He gave a faint smile. "Maybe two weeks. You will meet me again, yes?"

She nodded shyly. "The only reason I ask is because of something my father said. I heard him tell my mother about the Communist marches in Barcelona which made me wonder if something is about to happen and we must leave."

He shook his head and shrugged. "I have heard nothing."

"But he mentioned your cousin so perhaps he knows."

Maurici glanced up. "What does your father say about him?"

"I believe he said he was marching, with a banner..."

"With the Communists?" he demanded, his eyes narrowed.

Elizabeth drew back. "Why? Is it so important?"

Maurici made an effort to subdue his interest and took a steadying breath. "I like to know what my cousin does in the city, he does not tell me very much."

"Did you speak to him about the state he left your home?"

"Can you believe it, Elizabeth, I quite forgot!"

She laughed. "Then you are almost as bad as he!"

"But I don't go marching through the city," he murmured, his expression suddenly serious. "I believe in democracy, of course, but not when it is achieved by violence. There are other ways to gain freedom from suppression..." He paused, giving her a tiny lopsided smile as he continued, "People should make love, not fight."

She made no response but, aware she was trembling, he took her hand. "Maybe we should leave, it is becoming a little cool for you."

"Perhaps we should," she said looking up at the still bright sky. "It is so light, I'm inclined to forget the time."

Once he had delivered Elizabeth home, he drove back along the promenade, pausing in a quiet place to wrestle with his thoughts. What a coincidence she should mention Lluis; it had acted as an ice-cold shower, quickly dispelling the frustration he had been suffering. Convinced there was a connection between his discovery at Sant Adria and his cousin's political activities, he felt compelled to act upon it but, rather than cause a scene in Lluis' home, he would wait until tomorrow.

* *

Lluis had already left the house before Maurici could learn of his intentions for the day. His aunt assumed he had gone to Sant Adria to work on the burnt-out *celler* so, checking there was sufficient petrol for the journey, Maurici set off.

This morning he took the shortest route, along the winding coast road, past the gently swaying canes and twisted Carob trees, going north through the city to reach the vineyards of Sant Adria. The *masia* appeared deserted from the outside, but his tension increased as he quietly slid the key into the lock of the front door and stepped inside.

The sitting room was more or less as he had last seen it so he moved silently along the dim passage towards the kitchen. Throwing open the door, he saw Lluis seated at the table, studying a leaflet as he ate sardines from a can.

Lluis spun round, gaping in astonishment as he recognised his cousin, a thin trickle of oil escaping over his chin. Recovering quickly, he grinned and held out the partly empty can. "Care to join me?"

With a quick step forward, Maurici lashed out and struck the can from Lluis' hand, sending it clattering across the tiled floor. "What the hell are doing in here!" he cried, snatching the printed sheet Lluis held.

"Hey, that's private!" Lluis objected, reaching up and tearing it in his haste.

"Private!" snarled Maurici, thrusting him back on his seat. "Do you consider anyone's privacy when you use this house for your political activities! Papa would be horrified to learn of this."

"Papa, papa," Lluis mocked. "Who in hell do you think you are! Why can't you speak like the rest of us, you autocratic swine! Your father is no better than mine."

Maurici grabbed his shirt front, yanking him up from his seat to bellow, "But yours doesn't deserve a bastard like you for a son!"

"But your father is a shitting capitalist!" Lluis exclaimed scornfully.

"You don't know what you're saying." Maurici thrust Lluis away in disgust, sending him skidding on the spilt oil, overturning his chair. Standing over him, he continued, "All his life he has worked hard – *sí*, very hard – but to find some Communist pig in the family has ruined his business..."

"You're all Fascists!" Lluis snarled, attempting to get to his feet.

Lunging towards his cousin, Maurici pinned him to the floor. "You talk through your arse!" he hissed. "It's fools like you who prevent us from uniting against Franco – can't you see... ?"

He broke off as Lluis kicked out his booted foot, sending Maurici a sickening blow. *"Ui!"* he gasped, recoiling in pain. "You swine!"

Lluis took the opportunity to struggle his feet, his expression contorted. He swung his fist, making bruising contact with Maurici's jaw as he screamed, "and that's for your Capitalist whore!"

Unable to contain his fury, Maurici lashed out, striking the younger man one blow, then another with his sound hand.

Again Lluis fell to the floor, bringing Maurici down with him, each gasping and grunting as they wrestled to overpower the other. At last Maurici got the upper hand, his full weight on Lluis' body as he took a grip on his collar, holding him fast while he recovered his breath.

It was the sight of blood streaming from Lluis' nose that brought him to his senses and held back the blow he was about to strike.

"I'll tell you once more!" he ground out, glaring into his cousins face. "Neither I, nor my parents agree with the

Nationalist policies, so let this be the end of it. And, to avoid any trouble for them, I won't allow you, or your party, to set foot in this house ever again! Do you hear me? Take your filthy blankets and remember, in future my home is not to be used as a political meeting place!"

Intimidated by his cousin's formidable stare, Lluis attempted to speak but the constriction of his collar caused him to splutter and cough, splattering his blood in Maurici's face.

"B-but I must work here," he croaked, fear in his eyes as he tried to ease the pressure from his neck. "If my father hears of this he'll kill me..."

Repulsed by the smell of Lluis' breath, Maurici averted his head. "This is between us, not the family," he said tersely. "And your work is in the *celler*, not the house!"

Releasing his grip on Lluis'collar, he rose, staggering a little from exertion. Reaching for the bunch of keys lying on the table he removed those belonging to the locks of the house.

"Those are my keys..." Lluis began, putting a tentative hand to his rapidly swelling nose as he struggled to rise. But a look from Maurici cut him short and he shrank back, fearful of arousing a further attack.

"The keys will be returned to you when I am convinced you can be trusted," Maurici said shortly. "Until then, you keep out. Understand?"

Chapter 9

Wiping soap from the blade of his open razor, Maurici studied his reflection in the mirror. It had taken a week for the bruising to fade and he'd had to make the excuse of having fallen amongst rubble in the city. His thigh wound had stood up to the struggle well, whereas the skin covering the stump of his right index finger was inflamed still from gripping Lluis' abrasive clothing. It was the force of his aggression towards his cousin which caused him the greatest suffering; to become involved in physical violence over a political matter was totally out of character. His cousin had not returned home since the day of their confrontation so he concluded Lluis preferred to lick his wounds in private.

He sighed, to be labelled a Fascist filled him with fierce indignation. His parents had worked hard, providing employment for many local families. The vineyard had been successful, true, but they couldn't be classified as bourgeois, exploiting their employees, even Lluis should be aware of that.

To avoid Elizabeth seeing his bruises he'd sent a message giving a plausible reason for his absence. He hadn't been entirely deceitful, keeping an appointment with a doctor in Barcelona on one day, allowing him a ration of petrol for when he reported for duty the following week. At first his duties would not be entirely medical, part of his time would be spent teaching the lower ranks in the military hospital to read which, he guessed, ensured any battle plans formulated could be better understood. There was talk of Nationalist advancement to prepare Republican troops for the offensive which he feared may be not far ahead. Conflicting reports of the occupation of Fraga, with Republicans claiming they had dislodged the enemy while Nationalists claimed victory over the position, were confusing. Should the latter be the case it meant a large slice of Republican territory was surrounded by Nationalists on three sides with the river Ebre on the other. He'd heard considerable numbers of the International Brigade had been killed or taken prisoner. In the case of the British, he wondered what brought these men to fight for a cause their own government did not support. Was it their belief in democracy, or the enticement of a small financial reward that made the Brigade so tempting? But with news of more Republican militiamen crossing into France, the situation was anything but tempting. Should defeat be imminent, how would these foreigners make their escape? The troops, the journalists and their families, their daughters?

Thinking of Elizabeth, he reflected upon his clumsy attempt at seduction when last they had been together. Almost overwhelmed by the strength of his desire, once the surge of passion was suppressed he had respected her refusal to allow him to caress her intimately. In future, he would take more time over his enjoyment of her soft lips.

As it happened, Maurici's call to duty came earlier than he expected. He was to report to the barracks in Barcelona that very evening when lorry loads of troops would be moving towards the Aragón front, replacing those injured who were to be brought back to the hospital. Because of his imminent departure it was imperative he meet Elizabeth.

Waiting near the orphanage later that afternoon, he saw the delight with which she registered his presence. But when he gave the reason her smile faded.

"I wouldn't have thought you were fit enough," was her immediate concern.

"Only for light duties," he told her, "such as first aid, escort duties, that kind of thing."

"Oh, Maurici, I shall miss you," she said chokingly.

It broke his heart to see the pain in her beautiful eyes. "Please, Elizabeth, don't cry. Let us walk along the beach before we must say good-bye."

"You're going today?"

He nodded. "This evening,"

Once away from the houses he caught her hand, drawing her under the shimmering shadows of the palms. "I will not forget you, Elizabeth," he said softly, wiping away a tear that rolled down her cheek to replace it with his lips.

"I'll think of you every day," she promised as he enfolded her in his arms and kissed her. He wanted more but there was no time; perhaps it was better this way. A farewell kiss, and at the end of the road he turned to wave, misty-eyed over the pain of parting.

* *

William could sense tension in the atmosphere of the drawing room when he returned from his stroll in the grounds. Jane's expression of disapproval when she glanced up from the letter she held put him immediately on his guard.

"What is it?" he asked, noting the Spanish stamp.

"Your granddaughter has made the acquaintance of a Spaniard and has the audacity to tell me about it!"

William put on his spectacles. "He can't be unsuitable, otherwise James wouldn't permit it," he pointed out.

Choking with indignation she tossed the letter aside. "In addition, Molly has the impertinence to tell me not to interfere with their arrangements!"

He opened his mouth to speak, but she continued irritably, "She's so stubborn."

With the pages restored to order, William eagerly scanned each one, concealing his amusement when he read Molly's rejection of Jane's advice, merely commenting, "Such a relief to know they're safe."

She gave a derisive snort. "But for how long? This stupid little skirmish in Spain could go on forever."

"Hardly a skirmish," he objected, "there's been some very serious fighting and I'm afraid it looks as though the Fascists are gaining ground." He nodded vaguely as he added, "Mark my words, there will be more trouble in Europe before very long."

"Then I suggest you write to Molly, make her see reason. As for Elizabeth, well, encouraging a Spaniard, I don't know what Molly is thinking of."

"Actually, Jane, he's Catalan, and if you read on you will note he's a student doctor."

"Impossible! He's with the forces – Republicans, Unionists, or whatever they're called, not a suitable friend for my granddaughter."

"We don't know that. He may well be a very acceptable young man. I get the impression Molly and James are quite taken with him."

Jane rose. "I'm going to the rectory to congratulate our vicar on his Easter sermon. I'll ask Chapman to bring in tea."

"When shall I expect you?" he called as she was leaving.

"I really can't say, but do make sure Pincott keeps a good fire burning for when I return."

"Yes, dear," he replied on a sighing breath, and turned the pages to re-read the news from Sitges. Molly mentioned little of the fighting, he noticed, or were they withholding the facts? But James would ensure they came to no harm; he could depend upon him for that.

He put the letter aside when the parlour-maid brought in his tray. Spotting the girl's tear-stained cheeks, his expression changed to one of concern. "Something wrong, my dear?"

Hurriedly putting down the tray, Gladys Chapman pulled a handkerchief from behind the bib of her long white apron and blurted out the reason for her distress. "I-I'm sorry, s-sir," she spluttered, "it's mi dad, he's real badly."

"Oh, I'm sorry to hear that," said William, rising to his feet. "What's the problem?"

She could only snuffle into her handkerchief as she tried to contain her tears. Placing his arm about her shoulders he comforted her as she continued to sob, her face buried against the lapel of his jacket. He felt strangely disturbed consoling the girl, feeling the warmth of her flesh through the black cotton fabric of her dress as the smell of lavender drifted up from her abundant fair hair. Once her tears were exhausted, he said softly, "There, there, feel a little better now?"

The sound of a faint cough brought William's head up and he turned to see Pincott in the doorway.

"Beg pardon, sir, I didn't realise..." Pincott murmured, a faint smirk on his lips as he withdrew.

As it dawned on William what the butler had presumed, he took a swift step back to exclaim, "That dashed Pincott – always snooping about!"

"Oh, sir, he'd be wondering where I am!" she said in her strong Yorkshire accent. "I'd better get back te't kitchin!"

"Of course," he agreed uncomfortably, "but try not to worry, the doctor will attend your father..."

"Won't have 'im, says he's too dear," she said and hurried from the room.

It struck William just how unfair life could be; to be so poor one couldn't afford a doctor's fees had not occurred to him. He tried to imagine his own ailment remaining untreated; could he have tolerated such pain without hope of medical intervention? Filled with sympathy for Gladys Chapman's father he went down to use the telephone.

Fortunately, he caught Alex Wilson at home, and when he explained the reason for his call, the doctor agreed to visit Mr Chapman right away.

"But let me have the bill," said William in a hushed voice, "though not when my wife's around, you understand."

"It's good to know you show your staff such kindness," the doctor remarked, "but I propose we share the cost?"

"Dashed good of you, Alex, I don't like to think of the poor chap suffering. But, remember, this is between us."

Once assured his secret was safe, he returned the mouthpiece to its hook, smiling to himself as he mounted the stairs. His pot of tea was by now lukewarm but he drank it without complaint, his mind dwelling on the parlour-maid's warm flesh and the clean smell of her hair. He'd discovered it to be a sensual experience, a sensation he hadn't felt in years. Yearning for days gone by he began to sob, quietly at first, until each choking breath grew louder when he had to pace the room in an effort to drive the torment from his thoughts.

* *

As the convoy wound its way along the uneven road towards the borders of Aragón, Maurici reflected upon the horrors of the previous evening. There had been another raid on Barcelona when the authorities had called out the medical team to assist in coping with the amount of corpses that lay in the streets as they had fallen. He'd seen rows of them, awaiting identification, and watched grim-faced relatives searching along each line. Many were the tiny bodies of children, their clothing ripped to shreds by the blasts, clutched to the bosoms of their distraught mothers whose cries were lost in the turmoil of the night. The tragic scenes stayed with him as the lorries swayed on, travelling with lights dimmed for fear of attack. He knew not what awaited them and doubted the few medical supplies and food they carried would suffice. Well armed Nationalist troops had reached the Mediterranean and were gaining ground, and there had been reports of fierce fighting around Gandesa. It was all so depressing. And now the Catalan statute of autonomy had been abolished, the language ceased to be official. No Catalan was to be spoken, even in churches, restricting it to family life. Maurici ground his teeth in frustration; what kind of democracy was this?

One of his colleagues lit a cigarette, and in the glow of a match he saw the grave faces of the others, silent and thoughtful as they huddled together against the cold of the early hours. It was not yet light, though to the east he saw a hint of gold on the undulating line of the horizon. He hoped Elizabeth was sleeping, and to lighten the weight of his sadness he concentrated his thoughts on a time when he could take her in his arms. Stretching out his legs to ease his position on the narrow bunk he thought of the passengers in the open topped vehicles ahead, exposed to the chill of the early morning air. At least this old ambulance provided shelter, draughty though it was, and now April was almost at an end there was the prospect of warmer nights to come.

* *

Seeing Elizabeth's downcast expression at breakfast Molly asked, "Why not come to the orphanage this morning?"

Reluctantly she agreed and found the morning passed quickly, her sadness having little opportunity to surface as the children captured her attention.

"I shall come more often," she decided as she and her mother walked home. "The children have so little as a result of this dreadful war."

Molly glanced at her daughter with concern. "Yes, we're fortunate," she said, "though I had an awful feeling our visit here was about to be cut short. Your father tells me H.M.S. Hood is in Barcelona to discuss the safety of British subjects."

"But I feel quite safe here," Elizabeth objected, her thoughts returning to Maurici. She was fortunate, indeed.

* *

Since his arrival at the front, Maurici had worked non-stop. The number of casualties was far greater than he had been given to expect, and the difficulties confronting the medical team extreme. Going out over the mountainous terrain with the stretcher bearers to bring back the wounded was a hazardous task, performed mainly after dark when there was less chance of being fired upon by their opposition. He found walking over the barren, rocky hills with the added weight of first aid equipment a test of his endurance. Only the plight of the suffering men gave him the strength to continue. They'd set up a field hospital some kilometres behind the lines where men with minor injuries received attention to their wounds. The more seriously injured were taken to a village further back, whereas those without hope of recovery were patched up and made as comfortable as possible. He was filled with admiration for the troops whose morale was surprisingly high, though the conditions under which they laboured in an attempt to delay the Nationalist advance were the worst he had ever seen. The men were ill-equipped, many wore only thin canvas shoes along with a cotton shirt and khaki trousers and maybe a blanket tied across their shoulders. Hardly suitable attire for moving through such difficult terrain. And yet, although faced with an acute shortage of food and water, it was the scarcity of tobacco and ammunition they seemed to find most intolerable. He was glad he'd had the presence of mind to bring along a supply of cigarettes.

One of the smokers, who acted as stretcher-bearer, was a member of the British Brigade and Maurici enjoyed conversing with him in English when they took the ambulance to recover wounded men. The Britisher was a tough little character who didn't flinch when confronted by the most appalling of injuries. Maurici had begun to think him insensitive until, out in the gathering darkness on one particularly blustery evening, they came upon a young man, three fingers of one hand missing, attempting to bury a corpse.

"Wasting your bloody time," the stretcher-bearer pointed out when the young soldier looked up at their approach.

Maurici sent the Englishman a look of reproach when he saw the soldier was little more than a boy, slightly built and sobbing uncontrollably as he scraped the sun-bleached ground with a length of broken bayonet held in his other hand.

"Let the burial party attend to it," he advised, crouching beside the struggling youngster. "The ground here is too hard, they'll know a more suitable place."

The young soldier ignored him, jabbing at the stony terrain with increased ferocity, only stopping when his piece of blade snapped and his cries became almost hysterical as he flung aside the remaining scrap of metal. Furthering his attempts to console the weeping boy, Maurici gripped his heaving shoulders to ask, "Tell me, young soldier, you know this man?"

Saliva trailed from the youth's lips as he opened his mouth to wail, "My brother... he's my brother!" Then, exhausted by his efforts, he collapsed over his few centimetres of freshly dug earth.

"Poor little bugger," the Englishman muttered, coming to cradle the boy's head in his large, rough hands, "he's not old enough to be in the sodding army."

Surprised to see such compassion on the brigader's face, Maurici shielded his eyes from the rising dust to ask, "Englishman, what is your name?"

"Garbutt," the man replied, tossing back a lock of matted, fair hair. "Tom Garbutt."

"So, Tom, our patient suffers much shock. He was desperate to do the right thing for his brother, you understand?"

"But it's useless trying' to dig a bloody grave 'ere," Tom pointed out, "an' only a bit of fuckin' bayonet to do it with..." He fell silent as the youth stirred, raising his blood-caked hand before his eyes as though to ascertain his injury wasn't merely an awful nightmare.

Maurici bared the youth's arm, and reaching into his case he brought out a syringe. "This should ease the pain," he said gently, fitting a sterile needle. And after administering the injection he prepared dressings, instructing Tom to shield him from the flying dust whilst he applied them to the wound. The youth whimpered, his pain-filled dark eyes fixed on Tom.

Here, lad, your need is greater than mine," Tom said gruffly, sparks floating on the wind as he inhaled deeply on his last cigarette then placed it between the youth's quivering lips, muttering, "Poor kid. An' that bastard, Franco, expects us to surrender!"

Again, Maurici was moved; if this was an example of the British character, he was glad to have Tom along. Reassuring the boy his brother would be given a decent burial, he arranged for him to be moved off the hill-side for hospital attention to his injured hand.

This was only one of many such traumatic incidents that followed, and it soon became obvious to Maurici he had been coerced into this position when he learned the previous medical team had been wiped out and no replacements found. At the time, he'd welcomed a short spell of experience in emergency aid and minor surgery, though he had stipulated against selective treatment.

The military situation appeared unchanged, though he'd noticed the Republicans had gained time to consolidate their field position, build support lines. After hearing rumours of raids in Barcelona, a Sunday morning attack by German Junkers instead of the usual Italian planes, he wondered if the Catalan offensive had been postponed His concern for Elizabeth and his own family increased, so he was overjoyed to receive orders to return with the wounded in need of more intricate surgery than the field hospital could provide. But when the time came to leave for Barcelona new orders came through; a supply of medical equipment was on its way to the field hospital where he was to remain. A steady flow of arms, including field and anti-aircraft guns destined for the Republican army were entering Catalunya once more, decreasing their disparity in equipment. This could mean another fierce battle, the medical team stretched to its limit; there was no alternative but to stay.

As it happened, Tom Garbutt was suffering acute enteritis and in no condition to remain at the front. A replacement was quickly found in the ranks, and so Maurici managed to scribble a short note to Elizabeth and begged the ailing stretcher-bearer to make sure it reached its destination.

"Don't worry, Doc, I'll see she gets it," Tom assured, grinning widely as he added, "Better disinfect it first, don't want 'er getting the shits!"

"Please, just wash your hands, and do not give her those swearing words," he returned good-humouredly, and went back to the waiting ambulance.

* *

Almost a week passed before Tom Garbutt felt he dare venture out. Due to further raids there was a postal crisis so, because he admired the young student doctor, he took a tram into the city to deliver the letter to the news office himself.

Fortunately, James called at his office that evening, returning from a few days spent close to the front. It surprised him to see his daughter's joy on receiving the letter. Elizabeth uttered a sigh of pleasure as she read it then looked up to say, "He asks if you will call on his parents, let them know he's safe."

The following morning, Enric made a detour on their way to the city to call at the house where Maurici's parents were now living. He had experienced a tiny stab of jealousy over the note to Elizabeth. Not that he wished any ill to befall the young Catalan, but he'd felt a curious sense of relief when Maurici had been called to the front.

It was Josep Bachs who opened the door to them, his brown eyes flicking warily from one to the other until Enric explained they were merely bringing a message from their office. Josep was speechless with emotion on learning his son was safe, but Enric noticed his sullen nephew, Lluis, hovering behind as James spoke a polite farewell in Catalan.

* *

On a particularly pleasant day in early June, William and his doctor took a stroll through the grounds of Woodington Hall. For William it was a relief to spend a little time in the company of someone with whom he could share his anxieties over the war in Spain.

"Dreadful business," William tut-tutted, "and General Franco continues to demand their unconditional surrender." He shook his head slowly, ending on a sighing breath, "What is to become of them, I wonder?"

Alex nodded. "Indeed. And I hear Chamberlain discussed National Registration in the House of Commons only yesterday which makes one a trifle suspicious of what lies ahead."

"You know, I never cared for that damned Hitler, myself. If one can believe everything one reads in the newspaper, then I suggest this Government keep a close eye on him. And there's the piece I read concerning the Jews, well..."

"I know, and don't forget what is happening in London," Alex reminded him. "That Mosley fellow appears to have gained quite a following."

"It wouldn't pay to let Fascism get too strong a hold," said William. "Mark my words, Alex, it would mean the end of everything we hold dear to us."

As they came to a seat on the grassy bank bordering the river, William suggested they pause a while to discuss the progress of Gladys Chapman's father.

"Peritonitis, I'm afraid," said Alex with a shake of his head. "Poor devil must have suffered intensely." Then seeing William's puzzled expression explained briefly, "Infection from a burst appendix – should have been attended to earlier- had to get him to Malton hospital without delay."

William nodded. "Never did understand those medical terms..." A thought struck him and he turned to raise a bushy eyebrow in Alex's direction. "As he's in hospital, I expect the cost will be considerably higher, hm?"

"Don't let that worry you, I wouldn't have refused him treatment had he asked me himself. You know, sir, had you not intervened, Chapman could have died."

William clicked his tongue softly as he gazed upon the dark, slow-moving waters of the river. And for a while they sat in companionable silence, watching fish break the surface where insects hovered and smelling the heady perfume of lilac and honeysuckle drifting on the warm air. He uttered a breath of contentment, wishing Molly and her family were here.

Suddenly, from the other side of the house, the tranquillity was disturbed by the raucous cry of peacocks. "Feeding time, I expect," William supplied, wincing slightly as he straightened his shoulders and sat back to fan himself with his Panama hat.

"Noisy creatures," Alex commented and, with a nod towards the river, asked, "Did you ever swim here?"

William chuckled. "No fear, too damned deep for my liking! For years I've wanted it fenced off, but Jane won't hear of it. The horses, you see."

"Hmm, it's fortunate there are no children here, otherwise it would be quite dangerous."

"There are troughs in the stable-yard. Don't see why the dashed things can't drink there..."

Alex rose. "Here comes your wife now," he warned, sensing his patient may add something less discreet. William started visibly, and getting to his feet began to babble about the weather.

"Discussing the weather?" Jane queried with a humourless smile, and to Alex, "You must find it dreadfully boring."

"To the contrary, madam, I enjoy your husband's company," the young doctor replied, then glanced at his pocket watch. "But perhaps I shouldn't keep you..."

"You're not leaving?" William intervened. "I was about to ask Gladys to bring tea."

"Chapman is no longer with us," Jane broke in tonelessly.

"No longer with us?" he echoed, casting an anxious glance in Alex's direction.

"It is not something I intend to discuss here," she informed him archly, leaving William turning the brim of his hat through nervous fingers.

* *

Only days after receiving Maurici's note, Elizabeth caught sight of a young man alighting from a motor-cycle outside the house. Drawing aside the heavy lace curtain, she noticed he wasn't particularly tall and wore a leather helmet and clothing of a military style with a red neckerchief at his throat. Aware Maria was hanging out washing in the garden behind the house, when the stranger reached the door she went to answer his knock.

"Ingles, si?" he asked with a strangely twisted smile.

"Si," she nodded, recoiling from the smell of his wine-laden breath to enquire in halting Castilion, "S*eñor* Puig, si?"

Immediately she mentioned Enric's name, she recalled their visit to the cafe in the square and realised the identity of the caller. Although, with his unshaven appearance, Maurici's cousin was barely recognizable.

"No, *señorita*, you," he said with casual appraisal as he stepped over the threshold.

Finding the intensity of his dark stare unnerving, she backed into the house. "You have a message for me?"

"No, no message," he ground out, gathering her roughly into his arms, "My cousin's whore will oblige me?"

With a terrified cry, she struggled against him, only to be silenced by his bruising kiss.

Tearing her head aside, she cried, "I'll tell my father!"

"No, tell no-one," he thundered, "or this Capitalist's house burn!"

In her terror she reverted to English, pleading with him to let her go. But intent on avenging Maurici he pinned her against the table, perspiration beading on his face as he sought her lips once more.

Chapter 10

The persistent yapping of a dog followed by Maria's screeching admonition from the rear of the house halted Lluis' relentless demands. His head jerked up and he cursed, glaring into Elizabeth's frightened eyes as he reiterated his threat, "You speak, this house burn!"

Releasing her, he left and she heard the engine of his motorcycle leap to life as Maria came in, her dramatic gestures illustrating the antics of the dog that had brought down her line of clean washing.

Leaving Maria to rant about the animal she ran up to her room, knowing Lluis would have forced her to submit had Maria not appeared. But his threat continued to trouble her, she'd heard of houses in the area being burnt down. Dare she disregard it, or was he likely to return? The prospect horrified her; it would be prudent not to remain indoors alone.

* *

Towards the borders of Aragón, Maurici toiled without respite. Any sleep he managed was snatched between journeys from the field hospital to the trenches, when the shelling made it too dangerous to travel with wounded men.

There had been a lull in the fighting, but men suffering old wounds, odious, suppurating sores, unhealed for want of attention, came to the medical tent in great numbers. He saw gangrenous limbs, the skin blackened and peeling, which he dressed before dispatching the patient to the emergency hospital. Scabies he could deal with, though an inadequate water supply for scrubbing the infected areas made it difficult to treat with success. In the blazing sun the infected scratched continuously, whilst others sought comfort in the shade of the olives. Many were suffering because of insufficient vitamins in their meagre diet, and at times Maurici resorted to reflecting upon mouth-watering memories of a well-cooked *botifarra*, his favourite sausage, or a selection of grilled vegetables in a sizzling *escalibada*. But now he gazed disconsolately on the battered metal dish of watery bean soup brought from the makeshift cook house, and was reminiscing over an imaginary dessert of Catalan cream when a lorry drew up by the tent. Through the flap he saw two men jump from the rear, recognising one as the stocky brigader, Garbutt, the other, an auburn-haired stranger. The latter appeared to be in some discomfort, lagging behind Tom who strode towards the tent as the lorry pulled away.

"How do, Doc!" grinned Tom. "Surprised to see me?"

"Surprised, yes, also pleased you are now well."

"'I sure am', as the Americans say," he mimicked. "I met a couple of 'em today."

Maurici nodded towards the stranger waiting nearby. "And this man, he is American?"

"Nay, sounds Irish," Tom laughed, and signalled to the newcomer. "Come an' tell Doc what's up."

The Irishman lifted a sullen face when Maurici held aside the tent flap and indicated he should lie on the rickety examination bed. Already he had observed blemishes around the man's mouth and, on further examination, found similar sores in the area of his genitals.

"You have the indiscriminate relations with the ladies, yes?" he asked, cleaning his hands in a bowl of disinfectant as the man adjusted his clothing. "I believe you have symptoms of the syphilis which means injections will be required."

"Jesus, Mary and Joseph!" the man cried. "You sure?"

"The field hospital doctor will give a second opinion. Where is your unit?"

The man shrugged, but from the few words he had spoken Maurici noted an accent reminiscent of James', but much stronger. His eyes narrowed; the majority of Irish Brigaders were staunch Catholics who fought alongside the Nationalists.

"You are saying you are lost?" Maurici pressed.

"I did so," came the curt reply. "Why the questions?"

Without preamble, Maurici replied, "I suspect you were left behind because your comrades were nervous of infection."

"Aren't I telling you, I'm lost!" the man blustered, getting to his feet.

"Listen, I am willing to help any man who is in need, Republican or Nationalist!" Maurici broke in. "I assume you are with the latter?"

The Irishman stepped forward and Maurici gaped in horror when he saw him draw a gun. "Don't assume anything," he hissed, "treat me or I'll kill you!"

Just then Tom Garbutt burst in and kicked the gun from the man's hand. With lightening speed the Irishman backed out of the tent to dodge through the trees, regardless of his discomfort. Tom bent to pick up the weapon and aimed at the retreating figure but, guessing his intention, Maurici reached out to prevent him. Cursing in frustration, the tough little Britisher pulled free.

Maurici shook his head; what chance had he against such determination. It was ironic; two men, foreigners to this country, as politically opposed as were he and his cousin. It was a war within a war.

Shortly, Garbutt returned to find Maurici standing by the tent, his expression grim with disapproval. "What have you done?" he demanded, "I heard a shot."

"Nowt – I've lost the bastard!" the Britisher said, sliding the gun under his belt.

Maurici sighed. "I hope you speak the truth."

"Yes, Doc, but he were a bloody Nationalist!"

"Also a human being!" Maurici reminded him shortly.

"But he were armed, he would 'ave bloody killed you!"

"I appreciate your concern, but I don't believe he would have fired."

Confused, Tom asked, "You religious, is that why you wasn't scared?"

Maurici shook his head. "It is a risk I must take."

Turning back to the tent he wondered, had the man been killed should he have contacted a priest to carry out those offices required by the Irishman's faith? Yet he knew no priest would dare to make his calling known at this side of the line, and appealing to the opposition was out of the question. He didn't consider himself a strong believer but frowned upon the atrocities performed also in Republican areas. To desecrate the churches and imprison the priests and nuns had no place in a democracy. For many the price of freedom was too high.

Later, as Maurici was dressing an injured hand, he glanced up to ask Tom, "Are there any more waiting for treatment?"

"No, Doc, but this one reminds me of that poor devil we seen trying to bury 'is brother," replied Tom, wiping perspiration from his face.

Maurici nodded, reflecting upon the kindness the Britisher had shown that night, his faith in him renewed.

"But that Paddy could 'ave fired. Yer too bloody trustin'," Tom persisted.

Maurici saw a look of contrition on the other's sunburnt face. "Tom, I am not a military man. I offer treatment to everyone, whatever their conviction."

"But that mucky bugger 'ad got 'imself a dose."

Maurici knitted his brows. "Dose? What is this dose?"

Tom grinned. "Been dippin' 'is wick where he shouldn't, an' you guessed he were with the Nationalists."

"Right or wrong, all men believe in their cause."

Tom cast his eyes to the roof of the tent in disbelief. "But I 'ope you'll still have me."

Maurici hid a smile. "Ah yes, did you bring news from Barcelona?"

Tom frowned, pondering a moment before he revealed, "That French feller, Daladier, he's closed the border again and I 'eard it were 'cos Britain was pressuring him."

Maurici pondered this and concluded it would mean an end to the arms supply through the frontier. But would it mean an end to the fighting?

"More British registered ships lyin' off Barcelona 'ave been bombed," Tom went on, "and I hear enough stuff's washed up to feed an army."

"And to feed starving women and children."

Tom nodded. "I've 'ad nearly a year of it. Last August I were in Belchite. Terrible – real savage fightin', corpses everywhere – place reduced to ruins."

"Terrible indeed, such killing, such destruction of property," Maurici agreed on a long sigh. "And after Belchite?"

"Teruel, in December," Tom continued, eager to recount his adventures. "Hell of a battle on them 'ills and I had bloody frostbite! I'd never 'ave guessed I'd see snow in Spain, and now it's too bloody hot!" Gazing into space he added, "I'd like to give them soddin' Nationalists a kick up t'arse!"

Casting him an amused glance, Maurici reflected upon his own experiences in the town of Belchite; injured and dying huddled together in fear, without hope of finding sanctuary within the smoking ruins of their homes, the outer walls of many blown away by ferocious shelling. The bullet ridden walls of a partly ruined church had stood tall amidst the scene of destruction, its tower still erect as though protected by some super power. He sighed, regretting the impotence of his role; he had been powerless to stop the killing, the enormity of it all rendering his efforts ineffectual as the battle raged on.

Tom's voice brought him out of his retrospective mood and he cast a vague glance in the brigader's direction.

"Fancy one, Doc?" Tom offered two cigars for inspection.

"Thank you, it will be the first I have tasted in weeks."

Tom held out a match. "I were wonderin' what happened to that finger. Lose it in battle?"

With an ironic smile Maurici told him, "No, it was an accident."

"Another thing, you never mention your lady friend."

Maurici sat back and exhaled a ring of blue smoke. "Ah yes, Elizabeth. Like you she is from the region, Yorkshire – Woodington Hall – but you speak a different way."

"Well, her family'll be posh, but I'd be a bit worried about her being 'ere."

Elizabeth was constantly on Maurici's mind, but unwilling to share his fears he advised, "Better not to dwell on the future. I fear more fighting will come, and possibly very soon."

* *

"Alex tells me there was a slight earth tremor when he was in London last weekend," William related during dinner.

Jane nodded from across the dining table. "I saw it in the paper. Fortunately, Saint Paul's wasn't affected."

"Fortunate indeed," William agreed absently and cast a glance towards the door to remark, "Dinner is late tonight. I was looking forward to a little chicken, suits my digestion." He sighed, adding vaguely, "It's never been punctual since Gladys left us."

Jane glanced up. "Chapman went weeks ago, yet this is the first time you've mentioned her. I wonder why?"

William looked away. "No reason, dear, no reason at all."

Her eyes narrowed. "I believe you had become very close."

"Close? What in God's name do you mean by that?"

She gave a knowing smirk. "Gentlemen in your position should be more discreet. It doesn't do to allow the staff to get too familiar."

"That damned Pincott! He had no business to tell you – no business at all."

"You can't blame Pincott. I overheard him discussing your antics with Mrs Dowkes so I demanded he tell me."

"He got entirely the wrong impression. I was merely comforting the girl, her father, you know..."

"Of course, her father, I quite forgot."

"Believe what you will, it's the truth..."

At that moment, the dining room door opened when, with practiced charm, she said, "Ah, here's your chicken, dear."

By the time the meal had been served to them, William's appetite was beginning to wane. Yet, he reminded himself, he shouldn't allow Jane to make him feel guilty when he had committed no sin. No physical sin, he granted, though his memory of the moment when he'd held Gladys in that comforting embrace was still crystal clear.

"This smells delicious!" Jane exclaimed in gushing appreciation as Pincott returned the lids to the silver serving dishes on the long mahogany sideboard. "Molly tells me they had chicken the previous Sunday," she continued, but once alone added viciously, "I hope that creature Elizabeth's acquainted with didn't get a taste!"

"The poor devil's away at the front, I gather," he said with a shake of his greying head. "I don't expect there will be anything nutritious for him there."

"Speaking of nutrition, I asked Pincott to get your Phyllosan tablets. Cheaper than taking the waters at Harrogate as Wilson recommends. Don't forget, you owe me three shillings."

* *

"I'm worried about Elizabeth," James confessed when Enric queried his unusually preoccupied manner as they travelled back from near the battlefront one day. "I realise she misses Maurici, but she's curiously apprehensive, I feel."

"Yes, James, I also noticed she is not liking herself."

"Not herself," he corrected with a smile. "Every day at the orphanage, perhaps it's too much for her."

"You wish I take her outside one evening?" Enric offered. "We can go with the car."

"Bit risky on the roads, don't you think? These damned raids – one never knows where next they'll strike. Even so, a couple of hours in your company might cheer her up."

"But maybe you are right about the car," Enric conceded, "we have many bombings."

"You mean the petrol tanks, at the foot of Montjuich?"

"*Si*, the harbour. And now is much cargo from the ships, water is full with food."

"But did you hear what Winston Churchill had to say?" James queried on a note of triumph. "He's threatened to arrest Franco's ships if any more British are sunk or damaged."

Enric's brows rose. "Churchill is saying this!"

"I heard it from a good source, and since Daladier closed the frontier I expect they hope to bring in arms by sea."

"Then, James, you think this will help the British believe Fascism is bad?"

With a doubtful shake of his head, James considered a moment. "I really can't say, but I doubt if Oswald Mosley's Blackshirts will get much sympathy in London with their parades and Jew-baiting. They're merely Hitler's stooges, but too damned blind to realise it. The Jews in Berlin are having a rough time, too... shops defaced, slogans painted on windows... you know the sort of thing."

"And you think this Hitler has the power to win Europe?"

"God help us if he does," James murmured as he stared blankly through the windscreen. "It needs a man as tough as Churchill to stand up to him."

It was the penultimate day of June when Enric invited Elizabeth to take the promised evening stroll. That morning he had covered a particularly harrowing assignment when a train on a main line north of Barcelona had been bombed and machine-gunned by insurgent planes. He still could hear the screams of passengers trapped beneath the broken carriages, a sound which had haunted him throughout the day. But it was the feeling of helplessness that irked him most; standing by, permission to get closer refused yet, through the lens of his camera, near enough to see someone die.

"Are you all right?" Elizabeth queried as they strolled along the narrow road leading towards the church steps.

Unwilling to divulge the horrors of his day, he forced a smile. "Is very hot today, it makes me tired."

Pausing to look up at the church facade, she asked, "Will it be hot where the fighting is?"

At once he knew it was Maurici's comfort which concerned her and strove for a normal voice. "They have the tents."

She gave a small, satisfied smile and continued along to where the boats were moored where she stumbled. Instantly, he caught her arm and held her for a moment whilst she regained her balance, experiencing a curiously pleasant sensation from the touch of her smooth skin.

"Perhaps we'd better turn back," she said with a nervous laugh. "Mummy would be furious if I soaked her new shoes!"

He glanced down to the low-heeled courts she was wearing and couldn't help but admire her slim ankles and shapely sun-tanned calves.

As they retraced their steps the trauma of the day began to fade from his mind and he related events in the history of the town. "A few years ago," he began, pointing beyond the wide, golden beach to where a cluster of palm trees grew, "before the war, here was a cafe building, also with the dancing. Many people come, is enjoyable for us, but there was a big fire, is completely burned out."

"What a shame, I'd love to go dancing."

"I wish I could take you," he murmured, the thought of holding her in his arms growing vivid in his imagination.

"Perhaps Maurici will take me when he returns," she said softly, more to herself than Enric. His heart sank.

"Let us end our tour at the *Cap de la Vila*," he suggested, moving at a faster pace so that when they reached the square with its pile of sandbags, the cafe's evening trade had barely started.

Once seated he called the waiter who came over to whisper that a measure of brandy was available. Enric nodded, feeling the need of an added boost to his coffee.

"Could I try one of those?" she asked, eager to sample something a little more sophisticated. "Is it very strong?"

Enric chuckled. "I think so, but perhaps you will enjoy better with just drops of brandy?"

She agreed and after a short silence lowered her eyes to say, "Enric, may I ask you a question?"

Thinking she was about to reveal her problem he said eagerly, "Of course, Elizabeth, please, ask me now."

"Well, I hardly know how to say this, but whenever I speak of Maurici you go very quiet. Do you not like him?"

Surprised by her observation, it took him a moment to recover. "Is it this which makes you worry?"

"So you don't," she decided, her lower lip quivering.

"No!" he cried in consternation. "He is a very likely man."

A smile of relief fluttered on her mouth as she raised her startling eyes to his to ask, "You really do like him?"

"I really do, and when is coming back I hope he visits me," he reassured her, continuing shrewdly, "If this is not your worry, what it is?"

"I'm not worried," she denied as he put the drink into her hand, but realising her anxiety over Lluis' threat must be more apparent than she was aware, said teasingly, "You sound just like my father!"

Elizabeth appeared for breakfast after her father and Enric had started out.

"The coffee is reasonable," said Molly, "I suspect Enric found someone willing to exchange rations."

"Don't you think it's time we got ready? You're not even dressed."

"Elizabeth, there's something I'd like to discuss before we leave."

"Daddy hasn't been nagging about us going back to England again, has he?"

"No, nothing like that. It's you we're anxious about."

Elizabeth tensed, stirring her coffee with great concentration.

"I know something is troubling you, darling."

"There's nothing, mummy, really."

"I realise you are missing Maurici, but there's something else and I insist you tell me."

"Oh really, mother, I'm not a child!" Elizabeth cried, jumping up from the table.

"You certainly behave like one!" Molly retaliated. "Sit down when I'm speaking."

Elizabeth spread her hands. "Sorry," she mumbled, "but I wish you wouldn't keep on."

"But it upsets us to see you unhappy. You're not ill are you?"

Elizabeth shook her head violently, her eyes tightly closed against threatening tears. "I can't tell you…"

Molly drew her close, cradling Elizabeth's head against her shoulder. "Whatever it is, you know we'll stand by you."

"Y-you'd tell Daddy," the girl stammered through muffled sobs, "I know you would…"

For one awful moment Molly feared to continue, but in a controlled voice asked, "You're not pregnant, are you?"

"Mother!" Elizabeth exclaimed, pulling away. "It's nothing like that!"

"Well, what is it you don't wish your father to know?"

Elizabeth gave a long, shuddering sigh, her eyes downcast. "Promise me you'll keep a secret?" she begged, and when Molly nodded, little by little, she related the events of the morning of Lluis' visit.

"My poor darling, so that's why you avoid being here alone," Molly gasped. "But he must not be allowed to get away with such threats."

"He will!" Elizabeth wailed. "I heard Enric say a house nearby had been burnt out."

"Don't worry, darling. I'll keep quiet; you will come to no harm."

But even as Molly made that promise, she knew it was one she couldn't possibly keep.

* *

"Would you mind driving via the Bachs' place this morning?" James asked as he slid into the passenger seat. "There's a little business I wish to settle with the son."

Puzzled, Enric glanced across at James whose expression was unusually stern. "You have business with Lluis Bachs?"

James nodded, then noting his colleague's concern decided it only fair to enlighten him. "Something Molly mentioned last night..."

"*Ai!*" exclaimed Enric when James had finished speaking, "I am ashamed for this evil of my countryman."

"I could barely contain myself when Molly told me. I'll show him what evil is, I will so!" James hissed.

"*Si, si,* is very possible, he is with the Communists."

"Communists!" he echoed. "I'll tear out his Communist heart when I get hold of him!"

"No, no," Enric implored, "it will make trouble for you."

"Don't worry, I don't intend to inform the parents, or Maurici, but just let me get that young bastard on his own!"

"No, James!" Enric swerved to the roadside. "You are angry, you must not use the fists!"

"Have you a better suggestion?" he asked with a touch of asperity. "We can't let him get away with it."

"I have the idea, James, but not with the fightings."

"And just what is it you intend? Remember, she isn't your daughter, you can't possibly feel so strongly."

Enric raised one eyebrow and tapped his forehead to state vehemently, "I know the politics of these people, but you, James, you will speak nothing and I make it certain you have no trouble with Lluis!"

"I suppose you know him better than I," James conceded with a shrug. "But I'm going to find it damned difficult to stand by and do nothing."

"You will stay in the car," Enric directed, his mouth set in a firm line as he accelerated back onto the road.

They came upon Lluis Bachs just as he was leaving the house, a roll of paper tucked under one arm. Enric put out a restraining hand, reminding James, "Stay here, you promise," before alighting from the car.

James did as he was asked but couldn't resist rolling down the window as the two men drew together. And when he saw Enric raise a clenched fist to salute the younger man he gaped through the windscreen in total amazement.

"I salute you, Comrade!" Enric said in Castilian before lowering his arm.

Lluis cast an anxious glance in the direction of the house. "Please, not here," he whined, "my parents..."

Glaring at the younger man, Enric demanded, "Do you deny your beliefs?"

"No, no, but not so loud."

"But you are loyal to the Party?" Enric asked quietly, noting his look of relief.

"Is just my family," Lluis hedged, confiding in a lowered voice, "You see, I didn't know you are a Party member, but I'm loyal, believe me. I want to join the fighting."

"Then why wait, Comrade? You must go now!"

"*Si,* I'll go tomorrow," Lluis promised solicitously, thrusting the roll of paper towards Enric, "but first I must deliver these Party posters."

"Ah, good," Enric said, slapping the youth on the back. "Now you assure me you are faithful to the cause I have no need to report you."

"Is that why you're here – you thought I'm not faithful?"

Enric smiled. "I'm just checking."

"Then how did you know about me?"

"I know everything about all members," said Enric giving a cryptic tap to his nose. "I also work for the cause, secretly, you understand?"

Lluis cast a quick glance towards the car before he said in an inveigling tone, "Perhaps we can work together, heh?"

Enric frowned. "Never approach me about our work," he admonished in a hushed voice. "This must be our secret."

Although he hadn't caught their entire conversation, James was utterly bewildered by what he heard. "I sincerely hope there's no bloody truth in all that rubbish," he challenged Enric when he returned to the car.

Calmly starting the engine, Enric acknowledged Lluis' furtive salute as they pulled away. "No," he grinned, "but he believes me. He will give no more trouble to us."

"But damn it all, to confess to being a Communist..."

"No James, you are wrong. I said, I work for the cause, but not which cause, you agree?"

James' mouth tilted in a smile. "You conniving devil!" he growled and threw back his head and laughed.

"The young fool is too busy thinking of his loyalty to the Party to realise," Enric chuckled. But his expression grew solemn as he continued, "With the fists we have no success, there would be retaliation, this way he will not return to make Elizabeth unhappy."

"Or set your house alight," James acknowledged. "Yes, my friend, I must confess, yours was the wiser course to take."

Chapter 11

In the heat of early July Maurici and Tom Garbutt set out over the rough terrain, picking up those wounded in their efforts to repel the Nationalist advance towards Valencia. They also tended any civilians they came upon who had fled the bombing of the Valencia-Castellon road weeks before. One of these, a young woman, had died giving birth to a stillborn baby in a bombed building, its early passage into the world brought about by the trauma of war. And as Maurici covered the tiny infant's lifeless body any fanciful dreams he'd harboured of impregnating Elizabeth with his seed faded. He realised the foolishness of his desire and knew it was something he could only contemplate in peace, not war.

As he left the place where the woman had sought refuge in her labour, a great sadness descended upon him. It stayed with him throughout the day until he received news the Republicans had saved Valencia. He hoped this would mean the fighting would cease. But later that week, as he and Tom smoked a last cigar, he couldn't share the other's enthusiasm for the way the battle had been fought.

"I 'ear they dug trenches deep enough to withstand thousand pound bombs, and the Nationalist Infantry was kept back easy with machine-gun fire," grinned Tom, shaking dust from his sun-bleached hair as he related snippets of news he'd got from another brigader who had been at the scene.

"Yet the Nationalists possess a superior number of arms."

"Well, he said the 'ail of fire were constant and it 'eld back the advance."

Maurici uttered a sigh. "I hate this talk of military things, and the suffering it causes."

"No, Doc, it were the Nationalists what suffered 'eaviest casualties, not us."

"But it is suffering, whichever side. That baby I saw today, a tiny innocent being, dead because of this fighting."

"You're bound to think that way, Doc, specially if kids is involved. Mind you, there seems to be a bit of a stalemate in the fighting, even the Nationalists look worn out." He gave a deep yawn. "I'm bloody tired meself, 'umping stretchers is hard work in this 'eat."

Maurici suggested they catch up with sleep. Valencia may have been saved, but something told him he'd need all the rest he could get to conserve his energy for the coming weeks. With hunger pangs gnawing his stomach he eventually fell into a restless sleep haunted by dreams of Elizabeth, a baby in her arms, and Tom attempting to force a cigarette between its tiny purple lips. He awoke with perspiration standing on his brow.

For days the same dream would unexpectedly recur. This, together with the hunger and anxiety over what may follow, frequently kept him awake. And it was towards the last week in July, during a particularly sleepless night, when he caught the sound of voices, many voices, growing slowly nearer, bringing him to the entrance of the tent. There was no moon visible in the cloudy sky but he could see the dark shadows of an army of men heading in the direction of the *Ebre* with the intention of crossing the river that night.

* *

"Every available man is being called to defend *Catalunya*," Enric reported during dinner and sensed Elizabeth tense. "This could mean both Maurici and his cousin are at the front. Since Valencia is saved they are determined to drive all Nationalists out of the region."

"I believe you once said Lluis Bachs was with the Communists," she remarked with pretence of scant interest.

He shrugged. "Republican, Communist, is no important, both fight the same cause."

"Providing they can agree to pull together, which is something they are working on at present," James observed with a wink in his colleague's direction.

Elizabeth glanced up. "Does that mean an end to the war?"

"We hope so," sighed Molly, "though it is likely your father and Enric may be called to the front to report on the action.

* *

"Molly mentioned nothing of this," said Jane, a bitter edge to her voice as she pushed the paper across the table.

Adjusting his spectacles, William drew his attention from the dull sky outside. 'Republican offensive began yesterday with the crossing of the river Ebro at eleven points,' he saw and realised just where the battle was being fought. It had been bad enough to read of the bombing of Badalona, a manufacturing town not too far from Sitges, and then the district of Prat and Casteldefels which was even closer. This could mean a full scale battle which he feared would spill over into all Catalonia.

"Well," Jane said shortly, "what's your opinion?"

"I don't know what to think," William said on a wavering breath, "but I do know James would act if they are at risk." He gave a vague smile as he rambled on, "You know, I can sympathise with those who demonstrated their disapproval of the British government policy in London last week."

"I saw it in the Times, but they're no better than those Republicans who desecrate churches and kill priests. Ruffians, intent on fighting, not in the least like we English."

"We British have done plenty of fighting in our time," William remarked, "and it wouldn't surprise me if we're not soon fighting again."

"Utter rubbish!" she said. "We're a civilized nation. When I think of the Princess Royal when she visited York last week, so dignified, so elegant," She uttered a blissful sigh. "No, they don't have our breeding, and they never will."

"Do I take it you agree with the Nationalist policies?" William ventured.

"Well, of course. This Mister Franco, he's a man of rank, a gentleman."

"But he went against the Spanish government so I consider him a rebel." William gave a wry smile. "No, I wouldn't trust your Mister Franco, or any other Fascist leader," he said, "which includes that dashed upstart, Hitler."

"Really, William, you're obsessed with your mistrust of the German leader."

"Then tell me this," he responded sharply. "Why do you think they're inspecting road exits and studying the problem of evacuation in London in the event of an air attack? There must be a damned good reason for it!"

"I haven't the faintest idea, but it can't be anything connected with the Germans, they're our kind of people."

William gave a snort of contempt. "But greatly misled by their Fascist leader," he retaliated. "Mark my words, there will be trouble in that quarter before very long. Spain is simply an exercise for his troops, a bit of real fighting to keep them in practice."

"Merely your opinion," she rejected loftily, and referring to the newspaper, said, "It doesn't tell me why we haven't heard any of this from Molly."

"My dear, Jane, they can't tell us much, letters will be censored. James' position could be quite perilous if he overstepped the mark. In his opinion..."

"There you go again, James this, James that... try asserting your own views."

There was a look of undisguised hate in William's narrowed eyes as he rose from the table and snatched up the newspaper to hiss, "Then let this be a warning. In future, I shall endeavour to be much more assertive, and should I feel it necessary it may be directed towards you!"

* *

As the ambulance rocked over the precarious ground towards Mora la Nueva, Maurici packed the few remaining medical supplies in preparation for crossing the river. His premonition of something big about to happen had been realised when the team received orders to set up a first aid post beyond the south bank behind the advancing Republican army. It was decided to leave the ambulance on the north side of the river ready to evacuate any seriously injured personnel to the nearest railway station and, with the assistance of Tom and the driver, take his tent and supplies over the Ebre by boat.

A lot had happened since the men advanced on his sleeping quarters. He'd learned of pontoon bridges being laid across the fast-flowing river, and of the many small boats brought forward in readiness for the crossing that was to be made at various points during the hours of darkness.

The men had been in high spirits, excited by the prospect of action, arousing Tom with their talk. "We'll give them bastards what for!" he cried jubilantly, jumping from the ambulance.

"We will be dealing with the terrible results of this action," Maurici reminded him gravely. "Would you rather join the advance?"

For a moment, Tom looked abashed then replied, "No, Doc, I'll 'elp you."

"Then let us move our supplies to the boat. Quickly! I hear gunfire, we may be needed."

Tom enlisted the driver's help to lift the huge canvas bundle onto his back. "Christ, its bloody 'eavy!" he complained as, almost bent double, he moved off in the direction of the river bank.

Maurici couldn't resist a smile as he followed with his medical supplies to ensure all necessary equipment was stowed in the boat. It was a couple of local civilians who rowed them across, men familiar with the river currents. Over the last few days they had become used to handling their heavily laden boat, its gunwales sometimes precariously close to the surface of the water. But once securely moored on the other side, they set about enlisting the help of local sympathisers who were eager to lend their support.

The light was already beginning to fade by the time they reached the position where Maurici had been instructed to set up his first-aid station. First to be erected was the tent where his bed and equipment were to be stored. And it was here, beneath a clump of dusty olive trees, he learned the Republican army had reached a village north east of Gandesa where it was reported the road was littered with belongings of the fleeing insurgents.

"They were so busy boasting of their success in the valley of La Serena, they were unaware we had crossed the river," disclosed one man, a member of the Popular Front.

"We took hundreds of Nationalist prisoners," said another, his accent strongly Aragón.

"Were many injured?" queried Maurici as he eased off the sweat-soaked shirt which had clung to him uncomfortably throughout the journey.

"Only one, and we moved him to the village," the soldier told him, "but we've left the prisoners outside under guard."

"Any of them serious?" Maurici was packing a haversack with dressings.

"Our man caught the blast as we crossed. Shells were falling around us and one of our company drowned."

"And the prisoners, how serious are their injuries?"

"Two or three don't look so good," he revealed with a careless shrug.

"Then I shall attend all the injured men," Maurici decided, motioning for Tom to bring along the stretcher, "and if necessary bring them here."

"All?" the soldier sneered. "Only one infantryman needs attention."

Maurici's jaw tightened. "I am a doctor, not a soldier," he growled, "so take me to the injured man, also the prisoners."

He turned away to close the strap of his bag, his anger abating when he heard Garbutt defend his decision in halting Spanish. The soldier bent his arm in a vulgar gesture before moving away towards the building where his suffering comrade waited.

Once he had applied dressings to his first patient, Maurici asked to be taken to where the prisoners were held. It turned out their injuries were superficial, suffering mainly shock, but he sought out the man in charge, demanding the prisoners be moved under cover before morning when the heat of the rising sun would increase their discomfort.

Tom beamed in admiration. "He were a high ranker, but you don't care do yer, Doc?"

Maurici smiled. "I only advise, but if I speak with the authoritative voice they listen."

"You capped that snotty little bugger," the Britisher praised as they neared the tent where, from the unfurled stretcher, he produced a bottle of wine which he promptly uncorked. "It were in that buildin'," he explained giving it an appreciative sniff. "All right, Doc, eh?"

"Why not!" laughed Maurici taking a swallow from the bottle. But the constant sound of gunfire gave them little time to relax and very soon they were preparing to move up behind the advancing men.

Thankfully, the night delivered only minor flesh wounds as the troops dug in their positions. But the morning brought fresh fears when the Fascist air force detected them, strafing the groups of tired men as they advanced towards the hills near Gandesa. Huge clods of earth leapt up as bullets sprayed and machine-gun fire continued, drowning the agonized cries of soldiers who were struck. But they fought on, retaliating with their quick firing anti-aircraft guns, filling the Ebre valley with a cloud of dust and the acrid smell of high explosive. The insurgent troops resisted violently but the determination of the Republicans was at its peak, undaunted by the scorching rays of sun until all the main observation points had been captured.

During this time there were many injuries, some so serious Maurici doubted they would arrive at the field hospital in time to be saved. The plight of the wounded disturbed him; knowing they must endure hours of waiting under the relentless sun until darkness fell when they could be dragged over the rocks to a position of greater safety. Due to the skills of Tom and the driver, an abandoned vehicle was repaired and put to use allowing the first aid station to move forward. Under cover of darkness it made many life-saving journeys, bringing the injured from the battle-field beneath its bullet-torn canvas, the protesting roar of its engine as it toiled over the rough terrain drowned by the sound of perpetual gunfire. With each delivery came new cases when Maurici did his utmost to relieve them of their pain.

It was into the second week when Tom Garbutt brought news that there was very little petrol to be obtained. Maurici was already exhausted and this new problem only added to his state. The Government forces had launched a fierce attack which he knew from experience meant his work load would be increased, but without petrol it would be impossible to transport the number of injured men to safer ground.

"It'll not get us back tonight," Tom said, going round the vehicle to open up the back. "An' by the look of this poor sod it were a waste bringin' him in."

A fresh wave of despair washed over Maurici. "Let me see him," he said, hitching himself onto the tailboard to assist in sliding the patient out.

"He's a civvy," Tom observed with a short laugh, "and all he were bothered about were his fucking camera so we chucked it in the cab."

Easing the semiconscious man forward, Tom took the weight of his shoulders, carefully sliding him towards the tailboard as Maurici supported his legs. From there they carried him to the tent and laid him on the bed, but when Maurici straightened his aching back and reached for the lamp he gasped in astonishment.

"*Déu!*" he exclaimed softly, "*Senyor Puig!*" Quickly loosening the neck of Enric's shirt, Maurici proceeded with his examination. Enric's pulse was rapid but weak, his breathing laboured, skin cold and pale, and he was slightly delirious. But he was alive; only just...

"He's from Sitges, a war correspondent," Maurici said as he unfastened the belt at Enric's waist. "Come, help me remove his jacket."

"What's up with 'im?"

"*Coup de soliel*, I suspect," Maurici diagnosed, fanning the air over Enric's face. "Much sun, high temperature. I find no other reason for his collapse."

It was a while before Enric began to show signs of recovery, making sighing breaths as he struggled to focus on Maurici's face. Aware of his confusion, Maurici bathed his forehead with a little of the coolest water to hand and spoke gently to him in Catalan.

"*Senyor Puig, Enric* – it is I, Maurici," he said gently. "You are safe."

Enric uttered a faint moan, grimacing as he attempted to move. Maurici continued to bathe his body, using water as sparingly as he could, and to Tom he directed, "Make coffee, it will help to stimulate him."

When coffee arrived, he raised Enric's shoulders and held a cup to his lips. "Drink this, it will help you recover."

Enric took a few gasping sips and sagged back again, his face deathly pale. Maurici checked his patient's pulse before he bathed his face and body once more. He gave a sigh of regret. "If only we had ice, a cold enema would help."

"Bloody hell!" protested Tom. "Yer'd never shove ice up his arse!"

Maurici sent him a hard glance. "I must make him cool yet retain water for drinking." He paused, his words going unheeded when he saw Tom leave. But soon he was back to say the driver had gone to the river for water and Maurici's spirits lifted, though now their vehicle was out of action he knew the journey would take time and returned to fanning the air over his semiconscious patient.

Tom frowned. "I didn't know 'eat could do this to a man,"

Maurici nodded. "This man is not used to these conditions. With so many clothes it happens easily, and without treatment, phuf!" he exclaimed softly, his gesture clearly illustrating such a demise.

Supporting Enric's head, Maurici held the metal cup to his lips. He managed to take a little of the water and remained conscious, but drowsy, during the intervals between each sip. Even though he got no clear response, Maurici continued to speak to him until the driver returned with a can of river water when he felt the prospect of Enric's recovery was greater.

Tom grinned. "Amazin' what a few fags'll do. He also got a drop of petrol for a couple."

Maurici's eyes widened in disbelief. "But is it sufficient to return to the front? There may be more cases tonight."

Throughout the early hours of the morning Maurici continued to swab Enric's body, saving the few litres of drinking water for its intended purpose. Now his patient showed signs of improvement and, although still weak, he recognised Maurici and gave a feeble smile. As the morning passed they shared a few words of conversation in the language familiar to both, Maurici explaining why he had been brought to the tent the evening before.

"I can not believe it," Enric kept saying. "Thank God your men found me, otherwise I may have died."

"Your condition was critical," Maurici agreed. "Was *senyor* Purcell also at the front."

"Ah, James," he said, struggling to collect his thoughts. "No, no he went north two days before."

"Let's hope he fared better than you," Maurici said with a wry smile and, although he longed desperately to ask about Elizabeth, decided to wait until Enric recovered completely.

But it was Enric who first brought her into conversation. Maurici had saved his life by his untiring attention; he had not known a more compassionate man and could appreciate why Elizabeth had become enamoured of him. His lip quivered as he offered, "My dear friend, if you wish to send word to Elizabeth, I will ensure it is received."

It took two more days for Enric to regain his strength, resting in the shade while Maurici attended the soldiers. Once he was sufficiently recovered to travel, arrangements were made for him to be transported to the nearest railway station north of the river. Delighted to find his camera still intact he took several photographs before making an emotional farewell.

Although sorry to find Enric so ill, Maurici had welcomed his unexpected appearance which had somehow brought him closer to Elizabeth. And in the letter Enric promised to deliver he wrote of his longing to be with her again.

After this, Maurici's position was again moved forward. In the days that followed he laboured constantly in intense heat as Savoia planes with their distinctive markings flew overhead and the ground shook with the impact of falling bombs. The fighting continued with ferocious intent as Nationalist reserves were rushed to the front to defend their fortifications, a fusillade of rifle and machine-gun fire continuing day and night. Early in August, the Republican advance had been halted when fresh, devastating attacks began from the air. Planes swooped low over the trenches, machine guns blazing, but still the determination of the forces didn't waver, exhausted though they were from heat and lack of sleep. They almost lived in their trenches, crouching amongst excrement and blood, tormented by ceaseless swarms of flies. Only after darkness fell could the ground be cleared of the dead; young soldiers whose bullet-ridden bodies gave Maurici moments of almost unbearable anguish as he saw them dragged away. He laboured constantly as the number of casualties increased, their pain racked bodies writhing in the scorching heat as they waited in mounting dread of further planes. There was little relief; surrounded by the swoosh of trench mortars and the crack of fragmenting rock, row upon row of injured men lay under the inadequate cover of charred olives and battered fruit trees until he could treat them, or organise their transport to hospital. He felt near to defeat, overwhelmed by a feeling of helplessness as he surveyed the diminishing medical supplies. As the weeks passed the men were showing signs of exhaustion as they strove to defend their positions, manhandling their few supplies of ammunition, food, and water over the rocks at night.

It was becoming obvious to all the prospect of victory was fading and there had been word of the British International Brigade being withdrawn. Maurici recalled his conversation with Enric who, from reports, was convinced war in Europe now seemed inevitable. 'Peace in our time', the British Prime Minister was reported to have said on his return from

Munich but, like Enric, Maurici doubted the intentions of the Fascist German leader. He feared what lay in store for the future and wondered sadly if he would see Elizabeth ever again.

In despondent mood he sought out Tom Garbutt to query the rumour he'd heard. He would miss the stocky little Brigader who'd become indispensable to him in recent weeks. But Tom stubbornly refused to listen to suggestions of withdrawal.

"I'm not bloody goin' nowhere," he announced resolutely, "Any road, I 'eard river's flooded an' bridges is down."

"But you must obey orders, return with your battalion. That way you will have safe passage to England."

But Tom was adamant. "No, Doc, I'm staying. I'll help you or Red Cross. There's nowt for me back home, I haven't no job." He grinned. "Here, I've five pesetas a day."

"But the authorities, they will demand you leave."

"They won't know I'm 'ere, unless you tell 'em."

Maurici couldn't resist a smile. "If the Nationalists launch another offensive, I fear we all must retreat."

Tom grinned. "If you're retreatin', I'll go with you."

* *

In mid November, in Barcelona, as the men of the International Brigades marched past on their farewell parade, a cheer rose from the crowd lining the street. Some broke away from the throng, tears in their eyes as they ran out to hug and kiss the paraders, whilst others threw flowers and children marched proudly alongside. Enric wondered if Tom Garbutt marched with them and shaded his eyes, searching each line of soldiers as they went by. He recognised many well-known political figures seated above the crowd, listened with interest to the Communist leader's speech, praising the efforts of the Brigade, but he didn't see Tom.

"*Si*, we owe them a lot," commented one bystander.

"But what happens now?" asked another who turned in Enric's direction to demand, "Can you tell me that?"

Enric shook his head and with a sweep of his arm declared in exasperation, "It is only two or three weeks since the Nationalists launched their counter offensive and the Republicans were forced to retreat, yet look at everyone here – such enthusiasm – anyone would think the Reds had won! Believe me, before you know it the Nationalist forces will be here, in Barcelona!"

"You are serious, *senyor?*" asked one.

"No, no, the Communists will stop them," put in the other, "they are determined to continue the fight?"

"But these soldiers are leaving," Enric pointed out, "yet Franco still has the Italians and Germans fighting for him."

"What about the extra men conscripted from all over Catalunya – even from the prisons?"

"But untrained. I have been to the front line, seen the conditions, terrible!" Enric spread his hands in a gesture of hopelessness and wandered away. He lacked the enthusiasm of the cheering masses, he was anxious for James who had made a third visit to the front line. He waited in the Press office daily, saw the reports coming in; the Nationalists had reached the river – Mora la Nueva had fallen to them – the battle of the Ebre was as good as lost.

It was a few days later when James appeared at the Press office.

"I am thinking you are somewhere dead!" cried Enric, grasping his colleague's hands.

"The luck of the Irish!" laughed James. "But there was one occasion when I thought the Lord had forsaken me." He went on to relate how a grenade landed beside him but, fortunately, failed to explode. Then his expression changed. "I also heard about your misfortune. I trust you are fully recovered?"

Enric nodded. "But now, what is the present situation?"

James blew out his cheeks and said, "The last Republicans left the right bank of the Ebro last week. Since then I've detected movement on the Nationalist side, as if they're preparing for a new offensive, plenty of artillery and tanks. It's my opinion it will be absolute hell around there before the month is out."

"You will not go back?" Enric enquired anxiously.

"No, I've had enough and, although I'm reluctant to mention it, I must speak to Molly about leaving. Depends how risky the situation becomes, of course, but I must arrange transport, I can't have them stranded here."

"Is problems with refugees crowding the roads," Enric warned. "Many people go north."

James nodded, and with cheerful optimism said, "Let's get this dispatch away, then we'll discuss spending Christmas here."

Chapter 12

It was almost Christmas when Maurici delivered the last of the seriously wounded to a Barcelona hospital. By the entrance stood the familiar group of sad-faced women who thrust photographs of their missing loved ones under the noses of returning ambulance crews in the hope they may recall seeing them on their way. It had been a difficult and exhausting journey with many obstacles; bridges down, roads littered with burnt out vehicles, bomb craters, and the Nationalist air force still on the lookout above. The weather had cooled considerably and he would have welcomed the blankets lost when the first aid post received a direct hit; the parched canvas had burned to ashes in minutes leaving him without supplies. Fortunately, he and Tom were unharmed as it had happened when they were outside, preparing for the retreat.

"We must re-equip the ambulance when we meet," he told Tom after they had placed their wounded in the care of hospital staff. "Don't forget, be here the first day of January."

Astride a borrowed motorcycle with sidecar Maurici opened the throttle. With blue smoke billowing from the exhaust he drove away, through the desolate city streets. He passed a group singing revolutionary songs, saw old people and women with children queuing for food. More buildings had suffered in the raids and torn Republican posters urging unity fluttered from their crumbling walls.

Unity? He pursed his lips, recalling the retreat from the battlefront; men swimming the wide waters of the river *Ebre,* desperate to escape, others unable to contain their tears of relief on reaching the city. Would they be eager to unite?

He drove on, his spirits lifting as he left it all behind, his thoughts turning to Elizabeth.

* *

When a motorcycle drew to a halt outside, Elizabeth tensed. Peeping cautiously around the heavy brocade curtain she saw Maurici striding towards the house. With tears cascading down her cheeks she rushed into his outstretched arms, uttering cries of pleasure.

Indoors, seated round the table, they chatted until Molly realised it was time for her to go to the orphanage. Since hearing Enric's report on the conditions Maurici had left, Elizabeth prepared to make him a meal, but he followed her over to the cupboards, sliding his arms around her waist before she could bring out the dried sausage or the loaf of bread.

"I am not hungry for food," he murmured, his warm lips nuzzling her neck. As she turned in response, he took her in a close embrace and captured her mouth. Elizabeth gazed up at him adoringly; this was something she had yearned for throughout the long summer, and she moaned softly as they clung together, his mouth moving sensuously against hers.

But for Maurici, after so long without physical contact, the closeness of her body aroused the most tantalising sensations, the fire in his groin urging him to draw her even closer.

"Elizabeth, *estimada,* I have waited so long for this," he groaned, his breathing heavy as his searching hand explored the contours of her body, seeking to undo the buttons of her blouse. Uttering words of endearment in Catalan, he eased his hand under the silky fabric to cup her breast, the feel of the smooth, warm skin beneath his fingers driving him almost wild. Baring her breasts, he lowered his head, teasing and caressing first one pink nipple then the other with his tongue. Returning to kiss her lips, his exploring fingers reached down to gather up the hem of her skirt. Mistaking her stifled cries for those of pleasure, he pleaded between kisses, "Let me love you..."

Tearing her head aside, she cried, "No, Maurici – no!"

"*Sí,* you want me to love you," he persisted, passion darkening his gaze. "Tell me you want me..."

"We can't – someone may come."

"Then where," he demanded huskily, "tell me, where?"

"Please, Maurici, don't make me..."

With a hiss he turned away, his body taut with frustration, his accent more pronounced as he demanded, "Why you are saying I make you? You want me, I know it!"

Stung by his tone, she fumbled with the buttons of her blouse, her cheeks growing warm as she retaliated, "It's the only reason you came here – you don't love me!"

He swung round, his eyes glittering. "*Déu!* Can you not understand? I want you because I love you."

"Then you have a strange way of showing it!"

He spread his hands, reining his passion as he explained more gently, "When people love each other it is natural for their bodies to unite. You wanted love, I could feel it."

"You make it sound like a purely physical thing," she said, a trifle piqued to learn her desire was so obvious.

He managed a smile. "Love is many things – in the mind, the heart, the body – we must not feel ashamed."

"I'm not ashamed," she said petulantly, "I'm just not used to being... well, touched..."

"You are a virgin?" he asked softly, but she didn't have to reply, her expression confirmed it. Suppressing the ripple of desire that coursed through him, he promised, "I would not hurt you, Elizabeth, if that causes you worry."

"Of course not," she denied hotly. "I know all about the birds and the bees."

"Birds, and bees?" he echoed, frowning. "What is this?"

"You, a doctor, and you don't know!" she mocked. "It's human biology – you know..."

Relieved to find the tension between them had dissolved he moved towards her, the expression on his tanned features appealing. "And are birds and bees allowed to kiss?"

"I'm sorry, I shouldn't have laughed," she said, and standing on tip-toe she kissed him briefly on the lips.

"And I should not be angry," he admitted, raising his dark brows to ask, "Forgive me?"

"I suppose so," she murmured, allowing him to take her in his arms once more when, although her initial excitement had faded, she was filled with curiosity. What would it be like to have Maurici make love to her?

She pulled her thoughts back to the present to hear him tell of his plans. "I have leave until the new year, after that, a hospital near Barcelona. We have many cases to attend but I hope there will be some free time."

"Will you be living at home, or your uncle's house?"

He shrugged. "We usually spend Christmas with my uncle, but this year I am not sure, it was impossible to have letters."

"I still have the letter you sent with Enric," she said. "I was so relieved as we heard dreadful stories about what was happening at the front line."

"Conditions for the soldiers were bad, no food or water..." He paused when she uttered a cry of consternation.

"Oh, my goodness, I intended to make you a sandwich! You must be hungry."

He tried to persuade her it didn't matter, but she insisted, and he ate the first palatable sandwich he'd had for some time as they made plans for the following day. Then it was time to visit his family and he kissed her a fond farewell before going out to start the motorcycle.

* *

Although his mother appeared delighted to have him home, Maurici could see she was failing in health; anxiety and shortages had taken their toll. His father was more optimistic and invited him to inspect the progress made towards rebuilding the *celler*.

"I don't regret losing this year's crop," Josep admitted as they strolled together. "Friends of mine have been obliged to sell to the Fascists for safety's sake, whereas I was able to avoid the problem of refusing."

Maurici cast him a worried glance. "Had you the stock, it would have been unwise to refuse, you realise that?"

Josep acknowledged this with a nod of his head. "With luck, by the time I'm ready to produce again this war will be over and we can start afresh," he said as they examined the pile of roof timbers he had stored in readiness. "If only I could gain your mother's interest. Times are bleak, I know, but she seems to have lost all hope for the future."

"I'll have a word with her," Maurici promised. "The week in Sitges may do her good, providing she doesn't overdo it in the kitchen."

Josep gave a short laugh. "I doubt that! With food in such short supply, there won't be much cooking done this festive season." He sighed as he continued, "She needs another woman in the house, and perhaps a child to look forward to."

Maurici turned an amused gaze in his father's direction "*Papa!*" he laughed. "Are you suggesting I should marry?"

"Why not?" Josep returned indignantly. "The day will come when your mother cannot manage as well as she used to, and it is good for a man to take a wife, gives him something to strive for, keeps his feet on the earth."

Maurici dropped his eyes, tracing the edge of the paving with his foot. "As a matter of fact there is someone, though you won't know her, but I couldn't consider marriage until this war is over."

"Forget the war," Josep said, grasping Maurici's arm. "If you are happy with your choice, why wait?"

"Perhaps you're right, *papa*," he replied thoughtfully, "perhaps you're right."

* *

"Our Christmas pudding arrived wrapped in a pair of Mrs Dowkes' hand-knitted socks!" Molly told them laughingly.

"I expect your mother included those to boil it in," James grinned, "though I must say I enjoyed it, and Enric's traditional Catalan stew."

"My mother teaches me," Enric recalled sadly as he poured a dessert wine he had kept for Christmas day. "Today I am missing going to the church with her."

Molly gave his hand a sympathetic pat. "You can say a prayer without going to church."

He gave a brief smile. "This morning I have spoken the prayer, in a private house, with the priest attending. But I cannot tell where, is dangerous for him."

"Another contradiction to democracy..."

"Darling, not today," James interrupted. "We've had a dashed good meal, though I may put the damper on things when you hear what I've got to say."

She shot him a glance, her heart sinking when she noted his expression.

"Maybe you heard Enric telling me Franco's troops have launched a fresh attack across the river Segre...."

"As you told me, hardly the topic for today," she rejoined bitingly.

"Darling, please, this is serious."

She sighed deeply and took a sip of her wine. "Go on, James, I think I can guess what you're about to say."

"Darling, we've got to be sensible. I'm just as upset as you are, but I'd rather know you're safe in England and not here when the Nationalists arrive." He held up his hand to silence the objection she was about to make. "You can be sure, with their superior armour they will be heading across Catalonia damned quickly, with Barcelona as their main target."

"Is true, Molly," Enric put in, "he is determined to take this region. Before Christmas the Republicans hoped for support from all anti-fascists in Europe, but now is too late, better you go back."

"I suppose it had to happen," she said despondently. "We must warn Elizabeth."

* *

"Such a pity Elizabeth isn't here to see this," William paused to remark as he descended the stairs to where the Christmas tree glittered in the hall below.

"Do pull yourself together, William, you've been miserable all day," his wife remarked crisply. "It's almost seven, our guests will be here any minute."

Straightening his bow-tie, William sighed and prepared to meet the local dignitaries; the vicar and his wife, his accountant, the local veterinary, and the Grant's. And, considering the doctor's position equal to anyone on her guest list, he insisted Alex and his mother be included. He smiled to himself; he had become more assertive, just as Jane had suggested.

He saw her pause to give Pincott his final instructions and noticed she was wearing a dinner gown he'd not seen before. Irritated though he was, he couldn't help but admire the style; long sleeves, each with a row of small buttons at the cuff, and a full length skirt, softly draped across her slim hips. A pity it was grey, he thought, a colour reflecting his mood.

Suddenly aware she was speaking he came back to the present. "Yes, dear," he murmured vaguely, spotting the clover coloured flowers at the vee neckline. "I like the pink bits, sets it off somehow."

"Pink bits?" she queried. "What on earth are you babbling about?"

"Your dress, dear," he said, easing a finger under his stiff, new collar. "Hmm, very nice, very nice indeed."

"Fool! I was asking if you think one bottle of port will be enough, or shall I tell Pincott to bring up another?"

With a hoot of laughter he shot back smartly, "Better ask Grant. He'll be drinking most of it, without a doubt..." His retort was cut short by the ring of the doorbell and Pincott hurried to answer it.

"Don't speak to me in that tone of voice when Pincott is present," she hissed.

"And don't refer to me as a fool in his hearing!" William returned sharply, forcing his lips into a pretence of a smile as the first of their guests arrived.

As he expected, it was Miles Grant and his elderly parents who entered the oak-panelled hall adjoining the dining room. The Grant's were always first to attend, and to see Miles' smirking, pink countenance surveying the drinks trolley with gleeful anticipation made William's hackles rise. Pincott, his servile expression intact, proceeded to pour each request as seasonal greetings were exchanged. The vicar was next to arrive, also making his way over to Pincott with clear intent, leaving his wife alone, her fox fur dangling from her shoulders.

"Quite a fall of snow we had," the elder Grant remarked, warming his hands by the dancing flames of the open fire.

"Hmm, quite a fall," William concurred, "but I believe a thaw's setting in."

"Even so," Grant responded, his attention on Jane as he predicted, "you're in for a chilly ride tomorrow."

Of course, the Boxing Day hunt, William realised with distaste and moved closer to the group to inform them with a tight smile, "It's most unlikely Jane will be joining you, we expect to receive a call from Molly."

Jane's head snapped up. "Not hunting on Boxing Day!" she cried with a short laugh. "You can't be serious, William. Of course I shall go."

For a moment he gaped at her in disbelief. "Oh but I am, she'll wish to speak to us both."

"But she wouldn't want her mother to miss the fun," Miles broke in. "Remind her it's the hunt, she'll understand." Draining his glass he added with a grin, "Anyway, it's time they were back in Woodington. I'm quite looking forward to riding with Elizabeth – providing James hasn't placed her in a Convent, that is. Bit of a puritan isn't he, heh?"

William's face grew red. "What the devil do you mean by that!" he demanded, thumping his glass down on the table."

Miles laughed. "No offence, sir, but she's missing a decent social life. You should remind him of that when he rings."

"I'll damned well do no such thing!" William thundered, brushing off the vicar's restraining hand. "I must ask you to watch your tongue!"

"For goodness' sake," Jane hissed in his ear. "I shall decide whether or not I ride tomorrow, not you!"

"We'll see about that!" William roared, regardless of the astounded faces of those present, and strode from the room.

Ascending the oak staircase he moved purposefully in the direction of Jane's dressing-room. He'd seen her take delivery of new riding clothes and soon spotted the tailored jacket and habit hanging from the rail with shining leather boots standing beneath. Panting a little, he gathered the new clothing in his arms, the habit trailing as he made for the back stairs. Ignoring the astonished Pincott who'd rushed on the scene he snatched the key to the stables from a hook behind the door.

Outside it was dark and windy with a threat of rain, but William was so incensed the chill of the evening went unnoticed as he strode over to the riverbank, muttering, "I'll show you, woman! You'll not make a fool of me..." And struggling to keep his balance he flung the boots into the dark, swirling water one by one, following them with the breeches and the black habit and jacket. Still seething with rage, he marched to the stables and in the semi-dark saddle-room he groped for the new saddle resting on the wooden saddle-horse. On the other side of the partition wall, Jane's favourite stallion gave a snort of protest at the intrusion and clattered noisily about in its stall. William was fond of horses but the animal's sudden movement startled him.

"Quiet, you stupid bastard!" he roared, and heaving the saddle over one arm he struggled back to the riverbank to drop it in with an almighty splash. "There, now you know who's boss!" he declared breathlessly, rubbing his hands together. And for a while he remained by the river, cursing both the Grants and his wife as he stared down on the inky water.

Only as he fought to regain his breath did it begin to dawn on him exactly what he'd done. He cursed his impetuosity; Jane would never forgive him for this. With shoulders hunched, he turned to walk through the archway in the wall, towards the rose garden where he took a seat on a bench still sodden from the previous day's snow. For a moment, by the river, he had experienced a tremendous burst of elation, achieved something he'd often longed to do. But his satisfaction was short lived. Along with the anti-climax came the overwhelming torment of guilt. Now, head in hands, he became aware of a knot of pain below his ribs, brought about, he surmised wearily, by his over-rich, seasonal diet. He tried to relax but the cold was beginning to strike through the seat of his black trousers, and within minutes he began to shiver, teeth chattering uncontrollably as the chill about him increased. He spotted the light of a torch swinging from side to side coming from the rear of the house and assumed it was Pincott sent out to look for him. But he wasn't going back indoors whilst that damned Grant fellow was around even if it meant staying out all night.

"Mister Cussons! Are you there?" asked a gentle cultured voice which he immediately recognised as Alex Wilson's. "Are you all right, sir?" he heard him continue, and now the snow had begun to fall again he felt bound to speak.

Drawing a ragged breath, he pulled himself to his feet to reply, "I'm here, Alex, in the rose garden." But as soon as he stood upright he was overcome by weakness and fell back on the seat, gasping from pain.

"Experiencing a little pain this evening, are we?" Alex asked, advancing quickly towards him in the beam of light.

"I expect they've told you," he began weakly and retched, vomiting a brownish substance onto the snow at his feet.

"I understand you were rather upset," Alex agreed patiently, supporting William whilst he recovered from the violent heaving of his stomach. "Don't worry, we'll soon have you out of this cold air."

"I'll be damned if I'm going anywhere near that Grant fellow," he gasped, and coughed until he retched again.

"No need for you to see Grant – I'll make a suitable excuse, and as soon as you feel able we'll get you to bed," said Alex, offering his handkerchief. "Christmas can be an exhausting time, what you need is rest."

William raised his head. "But you don't realise what I've done?" he fretted. "I must have been out of my mind!"

Alex uttered a soft sigh. "I believe I do," he said, "and I'm not the least bit surprised."

* *

Lluis arrived home on the last day of December, and when he learned Maurici had been on leave for almost a week his attitude towards his cousin hardened.

"We don't sit on our arses," Lluis sneered. "I have distributed thousands of leaflets in *Catalonia* urging the people to continue the fight."

"My weeks at the front were hardly easy," Maurici retaliated. "Day and night, dealing with the injured and dying."

"Ah, yes, I read about it in a report from the front – how you saved the life of that fellow Puig."

"It was in the papers? But why, it is my work."

"If you'd known he was a Red would you have treated him?"

Maurici's brows drew together. "Of course, no one Party has precedence."

"I hear the young woman staying in his house means something to you, but what a treat for him having her there."

Maurici glanced up, but refused to be drawn.

"You gave him special treatment, yet for all you know she may be sharing his bed," Lluis jeered.

Realising he was being provoked, Maurici ignored him and opened his book.

"Or someone else's," Lluis went on, enjoying the situation, "you're not here to see."

"Stop your filthy insinuations!" Maurici managed in a reasonably controlled voice, his attention on the book.

Glancing to the Catalan literature Maurici held, Lluis commented, "For someone so patriotic, I'm surprised you entertain her, she's a foreigner." But finding his remarks failed to arouse his cousin he changed his tactics and smirked, "Capitalist snobs, I call them..."

Maurici smacked the book shut. "I don't give a damn what you call anything – shut your stupid mouth!"

"Oh I'm not stupid!" Lluis retorted. "I wouldn't let anyone hear me speak Catalan, or so was the comment in the paper."

Aware he may lose control, Maurici rose and left the house. He had arranged to meet Elizabeth that afternoon so, finding it to be a reasonably warm day, he considered inviting her to ride on the motorcycle. They'd had so little time alone, walking by the sea, or a few moments in Enric's house, but now he felt an impulse to drive to Sant Adria, to visit his home whilst his parents were away.

Elizabeth was already waiting when he pulled up outside the house, her downcast expression causing him concern. "I do wish we could spend some time alone," she said with a sigh. "There's always someone here."

"Exactly as I was thinking," he agreed, "so let's take a drive."

"I've never been in a sidecar before," she said, brightening, "You won't drive too fast?"

"No, no, and if the weather remains good we can do this often," he promised, glancing up to the cloudless sky.

Her smile faded as the memory of the dreaded words her father had spoken that morning returned. Seeing Maurici's frown of enquiry she explained in a flat voice, "But I don't know how much longer I'll be here. My father says the fighting is getting closer, we must leave."

Maurici assisted her into the sidecar's low seat. "I had anticipated this," he said, "so we must spend every possible moment together."

Though nervous, she soon found it exhilarating to have the wind rushing through her hair as they drove into the country in the direction of Sant Adria.

"You enjoy this?" Maurici called, his face lowered against the wind, his short, dark hair hidden beneath the black beret he wore.

"Wonderful!" she cried, managing a smile, though her heart ached when she thought of leaving all this behind.

Arriving at the *masia* he lifted his goggles, dismounted from the saddle, and came round to help her alight. Once inside the old house, silent but for the ticking of the long case clock, he drew back the shutters at the sitting room window, letting in the warm, slanting rays of afternoon sun.

Elizabeth slipped off her jacket and saw Maurici take a bottle from a cupboard in the whitewashed wall. "The eve of nineteen thirty-nine, we must celebrate," he said as he poured, and handing a glass to Elizabeth he linked his arm through hers to drink the toast.

Seated beside her on the repaired settee he opened a box. "Try this, it's a traditional dessert of the season."

"The sad season," she echoed, taking a piece of the nougat, packed full of almonds. "I only wish..." She broke off, her lower lip beginning to quiver.

Laying aside the box he asked softly, "What is it you wish?" and leaned across to kiss her before he repeated, "Tell me your wish and I will tell you mine."

"I wish I could stay here with you," she said, with tear-filled eyes.

He cupped her chin and drew her towards him, fluttering kisses on her eyelids, her lips, his gaze becoming intense. "And I wish for you to let me love you before you must go away; something for us to remember while we are apart."

Her heart missed a beat, she looked longingly into his eyes, her lips parting in anticipation of his next kiss. Quick to take up the invitation, Maurici drew her into his arms, his lips desperately seeking hers as he felt her hands slide up around his neck when the desire within him increased almost beyond his control.

Tense with excitement, he whispered against her cheek, "You like me to love you, yes?"

He caught a soft response from deep in her throat and heard her quick intake of breath as his hand slipped beneath the neckline of her dress. Fondling her bare, warm breast with infinite tenderness, he urged her to reply. "Tell me, *estimada*, tell me you do."

"Oh yes... yes I do..." she whispered tremulously, sending a fresh tide of desire through his body. He let out a shuddering breath, and in an effort to contain his ardour he concentrated on the soft skin of her neck, caressing it lightly until he felt her arch, her firm breasts pressing against him.

"When do you expect to go?" he asked softly, drawing slightly away as he continued his gentle caress.

"Next week perhaps, I'm not sure," she said on a sigh of impatience, reaching up to place her soft lips against his, urging him to kiss her again.

"We will see each other every day until then," he promised, his hand coming to rest on her thigh, "and we shall treasure this moment, always."

"Always," she echoed, allowing his exploring hand to caress her without objection.

Aware of her increasing desire, Maurici pressed kisses along her neck and murmured, "Let us go somewhere more comfortable, *amor meu*, I need to feel you close to me."

Regarding him from beneath her dark eyelashes, Elizabeth smiled and took his hand. Together they climbed the steps to the next floor, lingering a moment to kiss before continuing along the landing towards an open door.

"My room," he said softly, carrying her over to the bed where he laid her under the white damask cover. And in seconds he had kicked off his shoes, the bed-springs creaking as he climbed in beside her.

Elizabeth immediately buried her face, her cheek hot against his neck as he drew her closer to the length of his body. "This is better," he murmured, running his fingers through her silky hair. "You are comfortable with me?"

"Yes", she whispered, "but it's the first time tha...that I've been in bed with a man."

The very thought of her virginal state nearly drove him wild and he caught hold of her chin to take her lips in a passionate kiss. Her response was gratifying; his fingers went to the front of her already unbuttoned dress, easing it over her shoulders to slide her arms free. Resisting an impulse to tear away the lacy garment beneath, he took his time over baring her breasts, gently kissing each rosy nipple as he undid the remaining fastenings to trail his lips along the exposed, velvety skin of her warm body. Elizabeth was moaning softly; her dark hair fanned out over the white pillow, eyes closed, waiting to be loved. In his increasing need he quickly slid from the bed, fumbling wildly with the buttons in his haste to undress. But in seconds he was beside her, seeking her eager mouth as he reached down to caress her parted thighs. He kept reminding himself he must be gentle, though his urge was to thrust all caution aside. But when she pleaded for him, her voice husky with passion, he pressed forward, taking all the care he could possibly muster.

Her gasp of pain went almost unnoticed as he cried out her name, his awareness of her momentarily snatched away by a spasm of intense pleasure. He groaned and drew quickly back, suddenly concerned, but she held him there, imploring him to continue.

"Give me a few minutes," he gasped as his passion subsided, and returned to caressing her again as he whispered, "Did I hurt you?"

"A little, but I don't mind," she replied breathlessly, her arms around him, holding his hot, perspiring body against her. And in minutes he was pleasing her again until she cried out with uncontrolled delight before falling limp in his arms.

"You do love me, don't you?" she murmured, her sapphire eyes hazy with contentment.

"Of course I do," he smiled, dropping a light kiss on the end of her nose. "I adore you."

"And you'll still love me, after this...?"

"Yes, Elizabeth, I still love you, as before."

Chapter 13

When Maurici drew up outside Can Bachs the following morning to find an ambulance standing there, with Tom Garbutt in the passenger seat, his spirits sank.

"Happy New Year, Doc!" Tom called as he swung down from the vehicle.

"But why you are here, with the ambulance?" he asked, glancing from Tom to the driver.

"There's been trouble back at field 'ospital, a Colonel reported injured."

Maurici grimaced; his intention to bring Elizabeth here again before his parents returned was not to be.

"Driver says we can do it in a day," said Tom, climbing into the rear of the ambulance. "I were 'oping for a celebration."

Maurici shook his head in despair. Now Elizabeth may soon be leaving he had no intention of wasting precious time celebrating. With supplies already on board, there was a possibility he'd be back in time to meet her that evening. Locking the motorcycle combination in one of the outbuildings he climbed aboard the ambulance to travel towards Borjas Blancas, over familiar terrain.

Drawing up by the single-storey building that housed a few makeshift beds and instruments necessary to perform emergency operations, Maurici frowned. The area seemed uncommonly deserted with only a burnt out vehicle standing there. He noticed a sizeable hole in the tiled roof, and the trees nearby, once abundant with foliage, were reduced to scorched skeletons.

"Stay with the ambulance," he instructed when no-one appeared, and lowering himself from the cab he advanced cautiously towards the already open door. Hearing no sound from within he stepped over the threshold, hesitating when he detected a familiar odour and discovered a body lying on the floor just inside. Further into the building he saw another, that of a medical orderly who had served at the front, and on the operating table lay the corpse of the Colonel with bullet wounds to his head. Uttering a hiss of dismay he went out to signal the men; how many more lives must be lost – where would it end?

"They have been dead for twenty four hours, at least," Maurici speculated when Tom joined him, a stretcher in his arms. And after a moment's thought he decided, "We will take the bodies back to Barcelona for burial – their families, you know."

"Right, Doc, whatever you say..." Tom began when the driver rushed in, his colour drained.

"The enemy!" he cried, falling to his knees. "We're surrounded!"

"Ger up, daft sod!" Tom jeered, but Maurici silenced him and nodded to the open window where a soldier wearing a khaki side cap was sliding the barrel of his rifle over the sill.

"Christ!" gasped Tom. "We've had it now."

"But we are medics!" the driver wailed. "Tell him why we are here…"

"I intend to," Maurici growled, crossing to the door to find his exit barred as a second soldier stepped into view. Then he spotted a corporal advancing towards the building with another armed soldier in his wake and feared what their objective may be. At first, the corporal seemed a reasonable man, though he quickly dismissed Maurici's request to place the corpses in the ambulance for return to Barcelona. In a high pitched Castilion voice he declared he was holding them prisoner, they would remain in the building under guard.

"But we are a medical team sent here to help," Maurici protested in the man's own language. "We are not here to fight."

"Then we will make use of your services as we advance – particularly yours," he emphasized, his eyes on Maurici. "Our forces are advancing at speed so we will soon reach Barcelona. Now, let me see your papers."

"This man is English," Maurici pointed out, nodding in Tom's direction as he offered proof of his own identity. "You cannot hold an Englishman here."

Casting a dismissive glance in Tom's direction the corporal shrugged. "Already we have taken many English prisoner."

Tom's sun-bleached brows drew together. "Did I hear right, Doc, us three is prisoners?"

Maurici nodded, and urging the whimpering driver to calm himself he related his conversation with the corporal.

"Bloody 'ell!" Tom exploded. "Who wants to stay in this dump with three fuckin' stiffs for company?"

"I intend to ask for them to be moved," Maurici responded tersely, returning his attention to the corporal who finally agreed to the bodies being taken outside.

Tom made a gesture to indicate his stretcher was broken so the corporal called in his own men and instructed them to take their own. As the corpses were being removed, stirring up a stench in the already fetid room, Tom sidled past Maurici to whisper, "Gun's in ours."

Once the removal of the bodies was completed the corporal directed Maurici and his men to the far end of the building, leaving two armed soldiers on guard near the door. Avoiding the dark stain where one of the corpses had lain, the guards seated themselves against the wall, their guns pointing in the direction of their prisoners.

"At least we're alive, unlike those poor devils out there," said Maurici as they squatted on the floor, "so let us hope they don't consider our capture of great importance."

"I'm not waitin' to find out," Tom told him in a hushed voice. "When I get a chance, I'm bloody well off!"

"Then we must have a plan," he agreed. "My position is less precarious, they need me, but you two must escape."

"Silence!" a voice demanded from the other end of the room. "No talking allowed!"

"I must assess my stock of medical equipment with my men, and I require pen and paper," Maurici told him. "You heard the corporal, he expects me to assist with your injured."

The soldier uttered a hiss of annoyance and rose to his feet, going to rummage in a cupboard until he found what he wanted. "Here," he said grudgingly, tossing a wad of unused medical forms at Maurici's feet, and from his breast pocket he brought out a stump of pencil and warned, "but don't write in Catalan, it is not allowed."

"No, no, I won't," Maurici conceded, and taking the sheaf of forms he wrote in English, 'After dark I cause diversion. Be ready, take gun', and saw Tom glance to the low rafters above. He then wrote, 'Letter to Elizabeth, Woodington Hall, Yorkshire?' Again Tom indicated he understood; Woodington was not too great a distance from York.

Thankful he had divulged Elizabeth's name and home address once before, when he and Tom had taken a little too much wine, Maurici began to write on a second sheet. Should he be released in time, nothing was lost, otherwise this letter of explanation would await her in England.

For a moment he was thoughtful; if these troops had reached this far over the river *Ebre*, there could be others stretched along the bank making a rapid advance. The thought depressed him. Adjusting his grip on the stub of pencil to compensate for his part missing finger, he began, 'My darling', following it with a declaration of his love, vowing they would meet again. Reflecting upon his father's advice he included a brief proposal of marriage, promising the gunfire would be replaced by a celebration of fireworks upon receipt of a favourable reply.

Aware that Tom may read his letter, he dismissed any embarrassment he felt over the contents. He had to face it; he may not see his beloved Elizabeth for some time. Suddenly aware of approaching footsteps, and a certain unease in Tom's manner, he flung down the pad of paper and rose to his feet. Tearing the sheet with the escape plan into shreds he complained to the soldier coming towards him, "I cannot work in these conditions, it is impossible to see. I shall ask the corporal for better light."

"No need," the soldier said, convinced any work for his corporal warranted some consideration. "Sit by the window."

Returning to pick up the bulk of forms, Maurici saw the next sheet had gone and spotted Tom's flicker of assurance.

Waiting for daylight to fade, Maurici's thoughts drifted back to Elizabeth and the previous afternoon, experiencing a tingle of pleasure as he reflected upon the passion they had shared in his bedroom. Today he'd set out on an errand of mercy which he hoped she would accept as a duty he couldn't refuse. The journey to Barcelona would be swift, the corporal predicted, but this also meant the advancing Nationalists would alert James to hasten his family to the safety of England.

It was turned six o'clock before Maurici considered it dark enough to make his move. At the far end of the low building the soldiers chatted softly by the light of the only lamp. Resting their heads on the rolled up stretcher, Tom and the driver appeared to doze when, with an exaggerated sigh of frustration, Maurici signalled to the guards.

"I can no longer see," he complained, "I need a lamp."

One guard shrugged and shook his head.

"As you don't need that light, I could use it," he said authoritatively, though with a measure of politeness. "And I have a tremendous thirst. Please, have you water?"

With a reluctant grunt, one guard rose to go outside whilst the other made a lazy indication with his rifle for Maurici to take the lamp.

Nodding, Maurici moved towards him and reached up to take the flickering lamp from its bracket on the wall, then cried out in alarm as he let it drop to the floor. There was an immediate yell from the guard as flames burst forth, speeding after the spilled fuel which spread quickly over the stone floor. Hearing the commotion, the other guard rushed in, throwing the contents of the water can he carried at the fire. Grabbing a blanket they had brought from the ambulance, Maurici flung it over the escaping flames, plunging the place into darkness.

"Idiot!" screeched one of the guards as he grappled with Maurici, pinning him down.

There was a sound of movement, then a crash. "The prisoners!" exclaimed the other, his rifle at the ready as he fumbled his way along the building until his eyes adjusted to the dimness. "*Madre de Dios*, they are gone!" he cried, his attention caught by the clatter of roof tiles when he raised his gun to send a burst of fire into the rafters.

"This is your doing," snarled the guard, tightening his grip on Maurici as the other ran outside.

"But, the fire, I had to do something..."

"Idiot, you did it on purpose!" the man screamed, sinking his fist into Maurici's ribs.

From somewhere not too distant came the sound of shots and Maurici's heart sank. Gasping from the blow, he cried, "No! No killing! I am responsible..."

The guard uttered a harsh sound and sprang to his feet. Retrieving his rifle he swung the butt, striking Maurici a vicious blow to his head.

* *

"Don't forget, darling, once you reach Paris take a taxi to your hotel," James reminded his wife as they waited on the station platform in Barcelona. "I've included sufficient money to cover both the hotel and any shopping you may need."

She patted the leather handbag she was carrying. "Quite safe, but promise me you'll join us if at all possible."

James nodded then, as the great train beside the platform came to life with a burst of steam, he made a brave attempt to smile. "Look after Mummy for me," he whispered, hugging Elizabeth close. But she was too full to speak and merely nodded as he released her. Then he took Molly in his arms, admiring her composure as she fought back her tears.

"I'll soon be with you, darling, you'll see," he said in a choked voice, turning quickly away to instruct the porter to place the luggage in a first class compartment.

Enric was openly tearful as he bid them farewell and James hung on to Molly's hand for as long as he could, walking beside the train as it slowly puffed away.

"My God, it hurts!" said James as he and Enric watched the train go out of sight.

"Here, my friend, let us drink to democracy, it will help," Enric offered, withdrawing a small flask from his pocket as he patted his colleagues' shoulder.

* *

It was a day and a half later when Molly and Elizabeth finally reached their hotel in Paris. They had experienced delays at almost every coastal station where hordes of refugees and soldiers climbed aboard, fleeing to the safety of the French border. Molly found their plight disturbing and gladly shared the supply of food she carried with the fretful, hungry children.

Too miserable to contemplate food, Elizabeth had declined to eat throughout the long journey and spent her time gazing through the window or nursing a sleeping child as she struggled with her thoughts. How could Maurici desert her after they had shared such moments of ecstasy in his room, she asked herself, tears welling in her eyes. Did he not find satisfaction in their love-making, or was it as she'd once heard, rather vulgarly expressed, 'Once a man's had his way, you won't see him again'? Now Maurici had experience of her body, had his interest waned? Over and over she had tussled with these thoughts as the train rumbled along, and now, finally settled in a Paris hotel, they continued to invade her mind.

James telephoned the hotel that evening. "Thank God!" he said. "When I rang last night and you weren't there I was desperately worried."

Molly explained, and warned him of the difficulties he also may meet with on his journey back. "Do be careful, darling, I'm missing you already," Elizabeth heard her say as with growing impatience she awaited her turn to speak.

But James couldn't give her the news she had hoped for. "No, darling," he said gently, "I've not seen him yet, but try not to worry, I'm sure he'll turn up very soon."

During their stay in Paris, even though James telephoned each evening, there was no news of Maurici, and Elizabeth's heart ached as the cloak of misery descended upon her once more.

It was during breakfast in their room on the morning they were due to leave when Molly decided to have a frank word. "Elizabeth, we have a long journey ahead of us so I want to see you eat something more substantial."

"I'm not hungry," she declined, sipping disconsolately at her coffee.

"You don't realise how fortunate you are. Those poor souls on the train would have given the earth for a breakfast such as this," Molly reproved, gesturing to the warm croissants and steaming hot coffee on the tray. "You'll make yourself ill if you continue."

"You just don't care how I feel!" Elizabeth retaliated morosely, pushing the croissant to the side of her plate. "Any way, I didn't want to leave."

"Of course I care. How do you imagine I feel, leaving without your father?"

Elizabeth let out a shuddering sigh. "At least you know he'll be with us eventually, whereas I don't know anything."

Molly felt a twinge of guilt. "I know, darling, but quite frankly, this will be a real test of your feelings for each other. If Maurici wishes to continue having your friendship he'll find a way to contact you, and it gives you an opportunity to discover your true feelings for him."

"But I know how I feel..." Elizabeth began dismally, hesitating when she saw her mother's raised hand.

"No, no, let me finish, darling. Right now you may think you know, but in time you could change your view. However, should you both feel the same in a month or two, I shall be extremely happy for you."

"But we live so far apart," Elizabeth protested, though her mood had brightened a little.

"Your father was in Ireland for months after we first met in London," Molly pointed out, but our love survived."

"I suppose so," Elizabeth granted. "Perhaps Maurici may like to visit us one day."

"He'd be most welcome," Molly assured her.

"It would be simply wonderful if he came to Woodington," Elizabeth said dreamily. "I know Grandpa would like him."

"I'm sure he would, darling, and when you've finished breakfast I shall make a call to England. I know he'll be thrilled when I tell him we are on our way home?"

* *

Towards the end of the third week after making his escape, Tom Garbutt hobbled painfully along on a sprained ankle. It had been one of those careless accidents occurring when he'd been chasing a horse with the hope of using it for transport. He'd since realised, had he caught it he would never have managed to climb onto its back. And now, after clinging on to the back of a lorry which had carried him a fair distance, as he bathed the badly swollen joint in an icy stream at the foot of the Pyrenees, he reflected upon the way he had sustained the injury and cursed his own stupidity. It amazed him still just thinking of how he had jumped to the ground from the roof of the building where he'd been held prisoner, and run through the darkness without suffering any ill-effects, until now...

When Maurici first had indicated his route of escape he'd considered it impossible to achieve yet, when the time came, he'd found enough strength to follow it through. He owed his freedom to the distraction Maurici had caused. When flames from the upturned lamp had caught the guard's attention he had slung the rifle over his shoulder and jumped for the tie beam of the low building with more spring in his legs than he realised he possessed. Balancing on the beam, he'd paused to give the driver a hand up before making a grab for the rafters to haul himself through the hole in the roof.

Tom sighed as he studied the bruising on the outside of his leg, blue-black, almost to his knee. "You daft bugger!" he reproached himself aloud, repressing the desire to cry out as he tried to rotate the swollen joint. He thought of the driver whom he assumed to have been shot by the guard, compared it with his own good fortune; he had managed to get this far without running into trouble, so what did a sprained ankle matter?

Tearing strips from the lining of the khaki army jacket he'd found on his first day of freedom, he bound the aching joint as best he could, fishing in his trouser pocket for the safety pin he carried to hold it in place. Then, aware of hunger pangs and hoping he didn't have to travel too great a distance before he spotted his prey, he felt for the rifle lying by his side. But as he got to his feet with the help of the rifle, he noticed Maurici's folded letter on the grass, realising it had fallen from his pocket when he withdrew the pin. The brief address was on the outside and so far he'd resisted reading its contents, but a sudden desire to do so overcame him now.

Smiling to himself, he unfolded the sheet of paper to read Maurici's hurried note. He found the words quite touching and wished he could express himself so well. There was a proposal of marriage that he hoped Miss Elizabeth would be delighted to receive. But before he could return the letter to his pocket he was spun off his feet by a bullet and fell to the ground, the rifle still in his hand. The letter fluttered from his limp fingers to tumble along in the breeze, coming to rest on the bubbling waters of the ice-cold stream.

Chapter 14

William had felt no joy as he'd celebrated the coming of nineteen thirty-nine. The seasonal fare had been far too rich for his delicate constitution and during the past few weeks he had suffered a great deal. Since his virulent display on Christmas night, Jane had avoided him and he assumed she'd worn her old outfit when she rode to hunt the following day. His few pleasures over the festive season had been Molly's telephone call and, when weather permitted, driving his new Humber car. Jane preferred Nicholson to drive and would raise her hand in a most regal manner as they rode through the village. But William liked to have the wheel in his hands, feel the surge of power when he depressed the accelerator.

Molly had spoken of coming home if the Nationalists advanced further into Catalonia, and he'd seen from the newspaper report they were closing in from the south west. Should the advance gather speed he advised her not to hesitate, but wondered about the welcome James would receive at Woodington Hall.

With a deep sigh he closed the heavy curtains, shutting out the dismal scene as the house-maid brought in his tray. He saw it contained only one setting and assumed Jane was having tea with the Grants, a regular habit now he was in disgrace.

Elsie bobbed a curtsey and offered brightly, "Will there be owt else, sir?"

"Thank you. I'll not require anything more," he said, chuckling to himself over her strong Yorkshire accent, although he knew it irritated Jane. A servant's life was hard, he mused, as he uncovered the freshly baked scones and proceeded to spread one with local farm butter. Yet there were times when he considered Pincott quite fortunate as less demands were made upon his time than that of the women staff. Only the housekeeper, Mrs Dowkes, dared to contradict the demands he made upon them. Certainly, Pincott was more fortunate than himself; most likely listening to his wireless, he supposed enviously, whereas his own was awaiting repair.

Stretching out his long legs, he drained his second cup of tea. He'd had a reasonably comfortable afternoon when his stomach had been free of pain. Alex's prescription was working, the cost of his visits worth every penny.

"Where the devil is Pincott?" William muttered as he re-read an item of interest from the previous day's newspaper. It was the report on the Duchess of Atholl's address at a meeting in York which he had attended, donating two crisp, white five pound notes to the appeal for money to send food supplies to Spain. He'd applauded the Duchess' humanitarian beliefs, but found the account by a member of parliament of the dreadful sights he had witnessed on his recent visit to Barcelona quite unsettling. With a deep sigh he returned the paper to the rack, realising his reflections were stirring a twinge of pain. The report that

General Franco's army was fast advancing on Barcelona had increased his concern and he impatiently awaited further news.

It was some time later when the butler brought in the evening paper and by then William had got himself into a state of extreme agitation.

"Your tray, sir, I notice it hasn't been removed," the butler observed, "I'll speak to Elsie."

William's head came up. "You will do no such thing!" he interjected harshly. "Take the dashed thing yourself."

"As you wish, sir," Pincott conceded with a theatrical sigh and carried it from the room. Feeling a tiny glow of satisfaction, William turned his attention to the newspaper. Going first to foreign news, his blood ran cold when he saw the headline, 'Insurgents enter Barcelona' in heavy black print. The city had fallen to General Franco and was proclaimed to be the biggest prize of the Spanish Civil war. It appeared, the invading troops had been assembling at the city's gates for the last forty-eight hours and met with no resistance when they marched in. Barcelona, the greatest industrial centre of Spain had been taken by the Navarrese Division, a particularly heavy blow to the Republicans who had made feverish efforts towards a last, desperate stand.

He could read no more, the pain in his insides was now intense. He mixed himself a large port and brandy which in the past had proved a quick solution to his ailment, but twenty minutes later he was still writhing in agony, bent double on the Victorian settee. It is believed, General Franco was of the opinion the end of the war was in sight he'd read; for William the end couldn't come soon enough.

* *

From his position at the rear of the crowd lining the wide *Paseo de Gracia,* Enric watched the last of the Nationalist forces march past. He'd been on the streets since early morning but had kept well behind the lines of cheering supporters who raised their arms in a fascist salute. Cries of *'Viva Espana!'*, *'Franco, Franco, Franco!'* and *'Arriba Espana!'* still rang in his ears, and a vivid picture of the flags and banners bearing images of General Franco and the arrows of the Falange stayed in his mind. Men in an assortment of uniforms, khaki and blue, peaked hats, helmets and tasselled side caps, denoting their rank, had passed by. Booted feet clattered rhythmically over the stone setts, together with the rumble of tanks reverberating between the high buildings on either side. He felt desperately lonely, knowing he must return to his empty home with only memories of the family with whom he'd shared so many happy months. James had pleaded with him to leave, but now the crisis was upon them he'd been determined to remain, yet thankful his colleague had moved on before the enemy arrived.

Once he had learned the Francoites had entered Reus, and the *Generalitat* had held its last meeting in Barcelona, he'd urged James to leave with a friend who was travelling to the industrial town of Granollers, twenty-six kilometres north. Refugees had been streaming into Barcelona, pausing only briefly before starting the long trudge to the frontier along with deserters who had attached themselves to the line. Some wealthy Republicans were leaving their homes at frenzied speed, fearing what their fate may be; Franco demanded unconditional surrender.

* *

"Thank goodness!" Molly breathed, settling into her seat opposite Elizabeth as the train gathered steam towards London. "So many delays, it will be a relief to be home."

Elizabeth's eyes widened. "I would have thought you'd be dreadfully anxious after what Grandpa said about Barcelona when you telephoned."

"Of course I'm anxious, darling, but your father promised me he'd leave before the Nationalists marched in."

"I wonder if he's seen Maurici," she murmured dejectedly, gazing through the rain-spotted window.

"If he hasn't, then I'm sure Enric will," Molly responded, "but don't raise your hopes."

Elizabeth's face fell. "Grandpa didn't mention anything?"

Molly shook her head. "He was so excited he could hardly speak. I suggested we took the train to Woodington but he wouldn't hear of it."

"I expect he was disappointed to know Daddy isn't with us, though I'm sure Grandmother would be delighted."

"Elizabeth, please! I want our homecoming to be a happy occasion for everyone."

* *

Shortly after William had read the alarming newspaper report he was called to the telephone. He'd been choked with emotion on hearing Molly's voice, his only response being to insist upon driving to York to meet the train, and he resolved not to allow his ailment to cloud her homecoming.

Once he had calmed a little, he telephoned Jane at Grant's with the good news. "You could have told me later," was her unemotional response. Deflated he had gone to bed, hoping to recover by morning ready to make the journey to York.

But William experienced a terrible night, racked with pain and vomiting throughout the early hours until he felt utterly exhausted. Wearied by lack of sleep, he knew he hadn't the energy to drive to York and decided to ask Jane to call in Alex Wilson. He waited in agony until daylight came, but when Pincott came to his room to enquire about breakfast, he learned she already had gone out riding.

His disappointment was intense; he struggled against an overwhelming threat of tears as he directed Pincott to bring in the chauffeur who was delighted by the prospect of taking out the Humber.

Determined to gather his strength for when Molly and Elizabeth arrived, he decided a little fresh air might aid his recovery. After struggling to dress in his heavy tweed suit, he went slowly down the stairs, pausing to slip on his galoshes and overcoat on the way out. There was a chill wind blowing across the damp lawns as he made his way over to the gate in the boundary wall, lingering beneath the layered beech to scan the vast acres of farmland beyond. He took a few deep breaths of the sharp morning air when, quite suddenly, the trees seemed to whirl around him, as though he was in the centre of some crazy carousel. He thought he saw figures behind the spiralling uprights of the iron gate and taking quick gasping breaths he stumbled towards it. But he couldn't summon enough energy and let out a wavering cry as he sank to the ground.

"Hey up!" Chapman yelled, and calling his daughter he ran towards the gate. "Give us a hand, Gladys, t'master looks real badly!"

"You can't go in, Dad!" she cried as he pushed open the squealing iron gate. "She told me I 'adn't to set foot in there ever again."

"Bugger it all, lass, we can't leave 'im here!" Chapman rasped. "Ger 'old of his feet, we'll carry 'im inside."

"Such a gentleman 'e were." she remarked as they carried William's limp form to the house.

"He isn't a gonner yet, lass," Chapman reminded her as he braced his shoulder against the solid front door. "Any road, best fetch Doctor Wilson," he said, edging William onto the old wooden settle in the hall.

By now William was beginning to come round, moaning softly as he struggled to lift his head when fresh waves of nausea surged to his throat.

"Better not move 'till doctor gets here," Chapman advised. "He'll soon have yer right."

"Yes, get Alex," William gasped, his complexion deathly pale as he fought against the urge to retch.

Sensing he was being observed, Chapman looked up to see the butler advancing silently into the hall, his expression aloof.

"Who gave you permission to enter?" Pincott hissed, and jerked his head towards the door. "Get out, immediately!"

"Our Gladys has gone for Doctor Wilson..." Chapman began, but Pincott cut him short.

"I shall attend to the master," he said coldly. "You are not required here."

Chapman met Alex Wilson entering the grounds, pausing only to explain how he had found the master in a state of collapse. With a brief nod Alex rushed into the hall and saw the butler's icy regard for William's helpless form.

"Pincott, bring blankets, a pillow," he directed sharply, noting his patient's look of relief. To William he said gently, "Now, sir, what have we been doing this morning, hey?"

"Thank God you're here!" William exclaimed weakly, tears beginning to gather in his eyes. "I – I passed out in the garden – cold weather, you know."

"Quite probably," Alex agreed, "it's a chilly day."

William struggled to rise. "Molly is due home today, perhaps I allowed myself to get over excited," he said with a hint of a smile, but omitted to mention the black, tarry mass he had passed during his visit to the bathroom early that morning for fear of being confined to bed. It had occurred before, the previous night, but it wasn't something he cared to mention.

"Perhaps so," agreed Alex, though to him it was becoming very obvious excitement was not the root cause of his patient's trouble. He went briefly through all the usual preliminary checks to find William's pulse and respiration nowhere near their expected rate, and when he queried his bodily functions his patient denied anything was amiss. But his weak and pale condition and the fact he had passed out confirmed Alex's suspicions; William was bleeding from the stomach, his condition was grave.

When Pincott came with blankets, the doctor instructed he call the chauffeur so that William may be taken to his room.

"But, Doctor, Nicholson has already left for York," Pincott whined, "I can't manage the master alone."

"Then find someone else," Alex directed with an edge of irritation as he tucked a blanket round William's shivering form. "I expect Mrs Cussons has gone to meet the train."

"Madam went riding early this morning," Pincott supplied ingratiatingly. "She's not expected back until lunchtime."

"Riding!" Alex ejaculated then, suppressing his feelings, urged, "Off you go, Pincott. Get the groom to lend a hand, and ask someone to light a fire in the bedroom, will you?"

Returning his attention to his patient, Alex said, "You'll feel more comfortable once we get you to bed, then I'd like your permission to seek another opinion. I know an excellent fellow in York who specializes in your condition."

"But dash it all, Alex, I don't want to be confined to bed now the family are due," William objected, his voice strained as he winced from discomfort.

"Ah, but think of the good times you'll have together when your health improves," Alex pointed out with caring optimism.

Without protest, William allowed Pincott and the groom to carry him upstairs. Elsie had just finished lighting a fire that sent a bright flickering glow around the chilly panelled room.

William had to admit to feeling a little better in bed but Alex again broached the subject of calling in a specialist, and when William finally agreed he went immediately to the telephone. He also requested Mrs Cussons be found and brought to her husband's bedside, though doubted her presence would be of benefit. Aware of the strain his patient was under, Alex had to admire his strength of character, his desire to get well but, during the next hour, as William's condition worsened, he prayed Molly and Elizabeth would arrive in time.

* *

Shivering on the slatted bunk in his cell, Maurici thoughts were with Elizabeth, hoping she and her parents were safely back in England. His journey to Barcelona had been swift, as the corporal predicted, and his medical skills had been put to use tending Nationalist troops who had been injured as they advanced. Not that he had objected to ministering to them, as a medical man he must remain impartial, but now, to find himself in a cold and stinking prison block awaiting trial filled him with fierce indignation. He had been brought here the previous day, behind troops intent upon conquering the city, and heard cheering civilians raising the fascist salute, sickening him to the core. He'd travelled with prisoners under guard in the rear of a lorry when the only signs of resistance he'd seen were a few stone blockades constructed in a useless attempt at defence.

He looked across at his cellmate, an elderly drunkard, happily oblivious to the conditions in which he lay, brought in because he insisted on singing Catalan songs. Maurici wondered what would be the man's choice of language when he returned to a more sober state? He thought of Tom Garbutt, envying his freedom, trying to calculate the distance he would have travelled during the twenty-seven days since his escape. Smiling to himself, he imagined Elizabeth's expression when she received the letter containing his proposal of marriage, then fell into a light doze, continually waking to each loud snore from his cellmate.

* *

"Nice to see you, Nicholson," said Molly. "Is Daddy waiting in the car?"

"I'm afraid the master is not well this morning, madam," he replied as the porter came up with his trolley.

"Nothing serious, is it?"

"I really can't say, madam," he said, directing the porter to the car. "Doctor Wilson is with him now."

Molly frowned. She had spoken with her father the previous day and had the feeling all was not well. Her thoughts went to James, missing his support, until Elizabeth's burst of excitement brought her back.

"Look at Grandpa's new car!" she exclaimed as she trailed her hand over its gleaming, black bodywork.

"Yes, it's very handsome," said Molly, stepping on the running board of the big Humber to be met by the smell of new leather upholstery.

Once she and Elizabeth were seated with a tartan rug over their knees, Nicholson pulled smoothly away from the station, through the damp city streets onto the familiar country road. In poor visibility they drove past the bare hedgerows. Signs of a recent snowfall shrouded the slopes in a pale cloak, making the sunnier climes of Spain seem so very far away.

Molly shivered and slipped her hands into the wide cuffs of the woollen coat she'd bought in Paris; her thoughts dwelling on James until they turned off the main road at the signpost to Woodington when she transferred them to her father. Perhaps he was not so ill as she imagined, she tried to console herself as they covered the last mile of quiet road.

"A whole year away but everything looks just the same," Elizabeth remarked as they drew towards the entrance to Woodington Hall.

Molly nodded. "I see Doctor Wilson still drives the Morris," she commented as they came to a halt behind the small car on the pebbled drive.

Spotting Jane on the steps by the front door Elizabeth cried, "There's Grandmother! She's dressed for riding so Grandpa can't be ill after all."

But there was barely a smile on Jane's face as she embraced them and they realised immediately something was seriously wrong.

"Haven't been back too long myself," Jane explained when Molly queried her attire. "Obviously, had I known..."

"So it came on suddenly," Molly supposed as they entered the house, "since breakfast, I mean."

"I didn't see your father this morning. He was in bed when I left," Jane explained as Pincott came into the hall.

"Madam, Miss Elizabeth," he murmured expressionlessly, and to Jane, asked, "Do you wish me to delay lunch, madam?"

"I'm going up to see Daddy," said Molly, making for the stairs with Elizabeth following close behind.

In the doorway of his room she paused when Alex rose and beckoned her over to the bed. "I'm so pleased you're here," he said quietly. "Should you need me, I'll be downstairs."

Acknowledging Alex with a taut smile, Molly took her father's cold hands, stifling her initial shock when she saw how ill he appeared. He had aged considerably and it broke her heart to see tears welling in his eyes. Leaning over she kissed his cheek, fighting her own desire to weep as she said, "Here at last, Daddy... wonderful to be back with you again."

Closing his eyes against the onrush of emotion he responded feebly, "Too late, I fear..."

"Now, now, darling, you're going to get well again," she reproached gently. "I shall devote my time to nursing you."

Elizabeth stood by wordlessly, her lower lip beginning to quiver as Molly continued, "We love the new Humber, Daddy, such a comfortable ride, much warmer than the old car. And you'll be pleased to know Nicholson drove perfectly, had us here sooner than we expected."

At this, William appeared to brighten, and when Molly voiced a desire to get behind the wheel herself he smiled.

"And I'd like to learn to drive, Grandpa," Elizabeth put in once she'd regained control.

"Too big for you to handle," William responded with a weak grin.

For a few minutes more Molly lingered by his bed making light conversation, but she wanted a word with Alex Wilson to discover just what he had diagnosed.

With a smile of assurance for Elizabeth, she left to go downstairs, dismayed to hear her mother's indignant voice coming from the hall. "How was I to know he would be taken ill this morning!"

"But your husband can't have felt well for days," came Alex's cool reply.

"You saw him yourself last week!" Jane retorted and Molly hung back, unwilling to intrude in their heated exchange.

"True, but I asked to be informed should he not improve," he reminded her shortly. "Did he not complain of pain?"

"I think you'd better leave," Jane bridled. "Obviously, you're not competent even to administer to a simple case of indigestion. I'll call in someone else."

"Madam, I've already explained," he returned in a barely controlled voice, "this is not merely a case of indigestion as no doubt my colleague will confirm."

"Please, Mother, don't do anything hasty," Molly broke in as she started down the stairs.

"After all, Alex has dealt with father's case for some time, whereas another doctor would have scant knowledge of his condition. And before we say anything more I suggest we wait until the specialist gets here. Could you spare me a moment, Alex?"

Hurriedly excusing himself, he followed Molly up the stairs.

"I gather my mother is being difficult," said Molly, closing the sitting room door.

"Obviously, she's upset over your father's condition," he said carefully.

"No need to be diplomatic, I couldn't help but overhear," sighed Molly. "My poor father looks so ill I can't believe he will recover."

"I'm afraid you're right, the prognosis is grave. You wanted the truth?" he added quickly, seeing the increased anguish on her face.

"Yes, of course. Naturally, I'm upset, but I must know."

He drew a deep breath and continued gently, "I believe your father has a large haemorrhage in the duodenum – you know what that means? That's only my diagnosis, of course."

"I know, but for how long has he suffered like this?"

"I suspect it started yesterday or the day before. I noticed his clothing was stained. We've tried ice, I've given him morphia..." He raised his hands despairingly. "It's my opinion he needs an operation but his condition is too weak to withstand such a trauma. I've called in the best man I know but from our telephone conversation he fears it's too late. However, he still insists on coming over from York." He rose to his feet. "I expect him at any moment."

"We can only hope," she said on a sad sigh. "Thank you for being frank with me, Alex."

"I've tried to explain this to your mother. It's not merely indigestion. Even in a healthier man an operation is not without risk and serious after effects."

"Incidentally, when were you called? I assumed you'd been here quite some time."

Alex compressed his lips. "It was Gladys Chapman who came to fetch me," he said after a moment, "around half past ten. Her father saw Mister Cussons collapse in the garden so they brought him into the house."

"Ah yes, of course, Gladys would be here, but why didn't Mother use the telephone, it would have been much quicker?"

He hesitated, then said, "Gladys is no longer employed here, and I understand your mother was out riding at the time."

"Out riding!"

"My words exactly!" he bit out, turning away. "No, I shouldn't have said that, she wasn't to know. We got a message to her at Grant's place."

"At what time was this?"

"Pincott telephoned sometime before eleven."

Molly gasped. "But she'd just arrived shortly before we got here."

"Please... no point in allowing it to upset you."

"No, you're right," she agreed on a long sigh. "I'll go and sit with Daddy until the specialist arrives."

But William was barely conscious when Molly returned to his room, his long, bloodless fingers curled loosely round Elizabeth's hand.

"He's very poorly isn't he?" Elizabeth whispered through quivering lips.

Molly put a finger to her own. "A specialist from York is due any moment," she said with a brave smile, "so we'll have to leave him for a while."

Pulling aside the lace curtains, she saw a large black car draw to a halt at the front of the house and Alex going out to meet it.

* *

When the Nationalist troops marched into Barcelona, James had been waiting at the railway station in Granollers to take a train to Gerona. He'd sent his last dispatch from the press room in Barcelona two nights before when news reached him the insurgents were closing towards the river Llobregat. Unable to persuade Enric to leave with him, they'd spent that last night in the city, a sad occasion when he'd begged his colleague not to air his political views, concerned he may suffer under Nationalist control.

The following day, James roamed the streets of Gerona, a city teeming with troops and civilians, all heading north amongst much confusion. He saw young soldiers gathering outside the cathedral, men who had lost contact with their units, and a curious collection of vehicles, some horse-drawn, laden with families and their precious belongings. He was having difficulty making contact with his press office, also Woodington Hall, but he expected these problems could be surmounted once he had crossed the border into France. At least he could gather news as he travelled, an actual account of the plight of refugees on the move. Yet, as he mingled with them, it seemed as though they were only beginning to realise the war was lost, and those willing to make comment blamed France and Britain for failing the Republic in their battle against Fascism.

From Girona, travelling in an already crowded car, James moved towards France. The towns and villages they passed through were crammed to overflowing with people of all ages; at night the pavements and doorways were the only shelter for these shivering beings. He found the pitiful cries of children more than he could bear and bought chocolate on the black market to distribute amongst them. But he could do nothing about the cold they suffered and his heart ached to see their swollen fingers burning from the frost. In the drenching rain and icy snow of Besalu news reached him that the rump of the *Cortes* was holding its last meeting in Figueras, also of reprisals further south. Executions were being carried out in Barcelona, making him anxious for Enric and young Maurici, but he had to move on.

Nearing the town of Camprodon, close to the French border, he found the roads thickly crowded with carts and vans, hunger-stricken people carried suitcases, or sacks tied with string, some protecting themselves from the early February chill with blankets draped over their shoulders. Others less fortunate derived a little warmth by moving close within the crowds. He was appalled to see such hordes of refugees – wondering what their future may be – yet admired their dignity as they moved on, carrying children and overweight baskets, clutching their few possessions. He smiled as he noticed a child, contentedly hugging a toy horse, oblivious to any discomfort. The boy would be around six years of age and followed closely behind his parents, the father laden with their bundles while the mother carried a younger child. The man was encouraging the boy to keep the circulation moving in his hands and the child responded happily. With the toy clutched in his chubby fingers he swung his arms back and forth across his body until, with a wail of dismay, the horse flew from his grasp to disappear over the edge of the roadside which fell steeply away. The child immediately rushed in pursuit of his toy when to everyone's horror he toppled out of sight. James dashed forward, past the panic-stricken parents, to see the child sprawled on a rocky ledge almost two meters below. Giving no thought to his own safety, he dropped to his knees, lowering himself down the damp rock face to where the child lay. Hearing the mother's shriek, many had crowded the roadside to see James speaking calmly to the boy. Once his toy had been retrieved, the child became surprisingly alert, the only sign of injury a small abrasion on his forehead which he indicated James should kiss better by pursing his tiny mouth.

To James' relief someone let down a rope which he secured around the boy before signalling for the men to haul him safely back onto the road. But James was seized by sudden horror when he felt the rocky shelf give way beneath him, plunging him further down the steep cliff-side.

Chapter 15

A canopy of black umbrellas had surrounded the grave as William was laid to rest and it had continued to pour with rain for most of the week following the sombre occasion. Molly could picture it still; from the moment she had gazed upon her father's peaceful, marble-like features before his coffin was closed, to the slow journey behind the hearse up the hill to Woodington church. Behind her veil she had held back her tears, but once it was over and everyone had left the Hall she had wept. She was missing James at a time when she most needed him and was becoming increasingly anxious over the lack of word from him since she and Elizabeth had left Paris.

Elizabeth had been heartbroken over her grandfather's death which had occurred so soon after their arrival. And, following a news bulletin, she also was anxious for her father as well as being distressed over Maurici.

The Nationalists were heading north towards the French border, fleeing refugees had been killed in the bombing of Granollers and Gerona. Molly prayed her husband was now safely into France, away from the risk of persecution for sending reports to a left-wing newspaper.

They had heard of the open-air service in Barcelona, a Nationalist thanksgiving for the capture of the city. "How very Christian," Molly had scoffed, "particularly now the French frontier's virtually sealed."

"You're so like your father," Jane had remarked when Molly listened for the latest report.

Elizabeth had risen to her mother's defence, an expression almost akin to hatred on her grief-stricken face. "You don't know what it's like, Grandmother," she'd accused as they strained their ears to catch a few words before the battery faded. "Thomas used to change the accumulator weekly."

"The only thing to his credit that I can recall..." Jane began, sending Elizabeth dashing from the room.

Molly's eyes narrowed. "Ah yes, speaking of staff, I've been meaning to ask, why did Gladys leave? I understand she called Alex after Daddy collapsed?"

Jane snorted. "No-one was asked to call in Wilson."

Molly was too astounded to contain her fury. "It's a damned good thing she did – you weren't even here!"

"How dare you speak to me this way? And Elizabeth, she was most rude when I objected to her chatter about that foreigner. Such rubbish!"

"It's not rubbish, Mother, she was very upset over not seeing him before we left. He's a very nice young man."

"Hardly a desirable friend for Elizabeth."

"You may think not, but once she receives word from him she'll be happy."

Elizabeth had left the house in tears, a forlorn figure dressed in black, caring little for the direction she took as she trudged along the river bank. Coming to the break in the wall dividing the grounds from the farmland without, she slowed. Here the river widened, its icy waters rippling over the stony bed, the banks not as steep as those behind the Hall, enabling her to slip between the iron rails protruding from the wall. The flood had subsided but the bank was sodden from a recent downpour and her fashionable shoes sank into the sludge almost to her ankles. She swore, tears forgotten as she scrambled up the other side where a few snowdrops had escaped the grounds to grow wild amongst the grass. She stooped to admire the flawless white petals hanging bell-like from slender stems; the first sign of Spring, Grandpa always predicted.

It was the sound of hooves thudding over the damp field that caught her attention and she shaded her eyes against the pale February sun to see a horse and rider heading in her direction. She frowned as they drew near, not recognising the man in the saddle until he brought his mount to a halt.

"Elizabeth!" he exclaimed, raising his tweed cap. "Good to see you."

"Hello, Miles," she responded dully. "How are you?"

Swinging his foot from the stirrup, Miles Grant dismounted heavily and came towards her. "Welcome back," he said, "though I wish it could have been in happier circumstances. I was at the funeral, of course..."

"Yes, I noticed you were present," she broke in, her eyes downcast.

"He had many friends – big funeral," Miles said. "I had intended to call but felt it wasn't quite the time."

Elizabeth looked up and nodded. "I'm sure Grandma will be pleased to see you," she said, meeting his pale, grey stare.

He pushed back a strand of his thinning, equally pale hair and gave her a lopsided smile. "My dear Elizabeth, it wasn't only your Grandmother I was eager to see. You have become a most attractive young lady, if I may say."

Elizabeth looked at him in surprise. "Oh, thank you, Miles."

"I say, the old shoes are in a bit of a mess!" he grinned. "Like me to give you a lift back?"

Reaching up to stroke the velvety muzzle of the chestnut hunter, she shook her head. "I can't make them any worse."

The hunter snorted and reared its huge head, the movement reminding her of the stallion she had helped in Barcelona almost a year before. An unexpected twinge of pain clutched her heart as she recalled it also had been the day she met Maurici.

"I must go," she said, turning quickly towards the river bank, "It's becoming quite chilly out here."

Miles took a step forward. "Mind if I call on you one day? That is, if you don't think it's too soon."

"I expect it will be all right," she called over her shoulder as she swung round the rails to retrace her steps.

"I'll look forward to that," he said, placing a booted foot on the lower rail to re-mount his horse.

* *

Maurici glanced across the narrow cell to where the old man lay, noting his breathing had quietened; the deep snorting noises had faded to the more restful sound of sleep. His cellmate had suffered another early morning epileptic seizure, so suddenly violent even Maurici hadn't anticipated his heavy fall. He wondered if this increase in seizures had been brought about by his captivity together with the claustrophobia which troubled him a lot. It certainly was a small cell, intended for the seclusion of a single prisoner, he supposed. And the chill from the stone walls where a horizontal slit of light came in just below the ceiling told him they were confined in part of the cellars where conditions were unlikely to improve. He glanced down in time to avoid a thin stream of urine trickling across the stone floor; the man was beginning to rouse, blinking a little, his expression vacant until Maurici spoke.

"*Hola*, old friend, back with me again, hey?" he said gently, and leaning over to examine his cellmate's face, told him, "You've got a nasty swelling over your eye, but the skin isn't broken, thank God."

As the old man raised himself to glance to the floor, Maurici shook his head. "Don't worry I'll get you a change of clothing. They'll bring it for me."

"Give them a good salute," the man advised as Maurici helped him to a sitting position against the wall. And the harsh lines on his face deepened when he demanded, "Your hands? *Senyor*, hold out your hands."

Wary at first, Maurici drew back then, with an expression of faint amusement, unfurled his fingers, turning his palms upwards. "What the hell for?"

The man smiled. "Good, they're smooth. Make sure you keep them that way."

Maurici frowned, fearing his cellmate's fit had affected his sanity. "Why in God's name should I do that?"

"Smooth hands belong to the bourgeoisie," the other said wisely. "You've not fought against the Nationalists, they will see that." He shook his head and looked up to the flaking ceiling. "Really, I should hate you for it, but you're young, you haven't suffered as I have."

Maurici laid his hand on the other's bony shoulder. "But that is not the reason my hands are uncalloused, though I'll admit I've never used a gun. I'm a student doctor, my role is to save life, not end it by use of force."

The man lowered his head. "And that is why they put you in here, to look after me, heh?"

Maurici smiled. "More preferable than being confined with a noisy group of prisoners."

"Even though I piss my trousers from time to time?"

"You can't help that, it's the fits."

The old man pulled a face. "My father used to beat me when my trousers were wet. Only my mother had sympathy."

"Many people are ignorant of your condition."

"Or they think I'm mad!"

Maurici chuckled. "Far from it! You're very shrewd, which is why I prefer to be here."

"But don't forget," the other warned, "give the fascist salute, otherwise your family could suffer reprisals."

"I appreciate your advice..." Maurici began, rising to his feet as keys rattled in the lock of the cell door.

The old man also was quick to rise, thrusting out his skinny arms and pushing Maurici violently away as he screamed abuse. "Religious pig! I shit on your mother!" he yelled, and to the guard entering the cell demanded, "Why must I share with this Capitalist pig? Get him out!" And again he launched himself at Maurici, sending him off balance.

"Shut your mouth, you old fool," the guard yelled, dragging the old man aside. "You'll be going the way of your Communist friends if you're not careful."

To Maurici he directed briskly, "Come, you are due in court ten minutes from now."

"And save your fascist salutes for the courtroom!" the old man screeched, "I don't want to see them in here!"

Shocked by his cellmate's behaviour, Maurici walked ahead of his escort along the narrow stone passage of the old prison building.

"So, you're not one of them," his escort commented, jerking his head back towards the cell as they ascended a flight of steps. "That's something in your favour – could save you from execution."

Maurici was silent; it had soon dawned on him why his cellmate acted as he did.

* *

It was the fourteenth of February when Molly received the distressing news of James' accident. Her hands shook as she re-read the telegram sent from his London office while Pincott hovered uncomfortably nearby.

The details were quite vague; James had been injured in a fall somewhere near the French border and was now being cared for in a hospital in France.

"Thank you, Pincott," she murmured numbly as the message penetrated her mind. An accident, a French hospital; she drew a quavering breath, she must go there right away.

Assuming her mother and Elizabeth were already dining, Molly took a grip on herself, entering the dark panelled room where the table was laid for lunch.

Jane glanced up, her expression disapproving. "I sent Pincott to fetch you ages ago. Cook has made rabbit pie and I do so hate it served cold..." Seeing the expression on Molly's pale face, and the telegram she held, Jane paused to ask, "Is something amiss?"

"It's James, he's met with an accident, he's in hospital, in France. I feared this may happen..." Elizabeth's anguished cry startled her, but she continued to read out the telegram, relating its contents through a blur of tears. "I must leave immediately. If you will check the train times, Elizabeth, I'll pack."

"Pack?" Jane repeated. "It can't be so bad, surely?"

"They wouldn't trouble to send a telegram if it wasn't!" cried Molly. "I shall go to James' bedside at once."

"I trust he appreciates your devotion," she heard Jane mutter but resisted the urge to retaliate.

When Elizabeth joined her with train times and connections, Molly already had a small suitcase packed. "I would rather you didn't come, darling," she said, noticing Elizabeth had selected a case for herself. "Better I see how Daddy is; he may well be recovered by now. I intend to check with his office immediately I reach London, they may have received a further report."

"But it could be serious, you said so yourself."

"Don't worry, I'll send for you if he's likely to be there for any length of time," Molly promised, and with a note of concern reminded her, "You weren't too well yourself earlier. In fact, you still look a little pale."

"I'm fine now, Mummy, really..."

"Even so, I prefer you to stay and keep an eye on Mother," Molly said firmly, "and if you're not completely well by tomorrow, have a word with Alex. Perhaps you need a tonic."

Elizabeth conceded with an unhappy sigh. "As it happens, Grandmother wants me to accompany her to Grant's for tea this afternoon – the third time this week!"

"I expect it keeps her mind off things," Molly suggested, checking the contents of her bag. "Ask Cook to make sandwiches, will you? Nicholson will be here shortly and I've a long journey ahead of me before I reach the boat."

Elizabeth was relieved to hear her mother's voice two days later, to know she'd arrived safely in France. The call had come through just as she was leaving the bathroom when, for the third morning in succession she'd felt dreadfully sick. She wondered if the afternoon tea at Grant's consisting of tiny sandwiches and very rich cake, had upset her. Miles had pressed her to take another slice, just as he had on the previous day, so she was convinced this was to blame. On each occasion Miles had been utterly charming, but however pleasant his manner towards her, her thoughts continued to dwell on Spain. There were moments when she felt so bewildered and tearful over the lack of word from Maurici, she had to remain in her room. Communication could be difficult, she would remind herself, but his failure to make contact before she left Sitges was something she had to take into account. The awful realisation he may have tired of her was beginning to creep in; he had wooed her with one objective – to possess her body – and she bitterly regretted submitting to both his, and her own desires.

* *

Back in his cell, Maurici uttered a weary sigh as he sank gratefully to the floor and leant against the wall. Outside the room where the court was being held he had been ordered to stand to attention until called. For almost three hours he had waited only to be told his case wouldn't be heard until the following day. In addition to being physically tiring, it was intensely frustrating and it took all his self control to contain the bad humour he felt. His armed escort had informed him they had more important people to deal with that day; had that been one such important person he'd heard screaming for mercy in the courtroom? Had that same person been sentenced to death? He should feel thankful for the respite; perhaps he who sat in judgment would be more lenient another day.

Resting his elbows on his knees, he cupped his face in his hands and glanced to the other end of the narrow cell. The old man appeared to be sleeping on the low bunk, a kind of slatted, wooden platform on which they took turns to rest. Usually he insisted his cellmate used it for most of the night, but right now he would have given anything to lie on the uncomfortable slats rather than the cold stone floor.

Once he felt more rested, Maurici went over to check on the other man. He appeared to be sleeping soundly, but the strong odour of stale urine clearly indicated his companion was more likely to be recovering from another fit and needed a change of clothes. He'd have to plead with the guards for ointment to salve the raw folds of skin in the old man's groin, but who would care for him, Maurici wondered, if he was allowed to leave the cell?

Pondering this, he became aware of a bright eye focused upon him when the man cleared his throat and spoke.

"So, the Fascist is back," he croaked, a wicked smile on his wizened face. "You are to live another day, heh?"

Maurici frowned. "You have a devilish humour," he said as he moved the man's feet to one side and sat down, "but if you'd heard the noise up there you wouldn't joke."

The old man hauled himself into a sitting position and eyed Maurici blearily. "I spent a few hours up there after they brought me in, remember? I may have been drunk but I heard the shots that morning."

Maurici shook his head. "I don't advise taking alcohol with your disability, it could kill you."

The man gave a bitter smile. "Exactly what I was intending to do," he replied. "Who wants to live under that bastard Franco's rule, eh? I'm too old to fight; I've no family, whereas you're young. You have good prospects and a profession even the Fascists have a need for." He winked. "You'll do all right, but remember, keep those hands clean."

"I will," said Maurici, "and I realised what you were up to when the guard came in, but for Christ's sake, don't risk your neck for me."

"You could be right about the alcohol, nothing would be gained if I died from that, but I'd gladly give my life to save a better man – a pacifist like you."

* *

Slamming the heavy book closed, Elizabeth stared white-faced through the library window, her worst fears confirmed. For the fourth morning in succession she had suffered a terrible nausea on rising and today it had been even worse. Only this time she couldn't blame the cake, they hadn't visited the Grant's the previous afternoon. She had searched 'The Home Doctor' for a reason for this sickness to find appendicitis or food poisoning unlikely as the other symptoms weren't there. Just morning sickness, but she'd heard it wasn't possible to become pregnant the first time, and it had been her only intimate experience. Unable to resist the pages on pregnancy, her heart jolted painfully when she read of symptoms exactly like her own.

A feeling of numbness crept over her as she reflected upon her discovery, and she started violently as her grandmother came into the room.

"I've been searching the house for you," Jane complained then, seeing the book in her hands, came briskly across the room to mistakenly advise, "It's no use looking in there until you know what's wrong with him. I expect your mother will telephone later, then we shall know the worst."

The book slipped from Elizabeth's grasp. "Worst!" she repeated, her face ashen as she retrieved it from the polished floor.

"For goodness sake, child, you're allowing yourself to become far too upset," Jane reproved.

"I can't help worrying," Elizabeth said in a small voice. "I miss them."

"I know, so I've arranged for Nicholson to drive us to Helmsley after lunch, take your mind off things."

About to say she didn't feel up to it, Elizabeth thought again; it wouldn't do for her grandmother to suspect anything so she nodded. "Meanwhile, I'll go out in the garden as I don't expect Mummy will telephone before eleven."

"Good idea, you do look rather peaky this morning," Jane observed. "You did have breakfast?"

"Of course," Elizabeth lied, managing a convincing smile, "but I'm not used to eating much early in the day. We never ate large breakfasts in Spain."

"Spain!" Jane sneered. "Don't mention that place to me."

Elizabeth welcomed the fresh air. She had recovered completely from the nausea but her mind was in turmoil. Should she consult Doctor Wilson, she wondered? But she felt it was far too embarrassing to mention to a man, he may want to examine her and she couldn't bear that. Yet, the thought of confiding in her grandmother filled her with terror. Fresh tears rolled down her cheeks; should she try to contact Maurici? Or was this something he'd prefer not to know, the reason she'd not had word from him since she came back?

She slipped her hand under her thick coat, running it over her belly to find it strangely flat. Four months the book had said, or was it five when it would show? Or maybe there was nothing to show; dare she hope?

By the time she returned to the house, she had decided what she would do. Her grandmother regularly went to the stables before lunch, during that time she would put a call through to Spain. It was possible Maurici would be pleased to hear the news, after all they had been in love. Had? She loved him still. She had submitted to him with joy in her heart, but would Maurici welcome the result of their union?

Elizabeth had been on tenterhooks for more than an hour, concern for her father increasing the trepidation she already felt. When the telephone call from France came through, she was too choked with emotion to speak.

"Darling! What is it?" Molly cried in alarm.

"I'm-m worried about Daddy... how is he?"

There was a short silence before Molly told her solemnly, "I'm afraid it's not good news, darling. Your father has suffered injuries to his spine and must lie rigid for a time. But he is fully conscious now and I'm hoping to have him transferred to a Paris hospital very soon."

"H-how did it happen?" Elizabeth pressed.

"It's all rather vague, but I'm told he fell down a mountain-side in the Pyrenees – something about saving a child – near the French border. It was the refugees who got him to the border post where they found his passport and transported him to the nearest hospital. The journey made it worse, of course, but the International Red Cross were to hand, they brought him here."

"But he will get better?" she asked in an anxious whisper.

"We'll know more when he's had further tests, but he's reasonably cheerful, sends you his love..."

"Shall I come to Paris?" Elizabeth broke in. "I miss you so much, I'd love to see him."

"Better wait until I have the results of his tests," Molly advised. "I'll telephone you then."

"He didn't say anything else, did he?" she ventured, hardly daring to hope. "No message for me?"

"No, darling, but don't be too upset, conditions in Spain are very difficult."

"Yes, I expect so..."

"By the way, how's Mother? Is she coping all right?"

"I think so," Elizabeth replied bleakly, "we're going for a drive later."

"Oh, that will be nice for you. Give her my love, will you, and I'll speak to you again on Monday."

With a disconsolate sigh, Elizabeth hung back the earpiece. She longed to join her parents in Paris yet, if a letter came from Maurici she needed to be here to receive it. It was disappointing not to have news but she would try to make contact whilst her grandmother was out of the house.

However, quite some time later, she had not met with any success. International enquiries were unable to trace a number for the name and address she gave, and it appeared there were problems with communications in that area. And she had to stifle her sobs of frustration when Jane came back to the house, to convey her mother's message, relating on her father's state of health.

"A risk one takes when travelling abroad," was Jane's comment before she said briskly, "Let us go in to lunch. Nicholson will bring the car round at two, and I know you'll be pleased to hear Miles will be joining us for the drive."

* *

It was the last day of February when Maurici was called to appear in court. For two weeks he had waited with the fear of court marshal and the prospect of execution hanging over him, the tension increasing each time he heard the key in the lock.

The old man had died three days before, during one of his more frequent convulsive attacks. At the time, Maurici had been on another hopeless wait outside the courtroom when, with the onset of another grand mal, his cellmate had choked on a piece of bread. Often he had pleaded with the guards to let the man go, but the old fool would persist in annoying them by singing the Catalan Anthem.

At least his problems were over, Maurici had thought as they removed the body from the cell, but without his old companion he experienced dreadful bouts of depression when time dragged slowly by.

Now, as he climbed the flight of worn steps to the floor above, he hoped this would be his lucky day. He felt reasonably confident of the outcome of his court appearance. The old man had tutored him well. "Don't waste your life," he had advised, "do anything they ask of you to gain your freedom. This way the Republic will never die!"

With the old man's words still ringing in his ears, he gritted his teeth and returned the salute of the man standing at the courtroom door.

There were three men sitting behind a long wooden table when Maurici was marched in, the one in the centre a high ranking officer who raised his hand in casual salute. He was instructed to halt a few meters in front of the trio, his expression grave as he came to attention. The man on the right glanced over the papers before him and cleared his throat to demand curtly, "Name?"

"Bachs," said Maurici.

"Forename?"

"*Mauricio,*" Maurici responded quickly, changing to a Castilion pronunciation as the old man had said he should.

"Address?"

Maurici gave his address, adding fervently, "My family are good Catholics, they work hard to make a living."

Three pairs of eyes were directed his way. The officer made a note on the pad before him as he enquired, "And you?"

"I was raised in a good Catholic home," Maurici replied, "and I respect the views of my parents."

"But you do not share them?" The senior of the trio compressed his lips a moment before he continued, "You have been brought before this court accused of aiding the escape of two prisoners. What have you to say?"

"But I did not intend to aid their escape, sir. It happened when I assisted in putting out a fire..."

"Which, unfortunately, you caused, putting the lives of others at great risk."

"If I may say, sir, I am a student doctor, I would never intentionally put lives at risk," Maurici pointed out politely.

"And a student of the Catalan language, I understand," the man put in with a humourless smile.

"Merely newspaper gossip, I assure you."

"Newspaper gossip?" His accuser cocked an eyebrow. "The fact is, along with two other men, you were taken prisoner whilst trying to infiltrate behind the Nationalist lines."

"No, sir, I was sent there under orders to attend an injured officer."

"A Republican officer?"

"I was not aware of his status, but my profession requires me to alleviate the suffering of anyone who is sick, regardless of their politics."

The officer acknowledged this with a grunt and murmured something in the ear of his colleague when, looking directly at Maurici, he said coldly, "Did you kill your cellmate?"

Completely taken aback, Maurici could only stare.

"Well, did you?" the man thundered. "I believe he gave you a hard time."

"No, sir," Maurici replied, his brain whirling with thoughts of what the old man had told him to expect. "He gave me a hard time, I'll agree, but I realised he was ill, otherwise I may have been tempted."

The officer nodded and went into further quiet discussion with the other two before he returned his attention to Maurici. "I am given to understand you are extremely competent in your work. Therefore, to ensure your sympathies continue to lie with the Empire, and your skills be put to good use, it is the opinion of this court that you be conscripted to the Nationalist army..." The officer's eyes fell back to his notes when, with a dismissive wave of his hand, he concluded, "where you will serve your country for the next three years."

Chapter 16

66Fainting in the dining room indeed!" Jane hissed as she paced Elizabeth's bedroom. "Don't look at me with wide-eyed innocence; I've heard you vomiting in the bathroom."

"Please, Grandmother," pleaded Elizabeth, "I'm sorry."

"Sorry? You little trollop! What about your mother – you have told her?"

"No, I haven't told anyone."

"Just how long do you suppose you can keep it secret?" her grandmother continued to rant. "And the disgrace you'll bring upon us, have you thought of that?"

"I don't know what to think, or what I should do..."

"Do?" Jane snorted. "Well, obviously the father isn't interested so you'd better think of something. I presume it's that filthy little Spaniard your father encouraged."

Elizabeth shot bolt upright. "He's not a filthy little Spaniard!" she cried, "and no-one encouraged him."

"Then how did you arrive in this situation? Tell me that!"

"We were in love," Elizabeth sobbed.

"Don't be ridiculous, you're far too young."

"You don't understand," Elizabeth protested, "I tried to telephone him, and I've written to his friend, but there are problems with communication."

"Even so, your mother must be told, though you're not fit to travel to Paris in your condition."

"I don't feel up to the journey," Elizabeth admitted, "or to worry Mummy just now."

"I should think not, she has more than enough to deal with. I'll call Wilson, he'll know what to do, though I haven't much faith in him myself."

"But he may want to examine me!" Elizabeth gasped.

"A bit late to worry about that!" came her biting retort.

The following morning, as her grandmother gazed silently through the window, Elizabeth suffered the embarrassment of Doctor Wilson's attendance.

"That completes my examination, Elizabeth," he said, and directing his attention to Jane continued, "I'll have a word with her alone when she's ready."

Leaving Elizabeth to dress, they left the room. Dare she hope it was merely some minor illness she was suffering she wondered miserably, rolling up her lisle stockings. But when Alex Wilson returned she knew by his expression what his diagnosis would be. Did he imagine his smile would allay her anxiety as he settled himself into the chair opposite?

"I don't know if this will come as a surprise to you, Elizabeth, pleasant or otherwise, but I have to tell you you're pregnant. About two or three months, I'd say."

Elizabeth closed her eyes as the truth struck home and her fingers locked together until they hurt.

"Does your mother know?" he asked, noting her reaction.

"I prefer she doesn't, not yet, not with Daddy so ill."

"I understand," he said, his voice barely penetrating her numbed mind. "But Mrs Cussons is aware?"

She nodded and declared, "I'd like to go back to Spain, but it's impossible at present..."

"I assume that is where the father lives," he broke in quietly. "Does he know?"

Elizabeth lowered her head, her hair falling forward to conceal her flushed cheeks. "No," she said, so quietly he had to strain to catch her response. "I've not seen him since, you know, since it happened."

"At least you'll have your grandmother's support."

Elizabeth glanced up. "But the disgrace... she's warned me about that."

"Mrs Cussons will co-operate, I'm sure," he said kindly. "And I'll be here to take care of you, though there's no cause for concern as you're a perfectly healthy young woman."

* *

"Please, speak slowly," Molly said in her precise but limited French when the specialist looked up from his notes. "I've hardly used French since school."

The man smiled. "But you are a nurse, you will already be aware of the problem of your husband's injuries."

She nodded. "When they were performing the tests I noticed he appeared almost totally paralysed."

"I don't entirely agree, not yet, until he has recovered from the shock and the inflammatory reaction has subsided," he said with an optimistic lift of his brows. "Already, he can speak, his swallowing reflexes are fairly good, and there are signs of movement in his right hand."

He paused, referring to his notes before he continued, "As you will know, the extent of his disability depends on the level of the lesion, though in your husband's case it appears to be below the second lumbar vertebrae."

"Which could mean paraplegia," she supplied with an unhappy sigh.

"That depends on whether the lesion results in a complete or incomplete transection of the spinal cord, as you will be aware. However, I'm sure he benefits from your presence so I asked sister to allow you to visit the ward whenever you wish."

"I'm most grateful," said Molly, with a wan smile. "I would only worry if I wasn't here."

"You must not give up hope, these things take time."

* *

"I've grown extremely fond of you since you came home, Elizabeth," Miles said from across the dining table. "You must have noticed."

She glanced up. "But I've only been back a month, you hardly know me."

"Five weeks, actually, but you're forgetting the times we rode together before you went away. I was fond of you then, but you were rather too young."

"Only by a year! I can't have changed so much."

"Oh but you have," he said convincingly. "You've matured into a desirable young lady."

"It is kind of you to say so, Miles but..."

"It's a fact," he intruded earnestly, raising his hand to catch the waiter's attention. "I wish you'd been here to partner me at the Hunt Ball as there was no one in

Woodington I cared to invite. Now, how about another drink?"

"No, thank you," she declined hurriedly, nauseated by the very thought, "but don't let me stop you."

As Miles ordered another brandy from the hotel bar, Elizabeth studied him, noting he had taken great care with his appearance this evening. Instead of the usual tweeds, he was dressed in a dark suit of fine quality and his generally wispy hair was smooth and shining. An attentive escort, but what would be his reaction if her secret were revealed to him now?

She'd been unsure about accepting his invitation, but Jane insisted and had encouraged Miles to visit the Hall regularly since her mother left for France. It would take her mind off things, she had said, but how could she forget this tiny life within, or that her father was so ill and far away? And with no reply to her letter to Enric, it must mean Maurici no longer cared: as her grandmother constantly reminded her... and something she must accept.

"Elizabeth, you're miles away," she heard. "Sure you won't have another drink?"

"No, thank you, Miles," she replied in a flat voice. "I ought to go, it's half-past nine."

"Just one more drink, then we'll go," he promised. "The fog appears to have lifted so we'll soon be home."

When eventually they got into the cold interior of his car, Elizabeth felt exhausted. Over the past week she'd felt unusually tired and assumed it to be another symptom of her condition. During the journey, with a rug tucked snugly around her, she dozed and it was Miles' warm, brandy-laden breath on her face that startled her as she awoke.

"Sleepyhead," he murmured in an amused voice, then kissed her lightly on the mouth.

"Oh, Miles, I'm so sorry!" she exclaimed in confusion. "I didn't intend to fall asleep."

"That's all right – in fact, you looked very pretty..." He hesitated, hands on the steering wheel, he stared ahead to say, "You know, Elizabeth, I think you'd make me an ideal wife."

* *

With a groan of relief, Maurici broke away from the group and fell onto his hard, barrack room bed. For the past two weeks he'd cleaned the latrines before early morning drill in the barrack square and marched through every hour of daylight until he was ready to drop. Then came the lectures from a senior officer; obey the rules, speak only Castilian, the language of the Empire, serve God... The words reeled in his brain as he relaxed his aching body, wondering how he was going to survive the next two and a half months of this torture while still confined to barracks.

His mouth twisted in an ironic smile: should he be free to spend his evenings roaming the city he wouldn't have the energy to enjoy it. Not that he desired the all-night revelry of Barcelona; he needed his freedom to communicate with Elizabeth, a priority once the three months passed. There was no one in his barrack he could ask to post a letter, all were in the same situation. And the guards, already lacking in civility, were unlikely to oblige.

As he dozed, Elizabeth drifted into his thoughts and, as so often of late, he reflected upon the afternoon of New Year's Eve; her beautiful face, those eyes of sapphire blue, shining with love, her perfect body close to his, touching, stimulating his desire... titillated by his thoughts he rolled onto his side.

To ease his frustration he turned his mind to other things; his parents, his relatives in Sitges, and Enric whom he hoped soon to see. And Tom Garbutt, how had he fared? Had Elizabeth received the letter he sent?

* *

"Thank you, Pincott, I'll be obliged if you don't mention this," said Jane, taking the letter bearing a Spanish stamp from the butler's tray. "She's dreadfully upset about her father, you see, and word of that awful war will only add to her distress. I'll give it to her at a more suitable time."

"Certainly, madam," Pincott murmured. "Miss Elizabeth must be very worried just now."

Jane slipped the letter into the pocket of her cashmere cardigan and went up to her room. Seated by her rosewood escritoire, she slit open the envelope and withdrew the single sheet of notepaper. To her surprise she saw it was signed by someone called Enric, not this Maurici person as she expected, and for a moment she was struck by a twinge of guilt until she read its contents.

The letter was written in rather strange English and she had to go through it a second time to get the gist of the message it contained. 'I no see Maurici', she read, 'is in the prison. Sorry, is the war. Please, you write'. He also expressed sympathy for James and sent good wishes to the family.

A prisoner! Jane compressed her thin lips, convinced she was right in protecting Elizabeth from this disreputable man

– a criminal – who wanted no contact with the girl upon whom he had brought such shame. She had been infatuated with this foreign philanderer and was suffering as a result; better not to be reminded of him.

Satisfied her action would save further pain, she locked the letter away. But now there was Elizabeth's pregnancy to consider and Jane's thoughts went immediately to Miles Grant. It was obvious he was enamoured of her, only the previous afternoon he'd brought up the subject of marriage. Molly had not yet been told of the unfortunate situation, but if a marriage could be arranged it would help soften the blow.

From Molly's telephone calls she understood the improvement in James' condition was only very slight; he would be an invalid for the rest of his life. With this in mind, Jane decided to have a quiet talk with Elizabeth; perhaps now, while she was feeling at her worst.

"How are you today, dear?" Jane asked, seating herself on the edge of Elizabeth's bed.

Elizabeth sighed and pulled a face. "Awful," she said, glancing at the breakfast tray, "I couldn't face a thing."

Jane smiled. "I'm pleased you have taken my advice and stayed in bed."

"You really don't mind?"

"Of course not, dear," Jane assured her warmly. "Did you have plans for today – are you meeting Miles?"

Elizabeth shrugged. "I have little alternative, he's terribly persistent."

"He's very fond of you, Elizabeth."

"But I can't go on seeing him, particularly now when he's hinted at marriage."

"Has he really!" Jane exclaimed with feigned surprise. "Well, he would make a very good husband…"

In my condition! I can't even consider it."

"Why not? It would get you out of this predicament."

"But I'm expecting another man's baby…"

"About which the father doesn't wish to know!" Jane reminded her tartly then, reverting to a sympathetic tone, said, "It's unfortunate, but you've got to face it, he never wanted the responsibility."

Elizabeth uttered a long sigh, saying miserably, "If you knew him you'd understand why I find it so hard to accept."

"My dear, you must realise we'd stand little chance of bringing him to court, and the newspapers would have a field day!"

"Oh no, I wouldn't want that. Actually, I can go away as I understand there are places…"

"Nonsense, I won't allow it. No, I think you should consider Miles' offer."

"But he's almost twice my age."

"Does that really matter? A mature man can be much less demanding, you know. He's extremely taken with you, and he's from a wealthy family, you will want for nothing."

Jane rose from the bed, smiling as she continued, "Do remember, I won't always be here, so if you choose not to marry you will have an illegitimate baby to support. Have you thought of that, dear? And don't forget your poor father, I'm afraid he'll not work again. His treatment is so costly he'll barely be able to support your mother, never mind you and a baby. It would be an immense relief to him to know you are comfortably settled."

Elizabeth was thoughtful for a few moments before she replied. "But there's still the scandal, whatever I choose to do..."

Jane shook her head. "Oh no. No-one would dare remark upon it if you were married to Miles."

* *

"Are you sure, Elizabeth?" Molly asked when they spoke on the telephone. "You've never shown an interest in Miles."

Elizabeth took a steadying breath. "Of course. We've been seeing each other almost every day since you left."

"But don't rush into something you may later regret, darling. Remember, he's years older than you."

"It doesn't matter, Mummy, really, we get along famously. Grandmother says, providing you're agreeable, she will see to the formalities and fix a date for when you return."

"It could be towards the end of April, or early June, so you have plenty of time."

Elizabeth's heart sank. "As long as that?"

"As I explained, darling, spinal injuries take time, it's only nine weeks since his accident."

"It seems as though you've been away for ages."

"I suppose it must," Molly agreed. "But, as I've already told you, he's now showing signs of recovery, though it's unlikely he'll regain the use of his legs. However, despite everything, he's in reasonably good spirits"

"I miss him, and I don't know how you manage to sound so normal, you must be upset."

"One has to keep going," Molly sighed, "and I couldn't bear to leave him here alone. Even so, it shouldn't delay your plans too much."

Elizabeth took a deep breath. "I'm afraid it will," she began nervously, "you see – I – I'm expecting a baby."

There was a faint gasp, followed by a long silence before Molly said softly, "Oh, I see. You're quite sure?"

"Yes, that's why I want to get married as soon as possible," she hurried to say. "I'm sorry, Mummy, I didn't want to tell you yet, not while Daddy's ill."

"You and Miles certainly are getting along very famously," her mother responded coolly. "That changes everything."

"I'm really sorry. I don't know what else to say, but you must understand I can't wait much longer."

"Even so, don't let that rush you into making a decision you may later regret. Now, how are you – keeping well?"

"Quite well, actually," Elizabeth replied, relieved to hear her mother had taken the news reasonably calmly.

"You've seen Alex? No morning sickness?"

"Not yet," she lied, though she wasn't quite sure why.

"It may not affect you, just take it easy. Does mother know? About the baby, I mean."

"Yes, she's taken it well. She's doing the organizing."

"Well, it sounds as though everything's settled..." Molly hesitated, then went on to say, "providing you are absolutely sure, darling. You don't have to marry you know..."

"I know," Elizabeth rushed in. "My only regret is not joining you in Paris, but the seas have been so rough Grandmother says I'd be foolish to travel."

"Quite so, darling. And now I'm with Daddy I am pleased you are there with her. When I was speaking to her just now she sounded quite pleasant."

"Actually, she's changed," Elizabeth agreed in a lowered voice. "Perhaps it is because she doesn't have to worry about poor Grandpa any more."

"Maybe," agreed Molly, but without conviction, and said with a short laugh, "I'd better get your father used to the idea of having a grandchild."

"I hope he won't be too upset. I'd do anything rather than hurt him."

"We can't change things now," Molly responded wisely. "But let us know your plans?"

"I'll let you know the exact date as soon as arranged."

"I could fly over. It depends on how your father is."

"I understand," Elizabeth assured her, ending with gentle sincerity, "I can't wait for you both to come back."

After the telephone call, when Jane had gone out to the stables, Elizabeth went along to the oratory where, as a child, she had discovered her grandfather kneeling in prayer. And for a few moments she knelt there, absently turning her left hand this way and that, the stones in her engagement ring sparkling in the light from the tiny window.

"Please, God," she prayed softly, "let Daddy walk again, however long it takes. And my baby – Maurici's baby – help me to know what I must do..."

With tears glistening in her eyes, she continued to pray in silence in the hope it would give her strength.

* *

Elizabeth and Miles were married on the third Saturday in March of nineteen thirty-nine. It had been a bright, sunny day when the church at Woodington was decorated with spring flowers and packed with well-wishers, many fashionably attired. A telegram from Paris conveyed the good wishes of Molly and James. Elizabeth sent flowers to the hospital; she had missed her parents terribly, particularly her father who could not be beside her as she walked up the aisle. In the whirl of activity any moments of sadness and doubt were quickly dispelled by the social demands made upon her.

Although still in mourning, Jane felt the occasion called for something a little more fashionable in style and had insisted Elizabeth accompany her to York to help choose a suitable outfit. However, all went well on the day; Jane had been more than usually sociable, and Miles' relatives appeared delighted with his choice of bride.

But there had been anxious moments for Elizabeth when the reception was nearing its close, Miles had taken too much to drink and was barely capable of driving them away on honeymoon. When, finally, they reached their hotel in Harrogate he had fallen into a deep sleep still wearing his clothes. Afterwards, he'd been very apologetic, but was inclined to overdo the after-dinner brandy, the smell lingering on his breath, repulsing her as they lay together in bed. Thankfully, he had seemed almost impotent, though she endured his fumbling without complaint. At least, while he lay in a drunken slumber she had no cause to worry if his clumsy attempts at intimacy would harm the tiny life within.

The few days in Harrogate dragged by and Elizabeth was relieved when the time came for them to drive back to Miles' Woodington home. It was April the second and she had spotted in a newspaper the war in Spain had ended the previous day; All Fools day, she'd realised bitterly.

Miles hadn't considered it necessary to move out of his family home. After all, the house was large enough for two families to live in comfort, and as his parents were elderly he assumed Elizabeth would take over the running of the house. But as time went by it became clear her responsibilities were increasing. Miles' mother, a sweet-natured lady, required the services of a nurse, but he employed one for only a minimum amount of time, leaving Elizabeth to tend her during the remainder of each day. His father was quite demanding and, like Miles, enjoyed more than the occasional drink. Jane continued her visits, perhaps three times a week in addition to her morning rides in the company of the elder Grant and Miles.

It was after Miles had been out riding, whilst he changed his mud-splattered clothes, when he suggested Elizabeth should ride with them the following morning now he had acquired another horse.

"Seems quiet enough," he had said. "Not too highly spirited, you'd manage her all right."

Considering it a perfect moment to bring up the subject of the baby, she had replied a trifle apprehensively, "No, Miles, I'd better not. You see, I-I'm expecting a baby."

"A what? Baby, did you say?" For a moment Miles had looked quite amazed, then sniggered and said, "Well done, Elizabeth, hope it's a boy! When's it due?"

"Not until later in the year," she'd managed to reply, hoping the rush of colour to her cheeks had gone unnoticed.

"We must celebrate, have a drink," he'd urged. "It's not every day a chap learns he's going to be a father."

Downstairs, along with members of the family, Jane had raised her glass, directing a smug little smile in Elizabeth's direction as they toasted the coming child. But it was Miles' aunt who inadvertently divulged something of which Elizabeth had not been previously aware.

"He's certainly done well for himself. A pretty wife and an heir to all that wealth," the old lady had said as Elizabeth helped her on with her coat.

Seeing Elizabeth's puzzled look, she'd chuckled. "We had given up hope of Miles marrying, but his grandmother was determined he would only inherit if he continued the family line."

This news had astonished Elizabeth, and it was shortly after the family left when the baby first made its presence felt. The future heir to the Grant estate. But she had come to think of it as her own very special child, each tiny flutter of movement reminding her of Maurici and the love she had known. However wealthy Miles would become he could never take Maurici's place in her heart.

* *

The August skies were bright over Woodington Hall on the day Molly and James came home. When the ambulance that had brought them on the final leg of their journey turned into the drive, Elizabeth rushed out to welcome them, tears of happiness streaming down her cheeks. But she had difficulty suppressing her shock on seeing her father; looking years older he appeared to have shrunk into his clothes. Yet, as he released her from an emotional embrace, she saw the familiar smile brighten his vivid blue eyes.

And once inside the house even Jane showed less restraint when she bent over the stretcher to kiss her son-in-law on the cheek.

"You're looking extremely well," Molly commented, her glance coming to rest on her daughter's increasing waistline. "How long before baby arrives?"

"Oh ages," Elizabeth replied offhandedly, "I'm not sure."

"We may have missed your wedding, but we'll be here when baby's born." Molly smiled, settling into a chair as Pincott came in bearing a tray.

"Tell me more about France, Daddy," Elizabeth begged as she set out china cups and saucers and a drinking cup for her father. "Were they good to you in the hospital?"

"They were very considerate," James said, "and it was wonderful to have your mother with me, particularly now, with the situation in Europe as it is."

He went on to tell her about the treatment he'd received, but what troubled him most was his lost independence and the cost of employing the full-time nurse who had moved into the Hall in preparation for his arrival.

Elizabeth accompanied him as he was transferred to his room when just the way he held her gaze gave her a moment of intense discomfort. "Are you truly happy married to Miles?" he asked, his eyes searching her face. "From your letters, I was never quite convinced it was what you really wanted to do."

* *

Elizabeth's baby was born on a rainy day in October. England was now at war with Germany though little had changed in the Grant household, until this morning, the morning of the fourth.

"Miles, come and have a peep at her," Doctor Wilson smiled, inviting him over to the bed. "This will take your mind off the war."

"Like a skinned rabbit!" Miles exclaimed with a short laugh, looking down on the baby cradled in Elizabeth's arms.

"She's not, she's beautiful..." Elizabeth protested, kissing its tiny hand.

"Where mothers are concerned, all babies are beautiful," Alex Wilson put in with a chuckle. "And I must say, this one is exceptionally pretty considering she's so small."

"I suppose, being premature, she's bound to be small," Miles remarked. "But I expect she'll soon gain weight."

Elizabeth glanced up to meet the doctor's steady gaze. He had tried to persuade her to tell Miles the truth but she hadn't had the nerve, and after learning the reason he had been so eager to marry her, she no longer felt any guilt. Perhaps if Alex were made aware of this...

The baby moved in her arms just as she was beginning to doze. "Let nurse put baby in her cot then you can rest," Alex suggested. "By the way, have you decided on a name?"

Miles shook his head. "Didn't think of a girl's name. I was hoping for a boy."

"I have," Elizabeth murmured, her half-closed eyes following her baby as it was lifted away. "I shall call her Serena, it suits her somehow."

* *

After Serena's christening, Elizabeth took her regularly to the Hall. The weather was turning quite cold, with heavy frosts lingering on the lawns until after midday so she usually drove her there in Miles' small Austin. She was an adorable baby, good-natured and quiet, and James liked nothing more than to lie in his bed by the window with Serena beside him.

But Elizabeth was beginning to dread going back to the farm at midday when Miles came in from riding over his land. He regularly finished his meal with a very large whisky then fell asleep in a chair for the afternoon. At times his manner was quite belligerent and a crying baby made things worse, so to avoid a scene she took to walking Serena in the pram when the contented child left her alone with her thoughts. It was during these quiet moments when she wondered what the future held; had she been a fool to marry Miles simply to give her baby a name?

Chapter 17

Towards the end of February Maurici was released from the army. Returning home, he saw his mother sitting in the open doorway, the sun glinting on her spectacles, her attention on her needlework until she caught the sound of his footsteps on the gravel. Uttering a gasp of delight she thrust her work aside, heaving herself out of the chair as he hurried forward.

Carmen held her son close. "At last," she said, her eyes brimming with tears, "you are home where you belong."

A lump rose in his throat but he smiled. "Anyone would think you hadn't seen me during these last three years."

"I know, but this time you will stay." She held him away and clicked her tongue. "*Ai*, so thin..."

"That's due to the hard work, building roads." he said as she ushered him indoors.

Her hands flew to her cheeks. "Building roads! But what of your medical skills – such a terrible waste!"

"I worked with the medics also, but the roadwork got rid of any surplus flesh."

"But no home cooking, hey? I'll soon put some weight on you."

"On your meagre rations, mama!"

Her pendant earrings trembled as she tilted her head. "Your father does a little business in the market, we have not starved."

Maurici's eyes widened. "He shouldn't, it's too risky. The police may hear of it."

"So, what else? We have to eat. Three years since the war ended, and there's little food available, even yet."

"But it could mean imprisonment – something I don't recommend," he said wryly. "Have you thought of that?"

"Now you are home it will improve," she declared with smiling optimism. "Nineteen forty-two will be a good year."

"But now the rest of Europe is at war," he reminded her with a despairing shake of his head. "I could see it coming back in the Spring of thirty-nine and that damned Hitler won't be satisfied until he rules all Europe!" He grinned as he continued, "I hear the Fascists in Britain were interred some time ago. Their Prime Minister, *senyor* Churchill has the right idea. They won't tolerate it."

"Please, Maurici, let us not talk of war. We've had enough misery to last us all our lives."

"Forgive me for saying this, but we don't know what real misery is. Think of those wretched refugees, sick and dying, trailing over the Pyrenees into France as the war ended, in rain and snow, without adequate clothing, and for what?" He spread his hands in a despairing gesture.

"*Si, si,* I know, and many of them only children..."

"The reports were terrible," he broke in. "Families parted, innocent people thrown into camps, guarded like prisoners. Only God knows where they are now..." He lowered his head to conceal his emotion.

"But the French, surely they could have helped?"

"To have sided with Franco, or against him, may have plunged France into a civil uprising of its own." His expression hardened. "Look what they did with the President of the Catalan government. They handed him back to the Nationalists who had him shot."

Carmen heaved a long sigh. "Ach, politics!" she cried, dropping heavily onto a chair. "I will never understand why people cannot live in peace."

"The man in the street can, it's the power-seekers. Some time ago, when I heard of Fascists occupying France and the Channel Islands, I was concerned for the future. And London is bombed almost nightly, worse than we suffered here..."

Hearing his father enter he rose. "*Hola, papa!* I am a civilian once more!"

"Ready for work, I hope," said Josep, smiling. "I had a hard time this winter, pruning and ploughing in the cold. Now the sap is rising, the buds will soon begin to break."

"I hear a number of vineyards are being re-established," Maurici commented. "Is this so?"

"*Sí*, but some are cutting down on the area of land they cultivate. Even I have a few hectares less as you will see..."

"But your training, Maurici, the medical school," Carmen broke in, "do you not intend to continue?"

"I don't know, *mama*. For the time being I want just peace and quiet. Work in the vineyard will suit me very well."

It was only when Maurici relaxed in his own bed that he felt truly free. He'd chatted with his parents over a home-cooked meal and it was late when he retired. But then, comfortable and warm beneath the blankets, was when the sweet memories came flooding back, the afternoon spent with Elizabeth returning to torment him afresh. He could recall quite vividly how she'd snuggled shyly into his arms, the memory arousing him still as he imagined her young body lying naked next to his. Reflecting upon the intimacy they had shared, he beat the pillow with his fist. Whose arms embraced her now? How quickly her affection for him had waned; barely three months after they had been together in this very bed, Elizabeth had married. Enric had told him, albeit reluctantly, on his first day out of barracks when he'd travelled to Sitges in search of news. And in a moment of fury he'd torn the note she had left behind to shreds. To write of her distress over leaving only to marry so soon afterwards broke his heart.

Enric had told him of the accident James had met with on his way into France, and that Molly had kept up correspondence with him, though Elizabeth had not replied to his letter. Maurici could still picture Enric's discomfort when he had pressed him for news, and remembered his own reaction at the time; disbelief, fury, indignation, and getting terribly drunk. But what had become of Tom Garbutt? Had he not reached Woodington in time, or was he caught up in his own country's war?

Hours later he was still awake. For a while he had felt a free man, but now the past was back with him, holding his heart prisoner.

* *

"I do hate those strips of sticky tape over the windows, it makes it so dark in here," Molly grumbled as she sorted through the post. "And those dreary old blackout curtains, one wouldn't think it was the middle of May."

"Better than the glass shattering during a raid," James pointed out. "The Londoners spend most nights in the shelters."

"Perhaps you're right, we are more fortunate in the country, and there's always the cellar should we need it."

"Anything for me?" he asked as she came to his side.

"Ah yes, there's one from Enric. You know, I can't believe it's well over three years since we left!"

James opened the letter. "Things seem pretty bad," he said. "Repression, everything subject to Franco's restrictions, no Catalan literature available. It breaks his heart to think of the books burned in that cultural purge." He sighed. "At least he's working, lucky devil,"

"But you do your bit for the war effort, darling. Taking telephone messages, typing for the billeting officer. And looking after Serena means Elizabeth can help me with the Women's Voluntary Service."

James grinned. "Oh, you mean the knitting group."

"We don't spend all our time knitting..." she began, then saw his teasing smile. "Oh you know very well what we do."

"Yes, placing evacuees, first aid lessons, sending clothing to bombed out areas? That's more than my bit, darling."

"But guess what?" said Molly, her eyes shining. "I've even persuaded Mother to knit a balaclava."

"Jane, doing her bit for the forces, I don't believe it!"

"The British forces, of course," Molly laughed, mimicking her mother's manner of speaking.

With a grin for his wife, James returned his attention to the letter. "I say!" he began in surprise. "Enric had applied for a visa, he wants to visit us here."

"Oh, that would be wonderful, James, especially for you."

"But he says permission was refused, control is very tight. Such a pity, I would dearly love to see my old friend again."

"I'm sure you will, when this dreadful war is over," she sighed, and through the window she spotted Elizabeth's car. "Goodness me, is that the time! We must get you dressed."

James glanced at the clock and frowned. "She's earlier than usual. I hope every thing's all right."

Molly looked thoughtful. "You know, I never mentioned the letter we had from Enric a couple of years ago – you remember, around the time of Dunkirk – when he wrote to tell us the young student doctor had visited him. I often wonder if I did the right thing..."

"Of course, darling. Elizabeth was already married, and a mother, there was no point."

"I know, but it explained why he never appeared before we left, and the letter had taken ages to get here."

"Even so, it was still too late. When Enric told us he'd had no reply from Elizabeth to his letter, though she says she didn't receive it, I assumed she'd wanted to sever all connection with Sitges."

Molly sighed. "You could be right, yet she never seems really happy. Some thing's troubling her, I'm sure."

"Perhaps it's Miles. Never cared for the man, myself. He's rarely at home and spends no time with that child."

"Ah, you've noticed! And when someone of two and a half tells us her daddy keeps falling over, it makes me wonder."

"Poor child. She's such a dainty little thing, and so advanced for her age," he remarked with an indulgent smile."

"She's adorable," Molly agreed, "but one thing still troubles me. Have you noticed the colour of her eyes?"

James shrugged but remained silent.

Noting his guarded expression, she nodded. "So you have, and you will have realised why they're brown."

* *

"They look healthy and strong," Josep observed as he and Maurici surveyed the rows of young vines, their leaves turning a brownish red. "In two more years we'll have a good crop."

"The old ones would have been past their best, whereas these will mature at just the right time."

Josep nodded as they turned back towards the house where the leaves on the young shoots were a greenish yellow. "The stocks which grew in this area before it was bombed were almost fifty years old. My father planted them, they produced a perfect wine."

Maurici sent him an admiring glance. "You've worked hard to restock such a large area. What type are they?"

Josep raised his arm in a wide arc. "Beyond the house, *Xarel-lo*, here *Garnacha*. I like them, the clusters are very compact and give a wine with very little acid."

"I wish I'd been here to make it easier for you."

"If only Lluis were as enthusiastic, I'd consider taking him on again."

Maurici turned to him in shocked surprise. "No! After what he did?"

Josep pulled a wry face. "Family," he said, "Lluis is family, and the war is over. What else can I do?"

"Oh *papa*! Have you forgotten? He was party to the destruction of the *Celler*. He helped ruin your business!"

"*Si,* Maurici, but he was young. He's different now, my brother..."

"Different!" Maurici snorted. "Not every parent would have stood by him at such risk to themselves."

Josep spread his hands. "But he's their son."

Maurici pursed his lips. "I hope he appreciates it."

"He works hard at home, though the business doesn't make enough to keep the family and pay Lluis a wage."

"Well, it's up to you, *papa*. If you're serious about re-employing him, I'll suggest we call a truce."

"It would improve the situation," Josep agreed with a faint smile. "I can't help but admire my brother, he swore white was black young Lluis wasn't with the Communists. He got him off that prison sentence at great risk to himself."

"Pity he wasn't around when I was taken prisoner!" Maurici exclaimed bitterly.

Josep knitted his brow. "If only we had known where you were," he said sadly. "We had no word from you."

"I know, *papa*, it wasn't allowed. I suspect everything was censored, I doubt it would have arrived."

Later in the week, when Lluis called, there was a certain reserve between the cousins as they exchanged greetings, and to avoid further conversation Maurici led him into the sitting room where his father beckoned him to a seat.

"My father tells me you have work for me," he heard Lluis say.

"That is so," Josep replied as he held a match to his cigar. "Now the vineyard is well established we need an extra hand for ploughing and pruning."

"Ploughing and pruning..." Lluis began with obvious distaste. "But I thought..."

"Maurici can manage the rest," Josep interrupted. "After this crop is in I intend to retire. Meanwhile, you'll have to prove yourself before I allow you more responsibility."

Lluis turned a hard gaze in his cousin's direction when, regardless of his father's presence, Maurici remarked coolly, "Consider yourself lucky, and if we're to work together I suggest we call a truce."

* *

Maurici shook his head. "Mama, you can't fool me, I know what you're up to."

"But I thought you liked Dolors."

"I like her," he agreed with a lift of his shoulders, "but I've never considered her as more than a friend."

"She'd be a good wife, and if you like her..."

"Like her, yes," he began, glancing away as he rushed to add, "but I don't love her."

"You're twenty-eight now," the *senyora* said wistfully. "Am I never to see my grandchildren before I die?"

"Please, mama!" he chided her, but without real anger. His mother would never understand – even if he were to tell her of the great void in his heart – he couldn't expect her to. Elizabeth was married.

"Maurici, show Dolors the *celler*," his mother suggested, passing round the plate of biscuits she'd concocted from maize flour and black market sugar.

"I'm sure Dolors has already seen it," Maurici said as he replenished the glasses of their guests with dessert wine.

"I wouldn't mind seeing it again," Dolors put in eagerly, her velvet-brown eyes resting on Maurici.

Maurici stifled a sigh and smiled. He'd been observing her discreetly ever since she had arrived with her parents, noting the care she had taken with her appearance, from her shining dark hair to her freshly pressed costume and well polished shoes. And the way she crossed her legs, showing just a hint of the smooth skin of her thigh. Yes, Dolors was attractive, but not the kind of girl who would agree to sexual activity without first having the security of marriage. He could make love to her, of that he was sure, but could he love her as a wife? As they discussed last December's bombing of Pearl Harbor, he'd noticed she showed scant interest in world affairs. She lacked that essential spark, presented no challenge to his intelligence, nothing to stir his imagination, and marriage was for life.

He realised she was aware of his eyes upon her when she tugged down her skirt. Quickly averting his gaze, he suggested a walk outside to which she responded eagerly. Going ahead in the pale evening sun, as she sauntered down the path towards the *celler*, he eyed her from behind, seeing the swing of her shapely figure, imagining it naked against his own. A pleasurable thought yet, was it enough? But Elizabeth was already married, he kept reminding himself, it may have to be.

* *

Elizabeth checked the contents of her bag, listing them aloud, "Identity card, cheque book, purse." Then glancing around the room exclaimed, "Oh, my gas mask!" and picked up the square cardboard container in its fawn, waterproof case, slipping the strap over her shoulder to leave her hands free to carry Serena to the car.

"Daddy coming, too?" Serena asked, pointing a chubby little finger in the direction of Miles' room where he was recovering from the night before.

"Not today, sweetheart, Daddy's asleep."

"Not today," Serena repeated, "Daddy sleep."

"That's right, but Grandma will be waiting for you."

"Teddy's not sleeping," Serena said, pointing out her favourite toy as they hurried from the room.

"Oh, Serena, not now!" she cried, then relented and went back to snatch up the bear.

With Serena beside her in the car, she straightened her shoulders and rubbed a hand over the back of her aching neck and drove in the direction of the Hall. The child smiled, unaware anything was amiss, causing Elizabeth a pang of guilt as she drove along. It wasn't Serena's fault they'd had to change their plans. Miles had promised to drive James to his appointment with a specialist in York, even insisted. But that had been yesterday when he was sober, this morning everything had changed.

She cringed when she thought of the way Miles had jeered, "He'll always be a bloody cripple, I don't know why you bother," before he had turned over in bed and gone back to sleep. Thank goodness Nicholson was available when she'd telephoned, it would have been impossible to manage the wheelchair on the train.

"Miles isn't too well this morning," Elizabeth explained when they arrived at the Hall, "and it would be rather difficult to get Daddy into my little car. I assume you have an allowance of petrol for the journey?"

"Of course. It's such a filthy day," said Molly, "much better to go in the Humber."

"And warmer!" Elizabeth added, drawing her fur coat tightly around her. "November isn't the best month for travelling."

"Hope you get back before darkness falls, it may be foggy this evening," Molly warned, and placing her arm round Elizabeth's waist she gave her a quick hug. "It is good of you to go with him, darling, gives me a break."

"I shall enjoy the change of scenery," Elizabeth said, and to herself, 'anything to be away from Miles.'

"Ah, here's Nurse with your father." Placing a restraining hand on Elizabeth's arm, Molly smiled. "Nicholson will transfer him to the car. You look tired, darling, sure you're all right?"

Elizabeth nodded and gave her a convincing smile, and stooped to kiss Serena before going to the waiting car.

"Elizabeth, you're miles away!" James laughed as they drove along. "Yes, miles away – away from Miles." Seeing her blank expression he said, "Just my little joke."

"Oh," Elizabeth responded absently, her attention on the dull skies that hung heavily over the bare fields.

"I hear a German bomber crashed at Appleton le Moors," he continued. "Day before yesterday, I believe, the tenth."

"Oh yes," she murmured without real interest, her eyes still glued to the wintry scene.

James reached for her hand and, finding her fingers tightly clenched, commented with concern, "I say, Elizabeth, you're hands are like ice!"

"I forgot my gloves," she confessed with a quick smile. "You know how it is, rushing around, preparing breakfast, Serena to dress...."

"Breakfast?" James frowned. "You, preparing breakfast?"

"For Mrs Grant, I couldn't leave without, and it takes time for her to eat."

"But the staff, surely there was someone there?"

Elizabeth hesitated before she admitted, "There's only the daily, I can't expect her to cook as well."

"But I thought..." James began, squeezing her hand as he remarked, "Little wonder you look tired. I understand Miles is not too well this morning."

Her head averted, she merely nodded.

"Nothing serious, I hope?"

"No, nothing serious."

"Darling," he said tentatively, "is something troubling you?"

She drew her hand away to make a negative sign, but he caught sight of the single teardrop, glistening in the light as it fell onto the lapel of her coat.

"Would it make it any easier if you told me?" he pressed gently. "A problem shared, you know..."

She shook her head, saying chokingly. "Please, Daddy, I'd rather not talk about it..."

"Very well, darling," he murmured as he sought her hand to tuck it under the rug, "I'll say no more."

Remembering he had problems of his own, she made an effort to smile as she turned to him to remark, "Your grip is getting stronger, the exercises seem to be working."

"Considering it's going on for four years since it happened, I've not made much progress," he said despondently, "but your mother insists I keep it up."

"Daddy, you must!" she exclaimed passionately. "Great strides have been made in the field of medicine and new techniques are being discovered. You mustn't give up hope."

He smiled. "Exactly what your mother says. You're beginning to sound just like her."

"Even one of those modern wheel-chairs would make a difference, something you could propel yourself. I do hope the specialist can advise us."

"We'll see," he said, his smile fading, "we'll see."

* *

From the expression on Miles' face, Elizabeth knew he wasn't in the best of moods. "Where the hell have you been until now?" he demanded immediately she entered the room. "Mother's been knocking, she'll be wanting her tea."

"Oh really, Miles, you could at least have made a pot of tea," she admonished as she slipped off her headscarf and coat. "Anyway, considering the signposts have been removed, plus the fog, we're back in reasonable time."

"A bloody waste of time if you ask me." he said with a curl of his lip.

"Miles, please," she beseeched in a hushed voice.

Serena had been looking from one to the other and Elizabeth saw her face begin to crumple.

"Go to your room, darling, take off your coat and shoes whilst Mummy prepares tea," she suggested, forcing a smile.

"Not for me," Miles grunted. "I'm going out."

"Don't you think you ought to eat something first?"

"No I bloody well don't," he replied harshly, jerking to his feet. "I had a late lunch."

"As you wish," conceded Elizabeth, attributing his truculent mood to the empty whisky bottle on the sideboard.

"And don't make any plans for tomorrow," he said, flinging on his jacket, "Mother wants taking to the bank."

"So, you've finally persuaded her."

"Why the hell not, she can't take it with her!" He gave a humourless laugh. "No pockets in a shroud, as they say."

"Depends what you have in mind for it," she returned shrewdly. "It worries me to see you drinking so much."

"For Christ's sake, Elizabeth, not again!"

"But you'll make yourself ill. Try to cut down."

"No woman is going to dictate to me," he thundered, "and if you don't like it, you can bugger off!"

Sending the door clattering back on its hinges, he left the room. Elizabeth sighed; there's nothing more I'd like to do, she thought sadly as the front door crashed behind him. Just Serena and me, and...

Her heart gave a curious jolt as, for the umpteenth time that day, Maurici entered her thoughts. "I wish you were here," she groaned softly as her daughter came rushing back.

"Tea, Mummy?" Serena persisted, tugging at her skirt.

"Yes, darling," she said automatically, her thoughts faraway as she picked up the child to hug her to her bosom.

Looking into her daughter's beautiful dark eyes, she saw Maurici's warm gaze. Stifling a sob, she closed her eyes; what a fool she had been to marry Miles.

Seated before the fire at Woodington Hall, James warmed his hands while Molly poured tea.

"Was it so cold, darling?" she asked with concern, setting a cup and saucer within her husband's reach.

"Extremely," he told her, "the specialist's private rooms were poorly heated, and when one is pretty well naked it's hardly the most desirable situation."

She smiled. "Tell me what he had to say," she encouraged, taking a chair opposite. "Does he think there's any improvement since last you visited?"

"Very little," he replied, "though he's pleased with the condition of my skin – no pressure sores – and the fact there has been no recurrence of the old infection in my water-works."

"It was considered bad policy to allow a patient to develop sores, so once they decided it wouldn't harm to move you, I remembered my old matron's words. 'Turn the patient nurse, and keep turning,' is what she used to say."

James managed a smile. "Sounds like an ox on a spit!"

She laughed. "He sounds less pessimistic about your condition than some of the doctors we've seen, but Alex's strict observation of aseptic precautions account for much of your progress. He's been most encouraging throughout."

"So he has. The specialist noted I've built up muscle power, prescribes swimming, but there's no hope of getting back on my feet."

"I'm inclined to be slightly more optimistic than he," she said gently. "A lot of research is being done regarding injuries such as yours, and all as a result of the war."

"True," he agreed, meeting Molly's look of concern. "I won't let it get me down again."

"That's my James," she said, reaching for his hand as she reflected upon the anger and frustration he had endured during the first years of his disablement.

"By the way, he mentioned a firm who manufacture chairs," he said more brightly. "Costs are rather high, but it will give me more independence."

"That's wonderful, darling! Elizabeth would be pleased."

James frowned. "I'm not so sure, she seems preoccupied with her own troubles at present."

Molly shot him a glance. "To which troubles are you referring?"

He wrinkled his nose. "She declined to say, but seemed very tense – worried in case we were late back – and the clothing coupons you gave her for shopping are in my pocket still as we returned immediately my appointment was over."

"I see, then do you think she was worried about Miles?"

"I don't think it was that which concerned her so much as being late home," he said, and concluded, "Perhaps I'll have a word with Miles, maybe he can tell us what's wrong."

Chapter 18

Molly cast her daughter a worried glance. "Why, darling? Are you not happy?"

Elizabeth lifted a tear-stained face. "I can't live with him a moment longer, he's impossible!"

"But you've been married only a few years..."

"Four actually, and that's too long. He's forever drunk, and poor Serena gets terribly upset when he shouts at her." She closed her eyes a moment to continue more calmly, "It was stupid of me to marry Miles."

Molly leaned forward to capture her daughter's unhappy gaze, her eyebrows lifting as she asked quietly, "Was it because of Serena?"

Lowering her eyes, Elizabeth nodded. "You knew Miles wasn't her father, didn't you?"

"We guessed," Molly admitted. "She's a pretty child, as you were, but with those beautiful dark eyes, and her smile, she's the image of her father."

Elizabeth looked up. "You never mentioned it before."

"And you gave up waiting for a word from Spain?"

"I was pregnant, I had to do something!"she cried. "I had no reply to my letters, no word from him or Enric. Now I'm trapped in this farce of a marriage."

Molly reached out to her. "You married merely to save your reputation and that of the coming baby?"

Elizabeth glanced away. "I know, it was wrong of me. But Miles was determined and eventually I discovered why," she said dismally. "If marriage was the only way to release his inheritance, then marry he would."

Molly let out a long breath. "Then I suppose the only solution is to move out. But I hope you've considered it carefully, made no rash decisions."

"For the past few weeks I've done little else," she said, her mouth quivering. "Now he's hinting at my bank account, I'll lose the little independence I have."

"My father intended it to be yours, Elizabeth."

She spread her hands despairingly. "That's not how Miles views it. I've got to get away."

"Would you consider coming home – to the Hall I mean?"

"No, I couldn't. I love you and Daddy dearly, but Grandmother won't hear a word against Miles." She brightened a little to continue, "There's a house for sale in the Gazette, four beds, two reception, garage, and central heating... all for under three thousand. Reasonable, I thought."

Molly smiled. "You've already decided?"

"It's Ashdale House, I expect you know it, not far from the Hall."

As she babbled on about the house and its attributes, Molly saw her smile, the first she'd seen in ages. "So, you've made a decision. Does Miles know?"

Elizabeth's expression changed.

* *

Carmen glanced up, anxious. "What is it, Maurici, something is wrong?"

"To the contrary," he said, containing his own pleasure as he watched for her reaction. "You are to realise your dearest wish, but first you must guess what it is."

"Oh Maurici, don't tease," she gave him a playful slap. "Is it a new oven?"

"No, though we will have a new oven soon. Guess again."

"I can't!" she wailed. "Does *papa* know?"

He grinned. "No, not yet."

"And Dolors – does she know?"

"*Si,* she was the first to know..." he began and saw her expression change.

"A baby!" she cried, clasping his hands. "My first grandchild! Oh, my son, you have made me so happy!" Her smile was tearful. "When is it due?"

"November, soon after our first anniversary," he told her, then more seriously, "Dolors is feeling a bit wretched in the mornings so I think we should make allowances and prepare breakfast for ourselves."

The *senyora* nodded. "You know, son, I'm glad you decided against going abroad, we would have missed all this if you hadn't married."

"Hardly decided against it," he replied. "If you recall, permission to travel was refused."

She gave him an odd look and struggled from her chair, bustling into the kitchen to take Dolors in a warm embrace.

* *

In July of nineteen forty-three, the purchase of Ashdale House was completed. Elizabeth and Serena moved into their new home. When first her intention had been mentioned, Miles had caused a terrible scene. His father also had been annoyed to hear the news and his mother had wept which made Elizabeth sad. But it was Serena's happiness she must consider as it was obvious Miles' unreasonable behaviour caused the child distress.

Elizabeth had engaged old Thomas, Pincott's predecessor, also Gladys Chapman who felt honoured to serve the granddaughter of the late Mr William. Then she set about furnishing the house, using a considerable sum from her legacy to make a comfortable home. Her first visitor was Alex Wilson who called to enquire after Serena who was occupied picking daisies on the lawn.

"She's very settled here," Elizabeth told him as they took seats on the garden bench. "Sleeps well, no more nightmares, and she has a huge appetite."

Alex smiled his approval, but his expression grew serious when he asked, "But what is to become of Miles?"

Elizabeth glared at him from beneath the wide brim of her straw hat, her blue eyes darkening. "If that is the reason you called, you're wasting your time."

He nodded towards Serena. "I think you should have told him the truth about her, if you don't mind my saying."

"Yes, I do mind!" she repudiated indignantly and saw his colour rise. "If I had, what difference would it have made?"

"Quite frankly, you appeared to marry simply for the child's sake which must have upset poor Miles."

"Poor Miles? Let me enlighten you, Alex. Miles Grant wouldn't take no for an answer and only after we had married did I learn the reason why."

Alex's brows rose expectantly and she continued without reserve. "It's poor Miles this, poor Miles that – don't you think you should consider my feelings?"

"Certainly," he conceded quietly, flicking a speck from the sleeve of his dark suit, "but he is my patient."

"I suppose you may as well know, perhaps then you'll understand why I get so cross about it." She leaned back on the seat. "Miles stood to inherit a great deal of money, but only on the day of his marriage. I wouldn't have known if his aunt hadn't told me, Miles never spoke of it, so I'm not entirely to blame."

Alex screwed up his mouth before responding. "I see, so Serena isn't the cause of trouble between you?"

She gave a humourless laugh. "No, money is all Miles cares about."

"His mother seemed to think it was," Alex confided. "She thought a baby three months premature would have stood little chance of survival."

Elizabeth shrugged, her slender finger absently tracing the flowers on the skirt of her summer dress. "Maybe," she agreed, "though she and I always got on very well, but I worry about her having Miles around, especially when he's drunk."

"Yet, without you he's likely to get worse," he commented as he picked up the ball Serena had tossed at his feet.

"And when the money runs out," Elizabeth put in bitterly. I don't know if you realise, his mother also transferred a considerable sum into his account and that is dwindling fast."

"Good Lord, as bad as that!" he exclaimed, throwing the ball in Serena's direction. "I think I'd better have a word with him, otherwise his health is going to suffer."

"I'm afraid it's hopeless, which is why I left. I'd even thought of joining the forces but I couldn't leave her," she ended, gazing fondly in Serena's direction.

Alex shot her an amused glance. "You, in the forces?"

"Why not?" she asked with a lift of her chin, "If Princess Elizabeth can do it, so can I!" and holding onto her hat she looked up to the cloudless sky to add thoughtfully, "You know, if Miles hadn't been exempt from army service he may have never got into this state."

"Perhaps," he said, rising to his feet as Serena rushed over the lawn towards them. "Nevertheless, I'm sorry you felt it necessary to leave him."

"Lifting the child onto her knee, Elizabeth tilted her head to ask, "Will you stay for tea, Alex?" Adding wryly, "I expect we can discuss the latest news without arguing, and I'd like your views on Daddy's progress."

Alex looked down to see the appealing picture they presented; Elizabeth's beautiful face framed by the brim of her hat, and Serena's dark ringlets tumbling from beneath the organdie sun-hat she wore. Two pairs of smiling eyes, sapphire blue and deep velvet brown, melting the unexpected anger he had felt over Elizabeth's attitude. She had changed, grown up before he'd realised, displaying a maturity that came with experience of life.

* *

Shading his eyes against the glare of the late August sun, Maurici surveyed the ripening crop. Colour was appearing in the red grapes, they were full and juicy and showed promise of the good harvest his father predicted. Now retired from manual work, Josep had kept an interest in the progress of the vineyard, tutoring his son and nephew in the techniques of the grower from his vast store of experience.

"We'll show a profit this year," he told them, indicating the rows of fruit-laden vines with a wave of his stick."

"Profit, for whom?" Maurici heard his cousin mutter. Shooting Lluis a hard glance he fell into step beside him.

"For us all, which means you keep your job," he told him shortly, moving on in the footsteps of his father, along the dusty track towards the house.

Their afternoon meal was already on the table when the two younger men had finished scrubbing themselves at the stone sink. And Dolors' dark eyes were flashing as she ladled bean stew into their bowls.

"It was ready ages ago," she complained, the ladle clattering against the earthenware dish.

"I'm sorry, Dolors," said Maurici, attributing her irritability to her condition.

"It is annoying, I know," Carmen sympathised, casting a smile in her daughter-in-law's direction, "but they work hard, let them eat in peace."

Dolors flopped heavily onto her chair, her shoulders drooping. "It's this heat," she sighed, "it gets me down."

Maurici smiled at her. "You rest this afternoon. I will clear this away."

Carmen winced, easing herself into a better position. "If it wasn't for my old bones, I would allow no man in my kitchen."

After the meal was over, Maurici ushered his wife towards the stairs. "Go up and rest," he directed firmly, "we can manage here..." He hesitated as she reached for the banister rail to heave herself up the steps, frowning when he saw the swelling around her ankles. Taking her arm to help her up to their room, he waited whilst she eased off her canvas shoes, noting the indentation they left behind. Complications associated with pregnancy were not a subject he had studied in depth, yet he couldn't help but feel concern, certain his wife should seek professional advice.

"Your feet are very swollen today," he commented as she reclined on the bed. "You should mention it to the doctor."

Dolors laughed, brushing aside his concern. "In my state, every woman's feet swell. It's the heat."

"But you must mention it when you visit?" he persisted, pressing gently on the puffy flesh. "In fact, I suggest you call on the doctor tomorrow. I'll go with you if you wish?"

"No, no, you have work to do here, I will ask my mother to accompany me."

"Good, I shall feel happier if you do. Meanwhile, you must rest more often, and with your feet raised."

"Such a fuss," she protested. "My mother says hers were the same when she was carrying."

Maurici smiled down at her and sighed. "Please, Dolors, for me and the baby, yes? Do it for our sake."

* *

How perfectly sweet," Molly whispered, gazing down on the sleeping Serena.

"Quite angelic," Elizabeth agreed, "but only because Thomas bribed her with a story. He's an absolute treasure."

"Certainly more obliging than Pincott," Molly remarked, gazing absently at the grubby teddy bear, chuckling as she disclosed, "Mother wasn't aware of it, but he used to place bets for your grandpa, on the horses, you know..."

"You mean, Thomas acted as his runner?"

Molly shrugged. "I couldn't say, he usually went on his bicycle ..." She paused as Elizabeth started to giggle.

"Sorry," said Elizabeth, stifling her laughter. "Grandmother would have been furious if she'd known. "Financial security is so important to her, yet money can't buy happiness."

Molly could guess the content of Elizabeth's thoughts and reached out to clasp her hand. "Why don't we take a glass of sherry until Thomas returns with your father?"

Elizabeth peered through the window. "Dusk already," she commented closing the blackout curtain before putting on the light. "The cricket match should be over by now."

"I expect they're having a drink in the club bar," Molly chuckled as she poured the wine. "Now James covers the sports features for the local paper, in addition to his report for the daily, he'll be busy taking down results."

"I'm glad he's got more work, increases his independence."

"Yes, he needs the challenge, it's been so beneficial."

"You know, Miles always dismissed the possibility of Daddy working," Elizabeth reflected with a vague smile. "I'm pleased he's proved him wrong." Gazing at the pale, dry wine in her glass, she murmured, "This takes me back. I wonder what he's doing now?"

"Who?" asked Molly. "Do you mean Miles?"

Elizabeth's eyes rolled to the ceiling. "Good Lord, no, I was referring to the sherry, I meant Maurici."

"Oh, I see," her mother said with a twinge of discomfort as she took a sip from her glass.

"Do you still correspond with Enric," she asked, relaxing on the settee.

"Occasionally, though I usually leave it to your father."

"I believe I told you, I wrote to him a couple of times, after we came back to England, but never received a reply."

"Perhaps he had no news at the time, assuming you were asking about Maurici. It was a year later when we learned the reason for his sudden disappearance. By then you'd married so it wouldn't have made any difference."

"No," Elizabeth replied tonelessly, "I suppose not."

"But you have something to be thankful for, Serena's a lovely child."

Elizabeth smiled. "I wonder what he would think if he knew he had a daughter – Maurici, I mean."

Molly drew in an uncertain breath. "I don't know what his private thoughts would be," she said at last, "but it could be embarrassing. Perhaps you should know, according to Enric, Maurici married towards the end of last year."

* *

Carmen Bachs hovered agitatedly behind her son's chair as he gulped down the coffee she'd made, longing to gather him in her arms with words of comfort to take the sorrow from his eyes. "Maybe when you go back," she began tentatively, "the doctor will have better news."

Maurici lifted a haggard face in her direction. "Too late," he said hollowly "She is not fully conscious, little can be done to save her now..."

"The doctor has told you this? But you did not say anything when you came back this morning."

"I don't need the doctor to tell me, mama, I could see for myself," he said wearily, resting his head in his hands. "Her symptoms, I should have known, they all pointed to albuminuria. If only she'd done as I asked."

"But you weren't to know she hadn't visited the doctor," she consoled. "You thought all was well. Dolors told you it was, you couldn't have known."

"I shouldn't have listened, I should have gone with her, insisted on tests and seen the results for myself."

"Dolors is a grown woman, Maurici, you couldn't treat her as a child. And those fits, whatever you call them, could our doctor have cured her of those?"

"Eclampsia?" He shook his head. "It would not have reached that stage if earlier tests had been made." Sighing, he rose to his feet, knowing he couldn't delay the journey back to Barcelona. He glanced at the clock – it was nearly midday – the operation on Dolors would be almost over by now.

Even though he had prepared for the worst, Maurici was stunned to learn Dolors had died. However kindly the surgeon spoke, it didn't lessen the shock. And now, as he followed the nurse who was to take him to his wife's deathbed, the words of the surgeon returned to persecute his numbed mind: 'Your wife didn't recover consciousness after the caesarean delivery of a premature male child'. It had been too late to save Dolors, only the child had survived.

His fists clenched at his sides; he had a son, yet he felt no joy over this new life, just a heavy sadness for the one which had been taken away.

In a small room away from the ward, the nurse drew aside the curtain to allow him access to the bed where Dolors now lay. As he gazed down on his wife's still features the nurse withdrew, murmuring something about taking him to the nursery as she closed the curtain behind him.

Puzzled for a moment, then he remembered he had a baby to consider. Would he be expected to take it home? But he couldn't take a baby in a sidecar he thought irrationally, Dolors' pale face a blur before his eyes. A shuddering breath tore through his chest as his throat constricted on a gasping sob. "*Dolors, amor meu,* why didn't you tell me..." he wept as he stroked her faintly warm but motionless hands. "Dolors," he continued brokenly, his cheek against the still fingers, "why...?" He ended on another choking breath and leaned over to kiss her forehead, suddenly aware of the shaft of weak November sunlight sliding across the room.

He turned to see the nurse, her expression apologetic, and Dolors' parents, heads bowed, following behind. Wiping away his tears, he took one last look at his wife's lifeless form before he went to clasp his mother-in-law in an emotional embrace. Out in the courtyard, he smoked a cigarette, drawing a certain comfort from the strong tobacco as he tried to reconcile himself with Dolors' death. He should have checked with the family doctor, accompanied her there, and insisted on seeing the results of her tests. After all, even though she had begged him for a child, he was responsible. But this child he had fathered, somehow he didn't think he could face seeing it, not yet. He then suffered further pangs of guilt; he couldn't blame the baby, it was something he had to do. And when the nurse knocked on the window, beckoning him indoors, he flicked away the half-smoked cigarette and followed her down the corridor.

The cot in which his child lay was set slightly aside from the others and the soft whimpering noises coming from it sent a stab of pain through his heart. He looked down on the perfect features of his new-born son, its head thickly covered in fine, dark hair. Almost three kilos, the nurse had told him, and he thought of Dolors, of how proud she would have been. Then, for a few curious moments, the baby reminded him of the one he had delivered near the Ebre battle-field a few years ago but, unlike his son, it had lost the fight, its precious life snatched away. And it was as these memories filtered into his mind that he felt a sudden surge of affection for his child, and a strong determination to care for its every need. He recalled the surgeon asking if he had chosen a name for the baby and had decided right away; Jaume, the name of his late grandfather, and the Catalan equivalent of James.

* *

"You know, darling," said James, "I feel strangely relieved to know Elizabeth and Serena are at Ashdale."

"Sad, isn't it," Molly began vaguely, when he shot her an enquiring look. "About the young doctor, I mean, he hadn't deserted her as we thought."

"But now he's married I think we should forget about him. And so should Elizabeth if she has any sense."

Molly gave a despairing shrug. "With Serena there to remind her it's unlikely she'll ever forget."

James looked faintly alarmed. "I know, but I don't want her pining for something that cannot be, particularly now her marriage has failed. There again, Miles would not be my choice of husband – if I were a woman, that is."

Molly smiled. "Nor mine," she said, "though my mother once suggested I consider him. He's only a year younger than I, but my father forbade it."

"And now look what you're lumbered with," he said, his smile fading, "a penniless cripple…"

"James, enough!" She reached out to grip his hand. "No matter what, I still love you."

"But will you love me when this place is buzzing with army personnel?"

"I will," she assured him, giggling as she added, "Though you can never tell with Mother. Naturally, she'll only allow officers to be billeted in the house."

James' manner brightened. "Poor old Jane, she stuck out against the army requisitioning part of the house until now, but at least I'll get to know what's happening. The last real news I had was months ago when I managed a chat with that pilot who told me about the raids last August, when Hamburg was almost wiped out."

"When you were doing a stint of plane-watching, you mean? Well, I'm sure you'll get plenty more of that, but now there are no signposts I don't want you and Nicholson lost. The moors can be treacherous at night.

"Don't worry, the Home Guard will show us the way, they're usually about."

"You know, darling, we've been extremely fortunate," she said. "Except for the odd incendiary bomb on the moor, and the bombing of York station last year, we hardly know anything of the war. I feel guilty when I hear of people living in towns, many injured, homes destroyed, the hospitals overflowing..." She paused a moment to add softly, "like Barcelona all over again."

* *

It was the old village midwife who came to Can Bachs to offer help with the baby's daily care a short time after Maurici brought him home. His mother coped wonderfully, but he could see it was tiring for her, and on this particular afternoon, he had insisted she rest whilst he fed and nursed Jaume, now five weeks old. He, also, was beginning to find his new responsibilities quite wearing, particularly if the baby woke in the night. But his father was understanding and in the early mornings took his place in the vineyard. Thankfully, in December things were quiet.

Placing Jaume in the midwife's arms, he went to pour her a glass of wine. The woman chuckled and gently rocked the baby until he fell asleep.

"He's perfect," she said, tilting her glass, "just like you were at this age."

Maurici had thought the child had a look of Dolors, her mouth and the dark, curly hair. Nevertheless, he smiled and offered to take the sleeping child.

"*No, no, no*, leave him with me," she cooed, "poor motherless little mite."

It was almost as if she had struck Maurici. His head jerked up, his eyes filled with pain as he uttered harshly, "I don't need reminding of that!"

The woman was instantly contrite. "*Ai, senyor,* I did not intend to distress you. I speak only with sympathy."

Realising he was being over sensitive, he nodded. "Such a waste of life," he said at last. "Dolors need not have died. If only she had done as I advised, let the doctor examine her instead of pretending everything was all right."

The old woman remained silent, allowing him to release his distress.

"I suspected something was wrong but she insisted the doctor had assured her everything was fine," he continued, his eyes fixed on the sleeping child. "I blame myself, I should have gone with her, then I would have known..." He broke off and crossed to the window, tears welling in his eyes.

The midwife clicked her tongue. "You shouldn't blame yourself. Such torment is not good for you, or the baby."

"Forgive me," Maurici said shortly, returning to his seat. "I didn't intend to burden you with my troubles."

The woman gave a knowing nod. "Perhaps I can salve your guilt before this burden becomes too great to bear."

Maurici cocked an eyebrow in her direction. "What do you suggest?" he asked with a derisive curl of his lip. "I take to the wine?"

"Such a thought never entered my mind, *senyor*, but there is something about Dolors it may help you to know."

He straightened. "What can you possibly know that will help me?"

She took a steadying breath and glanced down at the baby in her arms. "May God forgive me, I swore to her I would never speak of this," she began, lifting her eyes to Maurici, "but I cannot bear to see your distress when I know her death was through no fault of yours."

"What can you possibly know that I don't?" he asked on a bitter note.

"I've known Dolors all her life – I delivered her into this world – and God knows she was not a sinner. No, poor Dolors fell to the devil..."

Maurici's patience broke. "For God's sake, woman, if you have something to say, say it!"

Ignoring his outburst, the midwife's voice didn't waver as she said, "The devil took her in the last year of the Civil War – a Republican soldier – she was raped during a raid and miscarried the baby five months later."

Maurici gaped at her as though she'd taken leave of her senses. "Dolors – raped by a soldier – you are sure?"

"Of course I'm sure!" the woman cried raucously, "I attended her, I saw the result of that maniac's doings!" She shook her head sadly, lowering her voice. "I saw the misshapen creature that came from her womb before its time."

"*Déu meu!*" he exclaimed, rousing his son to whimper. "If this is true..."

"Do you think I would lie about something like that?"

He put out a hand to quell her indignation. "No, no," he said, "but why did she not tell me this herself?"

"Did you not realise she wasn't a virgin?"

"Well yes – no, I mean..." he began, avoiding the woman's piercing gaze. "I assumed..."

"And that is precisely what worried her – she feared losing you. She avoided an examination by the doctor because you are friendly with him and she feared you would learn of her previous pregnancy."

"But it wasn't her fault, I'd have understood, she could have told me."

"It is not something a woman speaks freely about, particularly to a man," the midwife said. "Usually, in my experience, where rape is concerned, women are not considered blameless, there's always that seed of doubt. Only because you have medical training did I dare speak on this shameful subject."

"A great pity I didn't mention my concern to you two or three months ago, she may have listened to you then."

"Had I not been staying in Tarragona with my ailing sister I would have seen her condition for myself," she sighed. "Yes, Dolors would have listened to me. I was the only one who knew her secret. Her own mother never learnt of it so I hope I can count on you to let it die with her."

"You can trust me," he agreed. "Although it has explained a lot, I deeply regret my wife's passing." He hid his face in his hands as he hissed savagely, "While Dolors lies cold in the cemetery, some bastard of a rapist goes free!"

The woman reached for his hand as she advised, "No, he's not free, God will punish him for what he has done." And gently transferring the waking baby into Maurici's arms, she smiled and added, "But you have a healthy son to care for, you are blessed."

Chapter 19

Maurici peeped round the door of his son's bedroom. "*Hola,* Jaume!" he called and went in to open the shutters. "Who is two years old today, heh?"

"Me!" the small boy cried joyfully, leaping from his bed to be scooped up in Maurici's arms. "Me is two, *papa.*"

Showering the child with noisy kisses, Maurici wrapped a shawl over the boy's nightwear. He could feel the warmth of Juame's squirming body as he held him close, his childish laughter only ceasing when they came to the gilt-framed portrait of Dolors which hung at the foot of the staircase.

"*Mama* sleeping," Jaume said, pointing a chubby finger at his mother's likeness. Maurici lingered, giving the child an opportunity to study the portrait; today was not only Jaume's second birthday, but also the anniversary of Dolors' death when they would go to the cemetery to place fresh flowers in the entrance to the niche where she had been laid to rest.

The silence was broken by the tap of the *senyora's* stick as she came from the kitchen. "*Si,* Jaume, *mama* sleeps with the angels," she said, pausing beside them, the appetizing aroma of freshly baked bread following in her wake.

Jaume's attention was quickly diverted by the prospect of breakfast, and the hot, crusty bread. Seating himself at the table, Maurici took the child on his knee. He thought it wiser to save the surprise, a small wooden dog his father had carved, for after they had eaten when it would keep Jaume occupied until the time came to join Dolors' parents at the village church.

"Two years old," Josep chuckled, giving his grandson a playful prod. "How time flies!"

Maurici nodded yet, unlike his father, he found there were times when the hours dragged by. After Dolors died he'd devoted all his spare time to his son and, although he dearly loved the child, he was beginning to feel there was something lacking in his life. He missed the company of his contemporaries, had begun to yearn for the stimulating atmosphere he remembered from medical school. There were times when he regretted not returning to his studies. He'd read of a great discovery, a new drug which had successfully treated thousands of soldiers in the past two years, men who would otherwise have died. He reflected sadly upon the wounded he had attended in the Civil War – many with no alternative to amputation, some too badly injured to be saved – regretting this miracle drug, Penicillin, had not been available to him then.

It was his son's demanding cry that drew his attention and he saw that Jaume had dropped his bread. "Uhuh, it's dirty," he warned. "We will give it to the chickens."

"If you give it to the chickens, they will give you a nice brown egg," the *senyora* comforted, seeing the child's lip quiver. "Here, I'll get you another," she offered, dipping a second crust into the earthenware honey jar. Chortling with delight, Jaume crammed it into his mouth.

"The child is hungry!" Carmen cried, breaking off more bread. "Today he shall have what he wants."

"Providing he isn't sick in church," warned Maurici, ruffling the crumbs out of his son's dark curls.

"Give him to me," Carmen said, dabbing a corner of her handkerchief on her tongue.

"No need, *mama*. I will wash him and put on his new outfit which Lluis brought yesterday."

"Your aunt Elvira is gifted," Carmen remarked. "It takes a good needlewoman to make a child's suit from an old coat."

"Not so old," Maurici corrected her. "It was purchased just before our wedding, when good clothing was hard to find." He smiled to himself, recollecting the day it was bought. He'd persuaded Dolors it suited her; a dark blue coat in a style similar to that Elizabeth had worn when first they met.

He uttered a soft sigh. Elizabeth, there she was again, invading his thoughts at the most unexpected times, perhaps more noticeably so since the news of Great Britain's victory over Germany in May.

"Ah, yes," Carmen began, rousing Maurici from his thoughts, "your father tells me things are not going favourably for his brother at present."

Maurici glanced up to enquire, "Poor crop, you mean?"

"Worse than that," his father replied. "A number of their fruit trees are diseased, one orchard must be cleared. It has come as quite a blow."

"Indeed, it would," agreed Maurici. "It will be some time before new trees produce a reasonable crop."

Josep shook his head. "It has never been very productive, the frosts in forty-two didn't help, and now my brother has had enough. But I've had an idea..."

He stopped speaking suddenly when Carmen gave an ear-piercing shriek.

"He's got my earring!" she cried, making a grab for Jaume's sticky fingers which were fastened round one of the gold pendants.

Maurici reached over to loosen Jaume's grip but, enjoying the commotion, the child made a second grab. Quickly distancing the giggling child from reach of his grandmother's ears, Maurici uttered an impatient sigh. "If you will react like that, *mama*, he'll do it all the more." And returning his attention to his father, he asked, "What was it you were saying about Uncle Miquel?"

"Later. It is impossible to discuss anything just now," said Josep with an indulgent smile for his grandson. "Let the boy have his present."

Maurici glanced at the clock. "You're right, he can play until it is time to get ready for church."

"I'm so pleased you've gone back to the church," his mother smiled. "Prayer will have been a great help to you during these past two years."

He gave a thoughtful shrug. "At least your prayers were answered, *mama*, you have a grandson," he said, ending almost inaudibly, "whereas, I doubt there ever will be an answer to mine."

* *

"This is not a permanent arrangement," Elizabeth said after Miles reeled off a list of items he wanted brought to Ashdale

House. "I want your ration book, of course, but you won't need outdoor clothes until you go back home."

"Surely you don't expect me to stay in bed all the time," Miles complained. "Thomas will have to help me downstairs."

"He'll do no such thing," she contradicted firmly. "He's far too old to lift anyone as heavy as you."

"My God, it's like being in one of those German prison camps we hear about," he grumbled. "I can't think what sort of Christmas this will be."

She cast him a withering glance. "You'll be on your feet again by then."

"I doubt it; Alex told me it will be six to eight weeks before I can put my weight on this ankle."

"Nonsense, it isn't broken, a couple of weeks should be enough."

"Good God, woman, you've grown bloody hard-hearted!"

She gave a short laugh. "It wasn't my idea to bring you here."

"Ah, well, if that is how it's going to be," he said with an exaggerated sigh, "put a bottle of whisky on the list."

"Certainly not! It won't agree with your medication."

He put on a hurt expression. "I'm still your husband, don't forget."

"Forget!" she echoed shrilly. "I wish to hell I could!"

When Doctor Wilson called later in the day Elizabeth left him to find his own way to the room Miles was occupying, asking him to call in the sitting room afterwards.

"He's remarkably cheerful even though he's in a lot of pain," Alex commented as he added a little water to the whisky in his glass. "Considering Miles is an expert horseman, I'm surprised he took such a heavy fall."

"An expert liar, I think you mean," Elizabeth rejoined, and with an edge of scepticism to her voice continued, "He tells me you expect the ankle to take a couple of months to heal."

"Good Lord no! A month at the most."

"Exactly, so he needn't think he's staying on here."

Alex gave a faint smile. "Perhaps it's his way of trying to bring about a reconciliation..."

"Out of the question!" she cut in with a short laugh. "Remember what happened on V E Day? He soon reverted to his old ways. In fact, I suspect he was drunk this morning, the reason he fell from his horse."

"You may be right," he granted, "but you must feel some sympathy for him to have taken him in like this."

"No, Alex, merely a sense of duty towards someone to whom I'm legally tied, nothing more. His mother couldn't cope."

"Pity," he said softly, "I had hoped..."

"A pity! Have you tried living with someone like Miles? Have you ever had to put up with not knowing what sort of mood they'll be in? No, Alex, I don't think you have, and my sympathy is wearing very thin."

Alex looked thoughtful as he swirled his drink round the glass. "No," he admitted finally, "I haven't, but I'm convinced you are the only one who can help him recover from his addiction. There are places where he can get help of course, but he denies he has a problem." Studying her expression, he went on to add, "He says you use it as an excuse to avoid your, er, wifely duties."

She spilled a little of her drink. "What! Quite frankly, wifely duties, as you put it, are the least of my problems. In fact, thank God, they don't exist!"

"Could be the reason he drinks," he responded quietly.

"No, you're quite wrong. Miles rarely wanted me in the way you suggest." Her eyes downcast, she added quietly, "He never was the most romantic of partners, alcohol takes first place in his affections."

"Good of you to be so frank," he said, draining his glass. "If Miles would be as frank with me, I could do more to help you both."

"Help Miles, don't you mean?"

He met her gaze with slight reproach. "If he were more sober, would it change the way you feel about him?"

She gave a harsh laugh. "I couldn't arouse an ounce of affection for Miles if he stayed sober for the rest of his life."

* *

It was only days before Christmas when Lluis rode up on his motorcycle, his father seated on the pillion with tears streaming from his unprotected eyes. "You should wear goggles," Maurici advised as his uncle dismounted, wiping his jacket sleeve across his face.

"Lluis needed the only pair we possess," Miquel Bachs explained blindly.

"I have a spare pair," Maurici offered going to the building where his own motorcycle was housed. On a shelf, amongst oil cans and spanners, Maurici found the pair of goggles he'd not used in years. They were last worn when he drove Elizabeth here in the combination on the eve of nineteen thirty-nine. He pursed his lips thoughtfully as he polished the dusty lenses on a piece of khaki fabric he'd once used tied around his neck. An old khaki neckerchief, a pair of well-used goggles; just two more of those once-forgotten items which kept coming to his notice. He hesitated, deciding to exchange the old goggles for those he now used which were hanging on the handlebars of his motorcycle. Emerging from the shed he saw his father gesturing impatiently from the house.

Seated at the kitchen table, Josep addressed his younger brother. "Well, Miquel, I have discussed your proposal with Carmen and Maurici, and the conclusion we arrived at is this..." He paused to light a small cigar, savouring the flavour as he continued, "We will accept your offer, providing the work is not too much for Elvira." Josep raised a hand to halt his brother's words and went on to explain, "Carmen's arthritis bothers her these days, and there's Jaume to consider. Maurici is tied with the boy now, whereas he would prefer to give the business his full attention which would mean she'd also have Jaume under her feet. We have help in the house, of course, but Maurici insists we consider your wife's opinion of the proposed arrangement..."

"I already know what her opinion will be," Miquel interrupted confidently. "Only this morning she voiced her desire to spend time with the boy."

"He can be hard work," Maurici commented with a wry smile, "he's never still for a moment."

"But she has less years than your mother," Miquel reminded him, "and all women like caring for children, it's their main purpose in life."

"*Si*, but often they are expected to cope without regard for their health or age," Maurici pointed out. "They worked hard throughout the war years, gave up their food rations so their husbands and children would not go without. They were starved of proper nutrition..."

"You're not suggesting your Aunt is undernourished?" his uncle broke in coolly. "Elvira is a healthy woman, and strong, I can vouch for that."

"Forgive me, Uncle, I'm merely saying we shouldn't take them for granted."

Miquel shrugged and turned to Josep. "The young have such strange opinions. I suppose that's education for you."

Maurici stifled his annoyance but felt obliged to say, "During thirty-eight, I saw women weighted down with ailing children, elderly parents, queues, no bread or electricity. It made me realise how strong, yet vulnerable, they are."

"*Si*, Maurici, I agree, but we are going off the subject. If Elvira is sure, it is settled. Now production in the vineyard has increased, you have work, Miquel. We all benefit that way."

"I am grateful to you, Josep," Miquel smiled, rising from his chair. "I must go and tell Elvira the good news."

When his uncle left the room, Maurici hovered in the doorway, "There is just one other thing, *papa*," he began apprehensively. "I haven't mentioned this before as it was obvious you needed me here."

Josep raised his head, the beginnings of a smile deepening the lines on his face. "Speak up, son, tell me what it is you wish to say?"

"The fact is, I have a strong desire to return to medical school. I've made tentative enquiries and should I be considered would you have any objection?"

* *

"After the way Elizabeth behaved," Jane disputed as she and Molly faced each other across the breakfast table. "She seems to forget Miles is her husband."

"I see, so you would rather spend Christmas alone?" Molly retaliated. "If you won't have them here, James and I will spend Christmas at Ashdale House!"

"I still insist she should have allowed Miles to stay on. What will people think?" Jane clicked her tongue as she rose to go over to the window.

"What other people think is of no consequence, its Elizabeth's happiness we must consider," Molly argued. "She has given in to him more than once and he doesn't change. Remember last Christmas, he spent Boxing Day in a drunken stupor – was rude to the guests – and she fears it may happen again."

Jane swung round. "He's still a better choice than a low-class Spanish prisoner..."

"Oh, Mother, that's a stupid comparison to make."

"You must realise this puts me in a most difficult position. I don't want Miles to have the impression I'm encouraging Elizabeth away from him."

"But she's not living in the same house as Miles," Molly pointed out. "I thought you'd be delighted to spend Christmas with her and Serena – your great granddaughter, don't forget."

Jane uttered a drawn-out sigh. "Very well, I suppose I shall have to make allowances. Since the army have left the house seems so empty, somehow."

"This Christmas is rather special," Molly reminded her. "Our first in peacetime for almost six years." But as she was leaving the room something puzzled her. Her mother had used the term 'prisoner' when referring to Maurici, yet she had never discussed him in her presence so, how did she know?

* *

The coming of nineteen forty-six at Can Bachs was quite a jolly affair. Josep was enjoying an after-lunch cigar in the company of his brother, Miquel. In the next room their wives chattered and laughed more than they had in years. Young Jaume was spending the rest of the day with his maternal grandparents who were giving a party for the children. And Lluis decided to visit a friend in the village which left Maurici unexpectedly alone. At first he thought of getting out his old medical books, set aside during the war. But then he had a sudden urge to take a ride out to Sitges, a place he hadn't visited for over five years, not since the day Enric had given him the news from England – news of Elizabeth's marriage – the day he'd got terribly drunk.

So it was six years to the day since he had been taken prisoner during a mission to the front, he reflected; his aspirations to return to Elizabeth's arms that same day thwarted by his Nationalist captors when, instead of a beautiful young woman, only fleas had shared his bed.

Taking the country route to Sitges, he purchased two bottles of sparkling wine. The roads were quiet but the small seaside town was surprisingly lively with a number of restaurants open. He found Enric at home, peering into the gathering dusk until he recognised Maurici standing by the door.

"Won't you come in?" Enric welcomed him in Catalan..

"If I'm not intruding," Maurici replied, relaxing into the same language, and indicating the sidecar added, "I have with me a bottle or two."

"Then bring it in, we can toast the New Year together."

"*Gràcies*, Enric," said Maurici, crossing the threshold of the familiar little house, its furnishings unchanged since last he was here. "Still living alone, are you?" he asked with a smile. "No *senyora* Puig lurking in the kitchen?"

Enric chuckled. "The right woman has not yet come along," he said as he polished two glasses and set them on the table between them. His expression grew solemn. "But you, my friend, I hear you lost your dear wife. My belated condolences to you."

Maurici sighed. "*Sí*, it was very unfortunate, we were together little more than a year."

"So, you also are alone. What do you do with your days?"

Maurici compressed his lips and shrugged. "Not alone exactly," he said at last, "I have a very lively two year old son who takes much of my time."

"You should have brought the boy along."

"Today he is with relatives of my late wife," Maurici told him and went on to relate the unfortunate circumstances which had led to Dolors' death.

"So, you lost a dear wife, but God gave you a son," Enric observed thoughtfully. "A great consolation, I'm sure, but what of your career? Did you continue with your training?"

"I've been working in my father's vineyard," Maurici began, glancing towards the unopened bottle. "Let's have a drink and I'll tell you about it."

"A lively one," Enric remarked, the wine bubbling over as he withdrew the thick cork.

"The result of the journey," Maurici laughed. "I should have warned you."

"Salut" said Enric after an appreciative sip. "Now tell me, how are things with you?"

For the next hour they discussed the political situation, the continued repression in Spain, and the arrival of peace in Europe. With a surge of emotion, Maurici voiced his horror over the use of atomic bombs the previous year, the suffering they caused which had strengthened his desire to return to medicine. Unwilling to become too involved in such a depressing subject, Enric reserved his opinion and spoke of his work with a Barcelona newspaper.

"But I don't travel far these days," he said, adding with a wry smile, "particularly in hot weather." He shook his head and sighed. "I'll never forget what you did, my friend, and I'm convinced you'll make an excellent doctor."

Stimulated by their conversation, Maurici smiled yet, much as he would like to, he hesitated to ask about the Purcell family in England.

But it was not too long before the wine began to loosen Enric's tongue. He opened the second bottle, toasted Maurici afresh, then raised his glass to say, "And a toast to my good friends in England!"

"You still have contact?" Maurici queried tentatively, meeting Enric's bleary-eyed gaze.. "Yes, I hear from them occasionally. James is confined to a wheel-chair, though he manages to write for a local paper, and Molly has been involved in voluntary work – the war, you know – so they keep busy."

Maurici nodded, and drawing a quick breath, asked, "And Elizabeth, how is she?"

Enric smiled shrewdly as he refilled his glass. "You were very fond of that girl, I seem to remember..."

"Extremely," agreed Maurici, and with a lopsided grin, reminded his host, "But, if you recall, when I last visited, it was you who told me she'd married."

Enric spread his fleshy, uncalloused hands, his expression solemn as he went on to say, "Since then things have changed. I don't know if I understood James' letter correctly, but it seemed to me Elizabeth's marriage was suffering. She and her husband are living apart."

Maurici's reaction was immediate; his quick intake of breath as he swallowed a mouthful of wine brought on a fierce bout of coughing.

"Went the wrong way," he gasped, thumping himself on the chest as he struggled to recover. "Perhaps I've had enough."

"Si, rather stronger than I expected," Enric commented, raising his glass to examine its sparkling contents. "Already I feel a little drunk."

"Then finish the bottle, Maurici said. "They'll soon be bringing my son back home after the party, I'll have to go."

Enric pulled a face. "You will visit me again?"

Maurici smiled, and as they shook hands he said, "My good wishes to the Purcells when next you write."

Enric nodded and drawing the lace curtain at the tiny window, reminisced sadly, "We had great aspirations for the future until fate intervened to take charge of our lives."

Indeed, fate had intervened, Maurici thought as he drove home by way of the cliff road. It had stifled his aspirations, thwarting his plans for the future, until now... As he covered the winding road beneath a clear, starlit sky, he experienced a surge of determination. He would succeed, become a doctor, and prepare a secure future for his son. He'd had news of Elizabeth, his enthusiasm increased; dare he anticipate the future? He had to know.

Chapter 20

❝Jaume seems happy with Aunt Elvira," Maurici remarked as he and his mother dallied over a late meal. "I don't foresee any problems when I go back to medical school."

"It has worked out well," she agreed, "and your father is delighted with progress in the vineyard so pruning will be done in record time."

"I notice his brother sends him indoors when it rains, which means the bronchitis won't trouble as much."

"But then he's constantly under my feet!" she laughed, then leaned towards him to ask, "Does cousin Lluis aggravate you less now his father's here?"

Maurici nodded. "He's matured, and his political leanings appear to have changed."

"Strange, isn't it," Carmen said, staring vaguely ahead, "I've always had the feeling he was jealous of you."

"Perhaps he envies the opportunities I've had, my education, etcetera."

"Your education would have been wasted on Lluis, and his father thought studying a waste of time."

"But he's good with engines. He could have trained as a mechanic."

"His father is still bitter over losing his business but an empty stomach soon takes precedence over pride. It's my guess Elvira changed his mind."

"And the priest, no doubt he had a hand in it," he added. "I am indebted to him for the advice he gave me."

"The priest who had studied medicine, you mean?"

"Yes, but for him, and Sister Teresa, I doubt if I would have been allowed to continue my training."

* *

"How do I manoeuvre this damned thing!" cried James, striking the armrest of his chair.

"More easily than the old basket chair Grandmother unearthed," Elizabeth chuckled until she saw how cross he was.

"Dashed thing was no worse than this!" he snorted, steadying his cup in the saucer. "The chappie Alex brought here on Saint Stephen's Day spoke of a new hospital specialising in my type of ailment."

"Then why not contact him right away?" she encouraged, handing over a plate of homemade biscuits.

"First, I'll read up on the treatment he mentioned," he said, his eyes lighting up at the sight of something sweet. "If I must travel so great a distance I may as well attend to both matters at once."

Elizabeth uttered a sigh of longing. "I'd love to visit the London shops, buy something really fashionable."

James shot her an amused glance. "Tell me, darling, when would you wear it? You never go anywhere."

"I suppose you're right," she agreed, pouting a little. "But now Serena's at school, I ought to make an effort."

"Then why not travel with me, give your mother a break?"

Elizabeth's expression brightened. "Mm, I'd like that, and if we can scrounge a few of Grandmother's clothing coupons I'll do a little shopping."

"Anything rather than that dreadful article you made from old blackout material!" he exclaimed laughingly.

Smoothing down her skirt, pleated from a low waistline, she said in mock indignation, "Make do and mend, remember? Everyone's wearing them at the village hall dances."

"But it's no use to you, darling, You never go dancing."

"And I used to love it."

Sadness clouded his eyes. "Was I not damned well paralysed we could go tea-dancing in London, like your mother and I used to do."

Catching his emotion, she gave him a tender smile. "It's not important, Daddy. I shall enjoy just being with you."

"Then we'll have a slap-up lunch, there should be one decent restaurant without hundreds of damned steps!"

* *

"You do even more studying now you are back in college, Maurici," *senyora* Bachs observed one Sunday afternoon. "Why not take it easy, Elvira will keep an eye on the boy."

Maurici glanced up. "Actually, I'm re-applying for permission to travel to a conference in London."

"I hope you succeed this time. I can't recall why you were refused before."

"That was two years ago. The reason they gave was because I'd spent some time in that hell-hole of a prison."

"*Si*, now I remember, they accused you of spying for the Reds."

"I told them, my sole purpose for being anywhere near the front line was to minister to the wounded. Hardly military tactics, I would have thought."

"Will this conference benefit your studies?"

"*Si, mama*. It's concerned mainly with nutrition, a subject I find particularly interesting."

She sighed. "Or the lack of it which we've all experienced these past years."

"I believe certain foods are still rationed in England, so I am keen to see how they are managing."

"Then I wish you luck with this application," she said, going in the direction of the stairs, to remind him, "Don't forget our village priest, he will vouch for you being a respectable citizen, sound morals..."

Maurici smiled to himself and wondered; would the priest vouch for him so willingly if he were aware of the content of his recent thoughts? It was true he found the subject of nutrition extremely interesting, but ever since the London conference had been mentioned, visions of Elizabeth kept invading his mind. There were times when he indulged in fantasy, absorbing her into his erotic dreams, the like of which the priest would never approve. Dare he hope she no longer played the role of an English gentleman's wife?

The following morning Maurici placed his application form on the desk appropriate to his request.

"Left it a bit late," commented the clerk, tossing it into his overflowing tray.

"When do you suggest I call back?" he asked, concerned over the man's casual manner.

The clerk shrugged and took out a cigarette. "Who knows?" he said, his attention centered on finding a match.

"I'd rather hoped you would."

"You'll be lucky if it's attended to by the end of the month," he rasped, rummaging in the drawers of his desk. "I can't promise anything."

"Lucky!" Maurici exploded, causing the man to glance up from his search. "It is in the interests of this country we medical students be allowed to study abroad, so I hope you will give my application your prompt attention!"

On Friday morning Maurici returned to the office, striding purposefully toward the desk where the same clerk was seated.

"Si?" grunted the man without looking up, but immediately he heard the harsh note in Maurici's voice he reached for a wire tray to sift through the few papers it contained.

With a wary glance at Maurici he shook his head. "Nothing in the name of Bachs. No-one signed your application."

Not wishing to jeopardize his chances, Maurici stifled his impatience. "But you have passed it to the appropriate person?"

"Of course, *senyor*, the very day you brought it in."

"But it is imperative I have the result as soon as possible so that I may confirm my seat at the conference."

The young man spread his nicotine-stained fingers. "I'll make a note of the urgency."

Unaware he had attracted the interest of a man at the rear of the office, Maurici declared, "This conference is essential to my profession!"

Angry and disappointed, he paused on the pavement outside; it was more than he should have hoped for yet, since Elizabeth had begun to trickle more frequently into his daily thoughts, the desire had become an obsession.

Cursing to himself, he had gone only a short distance when he heard someone call his name and glanced back to see someone hurrying towards him, the man he had noticed in the office he'd just left.

"You have news of my application?" asked Maurici, his hopes rising as the breathless man drew alongside.

"I overheard you asking about it..."

"*Si*, correct. It has been signed?"

The man shook his head and glanced back towards the office. "And not likely to be," he said from the corner of his mouth as he smoothed the dark hair on his upper lip, a moustache reminiscent of that worn by Adolf Hitler.

"Why not?" Maurici demanded.

The man raised a finger to his lips. "Please, *senyor*, not so loud."

Maurici lowered his voice. "My references are good, I have committed no crime."

"But they know you have been refused before."

"That was years ago!" Maurici's eyes narrowed. "Look, exactly what are you getting at?"

"I overheard you say the London conference is important – you must attend."

Maurici studied him from beneath half-closed lids. "Indeed, I must," he agreed warily, "but of what possible interest is it to you?"

"Meet me in the cafe behind the cathedral – nine-thirty – I'll explain. It will be to your advantage," he ended, noting a look of scepticism in Maurici's expression.

It was only nine o'clock when Maurici entered the dim cafe in the old quarter of Barcelona. He took a seat at the end of the narrow, smoke-filled room with a view of the door and spread his newspaper on the table. Since that morning he'd been on tenterhooks, yet it had taken no time to deduce he was about to be offered some illicit service that would carry certain risks.

Ordering coffee with a dash of anise from the young waiter whose white apron reached almost to his ankles, he tried to concentrate on the print. But his mind wandered, transferring his interest to the curls of smoke rising to the yellowed ceiling until he became aware of someone breaking away from the crowd at the bar. Looking expectantly at the advancing figure he soon realised it was a woman heading towards his table.

"Lonely?" she asked, her ruby mouth parting in a smile as she unbuttoned her coat and slid into the seat opposite, enveloping him in the heavy aroma of cheap perfume.

"*Gràcies*, no," he replied politely, returning his attention to his paper.

"I could give you the time of your life," she offered, her coat falling open to reveal scantily covered breasts.

For a second he was transfixed, his gaze lustful as desire pierced his loins. He exhaled softly, dismissing her with a shake of his head. "Sorry, I'm expecting a friend."

With a shrug of indifference she rose, her leaving coinciding with the arrival of the man Maurici awaited. And when he indicated for the man to seat himself on the seat she had just vacated, her expression became one of disgust.

"Filthy bastards!" she sneered, glaring at Maurici as she turned away.

The newcomer grinned. "Have I interrupted something?"

"Thankfully, yes," he said, raising his hand to attract the waiter's attention. "Can I offer you a drink?"

The man chose a regional wine but, wishing to keep a clear head, Maurici ordered a second coffee and drew up his chair as a signal for him to begin.

"I couldn't say much this morning," he began and tapped the side of his nose. "You understand?"

Maurici looked up from lighting a cigar. "Care to give me your name?"

"Before I reveal anything, let's come to some agreement."

"With regard to my application, you mean?"

"Your failed application, to be more accurate," the man corrected. "You omitted to include your prison sentence yet you must have known it was on record..."

"So, what is the point of this meeting?" he broke in, sending the newcomer a hard glance.

"I make it my business to have all the facts, *senyor* Bachs, otherwise I would have little to offer you now."

"Quite frankly, unless you hold a senior position, I cannot believe there's anything you can offer me."

"My position there does not count, I was merely visiting, but there are ways, believe me..."

"As I appealed against the last decision, I'm not likely to be in favour with the authorities," Maurici disclosed ruefully.

The man shrugged and smoothed a hand over his dark, glossy hair. "I've looked at your file; you have good prospects, a reasonably wealthy family."

Maurici compressed his lips and nodded. "At last we get down to the basics," he said, rubbing his thumb against the tips of his fingers. "Well, come on, how much? And what do I get for my money?"

"An introduction to someone who can supply you with signed documents guaranteed to authorise your travel." His eyes narrowed as he leaned closer. "But I need to see the colour of your money before I even begin."

"How do I know you'll keep your word, or can you be sure I won't report you to higher authorities?"

The man met Maurici's stare and smiled. "*Senyor,* you need that document and you are sufficiently intelligent to realise I could report you for attempting to bribe an officer which would land you with an even longer spell in jail. It would be my word against yours."

Maurici gave a short laugh and leaned back in his chair, regarding the man at length. "Come to the point, you haven't yet told me the price, or who will supply me with this document – assuming it is within my reach."

The man cast a wary glance at the adjoining tables before leaning forward to name a price. "Not a pesseta less!" he stressed, seeing a look of incredulity on Maurici's face.

"But that's ridiculous!" Maurici hissed. "I'd expect to travel the world for half that amount."

"Take it or leave it," said the man.

"But I haven't got that kind of money to spare!"

The other lit a cigarette from the butt of the one he'd just finished and eyed Maurici.

"Perhaps we can come to an arrangement," he began, "I'll try to negotiate a lower price. What is the most you can afford?"

"I realise counterfeiting is risky, but I doubt I could raise half that amount."

"What about your family?"

"I wouldn't want them to be involved so it's no deal, not at that price."

The man sighed. "All right," he said at last, "meet me here, same time tomorrow, I'll see what I can do."

* *

Still unable to believe his good fortune, Maurici gave the waitress a grateful smile as he reflected once again upon the heart-stopping moment when his papers were scrutinized on his arrival in England.

It was his second night in the London hotel where many of the delegates attending the conference were staying. He'd already had dinner, yet it was only eight forty five, much earlier than he was used to. But he had found the meal interestingly different; a brown soup, by the name of Windsor, had been followed by two thin slices of meat served with vegetables and boiled potatoes on the same plate. The dessert, he'd quite enjoyed; a small portion of sponge cake dotted with raisins and smothered in a thin yellow sauce.

A Frenchman seated at the same table had made extremely scathing remarks about each course, whereas Maurici delighted in the experience of choosing items from a menu so foreign to his palate. But he'd considered the hushed atmosphere of the dining room quite extraordinary;

only during coffee had reserved conversation begun. All with the exception of his table companion who complained continually throughout the meal, and criticized those few English who had ordered wine which they drank to the very last drop. Yet, with wine so scarce and expensive, Maurici could appreciate why this was and merely smiled, preferring not to demonstrate his own fluency in French.

Excusing himself from the table he strolled into the lounge to seek out a fellow student from the Barcelona medical school. Seated in one of the deep arm-chairs with its brown velvet cushions, he ordered a drink and let his thoughts drift back to the meeting he had attended that day. Suddenly, the sound of female laughter caught his attention and he glanced round to see a young couple enter the lounge, the man catching hold of the woman's hand, interlacing his fingers with hers to lead her to a more secluded seat. Drawn into their seclusion, Maurici realised he'd been holding his breath for the few moments his attention had been taken. It was with Elizabeth he'd experienced that same careless rapture that comes with being in love.

"Like a drink?" his fellow student offered, his sudden arrival driving the vivid pictures from Maurici's mind.

Over a drink they exchanged opinions on subjects which came up for discussion that day, continuing the conversation as they took a stroll outside. But the chill of a strong March wind soon drove them back indoors where they retired to their respective rooms.

For Maurici, to retire so early made the night seem long. He lay awake into the early hours, his thoughts turning to Elizabeth for the umpteenth time. He toyed with the idea of contacting her by telephone, but had he got the true facts to risk making such a call? And should he be successful in reaching her, would she welcome the news he was in England? It wasn't too far from London to York, he'd estimated it to be just over three hundred kilometres, but unless he took courage to contact her she would remain as far away as ever. It was the possibility of seeing her that had finally persuaded him to hand over the exorbitant sum for his travel documents. He had experienced moments of inner panic on the journey during the official scrutiny of his papers at the border, also at the prospect of his return. He awoke with thoughts of Elizabeth lingering in his mind and, as he washed and shaved in the chilly bathroom, the more he thought about contacting her, the more convinced he became. She may welcome a word with an old acquaintance, he decided, and planned to make the call at midday rather than evening when the hotel telephone was in constant use.

After a morning spent analysing nutritional values, he came back to the hotel for lunch, first enquiring of the receptionist the telephone number of Woodington Hall. With remarkable efficiency, she soon had the number and indicated he should wait in the cubicle until the connection was made.

When the telephone rang he felt his heartbeat quicken and heard the operator say, "You're through now," before a male voice informed him he was connected with Woodington Hall.

"Woodington Hall," a voice repeated in precise tones. "To whom do you wish to speak?"

"Miss Elizabeth Purcell," Maurici replied quickly before he had considered any other than her maiden name.

"I am sorry, sir, this is not Miss Elizabeth's residence, though I understand she is out this afternoon," the speaker informed him as Maurici's spirits fell. "Do you wish me to give her a message?"

"To whom am I speaking?" he asked and heard the man give his position as the butler, renewing Maurici's courage.

"Please ask if she will telephone this number after five-thirty?" he requested, giving the number of his hotel.

"And who shall I say was calling, sir?" Pincott asked in the same polite tone, causing Maurici a moment's hesitation.

"A doctor, in London." he said. "I wish to speak with her."

"Certainly, Doctor," said Pincott, repeating the number.

Maurici smiled as he replaced the receiver.

* *

Grunting with effort, James heaved himself from the car into the wheelchair Nicholson held by the door. "Wonderful day," he said, grasping each leg in turn to drag it onto the footrest. "Nice to taste a drop of Irish for a change."

"I prefer Scotch," Jane declared, sending him a withering glance.

"Somehow, I thought you might," James laughed and added with a wicked smile, "But I didn't hear you refuse."

Jane's back stiffened as she continued indoors. Elizabeth pressed her gloved hand to her mouth to stifle her giggles.

"God love her, she enjoys a little teasing," James said, near to giggling himself. So, it was my birthday lunch, I'm allowed an extra drink or two."

"Of course," she agreed, then glancing at her watch cried, "Is it that time? I must meet Serena from school."

"Yes, it's half past, you'd better hurry," Molly called as she accompanied James into the house.

"We'll go again – after the London trip – something to look forward to." With a wave of her hand, Elizabeth set off along the drive, but she hadn't gone far before she turned to see Pincott puffing after her, a slip of paper in his hand.

"What is it, Pincott? I'm in rather a hurry," she said, pausing just long enough for him to catch up.

"There was a telephone call for you, Miss Elizabeth, a gentleman from London."

"Who was it, did he say?"

"A doctor, but he didn't give his name," Pincott related breathlessly. "He asked if you would call this number. After five-thirty, he said."

"I hope Daddy's appointment hasn't been cancelled," she said, taking the slip of paper. "Thanks, Pincott, must dash, Serena will wonder where I am."

It was almost six o'clock when Elizabeth spotted the slip of paper Pincott had given her that afternoon. She had propped it on the hall table while she made Serena's tea. Hoping she was not too late to call the doctor's consulting rooms, she lifted the receiver and gave the operator the number required.

As she waited, faint clicking sounds came over the earpiece before the operator confirmed she was through, but when a female voice came on the line giving the name of a hotel, she assumed there must be some mistake.

"I'm afraid I've been wrongly connected," she apologised, repeating the number required. "Sorry you've been troubled."

"This is the number you require, madam. Hold the line; I have someone waiting to take your call."

"With a sigh of impatience, Elizabeth waited until she heard a faint, "I'm connecting you now, sir," when she demanded, "Hello, who is this...?"

"Miss Purcell? Elizabeth?" she heard, and something about the way he spoke her name made her catch her breath.

"Elizabeth Purcell speaking," she said, inadvertently repeating her maiden name.

"Elizabeth! It is wonderful to hear you..." There came a soft chuckle and her pulse quickened at the familiar way the caller pronounced her name. "You recognise my voice?"

Her heart seemed to contract. "Maurici, it is you! Oh, what a surprise – what can I say..."

"Elizabeth," he repeated softly, in his attractive and slightly accented way, "it is wonderful to speak with you. Are you pleased to hear me on the telephone?"

"I'm delighted!" she replied breathlessly. "But what are you doing in London?"

"Can you speak? Do you wish I should telephone a different time?"

"No, no, it's all right, this is a private 'phone, we can speak for as long as we wish."

There was a pause before he asked, "You have no husband with you?"

"No, no-one, I'm alone," she assured, "but do tell me why you're here."

Briefly, Maurici gave the reason for his visit, his decision to resume his training which had led to attending this conference in London. "And now, although I feel closer to you, we are not together." he ended on a sad note.

"Oh, Maurici, it would be lovely to see you again..."

"You wish that we meet...?" he broke in hopefully.

"I was about to say, I shall be in London the day after tomorrow," she intruded eagerly. "Could we meet then?"

"*Si*, Elizabeth," came his instant reply, "I am hoping for this, there is so much to say. When you will arrive?"

She hesitated. "It's rather difficult. You see, I'm accompanying my father who has an appointment with a specialist there."

"Your father, he is ill, I understand."

"I'll tell you about it when we meet," she said, hurrying on to add, "I expect to be free in the afternoon, we can meet then."

"Perfect," he replied warmly. "You must return the same day?"

She gave a rueful sigh. "I'm afraid I must, we shall be leaving on the early evening train."

"Where we can meet, Elizabeth? Tell me a place."

"How about the National Gallery? Most likely someone will direct you to Trafalgar Square."

"Is not a problem, I will find it. But which time?"

"Oh, two o'clock I suggest. If I find I'm going to be delayed, I'll telephone your hotel, leave a message."

"I will wait for you, Elizabeth," he promised. "I look forward to be with you very much."

"Oh yes," she responded warmly. "It has been a long time."

"More than seven years," he said on a note of regret, but his tone brightened as he reiterated their plans to meet.

Staring, dreamy-eyed at her reflection in the hall mirror, Elizabeth lingered by the telephone, not wishing to break the spell. Seven years he had said, and so many questions she had been too overwhelmed to ask. She should have been angry over the years of silence and the reason he hadn't contacted her until now; had his promises that afternoon at Can Bachs meant nothing? But Maurici had married, and although she knew she had no right to deny him that, did he expect to take up the threads of their lives as though they had never been broken?

She blinked suddenly, turning away from the mirror; it was perfectly normal for an old acquaintance to keep in touch and she shouldn't read too much into what had been a short telephone call to someone with whom he could exchange a few words about days gone by. But it was the way he had spoken her name, conveying warmth and excitement, which convinced her it was more than just a simple desire to communicate. And there was her own reaction to the sound of his voice, the reciprocal emotions it had inspired, the wild jolting of her heart rendering her almost speechless when she had realised who was speaking.

Now she was beginning to experience twinges of guilt. Maurici was alone in London; was he hoping to continue their association, however briefly, on the same intimate level as it had been the day they parted? Was his marriage a failure, like her own? However much pleasure it had brought her, she must take care not to misinterpret the reason for his call. She would keep the appointment but purely on a friendly footing. Meeting an old acquaintance in the centre of London wasn't so unusual, was it? Or was it? She suffered the turmoil of her thoughts more keenly throughout the following day, reminded by the changing expressions in her daughter's beautiful dark eyes. Had her feelings for Maurici been nothing more than the foolish emotions of inexperienced youth; memories she had clung to only because of the torment of the years which had followed? Would he now appear less appealing to her mature eye, his manner not so charming as she remembered it to be? She began to doubt the wisdom of the arrangement, conscious it may result in a painful upheaval of her emotions. Part of her craved the affection she remembered, while the remainder clung to the security of her present independent state. She decided against mentioning the telephone call to her father, he may consider her both indiscreet and foolish to hope to recapture the past.

Chapter 21

"Tell you what, darling," James suggested as the train pulled out of York station, "why don't we have a light lunch and book a table for dinner on the return journey."

She smiled. "Perfect, but your first appointment is at eleven, you don't have much time."

"I had considered staying the night," he said. "Bit late to change things now."

Elizabeth glanced away. She hadn't felt able to mention her arrangement for that afternoon, but it would have been wonderful to spend more time with Maurici, although it may have proved difficult to explain.

Gazing at her fondly, he remarked, "I must say, you look exceptionally pretty today. I see you've had your hair done, it suits you a little shorter."

"I'm pleased you like it." She found herself blushing under his scrutiny and hurried to ask, "Like more coffee?"

He shook his head and commented, "I notice you're wearing high heels. Will you be comfortable in town?"

"Actually, they're Mummy's," she told him, uncrossing her slim ankles to display the navy, round toed shoes.

"Mm, they go well with your costume. Blue suits you."

"Hope Gladys had Serena off to school on time," she said, glancing at her watch.

"Thomas would make sure of it. Pity we didn't bring her, she would enjoy the ride," he said, looking through the dusty window to observe the changing landscape.

Elizabeth sent him a faintly startled look, imagining Maurici's reaction should she confront him with Serena in tow.

"She's rather young for such a long journey," she said, opening her handbag to cast a surreptitious glance at Serena's photograph, seeing the dark, sparkling eyes, just like Maurici's.

"You could be right," he agreed. "I think I'll have a nap, we had rather an early start."

"Good idea," she said and closed her bag, a pleasurable wave of anticipation washing over her. And as she arranged to have James lifted from the train at King's Cross station she endeavoured to contain her excitement.

* *

"You go ahead," Maurici advised his colleague between lectures. "Perhaps I will rest as subjects for this afternoon are of no special interest to me."

"Maybe the change of diet affects you," the other suggested, gathering up his papers. "They eat most peculiar food and I've seen little bread."

"Rationed, I understand," Maurici explained. "Two bread units for one of those small loaves, I believe, from an allowance of only nine units per week."

"They appear to thrive on it," his companion commented with scant interest. "But you do look a bit off colour."

"Merely lack of sleep," Maurici assured him. "We'll have a drink together later when you might let me take a look at your notes."

"Of course. I may forego one or two lectures myself – see a bit more of London whilst we're here."

Maurici left his colleague to attend the last lecture of the morning whilst he rushed back to his hotel. As it was situated away from the city centre he had to allow himself sufficient time to change and reach the National Gallery by two o'clock. He'd been on tenterhooks all morning, a trifle pessimistic after the misfortunes of the past, but when no call came for him by midday, he went to his room to change. As he showered he wondered if she would have the time to come back to the hotel with him, or would that be too much to expect after so many years apart? But when he splashed cologne over his still lean body the anticipation of her presence aroused him, making him feel more alive than he had in years. Smoothing lavender oil over his dark hair, which he now wore a little longer, he combed it into place. And taking care to ensure his tie was knotted in the present fashion, he slipped on the jacket of his dark suit.

Once into the centre of London, he asked a passer-by for directions and, although he found the man's accent difficult to understand, he was able to ascertain the National Gallery was situated not too far away. He had already visited places of interest such as Tower Bridge, Buckingham Palace, and the British Museum, and now found himself close to Trafalgar Square with twenty minutes to spare.

Striding past the Royal College of Physicians with a lightness of step, he approached the National Gallery with its trim green lawns. Ascending the steps between the stately Corinthian columns, he paused to look down, eyes narrowed, searching for Elizabeth.

At ten minutes past the hour he began to grow anxious, his eyes flitting from place to place as he descended the steps until he caught sight of her alighting from a taxi. For a second he was fixed to the spot, his heart swelling as though it would burst: there stood Elizabeth, elegantly poised, less than ten metres away. Choked with emotion, he moved eagerly towards her, catching her quick expression of delight when she saw him draw near.

"Oh, Maurici!" she whispered, her lovely mouth quivering.

For a moment he gazed down on her in speechless wonder before he reached out to take her hands, kissing her cheeks in a Catalan style greeting. "Elizabeth!" he said brokenly, holding her slightly away from him as he slowly shook his head and managed to smile.

"I'm sorry to be late," she said, her voice wavering.

"But now you are here, with me," he said softly, his own voice ragged with emotion. And pressing her gloved hands to his chest, he looked down on her to ask, "What do you wish to do? You are hungry perhaps, or prefer to walk?"

She uttered a happy sigh. "I just want to spend the time talking to you – maybe afternoon tea later."

"There's my hotel," he ventured, "but it is almost one hour distant," and named the area, away from the centre of the city, and she had to agree, it was much too far to travel.

"You see, I must join my father at half past four," she explained, "we'd not be back in time. We could take a walk in Saint James' Park, it's quite near."

Once the wild racing of his heart had steadied somewhat, he was able to assess more clearly just how he felt. His initial desire had been to crush her against him and kiss her rose-tinted lips, but he'd restrained the longing, his searching eyes lingering on her beautiful face. Then, with his hand beneath her elbow to guide her between the traffic, they strolled off towards the park, each enquiring after the other's well-being, a thin cloak of reserve still in place. There were so many questions he wanted to ask but was hesitant to begin, until she spoke of her father's disability, her voice growing sad.

"He was on his way home when it happened, not far from the border with France."

He slowed his stride to match hers. "Yes, I heard of his accident," he said and felt her draw to a halt.

"You knew?"

He turned to her. "Enric told me some time ago."

"I expect Daddy gives him all our news," she said in a casual voice, but her eyes fixed enquiringly on his face.

"He did tell me you had married," he said, experiencing a tiny stab of bitterness. "But now I understand you and your husband are living apart. This is true, Elizabeth, yes?"

She tore her eyes away and moved on, her back straight, head held high as she replied in a small voice, "I wouldn't have thought it of interest to you, Maurici, not when you already had a wife."

"*Si*, Elizabeth, had. I had a wife," he stressed, keeping the emotion from his voice, "after I left the army."

She turned to him with startled eyes. "Had?" she repeated almost soundlessly, and gathering her thoughts she indicated a nearby bench. "Let's sit here, shall we?"

"You will be warm enough?"

She nodded, hugging her fur coat around her, and for a moment they stayed silent as if gathering courage to begin.

About to speak, Maurici checked himself as she began softly, "My parents received word from Enric, some time ago, said you'd been taken prisoner, the first I knew..."

"*Ai!* He told me he also wrote to you, soon after you left, but received no reply."

When she told him it had been in late summer after their return to England when her parents first had news of him, he captured her gaze to ask, "And if news had come earlier, you would have waited for me?"

She dropped her eyes and gave a small shrug. "But if it had, you couldn't leave Spain..."

"So you decided you could not wait, yes?" he broke in, a strained note in his voice. "And you were married only two months after you returned."

She shook her head and looked at him, her blue eyes filled with anguish as she whispered shakily, "You don't understand, I was desperate, I had no choice..." She turned away, a spot of colour staining her cheeks.

Realisation dawned on Maurici like a sudden cold shower, its icy slivers piercing every nerve in his body. "You mean..." he began, and rushed on to demand, "How old is your child? When was it born?"

For a moment she didn't reply until he reached out to cup her chin, gently turning her to face him to ask in a more controlled voice, "Please, Elizabeth? When...?"

"The fourth of October," she replied, and avoiding his eyes, continued, "But this isn't the way I intended to tell you."

"So, it is my child!" he exclaimed, suppressing a surge of emotion that made him want to shake the beautiful creature beside him. "*Déu!* Why didn't you tell me before?"

He saw a flash of indignation in her eyes as she said, "I wouldn't have thought it the most welcome news to send to a married man."

"I didn't marry until forty-two, but had I known..."

"At the time I thought you didn't want to know me. I had no word from you after – you know, after we'd..."

"Made love?" he supplied, one dark brow slanting upwards. "Believe me, I would have accepted my responsibilities, you know that, we could have sought permission to marry..."

"No, I couldn't bear to think you'd married me purely from a sense of duty." She uttered a sad sigh. "And how was I to know where you were?"

He gave a nod of acceptance, reflecting on Enric's words. "True, you couldn't have known I was in prison, or the army. It was one of the misfortunes of war." He felt for her hand in support of what he continued to say, "But you must believe me, had it been possible I would have wished to marry you, because I loved you..." Holding her gaze he went on softly, "Perhaps I still do."

He saw a flicker of warmth in her expression, her lips parted as though to make a response. Then she broke the spell, saying gently, "We shouldn't allow ourselves to get too carried away, I'm still legally tied."

"Of course," he accepted ruefully, "but here, under English law, will you not consider the divorce?"

"I already have, it's crossed my mind a hundred times, but he simply refuses to discuss it."

"He? Your husband?"

She nodded, staring vaguely ahead. "I suppose there was no urgency," she murmured, "but I'd rather not go into detail, not now."

He conceded with a shake of his head. "Then tell me about my child, the name, how it is looking."

"Her name is Serena, I have a photograph with me." She reached into her handbag, and leaned towards him. "This was taken last year, on her first day at school."

"She is now more than six years, yes?" he said, eager to see. And as he looked at the picture of his daughter he had to steel himself against the almost overwhelming tide of emotion. It was almost like looking at a photograph of Jaume, he realised in a moment of shocked surprise; the same large, dark eyes, sparkling with mischief, and dark, curling hair which was slightly longer than that of his son.

"My daughter..." He clenched his jaw in an effort to control his quivering chin. But he knew Elizabeth had sensed his emotion when he felt her hand creep into his.

"Now, tell me what has happened in your life," she said in sympathy of his mood. And her own expression grew sad with concern when he spoke briefly of his late wife, Dolors.

"How terribly, terribly sad," she said with feeling, "and not to have known her baby. Do you carry a photograph?"

He brightened and withdrew his wallet, taking out the likeness of Jaume which he carried when away from home. And with their heads together, cutting off all thought for the rest of the world, they exclaimed over the similarity of features of their children and spoke of their years apart.

"There's no disputing who the father is!" she said, laughter in her voice. "They both look so like you."

Smiling, he leaned back on the seat, his handsome face relaxed as he turned towards her. "I can't believe I am a father twice," he said, his look melting any remaining reserve between them. "Yet, I can remember every detail of that afternoon at Can Bachs as if it were yesterday, though afterwards I did wonder if I had been reckless."

Her cheeks flushed prettily as she cast him a sideways glance to disclose, "I don't recall making any objection at the time."

"I'll admit, I was overcome by the passion of the moment. Do you regret what we did?"

She smiled. "No, I wouldn't be without Serena, she has been my life, a constant reminder of you."

"Your husband, does he know?"

She shook her head. "My parents, they do."

"And what do they say? Are they in sympathy with you?"

"We've not really discussed it, though they are extremely fond of her."

"And they don't mind you are here with me today?"

She coloured slightly. "Actually, I haven't told them. It isn't that I'm ashamed," she was quick to assure him, "but if I'm to seek a divorce, then discretion is something I must consider very seriously."

"And that is the only reason our meeting is secret?" he asked, raising one dark brow.

She drew a deep breath and began a trifle awkwardly, "To be frank with you, Maurici, no. You see, I didn't want to attach too much importance to this meeting, particularly as I thought you were married." She paused, uttering a tiny sigh. "Over the years people change – we could have changed – we may have found we had nothing in common..."

He shot her a look of incredulity and raised his hands. "But we have a child! That is something in common, no?"

"Of course it is, but until now I didn't know how pleased you were likely to be."

"Maybe not," he granted, taking her hands. "I also realise you are married and I was anxious about how you would react to meeting me again, if we still had the attraction of more than friends. This is what worried you?"

She smiled as she searched his eyes to confess, "It is exactly what worried me. I dare not allow myself to hope for anything more."

"Darling Elizabeth," he breathed, "I am indeed a happy man."

As he smiled she noticed the tiny lines at the corners of his eyes. Lines etched more by suffering than maturity, she guessed, assessing he would now be almost thirty-two years old.

A sudden gust of wind made her shudder and she looked around her, aware they were no longer alone. A child stared at them with interest until Elizabeth laughed when he skipped away to join his nanny who strolled sedately along in charge of a large, gleaming pram.

"Is your son about his size?" asked Elizabeth, suddenly short of something to say.

"Slightly taller," he replied after a brief glance. "One day I hope you will see." His expression grew serious as he reminded her, "He is the brother by half of Serena, yes?"

Elizabeth couldn't suppress a bubble of laughter. "I think you mean half-brother. Jaume is her half-brother."

His response was good humoured, and sliding his arm about her shoulder he pulled her close, his face snuggling into the softness of her hair as they both shook with mirth.

As they drew apart their eyes met, sending a tingle of desire through every fibre in his body when he leaned across to place his lips on hers in a tentative kiss. At first she was motionless against him, but as his lips explored hers more boldly she drew back, nervous of who may see them in so close an embrace.

"We shouldn't, not here," she said with a gentle smile.

"Then where, Elizabeth? It is too late for my hotel?"

"Much too late, I'm afraid," she agreed, glancing at her watch to gasp in dismay, "I've got less than an hour."

"*No!*" he cried in frustration, his dark eyes glittering. "Why must we be ruled by time?"

"Believe me, Maurici, I don't want to go..."

"But we must meet again, very soon," he insisted passionately. "I love you, and I don't intend you will forget me."

"I'll not forget you, never in a million years," she promised, her reserve melting away, "but it's going to be difficult to arrange a meeting."

"You must return home today?"

"I can't possibly do otherwise. How long are you here? Maybe next week I can find an opportunity to get away."

"Two more days and I must leave," he said with a groan of regret. "But maybe it is possible for me to come again to London, quickly for the week-end, by the areoplane."

Her expression brightened. "That would be wonderful! Will you write or telephone, let me know when?"

"I intend to write regularly, and telephone when I have the opportunity," he promised with a smile. "But you must give me your address, the number of your home."

"And I must have yours," she said eagerly. "Let's go and have tea somewhere then I can write it down."

He rose to pull her gently to her feet, looking down on her with an expression of deep regret. "So many years apart," he murmured, then drew her close to capture her lips in a tender kiss, reluctant to let her go.

As he released her she opened her bag and took out the photograph of Serena to say softly, "Would you like to have this?"

He looked at the picture and smiled. "You will send to me one of yourself?" he asked, tucking her hand into the crook of his arm.

"In exchange for one of you and Jaume," she promised as they retraced their steps, crossing the little suspension bridge over the lake at a slightly quicker pace.

"I didn't expect to see fig trees in a London park," he commented in surprise. And, although time was getting short, they lingered a moment to watch the wildfowl and ducks, and had a glimpse of Buckingham Palace, just visible through the trees.

Once out of the park they found a small cafe and ordered afternoon tea. Maurici purposely kept the conversation light to ease the parting they must shortly make. He enquired after her parents and mentioned his own as he watched Elizabeth pour tea in the traditional English way, and he tasted scones for the first time, spread thinly with margarine and jam. They exchanged addresses and telephone numbers, chatting until it was time to leave.

"No, I'd rather you didn't come with me," she begged him as he paid the bill and made to follow her outside. And seeing the sparkle of tears in her beautiful sapphire eyes he nodded, leaning forward to brush her cheeks with his lips as he murmured a soft farewell.

"*Adéu*, Elizabeth," he said, his breath warm on her face. "Until we meet again."

* *

James had been still in the treatment room when Elizabeth arrived. Glad of a few moments in which to recover from her hurried ten minute walk, she'd gone to the cloakroom to bathe her eyes and apply make-up to her tear-stained face. What had been a most wonderful afternoon had ended all too soon, the moment of parting so painful; a picture of Maurici, his dark eyes glittering in the light thrown out from the cafe as he had watched her walk away lingering in her mind. She'd looked forward to this meeting with such longing it hardly seemed possible it had already passed, leaving her sad yet, at the same time, elated, knowing he still cared.

And now, on the train journey home, she was aware of her father's elation over his medical assessment that afternoon. "Considering I've not been hospitalized for most of the time, they are amazed at my progress and the lack of flare-ups of the old infection."

He smiled to himself as he continued, "By what the consultant tells me, my darling wife has been nursing me in exactly the way he recommends. I told him she wouldn't allow them to keep me in the plaster bed for longer than was necessary, and she'd organised the alterations, ramps, and wider doors." He shook his head and admitted sadly, "There were times when I made the most unreasonable demands; I didn't deserve such devotion..."

"But that was part of your illness, Daddy, knowing you wouldn't walk again, it must have been a terrible blow."

He nodded. "She never complained, not once, yet it took me a long time to accept I must help myself."

"Quite simply, Mummy loves you," she smiled, "though I'm sure you know that by now."

His expression brightened. "She'll be delighted to hear about the physiotherapy to help these muscle contractures she's been worried about. And now there's a place near Leeds dealing with this kind of thing it will make it much easier for us." He grinned as he exclaimed, "And what do you think, darling, they suggest I take up swimming to strengthen my muscles, get the circulation flowing!"

"That's wonderful news! You know, Daddy, since the Disabled Person's Act was passed a year or two ago, there's been more help available for people like you."

"True," he smiled, "and that reminds me, they advocate work as a therapy so I should take a look at the newspaper. Pity we didn't have time to visit my old firm, I'm sure I could manage a regular article for them."

Once her father appeared to be engrossed in the London evening paper, she rested her head against the backrest of the seat, pressing her hand to her cheek where Maurici's lips had brushed as she wallowed in the luxury of undisturbed thought. And as the train steamed along into the gathering dusk, she continued to reflect happily on almost every word

Maurici had spoken, her sadness eased by the promise of a future meeting, and lulled by the rhythm of the wheels.

"A penny for them," said James, glancing across the carriage as he tapped the newspaper against his other hand.

Elizabeth blinked, reluctant to relinquish her pleasurable reverie. "Sorry, did you say something?"

"I expect you're tired," he remarked and looked up at the luggage rack. "Incidentally, where are your parcels? You haven't left them behind?"

"Parcels?" she repeated blankly, following his eyes to the rack above.

"Your shopping, the things you bought this afternoon?"

She gave a guilty start and pointed to her handbag. "Oh yes, I got a little book for Serena, nothing else."

James shot her a faintly curious look. "Nothing else?"

"Actually, it was nice just to stroll in the sunshine – walk through the park – see the trees. They're coming into bud much earlier down here than at home."

James pulled a face and shook his head. "And you told me you were longing to buy clothes," he reproached with a chuckle. "Dear girl, what am I to make of you now?"

It was turned half-past eleven before Elizabeth finally arrived at Ashdale House after a quite exhausting journey. Nicholson had met them at York station when he and a porter transferred James to the waiting car, the porter hovering hopefully until she passed him a sizeable tip. She found a sleepy-eyed Gladys in the sitting room who reported Serena to be fast asleep before she mentioned a telephone call she had taken earlier in the evening.

"Twice 'e rang, but I told 'im you wouldn't be back for ages, Miss Elizabeth," Gladys called from the kitchen where she had gone to heat a pan of milk.

"Did he give his name?" Elizabeth queried as she kicked off her elegant high-heeled shoes.

"No, but he says he'll call again tomorrow," the woman related. "Real polite he was. Sounded quite a Toff."

Elizabeth smiled to herself, convinced it was Maurici who would have no idea how long her journey would take, and felt suddenly compelled to look in on Serena who lay peacefully asleep, the thumb of one hand still moist from sucking, her teddy bear clutched tightly in the other. As she gazed down on her she reflected on the emotion in Maurici's expression when he learned of her existence. How wonderful if they could meet, she thought, her own expression tender with love, yet she had no wish to put her friendship with Maurici in jeopardy, or expose Serena to such an encounter whilst she and Miles were still legally tied. The courts were inclined to look upon an erring wife none too favourably.

As she undressed, her thoughts returned to the subject of divorce which in the past she'd only fleetingly considered. But now it was imperative she consult a solicitor, someone in practice not too close to home.

* *

Since dinner, Maurici had spent the evening seated in a secluded corner of the hotel lounge. Disappointed over not finding Elizabeth at home when he'd telephoned, he ordered a drink and returned to his seat. "It'll be ages afore she's back," the woman on the line had informed him, and he wondered how long 'ages' would be. It was not that he had anything urgent to say, he simply wanted to hear her voice, convince himself the afternoon had not been merely a dream. He took out his wallet and withdrew the photograph of Serena, smiling as he imagined his children together, squealing with delight as they raced between the rows of vines as Jaume now did. Imagining his mother's astonishment he almost laughed aloud, but quickly composed himself and slid the photograph out of sight when he saw his colleague coming towards him bearing a tray of drinks.

"One for you, and two for me," the young man said. "I haven't had a drink all evening." He grinned. "Too busy pleasuring myself. But, my God, they charge the earth!"

Maurici shook his head, "Never mind the cost, think of the risk."

"Don't tell me you haven't fancied a bit of female company?"

"I don't relish the possible consequences," Maurici replied truthfully as he reached for his drink.

"You're not queer, are you? You know, one of those."

"I'm aware of what you mean," Maurici replied shortly. "And when you get into your next year, you'll see the horrific results of risks taken by people like you."

The younger man's grin faded as he raised his glass. "Got to get it down, the bars close at such odd times."

"Don't forget, we have a hospital visit tomorrow."

"Did you pick up the notes?" the other asked. "Just two pages, there was only one subject this afternoon."

"Yes, I'll return them in the morning," Maurici promised and went to collect his key at reception where his eyes were drawn involuntarily to the telephone. Almost midnight, too late to call Elizabeth.

After dinner the following evening, Maurici telephoned Ashdale House. He noted with pleasure how quickly the call was answered and detected the pleasure in Elizabeth's voice.

"I thought you may ring," was her slightly breathless response. "Was it you who rang last night?"

"Mm, twice," he replied, "but obviously, you arrived back safely. You enjoyed the afternoon?"

"More than I can tell you," she murmured, sighing as she added, "Oh, I do wish I was there with you now."

"Then come to London again tomorrow, yes?" he broke in hopefully and held his breath.

"I wish I could," he heard, his spirits sinking as she continued, "but it's impossible for me to get away."

"I could come to you," he persisted hopefully. "Tell me how I must travel to Woodington with the train."

"You can't, people would see you. We couldn't..."

"Because of your husband?" he queried coolly, then reasoned, "Surely, there is somewhere we can meet?"

"Please," she begged, "don't ask me, not yet."

"So when, Elizabeth? You have not changed your mind?"

"No, I've not changed, I promise you. But before we make any further plans I've decided to consult a solicitor concerning the matter we spoke of yesterday afternoon."

Chapter 22

It was Maurici's last day in London. The final post-lecture discussion was over by midday when delegates were free to leave, most in a hurry to be home for the weekend, whereas he had time to spare and went in search of gifts for the family. For Jaume he chose a model of a red London bus, for his mother and Elvira a small bottle of English lavender. It was more difficult to find something suitable for the men, confectionery still being rationed, but he managed to purchase a few English cigarettes and a quarter bottle of whisky. For himself he chose a book about England, its colour plates of the Yorkshire countryside catching his eye. And before returning to his hotel to pack, he visited the cafe where he and Elizabeth had taken tea, taking a seat at the same table, hoping to recapture the precious moments they had shared. But it wasn't the same; he realised sadly; the tepid tea, a scone like sawdust, the loneliness...

That evening he spoke with her on the telephone, his heart growing heavy when the time came to say a final goodbye. As he returned the telephone to its cradle he spotted postcards at the reception desk and bought a selection of views to take home, keeping one aside.

Early the following morning he took a taxi to the station where he would board the boat train. And with minutes to spare he gave in to the longing to hear Elizabeth's voice and found a public telephone.

"Elizabeth?" he said breathlessly, one eye on the waiting train. "It is the moment I am leaving."

He heard her gasp his name and caught the high pitched sound of a child's voice. His throat constricted painfully. "Do I hear Serena?" he managed to ask.

"Yes," Elizabeth said, a smile in her voice. "She's here."

"Kiss her for me, Elizabeth. And let me know what the solicitor says, will you? I love you, darling..."

There came an urgent tapping on the glass. "*Apa, home!*" he heard his colleague shout.

"*Si,*" he called, and to Elizabeth a hurried, "I must go, the train is waiting. *Adéu...*"

Elizabeth clung to the telephone for some moments after she whispered a sad farewell and the rapid beating of her heart began to subside when Serena caught her attention.

"Mummy, can we have breakfast now, please?" the child pleaded, rattling the brass knob of the dining room door.

Elated by the call, Elizabeth scooped Serena up in her arms to kiss her soft, warm cheek. She devoted the day to her daughter who, it being Saturday was not at school. They walked across the fields to see the new lambs, pausing by the hedgerow bordering a wood to gather the first spring flowers. Watching her child she felt a glow of happiness linked with a more optimistic view of the future.

The Monday morning post arrived as they were having breakfast. As usual, Serena rushed to open the wire basket behind the front door.

"Mummy, there's a letter with a picture!" Elizabeth heard as the child came dashing back to thrust a postcard under her nose.

When Elizabeth saw a picture of the National Gallery she quickly turned it over to read the message on the reverse.

"Is it for me?" Serena asked, tugging at her mother's arm.

Elizabeth lifted her onto her knee. "Actually, it's addressed to me..." she began, the words blurring as she read 'Good wishes for the future.'

"But, Mummy, who is it from?"

"No-one you know, darling," she said with a twinge of regret and propped it against the teapot.

But once Serena had left for school she went back to the dining-room to gaze at the card again, recapturing the moment she and Maurici had met in front of the building pictured there. Turning it over she studied Maurici's bold handwriting and knew his brief message had been written with love. The future was in his thoughts just as it was in hers; she pressed the postcard to her breast for a moment, and then went to the telephone to make an appointment with a solicitor in York.

* *

Carmen dabbed a few spots of lavender on each wrist and inhaled, her eyes closed. "Mmm, so fresh!" she said, adding with a chuckle, "Elvira was delighted you remembered her."

"We had little free time when the shops were open," Maurici explained. "There were many buildings I would have liked to see, perhaps next time," he ended absently as he opened the book he had purchased.

"Speaking English would be easy for you, but what of the people?"

"I found the people friendly enough, but London was very cold."

"And the food, it was good?"

"Well, different, but I enjoyed it, though certain items are still rationed."

"It appears to have suited you," she remarked. "You seem cheerful since your return.

He smiled to himself. "Do I? Yet it was a tiring journey, the sea crossing rough, and I was a little anxious about leaving Jaume for so long."

"He's been no trouble, though it's a pity the postcard didn't arrive while you were away."

"A week is hardly long enough for the post to get here. Next time I'll write one before I leave, I have some views of London in my case."

She shot him a shrewd smile. "Next time, heh? Perhaps there was something in what Lluis said when he suggested you may be too busy visiting your English friends to spare the time to write home."

* *

Jane was riding across the field adjoining the Hall at a steady canter when someone hailed her from behind. Pulling on the reins she drew her mount to a halt, her eyes narrowed as she turned, peering through the early morning mist to see Miles mounted on his hunter advancing her way.

"Good morning!" he cried breathlessly, bringing his horse to a snorting standstill beside hers. "Just the person I wish to see."

She smiled. "If it's a chase, count me out. I'm afraid my hunting days are over."

"No, Mrs Cussons, not the hunt. No, it's Mother. She's taken ill again, and I wondered if you'd mention it to Elizabeth."

"Have you tried ringing her?"

"If she knows it's me, she won't answer the telephone."

"I see," Jane sighed. "So what do you expect me to do?"

"Well, if you ask her to call she may agree." His voice took on a whining note as he continued, "She refuses to do anything for me."

Jane clicked her tongue. "Don't know what's got into her. I blame the war for these silly modern ideas women have today."

"Quite so, Mrs Cussons, you have a point," he agreed with an ingratiating smile. "I do hope she'll give up this independence thing."

"Not much of a life for you, Miles," she sympathised. "Not that she discusses anything with me, you understand, but she can be so obstinate at times, just like her father."

"I've always endeavoured to be more than generous, what more can one do?" He replaced his cap. "Won't delay you, Mrs Cussons. Good day."

Raising a gloved hand, Jane urged her horse to move on. Miles clenched his flabby jaw and digging his heels into his horse's flanks he gave it a savage flick with his crop and rode off in the direction of Grant's farm.

Elizabeth had not been home ten minutes when the telephone rang and she heard her grandmother say accusingly, "You were out when I called this afternoon."

"Yes, I was," Elizabeth agreed, determined not to be drawn. "Was there something you wanted?"

There was a tiny pause before Jane told her, "Miles spoke to me earlier. His mother's not well, wants you to call."

Elizabeth uttered a sigh of dismay. "That is awkward. Not that I object to calling on Mrs Grant, I'm sorry for the poor soul."

"Poor soul!" Jane echoed derisively. "That woman is always complaining about some ailment or other..."

"Little wonder, living with that beastly husband and son of hers!" she interrupted heatedly.

"Nonsense!" Jane retorted. "And in case you'd forgotten, you owe Miles a great deal."

"I owe him nothing! I've already paid for my mistake."

"Obviously, I'm wasting my breath on you, Elizabeth. You can be most impertinent at times."

"I'm sorry, Grandmother, but you don't appreciate my position. I'll call in the morning, when she's alone."

The following morning, after Serena had left for school, Elizabeth prepared to visit Miles' mother in the rambling farmhouse on the outskirts of the village. Since her meeting with Maurici she'd been in high spirits, until the previous afternoon when, as a result of her visit to the solicitor, she was again enveloped in gloom. And the prospect of visiting the Grant household didn't do anything to alleviate the feeling. She was doomed to remain legally tied to Miles for seven years for him to file for divorce on grounds of desertion, unless she could prove infidelity or cruelty on his part. It seemed like a life sentence, and would Miles act, or would he force her to remain in a loveless marriage purely out of spite?

She could see Mrs Grant at the bedroom window and noticed her expression brighten as she drew the car to a halt and reached for the fresh tulips on the back seat. A girl from the village who looked little more than sixteen years opened the door to her. Only recently employed by the Grants, she already appeared harassed and over-worked.

"The gentlemen are out riding," the girl informed her. "I don't expect them back 'till lunch, so it'll be nice for Madam to have company."

Feeling less cautious about spending an hour or two with the invalid, Elizabeth smiled. But on entering Mrs Grant's bedroom she detected an unpleasant odour and thought the lady had aged considerably. Also, she appeared not to have been washed that morning, or had a comb through her hair, and the crumpled bed-linen needed changing.

"Are you warm enough?" Elizabeth asked, noting the icy-coldness of her mother-in-law's hands. "It's a north-facing room, you ought to have a fire. I'll light one if you like."

"Miles says it's dangerous," Mrs Grant explained, tucking her hands into the sleeves of her winceyette night-dress.

"Then I'll bring a fire-guard," Elizabeth insisted. "It's much too cold for you in here."

Downstairs, she found the young maid cleaning out the grate in the drawing room and shook her head in dismay at the sight of the empty bottle and dirty glasses on the mantelpiece.

Picturing the men folk drinking, while poor Mrs Grant shivered upstairs, Elizabeth told her, "I'm going to light a fire if I can find paper and wood."

The girl shot her a startled look. "The master says I'm not to bother wi' that room, he'll see to her 'imself."

"Don't worry, I shall attend to Mrs Grant. It appears to me you have quite enough to do down here."

The girl looked astonished and admitted, "I 'ave worried about the missus, she don't look too well."

Once the fire was alight the room felt more cheerful. Wrapping Mrs Grant in a blanket, Elizabeth sat her in a chair while she changed the bed-linen and filled a bowl of water to wash her hands and face.

"There," said Elizabeth with a satisfied smile, "you look better already. We'll brush your hair before you get in, then I'll make you a hot drink."

"I do miss you," said Mrs Grant once she was tucked up in bed. "Won't you consider coming back here to live?"

Elizabeth merely smiled though inwardly she seethed; how dare Miles allow his mother to be treated this way! She vowed to tackle him about it at the first opportunity.

The opportunity came sooner than she expected. As she was leaving, both Miles and his father galloped into the yard.

"Been to see Mother?" Miles said airily as they dismounted. "That would please her."

"More than it pleased me, considering how I found her!" Elizabeth shot back and saw her father-in-law hurry away.

Miles gave a long sigh. "Don't tell me she's been moaning again?" he responded in a bored voice. "I don't know what she expects us to do."

"What she expects!" Elizabeth expostulated. "My God, you have a nerve! She should be kept warm, have a good, wholesome diet, plus a lot more care and comfort."

"Wouldn't mind a bit of care and comfort myself." he grinned, turning in the direction of the stables.

"Oh do be serious!" she hissed, following him across the yard. "You need to employ someone for her, more staff."

Miles' colour deepened. "Has that snotty little bitch been complaining..." he began, disappearing into the saddle room where he took a bottle part filled with whisky from amongst the tins of polish and oils on the shelf.

"She doesn't need to," she cried in exasperation, "I can see for myself. You can't expect the girl to do everything."

"Just a minute," he said, about to raise the bottle to his lips. "Don't think you can come here giving orders."

Elizabeth's colour rose. "Have you no compassion?" she cried. "For God's sake, Miles, she's your mother!"

Miles drank greedily before he lowered the empty bottle to look down on her with contempt. "And you, Elizabeth, are my wife!" he roared, flinging the bottle aside. "It is your place to see to things here, not mine!"

"You were keen enough to help her spend her money!" she retaliated furiously. "As for being your wife, that's nothing but a farce. We may just as well divorce!"

"Divorce?" he repeated, curling his lip. "Oh no, there'll be no divorce. It was you who deserted the marital bed so you can't use that as grounds."

"But if I can prove I had good reason..."

"Exactly!" he returned harshly. "Prove it, if you can!"

* *

"Good of you to invite me, Elizabeth. A very pretty cook, too," Alex remarked as he shook off his dark overcoat.

Surprised, Elizabeth cast a brief glance in the hall mirror to view the informal crepe-de-chine dress she was wearing.

"You're most welcome," she said. "This way I don't feel quite so guilty about taking up your time."

"I believe you've been to see Mrs Grant," he said as they went into the sitting room. "How did you find her?"

Elizabeth sighed as she poured their drinks. "Well, I'm in a most difficult position, Alex, and you are the only person to whom I can turn." She went on to relate the state in which she had found Mrs Grant that morning and Miles' indifference to his mother's health.

Alex nodded thoughtfully. "The solution would be for you to move back, but I assume that would be asking too much?"

"I do wish you wouldn't make me feel so guilty, you know very well I can't." She turned away, her lip quivering. "I've suggested we seek a divorce but he won't hear of it, yet it's madness to continue."

Alex's eyes narrowed, and with unexpected directness he asked, "Is there someone else?"

Elizabeth felt hot colour flood her cheeks. "Of course not!" she insisted, her voice pitched unnaturally high. "You may not believe it, Alex, but I'd rather die than remain tied to Miles!"

Unprepared for such a dramatic response he quickly changed the subject. "Regarding Mrs Grant," he said as they entered the dining room, "I could ask nurse to call."

Striving to regain her composure as Thomas brought in their first course, she managed to ask, "Do you mean that rather fearsome lady who helps out at the surgery?"

Alex nodded, but remained silent while Thomas uncovered the tureen of homemade soup.

Once served, he took up the conversation, smiling as he said, "I assume you're referring to Miss Holmes, though I don't find her particularly intimidating myself. She'd be ideal, won't stand any nonsense, yet extremely kind. Of course, I must have good reason to make a preliminary visit as I can't demand to see Mrs Grant without being called."

"I hadn't thought of that," she admitted. "Can't you say I mentioned she didn't look too well?"

"After what you've told me, Miles may resent your interference and I don't want to cause you further trouble."

Elizabeth's head shot up. "Actually, Alex, I don't give a damn! My only concern is for Mrs Grant."

He smiled. "Never heard you put anything quite so strongly before, my dear, but don't worry, I'll see to it first thing in the morning."

"Thank you, Alex, now we can relax. Will you have more beef?"

"Splendid! Now, about the cocktail party you're organizing, when is it to be?"

"Providing the weather's good, next month, but you're welcome any time, as you know."

"Elizabeth!" he said in mock reproach. "Should Miles come to hear of that he'll be citing me as co-respondent."

She shot him a startled look as he continued, "At this time of day it doesn't do to have the car parked outside for too long."

* *

It was a hot July evening when the insistent ringing of the telephone sent Elizabeth rushing into the house, snagging her dress as she took a short cut across the rose-bed.

"I'll get it for you, darling," Molly called through the open kitchen window where she was helping Thomas arrange a tray of tiny savouries to go with the drinks.

"It's alright, I'm here," called Elizabeth, snatching up the telephone to relay her number in a breathless voice.

At the sound of her name her heart seemed to contract, and she took a cautious glance towards the kitchen door before making a reply. "So wonderful to hear you, such a clear line! Yes, I have your letter, it came yesterday. Did you receive mine?"

Smiling to herself as she listened, her expression changed suddenly and she uttered an exclamation of sheer joy. "Oh, that's marvellous! When?"

Maurici gave her the date he planned to fly to England, causing her to flush with excitement.

"A week tomorrow! I never expected you to manage it so soon."

She heard his throaty laugh before he enquired after her own arrangements. "No, no problems at this end," she told him confidently, and to his next question she nodded. "Yes, Serena's fine. I agree, it would be nice if she could travel with me but better not this time."

A tiny frown stole between her brows as he went on to pursue her present problem. "I'll tell you when we meet, though there's little I can add to what you already know."

Maurici's final expression of affection stayed uppermost in her thoughts as she returned to the garden where her guests were enjoying the savouries Thomas served, together with glasses of wine. And a soft smile played on her lips as she crossed the lawn to where her father and Alex appeared to be making serious conversation.

"This is supposed to be a happy occasion, not a funeral," she chided them laughingly, catching the vicar's attention. "Sorry, Vicar, that wasn't a nice thing to say."

"To the contrary, my dear, on such an occasion as this we should remember how indebted we are to our good Lord," the vicar said, appearing quite flushed as he held out his glass for a refill of wine. And his speech sounded faintly slurred as he continued, "As I was saying to Mrs Cussons only moments ago – and your late grandfather would have agreed – we should make time each day to thank the Lord for all He provides."

"In this instance, it's thanks to Thomas!" she heard her father say. As her mirth threatened to bubble over, she turned an appealing face to Alex.

"Jolly good evening, Elizabeth," he complimented warmly, "but you're never away from the place."

"Actually, I've resolved to do something about it," she told him brightly. "I promised myself a day in London... possibly next weekend."

Behind, Molly's head jerked round. "When did you say, Elizabeth?"

Elizabeth hesitated a moment before she repeated, "Next weekend."

For a moment Molly merely held her gaze, a faintly calculating smile on her crimson mouth as she replied softly, "I know it's none of my business, darling, but I hope you know what you're doing."

Chapter 23

With so much to organise the week passed quickly, and when Elizabeth drove Serena to the Hall early Saturday morning she could hardly believe her special day had arrived. Serena was excited about staying with her grandparents and jigged up and down on the passenger seat of the little Morris. Once there she grabbed her Teddy bear and rushed indoors leaving her mother to bring in her night-wear and change of clothes. Elizabeth was relieved there was no time to spare before she left for the station, giving her parents little opportunity to question her about where she would be spending the night.

It was only a short drive to Woodington station where she intended to leave her car overnight. Once parked, she went to purchase her ticket, handing her small suitcase to the elderly porter who, assessing its weight, said with a smirk, "A long week-end, Mrs Grant?"

His use of her married name touched a nerve and she shot him a cool glance. However, it caused her to wonder, if a simple, elderly porter could surmise that much, for how long would her secret remain safe?

The journey to York was slow, but once she'd boarded the London train they seemed to gather steam and move at greater speed. She'd bought a magazine to read on the journey but found she couldn't concentrate so slipped it into her case. Her thoughts were racing ahead, and a smile quivered on her lips as she closed it and returned it to the rack. She had spotted the layers of tissue protecting her new satin underwear; lace-edged French knickers and slip in a soft powder blue, with matching peignoir. A glow of anticipation brought her out of her reverie and she checked her fanciful thoughts; would Maurici assume they would share a room or, in the light of her married status, would he expect her to insist she sleep alone? Yet, reflecting upon the last time they were together, just the way he'd looked at her – the ripple of excitement evoked by a mere kiss – clearly expressed his desire. Without doubt, had there been time enough, they would have gone to his hotel. And now, as the train drew closer to London, she was certain the same signals would be obvious to her again.

Maurici was waiting on the platform when she alighted from the train, his expression relaxing the moment he caught sight of her. And when he reached for her hand and stooped to brush his lips on her cheeks, the months they had spent apart simply melted away.

"First the hotel, yes?" he suggested, and indicated the porter should take their cases and call a taxi. And whilst this was being attended to he sorted a three-penny piece from the change in his pocket to purchase a copy of the Times.

The hotel Maurici had chosen was south of the Thames in a quiet area overlooking parkland. He'd telephoned from the airport, reserving only one room. "I hope this arrangement is suitable to you," he whispered as they rode through the busy London streets, "unless you would prefer I reserve another room for myself,"

"You mean, we're staying as man and wife?"

He looked at her, his dark brows raised. "We have a daughter, it is almost the same, no?"

She lowered her eyes and nodded. "It will give us more time together."

He leaned towards her to murmur, "You are hoping we will sleep together?"

"Well, I had wondered," she responded softly, sensually aware of his cologne.

He sat back with a contented sigh, his attention focused on the busy streets. Elizabeth was too engrossed in thought to notice what was happening outside and cast a glance in his direction, admiring his handsome profile and the tailored lightweight suit he was wearing. Sensing her eyes upon him he turned and smiled, indicating the hotel just ahead.

As he signed the register Elizabeth stood a short distance away, attempting to show wifely indifference towards the man who accompanied her. The situation was playing havoc with her nerves until they moved towards the lift, away from the receptionists assessing gaze.

In the privacy of their room he immediately took her in his arms. "My darling, I have longed for this moment," he breathed, capturing her lips in a lingering kiss.

Overwhelmed to find herself so soon in his embrace, she drew back, her voice husky with emotion, to whisper, "I can't believe this is happening."

"You are not happy?" he cried in alarm, cupping her face in his warm hands to gently draw her close.

She shook her head in silent denial, a tear splashing down her cheek."

"But you are crying," he said, holding her against him and stroking her hair. "Please, Elizabeth, do not cry."

Soothed by his caress, she let her cheek lie against the smooth cotton shirt covering the hard wall of his chest, and confessed, "I am crying because I'm so happy."

"I also feel emotion. To hold you in my arms after so many years is almost too much..." He gave a harsh, shuddering sigh and released her to go and stare through the net curtains draping the high bay window.

Elizabeth followed, sliding her hand into his to say in dismay, "I hadn't realised it was raining quite so heavily. What do you suggest we do?"

Chuckling softly, he gestured to the dismal scene outside. "This is how I expect London to be. Bowler hats, briefcases, rain, and umbrellas." He turned to her, raising her hand to his lips as he murmured, "You English and your preoccupation with the weather. With you beside me, I don't care if it rains all the time." He studied her a moment, a sparkle of amusement in his eyes as he proposed, "We could have lunch if you wish, then decide."

"It may have ceased by the time we've dined. I'm sure there are parts of London you particularly want to visit."

"Only this room, and you in it."

She gave a faint gasp, excitement flooding her body. "Oh, Maurici, you make me so happy."

He smiled to himself as he lifted the lid of his case. "You like the room?" he asked. "You said you preferred somewhere less known, but I insisted we have a bathroom."

"Perfect, Maurici, no-one could possibly know I'm here."

He looked away to hide the twinge of pain caused by her remark. He hated the secretiveness associated with their meeting, felt she was taking caution to extremes. He wanted to declare his happiness to all London.

Realising it was a purely selfish desire, he dropped the lid, and glancing through the window said, "Let's have lunch before we unpack. By the look of it out there we have the rest of the afternoon to do that."

Sensing his change of mood, Elizabeth willingly complied. They found the dining-room to be well patronized, the menu surprisingly varied, and the view from where they were seated was a verdant, rain-washed scene of the park across the road.

Maurici soon appeared to shake off whatever was troubling him and insisted she order anything she desired. Throughout the meal he was attentive and charming, to the onlooker a vision of a doting husband. But a tiny pang of unhappiness pierced her as she wondered if this cosy scene of apparent marital harmony could ever become reality.

"You look very serious," he remarked suddenly.

"Choosing a dessert is a serious business," she returned, laughing to cover her emotion. "I'm trying to decide which will have the most cherries on top."

They laughed when the desserts were served, his with a cherry, and hers without. But thoughtful as always he caught her attention, his eyes holding hers as he reached out his spoon to place the cherry between her lips.

There was something very sensual about the way he looked at her then, contact without touching, and only the arrival of the waiter broke the spell.

"Coffee?" Maurici enquired, suggesting they take it in the lounge where he unfolded his copy of The Times to glance down the entertainment column for that evening. "We could try Ivor Novello's Perchance to Dream at the Hippodrome, or would you prefer the cinema? I see My Reputation, with Barbara Stanwyck, is showing at the Warner cinema in Leicester Square."

"My Reputation?" She rolled her eyes and smiled. "Maybe not, but I've heard good reports about the Ivor Novello show." Leaning closer to glimpse the paper she observed, "It is in its second year; perhaps we could try for seats."

"Sounds very British," he said and sent her a teasing glance. "I enjoy theatre. Occasionally, my mother accompanies me to opera at the Liceu in Barcelona."

"Tell me more about your family," she said as she poured coffee.

"Ah yes, I have photographs in my case."

Finally deciding on Perchance to Dream as their evening's entertainment, Maurici made a booking at reception and, because of the continuing inclement conditions outside, arranged for a taxi to take them. Once arrangements were completed, he suggested they go to their room to unpack and relax.

Relax? Elizabeth felt tense with excitement. Did he anticipate the magical experience of so long ago awaited them once again?

"I have very little to unpack, though I have brought a change for this evening," she said, lifting the pretty, flowered voile dress from her case to hang it away.

"And I, a change of shirt. And..." paper rustled as he uncovered a bottle of sparkling wine, "from my region. The perfect drink for lovers."

Lovers! She paused, the blue satin night-dress in her hands; the word conjured up something exciting but illicit; a pleasurable but immoral act, though she didn't consider herself sexually unprincipled. But how would the population of Woodington view it? What would they think if they knew Elizabeth Grant had a lover?

"I remembered you liked it," Maurici was saying as he went into the bathroom. "I'll stand the bottle in cold water, that should improve it."

Roused from her thoughts, Elizabeth laid the matching nightwear over a chair to one side of the bed then took out the album she had brought with her and began to describe its contents.

"Better you sit here on the bed," he said, patting the quilted satin coverlet beside him. And he held open the leather-bound album for her to name the family photographs taken in the gardens of Ashdale House, and Woodington Hall.

"I recognise your parents," he remarked, then uttered an exclamation of pleasure as he turned over a page. "*Carai!* She is beautiful," he said, gazing at a picture of Serena feeding peacocks in the grounds of the Hall.

For almost an hour they looked at photographs, Maurici also having brought with him a small collection. One in particular, a picture of his home, recaptured memories that made Elizabeth smile, and she looked up into his eyes, tears of happiness sparkling in her own.

Her head resting against his shoulder, she reached across to select a photograph. "I like this of you and Jaume picking grapes. May I keep it?"

"Of course," he replied, catching hold of her arm, "Also, I have gifts for you both." He reached into the inside pocket of his jacket and produced a small chamois pouch, and from it he withdrew a gold ring mounted with deep purple amethysts. Taking her right hand in his, he slipped it onto her finger, saying, "It belonged to my grandmother. She bequeathed it to me with the instruction I give it to the woman I choose to be my wife."

Elizabeth gazed at it admiringly. "How beautiful," she murmured, "but I'm not sure if I should wear it..."

"Dolors never wore it," he put in quickly, "said it was unlucky. But it is your birthstone, I want you to have it as I think of you as my wife."

"I'll treasure it always," she promised, reaching up to kiss his cheek.

Quick to take advantage of the mood which prevailed, he took her in his arms and kissed her fully on the mouth. "I wish that we can marry," he said softly as their lips drew apart. "Tell me, have you news?"

Elizabeth felt the cold draught of reality and shook her head. "I have no more news since last I wrote..."

"But I want you," he groaned, drawing her close again, "you don't know how much I want you."

His words were music to her ears. "I think I do," she whispered, aware of the tension within him. And as the intensity of their kiss deepened she felt herself being lowered to the bed.

Lying in Maurici's arms was like being transported into another world where tenderness and affection were a natural part of life. He feathered kisses over her face and neck, his lips trailing down to the base of her throat, but no further, teasing her, as he caressed the smooth skin of her arms. Suddenly, he let her go and tugged off his tie to toss it aside. She heard his shoes drop to the floor, one by one, before he slipped off her court shoes and eased her further onto the bed.

"You love me, yes?" he asked, leaning on one elbow to look down on her with darkly glittering eyes.

"Mm, very, very much," she murmured, wallowing in the comfort of his embrace. And as he kissed her she felt the warmth of his hand sliding along the silky curve of her leg to caress her thigh.

Her response was everything he had hoped for when she reached out to rake her fingers through his hair, her lips parting enticingly beneath his as his exploring hand discovered the sensuous smoothness of her satin underwear.

From somewhere deep in her throat came a soft moan of desire, and she pulled him down against her until his lips were level with the neckline of her blouse.

"I want to love you, Elizabeth," he breathed as he drew slightly away to unbutton her blouse. But her fingers were already there and soon the silky garment was cast aside, her skirt quickly following so that he could gaze upon her with increasing excitement. And as he slowly slipped down her sheer stockings, and the few remaining items of lacy underwear, his eyes were drawn to every inch of her as he fluttered kisses on the exposed milky hue of her flesh. As he delighted her, he tugged at the belt encircling his narrow waist and slid out of his clothes to return to her impatient embrace.

"Not so quickly this time," he smiled reflectively as he took her naked in his arms. "I want to please you, but we must take the precautions..."

She uttered a groan of frustration. "I don't care, Maurici, just love me. It's a safe time, anyway..."

He gave a short laugh. "It is never safe, not for sure."

"It is, I've calculated the date," she said in a most appealing way.

"How can you be sure?" He drew slightly away to ask. "You do this with your husband?"

"No, of course not, I told you. Not since..."

"Since when, Elizabeth?" he demanded, gripping her shoulders, his eyes bright with passion. "Since when?"

She shook her head violently. "Not in years!" she cried, sounding as if she were about to burst into tears. "And then, hardly ever."

"Forgive me, darling," he murmured hoarsely, burying his face in her neck. "It is because I love you so much. I was your first – I can't bear to think of anyone else..."

His voice faded as he became acutely aware of the warm peaks of her breasts beneath him. Unable to resist the urge to caress them, he lost all hope of remaining in control.

The following day she awoke to find Maurici's eyes upon her, glittering in the early morning light. From the pillow next to hers he smiled a very tender smile and she reached out to touch his cheek, her eyelids still heavy from a deep, contented sleep.

He found her hand and kissed it, then took her fingertips in his even, white teeth, biting each one gently as he held her sleepy gaze, declaring softly, "Darling Elizabeth, you are so very lovely, I could eat you."

"Cannibal." she murmured, pouting provocatively. "Breakfast time, already?"

"No, no, is only half past seven, we have plenty of time," he assured her, sliding his arm under her shoulders to draw her close and kiss her eager mouth.

"Dearest Maurici, it's so wonderful being here with you," she said dreamily as she reflected upon the previous afternoon; their lovemaking, the wine, and the untouched tray of afternoon tea. "And I did enjoy the show last evening. You made it a perfect day."

She lay back against his arm, her hand on his chest, fingers travelling through the dark hair growing there as her mind went back to the shower they'd shared before dressing for dinner and the theatre.

"And after the show, you enjoyed this also?" he queried throatily, a fresh wave of desire surging through him as he recalled the frenzied strength with which she'd clung to him, unwilling to release him before a million stars exploded along every fibre of his being.

"Mm, even more," she responded huskily, her hand on his waist.

"*Ai!*" he interjected softly in Catalan as he felt himself respond. "We must be careful; I don't want you pregnant again."

"I don't care!" she cried recklessly, pressing against him.

"Elizabeth, we can't," he groaned feeling his will power melt away.

"You don't want me?" she murmured petulantly against his ear.

"I'll always want you," he said, seeing tears glisten in her eyes. "But we must make love without taking risks..." he continued as the nearness of her body further stimulated his desire.

They ate breakfast in a sunny corner of the dining room when Maurici's eyes hardly left her face. He hated knowing they must soon part after they had shared so much; life without her would seem empty. They belonged together. Could it really be that six more years must pass before Elizabeth was free, or should he make known his love for her in the hope her husband would sue for divorce? He could ignore the disgrace and scandal, but what of Elizabeth, and his daughter, would it be fair on them? He couldn't suggest they live together; envisaging the problems they would encounter if Elizabeth applied for permission to live in his country in any position other than that of his legal wife.

"What are you thinking?" Elizabeth asked, regarding his rather solemn expression with an anxious little frown.

"I'm thinking I must make the most of the opportunity to look at you whilst I may," he said with a slightly lopsided smile before taking a bite into a slice of toast.

Elizabeth glanced over to the window. "Such a lovely day," she remarked with a sigh. "There are lots of couples in the park this morning; it's a perfect day for them."

"But we made our own sunshine," he said, feeling a tingle of satisfaction as he reached over to squeeze her hand. "And we will again," he added convincingly when he saw she was near to tears.

She lowered her gaze, absently fingering the amethyst ring as she said, "At least I'm fortunate in having Serena for company, she's such an affectionate child."

"Like her mother," he remarked softly. "You will kiss her for me?"

"Of course I will, a hundred times," she promised, managing a smile. "Yet, it seems wrong that you should be denied the company of your own daughter, and she of you. I'd like to show her your photograph, explain you are her father, but I don't dare, not yet."

"Perhaps she's a little too young, " he suggested by way of consolation. "She may not understand."

"That's not quite my reason," she explained. "You see, if he, Miles that is, were to insist she belongs to him, and it became known that I had acted without discretion – this weekend, for instance – he could be granted custody." She lowered her voice to add emotionally, "It could mean I may lose her, Maurici, and I couldn't bear that."

Again his hand tightened on hers. "I know," he said, drawing a long, thoughtful breath. "I wish I could do something to help, but laws relating to these problems will be different in my country."

Her mouth set in a determined line. "I shall pay my solicitor another visit, there must be something he can advise."

Maurici insisted he accompanied her to the station before he made his way to the airport. And as the train pulled away he saw her at the window, a lace-edged handkerchief fluttering from her hand as she faded from sight in the blur of his own tears. Quickly brushing them away, he picked up his case and left the station to make his way to Northolt, purchasing a newspaper on the way. If only every weekend could be like this, he thought with longing, or better still, every day.

Chapter 24

Elizabeth arrived home from the station to find Alex waiting in his car. "Will you be at home this evening?" he called. "I'd like a word, if I may."

"Of course. Is it anything urgent?"

"Actually, I called yesterday, but it will keep."

"By the way, Alex, how is Mrs Grant?"

"Much improved, I'm pleased to say," he said, putting his car into gear. "Tell you later."

As she garaged her car she wondered what had brought him to the house; concerned as she was over Miles' mother, she was in no mood to discuss the Grant family affairs. Her thoughts dwelt still on Maurici and the pleasures of that morning, clouded only by the moment of parting and the uncertainty over when they would meet again.

Preferring to change into more casual attire before she went to collect Serena, she took her case upstairs. She'd allowed Gladys an extra day free, and Thomas had gone to visit his elderly sister in York, so the house was quiet, giving her time to enjoy her memories and adjust to everyday life.

Emptying her case, she laid the barely crumpled satin night-dress and negligee on the bed, putting aside the small velvet box intended for Serena to gaze at the photograph of Maurici with his son. Engrossed in her thoughts, it was a moment before she realised someone was calling her name and recognised her mother's voice coming from the stairs. Concealing the photograph in her case, she opened the bedroom door just as her mother reached the landing outside.

"There you are!" Molly exclaimed and signalled for Serena to come up. "We noticed your car in the garage, have you been here long?"

"Only minutes," she replied, taking her daughter in her arms. I thought it best to change before I brought Serena home."

"Mm, that is pretty," Molly remarked, fingering the satin nightwear lying on the bed. Then, looking directly into Elizabeth's eyes commented, "Rather glamorous for a solo weekend, I would have thought."

Elizabeth flushed and buried her face against Serena to plant a promised kiss on her warm cheek. The child giggled and struggled out of her mother's arms, and in seconds she was over by the dressing table reaching up for the small velvet box Elizabeth had taken from her luggage. Then, before Elizabeth could stop her, she had opened it, revealing the delicate silver bracelet that lay within.

"Oh dear, was it to be a surprise?" asked Molly. "She's so quick."

"Don't worry, I brought it for her," Elizabeth said, slipping the bracelet over her daughter's hand as she instructed; "Only to wear on special occasions, darling, otherwise it may get lost."

"Today, Mummy?" Serena asked as she raised her arm to admire the gleaming band of silver round her chubby wrist.

"Yes, you may," Elizabeth said affectionately, unaware of the anguish in Molly's expression when she spotted the name of a Barcelona jeweller inside the satin lined box.

"I can't stay," said Molly. "I left your father by the river with Nicholson. He is determined to catch a fish, though I've insisted he doesn't go there unaccompanied."

Elizabeth nodded. "Yes, it's very deep behind the Hall, though he should be safe with Nicholson. I've got Alex calling this evening, something he wants to discuss."

"I won't keep you," said Molly, casting her an anxious glance. She had heard of Miles' sudden collapse the previous day but decided Alex was better suited to break the news.

Once Serena was settled in bed, Elizabeth took the bracelet back to her room. As she returned it to the box she noticed the jeweller's name in the lid and realised it was something her mother may also have spotted. She had been quick to comment on her items of luxury nightwear, Elizabeth reflected with a spasm of discomfort, and if she had noticed the Barcelona address she was sure her mother would have reached her own conclusion and would be unlikely to condone an illicit weekend in London while she and Miles were still legally man and wife.

Sighing, she closed the box, putting it into her dressing table drawer along with the photograph of Maurici which she gently kissed before locking them out of sight. It was time to get ready for Alex's visit. With a certain reluctance she stepped into the bath, her thoughts on Maurici as she sponged herself. It felt as if she were washing away the invisible print of his caressing fingers, but it would take more than simple soap and water to dissolve the memory of his touch.

Alex arrived earlier than expected so she poured an extra cup of coffee.

"Haven't interrupted your meal, have I?" he asked as he took it to one of the easy chairs by the French window. "I was in rather a hurry when I saw you earlier – Mrs Allenby was having a difficult confinement."

"What did she have?" Elizabeth enquired. "Boy, or girl?"

"A seven and a quarter pound boy," he told her with a smile. "She's tired, of course, but they're both fine."

"Oh good," said Elizabeth. "We were at school together, though I haven't seen her for simply ages."

"I notice you don't keep in touch with your old school chums and it's not good to cut yourself off like this."

Elizabeth's expression darkened. "I expect my mother sent you as it's just the sort of remark she would make."

He clicked his tongue. "You should know me better than that. Actually, I'm here to appeal to your better nature."

"Now you're making me feel guilty," she said with a short laugh. "I assume you are here on behalf of Mrs Grant."

"No, it is Miles who needs you now. He collapsed yesterday."

Elizabeth's coffee slopped into the saucer. "Oh no! What's wrong now?"

"He is your husband, don't forget..."

"Forget!" she cried. "How the hell can I when you keep reminding me!"

Alex regarded her with shocked surprise. "Elizabeth, this isn't like you..."

"I'm sorry, Alex. I'm a little on edge today. I do apologise."

"That's all right, but I'm afraid things look pretty bad. His abdomen is very enlarged. I've arranged for tests – he's in hospital, of course."

"Attributed to his drinking, I suppose," she said dully. "You know, Alex, however hard I try, I don't find it easy to be sympathetic."

"I know, but you must realise, the strength of his addiction to alcohol makes it difficult for him to resist."

"But I've tried talking to him so many times – all to no avail – he will not listen."

Tilting his head a little, he drew a slow, thoughtful breath. "I see. However, whatever you may say, I think you're still the strongest influence, and now his father's been advised against alcohol, there's a chance things could improve."

"Is Mr Grant ill?"

Alex nodded. "Heart problems – frightened him rather – but only a mild attack." He levelled his gaze at her before he continued, "So you see, once Miles is out of hospital there's a little more hope."

"Do you expect him to make a full recovery?"

"Difficult to say, depends on what they find, but with careful nursing..."

"And that is where I come in, I suppose," she concluded with a twisted smile. "Well, Alex, if I must be involved in getting Miles back to better health, I may as well tell you now. I want a divorce and once he's well enough I intend to discuss the matter with him."

"Good Lord, I hadn't realised you were serious. I thought it was just the usual marital hiccup."

She uttered a long sigh. "I'm afraid our marriage has been one long hiccup, it's time it was brought to an end."

"Elizabeth, I don't think you're aware of the seriousness of Miles' case. I suspect cirrhosis, but there's a possibility a tumour may have developed so I hope you'll forget any talk of divorce, for the time being at least."

That night Elizabeth lay awake for hours, struggling with the turmoil of her thoughts; trapped in a marriage from which her conscience would allow her no escape. She couldn't abandon Miles, whatever sacrifice she must make: in sickness and in health – regardless of her heart's desire – she had promised. Tears slid over her cheeks as she prayed for the strength to fulfil this marriage vow.

She was still sleeping the following morning when Serena came into her room, and as she pulled herself up to glance at the clock on the bedside table, her thoughts went immediately to the battle with her conscience in which her sick husband had won. She remembered Alex had offered to take her to the cottage hospital that morning when he made his usual rounds, and forced herself to be cheerful as she slipped on a dressing gown and went down to prepare breakfast for Serena.

She was only just ready when Alex's car drew up, and they covered the few miles to the hospital with hardly a word exchanged. On the train from London she had planned to make an appointment with her solicitor as soon as he opened for business. Now everything had changed would Maurici accept the delay in obtaining her freedom after she had insisted she and Miles no longer lived together as man and wife? Would he now accept that she felt duty bound to care for Miles in her own house?

With this predicament weighing heavily on her mind, she followed Alex into the office adjoining the small ward. The sister explained that even though Miles was now showing signs of recovery, he still had a fever, his speech was slightly incoherent, and he would remain in their care for some time. They were weaning him off the alcohol, but only gradually to avoid the risk of delirium tremens.

"You will want to see your husband," she said, her starched white cap bobbing about with the movement of her head. "He's been asking for you which is a good sign." Leading them from her office to a room off the ward, she ushered Elizabeth inside.

"Your wife is here to see you, Mr Grant," she announced briskly before she withdrew to continue her duties.

Not knowing quite what to expect, Elizabeth held her breath as she moved closer to the bed, feeling a wave of compassion as she looked down on Miles' tear-filled eyes. "No need for that," she said gently. "You know I wouldn't refuse you a visit at a time like this."

"I've been such a fool," he whimpered, his lower lip trembling as he groped for her hand. "Doctor says I'm lucky to be alive – you've got to help me, Elizabeth.

"Yes, but you mustn't let it upset you," she advised quietly, sliding his hand back under the bedclothes as she struggled to find a suitable response.

He uttered a wavering sigh. "I'm so pleased to see you, I didn't think you'd come."

She forced a smile. "Well, I'll be here again tomorrow, Miles, maybe in the afternoon."

"We can start again," he said suddenly. "Come back to the farm. I'll employ more help, make it easier. I realise it was too much for you..."

"Not now," she pleaded, her expression filled with pain. "We'll talk about it when you're feeling better."

"I'll change, just give me a chance, please," he gasped, his voice growing stronger.

"Don't rush me, Miles..." Hearing a footstep she turned to see Alex in the doorway, ready to leave.

"Don't forget what I said," Miles begged, drawing her towards him with surprising force so that she felt obliged to drop a brief kiss on his forehead before she walked away.

* *

Struggling to conceal his dismay, Maurici rose from the breakfast table.

"Something wrong?" queried his mother, her keen gaze fixed on the letter he was holding.

"No, no, everything is fine," he replied with feigned cheerfulness and slid the letter back into the envelope. "I'll read it later; I didn't realise it was so late."

"Do your English friends also send you newspapers?" she asked with a curious little smile. "I noticed one in your room when I took in your clean linen."

He looked at her for a moment, his brow furrowed. "Oh, that," he said and reached for his brief case. "Must rush – tell you later."

Barely two kilometres away he drew his motorcycle to the side of the road and switched off the engine. He'd found it impossible to concentrate on the contents of Elizabeth's letter whilst his mother hovered near and, after the first glimpse, he'd dreaded to read further.

Withdrawing the letter from his pocket he read the contents a second time. What was Elizabeth saying? he asked himself, gazing miserably over the leafy vineyards. Were they never to be together? How long must he wait? He saw the letter had been written only days following their meeting in London, and he read again the first page where she wrote of her disappointment over not being able to consult her solicitor. Something unexpected had occurred that would prevent her from receiving his letters, or taking a call. She must behave with the utmost discretion, he read, and groaned in frustration when he turned to the next page. Her husband was seriously ill, his future health in doubt, and when discharged from hospital he would require constant care. She went on to explain, his only hope of recovery was for him to be nursed at Ashdale House.

He lit a cigar and exhaled thoughtfully, the thin stream of blue smoke unbroken in the still, warm air. Elizabeth and her husband would be living in the same house, though not, she assured him by underlining the words, in the same room. They may be sharing the house, she wrote, but only he, Maurici, would ever share her bed.

"But when!" he hissed, flicking his half-smoked cigar onto the dusty road before turning over the page where she begged him to understand her difficult situation, her moral duty. For how long could he bear the waiting, he wondered as he perused the final paragraph in which she expressed her love for him, her hope to meet again. Only The Lord knew when.

* *

After two weeks in hospital, Miles was considered well enough to be discharged into Elizabeth's care. "I think you'll find him a changed man," Alex said as they drove to hospital on the day he was to be discharged.

"We will see," Elizabeth murmured. "For his sake, I hope you're right."

"The Sister considers him a reformed character," he said and glanced her way to add, "She could be right, you know."

Elizabeth's smile was twisted. "A very optimistic view for someone in her profession, I would have thought."

"That's rather a defeatist attitude to take."

Elizabeth's head shot round. "When you've struggled to get someone undressed, cleaned vomit etcetera from their clothes, listened to their whining apologies, day in day out, you may criticize. Until then, don't dare to call me defeatist ever again!"

He laid his hand over her clenched fingers as he brought the car to a halt by the hospital door. "I'm sorry, you're right. It's just that you're usually determined to succeed it surprised me to hear you sound so unsure."

"I've said I'll look after him, haven't I?" she returned shortly as she flung open the door of the car.

"True, and maybe the future will look brighter once you have adjusted."

"Huh, another optimist!" she said with a humourless smile. "Let me tell you this, Alex, just being in the same house as Miles is something to which I'll never adjust."

* *

It was the week following his receipt of Elizabeth's letter when Maurici spotted Enric hurrying towards the railway station.

"Why not pay me a visit?" Enric called before he disappeared into the huge building. "And bring the boy."

Strangely, Maurici had already thought of calling on him after he'd received her letter; if he couldn't correspond with her, then perhaps Enric was still in touch with her parents, could keep him informed.

So, the Sunday morning after their brief meeting, Maurici changed his son into clothing more suited to the heat of the August day.

"You can have a little peace today," he told his mother as she held the boy still whilst he combed his thick, curly hair. "I hear there's a new restaurant in the village, why don't you and *papa* go there?"

"We'll see," she said, "though as Elvira and Miquel are going out I was hoping we'd have time for a chat..."

"Nothing urgent?" Maurici butted in as he took out cushions and a blanket to ensure Jaume had a comfortable journey.

"No, not urgent exactly," she said as she limped behind them and reached out to kiss the child on each cheek.

"Perhaps another time, *mama*. Make sure you rest today."

Coaxing the excited child to sit still in the sidecar, Maurici adjusted the harness to hold him safely in the seat. He'd felt sure his mother had been going to bring up the subject of the English newspaper she'd brought to his attention earlier. He'd caught her studying him often and wished she wouldn't concern herself over his private life. It wasn't that he minded her knowing, but at the moment he couldn't bring himself to discuss the situation between himself and Elizabeth without becoming emotional.

Ensuring Jaume was comfortable, Maurici stood astride the machine and slid the goggles down over his eyes. "Give grandmother a wave," he prompted, raising his own arm as the engine fired and they pulled away from the house.

Also in the sidecar he'd stowed a few eggs wrapped in newspaper, bottles of wine, and a jar of Cabell d'Angel, the delicious preserve of melon and sugar that his mother had made, all out of reach of Jaume's exploring fingers. Remembering Enric enjoyed an occasional foreign cigarette, he'd added a packet of Craven A purchased on his last visit to London.

London. He scowled as he drove the now familiar country route, his thoughts going back to that weekend with Elizabeth, every little detail still fresh in his memory. They'd been happy together, loving only each other, so what had possessed her to agree to take her husband into her home? Was there no-one else to care for him? Or had she been overcome by compassion? He clenched his jaw, cursing himself for allowing his thoughts to wander yet again. From his eye corner he saw his son smiling up at him, his wide-eyed, trusting gaze easing away a little of the pain.

"Nearly there, Jaume" Maurici mouthed as he turned his face from the wind to glance along the track leading to the house where his relatives used to live. Soon they were dropping down into Sitges with its fringe of palms and, beyond, a calm, blue sea.

The moment Maurici brought the motorcycle combination to a halt, Enric was out of the house. And Jaume shrieked with delight when he was lifted from behind the windscreen, his chubby finger pointing in the direction of the sunlit beach.

"I don't envisage a moment's trouble from him!" Maurici laughed as Jaume toddled off onto the sand. And when

Enric brought out a garden trowel and a small enamel bowl the child played happily whilst he and Maurici seated themselves outside the house to enjoy a glass of wine.

There were newspapers spread over the table, held there beneath a jug of wine, so reminiscent of another visit, Maurici thought as he visualised the scene. It had been a warm Sunday morning such as this when he had met Elizabeth and her parents socially for the first time. Raising his glass he glanced across to catch a smile from Enric.

"Reminds me of another time, years ago, when our English friends were with us" his companion remarked. "They were happy days even though the war was coming our way." He shook his head slowly as he puzzled, "What year would that be, thirty-eight, thirty-nine?"

"April thirty-eight," Maurici replied promptly, "and almost as warm as today."

Enric nodded towards the beach. "Let us hope the boy never has to live through a war."

As though he knew he was being spoken about, Jaume glanced up and laughed, and picking up the bowl he'd filled with sand he came up the beach to empty it at Enric's feet.

"Oops!" Enric exclaimed with a grin, then paused and leaned forward to look down into the child's wide, sparkling eyes. "My God, Maurici, it is amazing! Wait here a moment..." And he dashed into the house.

Mystified, Maurici scooped the spilt sand back into the bowl and followed Jaume onto the beach where he showed him how to turn it upside down to make a neat mound.

"How old is Jaume?" Enric asked, coming to join them on the sand.

Maurici looked up, noting the photograph in Enric's hand. "Three in November," he replied, wrinkling his nose against the bright sun. "Why, what have you there?"

"James sent me this picture of Elizabeth's daughter when she was about his age. An amazing likeness, don't you think?"

Maurici studied the photograph, similar to the one Elizabeth had given him when last they met...

"You see what I mean – the likeness?" Enric persisted. "They would pass for brother and sister any day."

Maurici glanced up. "They are," he said quietly. "Well, half-brother and sister, the half that looks like me."

Enric frowned. "Are you serious, my friend? Are you telling me the child of Elizabeth is yours?"

Overcome by a wave of emotion, Maurici nodded and turned away. Sensing his visitor was overwrought, Enric put out a comforting hand, suggesting he take another glass of wine.

"*No, gràcies,*" he declined once he had recovered his composure, and nodding in his son's direction explained, "I must stay sober today."

"Sorry I brought up the subject, I didn't realise..."

Wordlessly, Maurici gestured in his son's direction, finally managing to say, "I'm a little over-emotional today. But I wish to ask a favour concerning Elizabeth."

"You still think of her, after so many years?"

"All the time," he admitted. And once he had contained his troubled thoughts, continued, "Of course, you're not aware of our recent meetings in London." And he went on to explain all that had occurred in Elizabeth's life in the intervening years, concluding with the letter he had received from her only days before.

"So, she didn't know you had been taken prisoner until after she'd married?" Enric queried, inhaling on one of the cork-tipped cigarettes. "Did she not receive my letter?"

"Unfortunately, no. I suppose it was a difficult time for everyone," Maurici said, keeping a watchful eye on Jaume.

"Only when Molly wrote to tell me how James was progressing did she mention that Elizabeth had married. After that I thought it best to be discreet, particularly as I'd had no reply from Elizabeth."

Maurici shot him a rueful smile. "Indeed yes. But when next you write, perhaps you will enquire after Elizabeth and Serena on my behalf. Without mentioning me, of course, just so that I know what is happening there."

Enric nodded, and slanting one eyebrow in Maurici's direction, said, "It is obvious you have great affection for her, but what do you think the future holds for you now?"

Maurici raised his hands, then let them fall to his sides in a gesture of despair. "I adore her," he admitted softly, "so all I can do is hope..." and felt his throat constrict with the ache of unshed tears. To hide further signs of emotion he slipped off his shoes and went over to his son. And as they wandered barefoot towards the warm sea, Maurici looked down on the dark, curly head, murmuring, "Yes, my sweet one, we still have hope...

Chapter 25

Miles had been out of hospital almost two months and was making a slight improvement each day. Only once during the first week had he slipped from grace when he sneaked the bottle of cooking sherry from the kitchen cupboard. As a result he had become unreasonably aggressive, his language quite shocking, until Serena was almost hysterical with fright. Unable to reason with him, Elizabeth had called Alex who, with Thomas' assistance, heaved him semi-conscious into bed. The following day he'd suffered the torment of guilt, apologising profusely as he lay in his single bed.

"Oh, God, I do feel ill," he had groaned. "It won't happen again, Elizabeth, I promise, it's not bloody worth it."

Since then there had been no problems, and although Elizabeth was repulsed by his manner she had sympathy for his condition. She managed to praise him over his progress and cajole him into taking the drugs Alex prescribed, and as his appetite improved he began to appear in better health. James and Molly called occasionally, though Elizabeth thought their conversation with him sounded stilted. Jane looked in most days whilst out for her morning ride which enabled Elizabeth to give more time to Serena when she wasn't at school, or visit her parents at the Hall.

It was nearing the end of September, a time of the year when Elizabeth loved to walk through the Hall gardens to linger beneath the shining copper leaves of the layered beeches and watch the peacocks strutting over the lawns. Today when she called, James was seated at the front of the house, his writing materials balanced on his knees.

"Your mother is organizing someone to bring my table," he told her. "I want to get a letter off to dear old Enric."

"I'm pleased you keep in touch. Do give him my kind regards."

"Wouldn't surprise me if he turned up here one day!" he said. "They'll ease up on travel restrictions eventually, and I believe by early next year it will be possible to fly directly to Northolt, via Paris I believe, from Madrid."

She frowned; Maurici hadn't mentioned a problem visiting London, although he had chosen a more complicated route. "It would be wonderful having Enric to stay," she agreed warmly, "though I hadn't realised restrictions pertaining to travel were still in force."

"According to Enric they are," James told her, taking his weight on the armrests of his chair to ease himself into a more comfortable position. "Also, he tells me that doctor chappie, Maurici something or other, and his son spent the day with him a few weeks ago."

"Really," Elizabeth responded carefully. "Well, I suppose there's no better place for any three-year old to play."

"I didn't realise you were aware of the child's age."

Embarrassed, she looked away. "I merely guessed."

James' eyes narrowed. Molly had been right about Elizabeth and the young Catalan. His heart ached for her; twenty-six, no longer the naive girl upon whom he could impress his will, he thought irritably. Even so, he hated to think of her wasted life with Miles.

The sound of rattling crockery brought him out of his contemplative mood and he turned to see Pincott carrying a table on which Molly placed a tray before directing the butler to bring out chairs. As they waited, coffee cups in hand, Molly caught Elizabeth's faint gasp and saw she had turned deathly pale.

"What is it, darling?" she cried, but before she could reach her she saw the cup and saucer slip from Elizabeth's hand as she sank helplessly to the ground.

Hearing the crash, Pincott dashed forward with a chair but Molly, assuming Elizabeth had fainted, wisely let her lie. "She'll be fine in a moment," she said, dropping to her knees to waft the morning paper over her daughter's face. And as she began to stir, observed, "There, she's coming round already."

"Pincott! Telephone Doctor Wilson," James directed and, to silence the objection Molly appeared about to make, insisted, "Just to be on the safe side. Can't be too careful, there may be something going about."

Looking pale and distressed, Elizabeth was helped to a chair. "I'll be all right in a moment," she resisted weakly. "No need to call Alex, it's just the heat"

"We'll let Alex decide," Molly said, brushing grass from her daughter's back.

"Then I shall see him indoors!" Elizabeth announced through tight lips as she rose and marched off towards the house. But seeing her mother following, said shortly, "Do stay there, Mummy, I'm perfectly all right."

Molly hesitated and sighed; there it was again, that strange new secretiveness and sharpness of manner.

Elizabeth glanced back, her expression strained as she said, "Sorry, I thought you were intending to fuss over me."

"No, darling. I realise having Miles at Ashdale must put you under a great strain, but if you need to confide in someone, I'm here."

Elizabeth felt tears of remorse sting her eyes, and with a murmured apology she went indoors to await Alex.

Molly was anxious, convinced Elizabeth's manner was connected with her recent meeting with the young Catalan and she feared renewing his acquaintance would bring only further distress. Returning to where James was seated, she nodded towards the house, her voice wavering as she whispered, "Oh, James, I do hope I'm wrong, but the only time I ever knew Elizabeth to faint was when she was pregnant."

With her elbows resting on the polished library table Elizabeth waited by the open window for Alex to arrive. Fainting here, in front of her parents, was the last thing she had wanted, and now they were fussing over something she had suspected for more than a week. Not that Maurici was entirely to blame. During those deliriously happy hours in London she had been reckless, dismissing the need for caution as she had urged him to abandon himself to their every desire. But since that blissful weekend much had changed; Miles was in no fit state to discuss divorce and completely dependent upon her for his continuing better health. She sighed, a baby would be another obstacle to her gaining her freedom. Miles was a practised liar, once threatening to stop her from taking Serena away. Possibly, this baby too?

She gave a start when Alex entered. "They had no business to call you, it's just the heat."

"Perhaps you've been overdoing things at Ashdale," he said, taking her wrist. "You're rather tense, pulse a little fast. No problems with Miles since I changed his prescription?"

"None at all. Apart from that one lapse, he's done well and I'm beginning to have a better understanding of the problem. I realise it can't be easy for him."

"All the credit is due to you, Elizabeth, and I notice you and he seem to be getting along reasonably well."

She shrugged. "Reasonably, I suppose."

He gave a faint smile. "You're not pregnant by any chance?"

She pursed her mouth and looked him straight in the eye. "Yes, Alex, I am, so what do you say to that?"

He lifted one eyebrow. "Then I think you and Miles are getting along more than just reasonably well, don't you? Come and see me after surgery and bring a urine sample with you. One never knows, this could be the making of Miles."

Miles? She laughed aloud, an almost hysterical sound. "Oh no, don't tell him, not yet..."

"Indeed not, Elizabeth, I'll leave that entirely to you."

* *

Saddened as Maurici had been to receive Elizabeth's last letter, it had brought with it a small measure of relief. Because of the pressure of work, until he qualified, he knew he must forego taking days off from his studies as he had done two months earlier when he'd travelled the roundabout route to London.

It had been a busy year, he'd sat in on operations, assisted in the theatre, and now he was to complete a course on psychiatry at another hospital, a subject he enjoyed. He would be studying under a well known professor who demanded his students give one hundred percent attention, and there would be little free time. This would mean less temptation to travel, and less financial worries. His journey to London had been worth every pesseta but, in addition to his fare, the price he'd paid for an illegal signature on a travel permit had been exorbitant. And now, with the increased annual cost of books and medical equipment, he began to doubt if the money set aside for his training would see him through. Not that he would turn down an opportunity to meet Elizabeth, should he be fortunate enough to receive an invitation.

He sighed heavily as he wondered about her; he had yet to learn of the situation at Ashdale House, discover why this husband of hers had returned and what did he suffer. He thought of Serena, in the company of a man who was not her father, yet knew he had no right to object.

No right to object? The question dogged his weary mind until he lost all power of concentration and pushed his books aside. But he must complete his studies to qualify for an honourable profession. He needed something to offer Elizabeth, provide a future for Serena and Jaume. Even then, it all depended upon her success in the pursuit of freedom.

* *

"So, you already know," said Miles as the doctor took a seat by his bed.

"Naturally, Elizabeth felt she should have it confirmed," Alex said, reaching into his bag.

"Now, can you sit up for me whilst I listen to your chest?"

Miles did as he was asked. "Hope it's a boy..." he began, then jumped as Alex proceeded to place the cold stethoscope on his pale, smooth skin.

"So, you're hoping for a boy," Alex took up when he'd completed his examination.

"Most definitely!" Miles emphasised, giving his blanket a tug. "Horses, rugby, cricket – much more fun to be had with boys. I'll have to get myself fit for a bit of bowling practice if I'm to make a cricketer of him..."

"Hold on, it's not yet born." Alex began but Miles' enthusiasm ran on.

"It will be a boy this time, I'm sure. It has to be."

"Either way, for baby's sake, you must keep off drink"

"Good God, man, you don't need to tell me that!" Miles cried, flushed with indignation. "I'll not allow another drink past my lips, Elizabeth would be furious."

"Without her you wouldn't be alive today," Alex reminded him, unconvinced. "She's been through a lot recently."

"Which is why I've decided to stay on here," Miles said smugly. "Otherwise I can't guarantee to remain teetotal."

* *

The fourth of October, the seventh anniversary of his daughter's birth, Maurici realised with a stab of guilt as he left the examination room. The question paper had brought the date to his notice and he longed to be free to telephone her, offer his love and good wishes. But Elizabeth had not yet rescinded her wish that he cease contact with them until her husband's health improved sufficiently for him to move out. He once tried to reach her by telephone but hearing a male voice on the line he had made the excuse of having a wrong number and realised he may make it difficult for her.

He stifled a sigh as he left the building, pausing to gaze thoughtfully onto the quiet street. He could clearly remember the morning in March when he'd heard Serena's high-pitched laughter in the background as he spoke to Elizabeth on the telephone; the same childish excitement he heard when his son welcomed him home, a sound he'd grown to love.

"Maurici! *Bon dia!*" he heard and raised his eyes to see the stocky figure of Enric emerging from a car pulled up by the pavement.

"Good to see you!" Maurici exclaimed, his spirits lifting as he extended his hand. "What brings you to this part of town?"

"On my way back to the office," said the other. "That is, after I've had a bite to eat. How about you?"

The corners of Maurici's mouth went down. He said, "I had another exam this morning."

"I don't think you need worry over the result!" Enric laughed. "If you're free, why not join me for a drink?"

Maurici's expression brightened. "Perhaps I will," he said, turning to walk beside the older man. "My daughter is seven years old today, I can drink to her good health."

At the tapas bar they selected portions of sea-food and crusty bread, and shared local wine from a narrow-spouted vessel as Maurici spoke of further exams and interviews he had yet to attend. Then, after what he considered was a reasonable pause, he enquired about the Purcells. Enric merely nodded, reluctant to divulge the content of the letter he'd received until Maurici pressed him further.

"It is not good news," Enric began with a slow shake of his head. "I wasn't going to mention it if you hadn't asked."

"As bad as that, heh?" said Maurici despondently. "I realise it is a private letter, and perhaps I shouldn't ask, but if it's news concerning Elizabeth I must know."

His companion reached into his briefcase. "I have it here. You'll find a bit of family news on the last page."

Maurici took the letter and saw the typewritten script had almost cut through the flimsy sheets of light blue paper. He skimmed over the first two pages, noting Elizabeth's name appeared only in the last paragraph where her father wrote of having lunch at her home. His heart contracted painfully when he read, 'Elizabeth and her husband may have resolved their differences now he's back at Ashdale House. They appear to be a reasonably happy family', James had written, and went on to mention his beautiful granddaughter, Serena, who would shortly reach her seventh birthday and was growing fast. James' bold signature followed, and beneath it a postscript that read, 'Elizabeth sends her kind regards'. But there was no reference to an item Enric had included in his letter, conveying the good wishes of the visitor he'd had.

"Sorry, my friend," Enric murmured, his hand on Maurici's shoulder, "but it says only 'appear happy', nothing more."

Seeped in misery, Maurici seemed oblivious to the other's presence as he re-read the final paragraph. The woman who had lain so lovingly in his arms barely three months ago was now part of a happy family, it told him. So, did Elizabeth truly desire her freedom, or was he merely an occasional spark of excitement in her preferred way of life?

* *

On the first day of Spring the following year Timothy James William arrived, a few weeks before the expected date, after a short but painful labour which left Elizabeth exhausted.

"Six and a half pounds, quite big enough," Alex said as the nurse handed her the cleanly wrapped bundle. "Imagine the size of him if you'd gone full term!"

Elizabeth gave him a wry smile. "I'd rather not, Alex, although I must admit it all happened rather quickly."

The doctor smiled. "Well, he's in excellent health, and it's only five minutes to one so you'll still get a good night's sleep. Don't worry about Miles," he added in a lowered voice, "I've given him a sedative which should keep him quiet." As he took up his cup of tea he nodded towards the nurse, saying, "Nurse Holmes will stay until morning. She's been aware of Miles' problem ever since his mother died."

Elizabeth nodded and gazed down on the tiny bundle, a smile on her lips as she smoothed a forefinger over the wisps of still damp, dark hair covering the baby's head, just like Serena's had been at this age. And her heart seemed to swell as she listened to the soft whimpering sounds, typical of the newly born, and thought longingly of Maurici as she cradled his child in her arms.

Suddenly aware of Alex's eyes upon her, his expression difficult to read, she gave him a tired smile. "Sorry, I was miles away. What was it you were saying?"

Alex chuckled. "I merely said, I'm pleased you included the name William, after your grandfather."

"I think it will please both Mummy and my grandmother," she said, half expecting him to query the first name she had chosen; Timothy – the English equivalent of Timoteu – Maurici's second name.

* *

"I want a brother to play with," Jaume insisted petulantly, scuffing the toes of his shoes on the dusty surface of the village street.

"Don't do that, you'll ruin your shoes," Maurici rebuked, making a grab for his son's hand as he tried to dash away.

"You've got a handful there," his late wife's sister said, laughing as she rocked her baby's pram back and forth. "How old is he now?"

"He'll be four on the ninth of November and already shows a fierce determination to have his own way," he told her with a rueful smile."

"Then he takes after you, Maurici. I can't recall Dolors having ambitions to be any other than a wife and mother; God rest her soul." The young woman made a fleeting sign of the cross and to Jaume she said, "When my baby is older you can play with him. *Si?*"

Jaume scowled. "I want to play now!" he wailed, trying to escape his father's grip.

Maurici uttered a sigh of exasperation. "I think we had better go, he's out of sorts today. No doubt my mother will pacify him with a few sweetmeats from her bag."

"Perhaps that is what he misses, Maurici, a little loving care. Not that you neglect him," she hurried to add, "but he's very young to be without a mother."

Maurici nodded and looked down on his son's upturned face with its big, pleading eyes. "I know what Jaume likes," he said and lifted the child onto his shoulders. "He likes to ride up there so that he can look into the fountain to see where the water comes out."

Wishing his late wife's sister a pleasant day, and with Jaume now shrieking with delight, he jogged off in the direction of the village square where his mother rested beneath the large leaves of a mulberry tree, fanning herself in the heat of late morning.

"Have you been a good boy?" she said, rummaging in her bag until she found a tit-bit for the child who then went to make a closer inspection of the pigeons pecking at scraps of bread littering the rough ground. And whilst the child's attention was taken she enquired, "Now, tell me, Maurici, what have you been doing with yourselves?"

"We met Dolors' sister with her new baby and that started Jaume off again. You know, this playmate he wants. He's been pestering me for weeks," he said with a long-suffering sigh. "But something she said made me think, I wonder if he does miss the affection of a woman."

"A passing phase," said Carmen with a dismissive gesture. "You give him all the love and attention any child could wish for. What you don't realise is, she's trying to find a husband for her sister-in-law, and someone in your profession will be considered most eligible."

"You mean her husband's widowed sister? Do I know her?"

"Of course you do, she's the one with protruding teeth. She brought her to the house a week or so ago, the one I overheard blaspheming."

Maurici smiled. "Ah, yes. Not that the poor woman can help the way her teeth protrude, but she'd hardly be my dream-girl if they were perfect. And the political views of her family are far too militant. Marriage to such a woman would be like being constantly at war!"

"I didn't care for her manner," she agreed. "Even so, I don't expect you to remain single all your life."

Maurici shrugged but remained silent. His eyes were on Jaume yet his thoughts were with Elizabeth. The woman he longed to make his wife, an ideal mother, and Serena, the playmate Jaume yearned for...

"I hope you're not still hankering after that English girl you met again in London," Carmen ventured and glimpsed his surprise. "Not that I object to foreigners," she added shrewdly, "but it's too great a distance over which to conduct a serious courtship, don't you think?"

"Forgive me, mama, I'd rather not discuss it."

Noting his guarded expression, she raised her plump shoulders and said gently, "As you wish, but I don't want to see you grow into a bitter and lonely man."

A good description of my present state, he thought with a gentle shake of his head; lonely for Elizabeth, and bitter because he'd had no word for almost a year. And to read in her father's letter to Enric that she appeared to be living in harmony had increased the torment. What was he to do? Should he try to forget her, give up hope of seeing his daughter, not risk breaking up a marriage she may have salvaged? He knew it was pure selfishness, but the strength of his love for Elizabeth overrode his desire not to jeopardize her happiness. He would telephone Ashdale House just once more.

* *

"Miles, I won't tolerate it, you must leave this house!"

"For God's sake, Elizabeth, shut up!" he yelled, pulling the bedclothes over his head.

"But you know it doesn't agree with you – you're so damned rude – and you promised not to touch another drop."

"I know, but it's one of York's main race meetings," came the muffled response. "You can't expect me to miss that. Even old Jane would agree."

"Leave my grandmother out of this, she's not going, and don't blame me if you're ill. Alex will be furious..."

"Alex, Alex, Alex! That's all I ever bloody well hear from you. It wouldn't surprise me to discover you two are having an affair! And it makes me wonder if the boy is mine..."

She stood her ground, her cheeks flushed as she demanded, "And if we are, what would you do about it?"

"Absolutely nothing," he thundered and winced, "so you'll not get rid of me that way. You wouldn't want to lose Timothy, and I know that other brat's not mine, but I'd make sure I got custody of her as well." He winced again and continued with a smirk of triumph. "If you walk out on me you'll be on your own. Now, for Christ's sake get me some Aspro!"

"Look here, you either pull yourself together or leave. If you want to kill yourself with drink that's your affair, not mine!" At the door she turned to add furiously, "And you can get your own damned Aspro!"

It was not long after this heated exchange when Doctor Wilson called. Going towards the stairs he paused to ask, "How do you think Miles would react if I propose he goes into a private hospital for a couple of weeks?"

"An excellent idea, provided he'll go," Elizabeth agreed. "Already he's mentioned celebrating during the racing season which I always dread. You know, if I didn't risk losing the children, I wouldn't hesitate to seek a separation."

"I'll see what he says," he began, but she laid a restraining hand on his arm.

"Before you go up, Alex, I ought to warn you, I allowed myself to be drawn into an argument with him this morning. His manner was most infuriating, even suggested you and I are having an affair merely because I mentioned your name."

"I suppose he has to pin his inadequacies on someone." He smiled, glancing to the child she held who was shrieking to be put down.

"Perhaps," she said, containing the wriggling youngster. "But do let me know what he says before you go."

He nodded, his eyes on Timothy who sought to reach the bright fastener on his medical case. "He's a determined little fellow for five months," was his laughing comment. "Takes after you, I would say."

Elizabeth gave him a serene smile. "I've got to be strong, otherwise I'd never cope."

More than half an hour passed before Alex came downstairs. Elizabeth was growing anxious, convinced he was having difficulty persuading Miles to agree.

"At the moment he's filled with remorse, though that made it rather easier for me," Alex told her, accepting the coffee she poured. "But, providing you and Timothy visit him regularly, he's agreed to go. I've warned him of the consequences of imbibing alcohol, although I think he's still feeling pretty rotten after last night which helped me get the message home."

"I suppose it got really out of hand after his mother died. She left him quite a sizeable legacy, you know."

"I advised him to invest it for Timothy, and do himself a favour at the same time." His expression grew serious. "I wasn't joking, he is seriously endangering his life by his continued drinking."

"As bad as that, is it? Well, I hope he has taken notice of you as I lost patience with him this morning, threatened to turn him out if he gets drunk again."

"Well, you can forget divorce," Alex interrupted, his expression grave. "If he continues at this rate you'll be a widow much sooner than you realise."

"I see, that rather changes things," she said in a barely audible voice. Then, gathering her thoughts, said brightly, "At least, with Miles in hospital, the children can enjoy the next couple of weeks in peace."

Alex raised his brows. "And after that?"

"I'll cope," she resolved in a manner faintly reminiscent of her mother. "It would be very selfish of me to put his life in jeopardy, my conscience won't allow me to do that."

* *

It was the end of August before Maurici had the opportunity to use a private telephone. At first he couldn't get through and began to feel guilty over using the professor's own line. Deciding to make a last attempt, he asked for the international operator once more.

Suddenly it all happened, he was connected with Great Britain then Ashdale House. He held his breath when a woman's voice came on the line. He knew it wasn't Elizabeth, yet he continued in precise English, "I wish to speak to Mrs Grant," as he had rehearsed for the past hour."

"Who is it calling, please?"

"Doctor Nightingale," he said, the first name that came to mind.

"Well, I'm sorry, Doctor, Mrs Grant is at the hospital with the baby."

"Baby?" Maurici queried in alarm. "You are speaking of her daughter, Serena?"

"No, Doctor, the new baby," she corrected him distinctly, "the little boy."

Elizabeth in hospital? A new baby boy... An awful numbness enveloped him as he stared abstractedly at the opposite wall when it was a few moments before he realised the line was still open.

"No, no message," he managed, his hand tightening on the receiver. With a new baby to care for Elizabeth's responsibilities lay with her family. There was no room in her life for him. Dejectedly, he repeated, "No message."

* *

"Tell Gladys about the lovely picnic we had on the way back," Elizabeth said brightly as she lifted Timothy from the car and ushered Serena up the steps of Ashdale House. And handing the hamper to the housemaid, she asked, "Any calls whilst I was at the hospital?"

"Two," Gladys told her. "One from the vicar, and another from a doctor – a Doctor Nightingale I think it were. The vicar says he'll call on Mister Miles tomorrow when he does his hospital visit, but the doctor asked to speak to you and wouldn't say what about."

Elizabeth frowned. "Doctor Nightingale? I've never heard of anyone of that name..." She broke off, smiling. "Probably Doctor Wilson having a joke."

But it was Alex who thought she was joking when she told him why she had rung. "No, Elizabeth," he said, "I didn't call you. As a matter of fact, I've been on my rounds this afternoon. Most likely Gladys misheard, I know of no doctor around here who practices by that name."

Chapter 26

Serena smiled at her mother's reflection as she stood before the mirror combing her newly-washed hair. "We really are alike," she said, "except for our eyes."

Elizabeth met her daughter's enquiring gaze. "I took after my mother, I suppose."

"But Grandpa's are also blue," she said and raised a pointing finger in the direction of Miles' room to add, "His too."

Elizabeth shrouded her daughter's head in a warm, fluffy towel. "I know. Now come along, dry your hair."

In a muffled voice, Serena continued, "Someone at school said he's not my father, and that's why my eyes are brown."

Elizabeth stiffened. "You shouldn't heed silly gossip, darling."

"It doesn't matter if he isn't," came the shrugged response from beneath the towel, "I don't like him, anyway!"

"Serena, that's not a very nice thing to say!" her mother reproved, but the girl merely grabbed the towel from her and dashed off, shutting herself in her own room. Troubled by Serena's frank statement, Elizabeth closed her eyes.

Miles rarely missed an opportunity to find fault with everything she did. In his eyes, the poor girl compared unfavourably with Timothy. She had tried to explain Miles' unreasonable behaviour, could appreciate the shame a girl of thirteen must feel each time he was brought home drunk. Thankfully, she showed no animosity towards her younger brother and had bought a present for his fifth birthday, the following day.

Elizabeth gazed sadly at her own reflection; how could she expect someone so young to take an adult view of Miles' sorry state in addition to worrying over rumours about the true identity of her father? How was she to deal with it when she felt unable to confide in her own mother? She considered her father more approachable, though he never intimated that he realised anything was amiss, and she didn't want to worry him unnecessarily. Alex was aware of the facts, but would he be sympathetic, or merely remind her she had brought these problems on her own head?

"Your husband is such a gentleman," beamed one of the young mothers, ushering her child into the hall at Ashdale.

Elizabeth put on a brave face, knowing Miles was at his best in these situations, fussing over the ladies whose children were attending Timothy's birthday tea party, and taking credit for the polite and gentle personality of the boy as though Timothy's upbringing had been entirely his own doing.

"Yes, he'll make a good sportsman, just as I was,." Miles boasted, patting Timothy's dark head as he greeted the new arrivals."

Elizabeth then overheard him saying, "We ought to offer the ladies a drop of sherry, Thomas?" And her heart sank as he volunteered, "I'll just nip out for another bottle."

She saw the discomfort in Thomas' expression and followed Miles out to his car. "Please, Miles, not today."

"Hell's Bells!" he hissed as he got into the driving seat and crashed the vehicle into gear, gravel flying as it sped away.

A harsh sob escaped her and she fought to regain composure before returning to the house. Startled by the sudden pressure of a hand on her shoulder, she turned to find Alex close behind. "Try not to upset yourself," he said, "he's better out of the way this afternoon."

Elizabeth forced a smile. "You're right, it wouldn't make any difference whatever I said. Luckily, the family aren't here." A tear coursed down her cheek as in a wavering voice she continued, "I just can't cope with any more."

With a word of sympathy Alex drew her back to the house where Thomas had ushered everyone into the dining room to announce tea was served. It worked like magic, silence fell as each child tucked into the party fare with gusto. Serena glanced up as she entered, her beautiful young face showing concern, but Elizabeth smiled to assure her all was well, her misery fading a little as the party progressed when she joined in the laughter as Timothy blew one candle completely off the cake. Games kept her busy for the next hour until the yawns of the little guests told her it was time to call a halt.

"What a pity your husband missed the fun," sympathised one lady as she buttoned her daughter into her coat.

Yes, such a pity," agreed another, tying her son's shoelaces.

"He must have been delayed at the farm," she explained with a tight smile as she saw them out, fervently hoping Miles would not return until all the guests had left.

All was quiet at Ashdale. The children were in bed, and once everything had been tidied away Thomas and Gladys were given the evening off. Slipping off her shoes, Elizabeth curled her feet beneath her, about to reach for a magazine until she heard a car draw up outside. For a second her heart stopped, but a tap on the sitting room door brought relief when she realised it wasn't Miles.

"Miles not back?" Alex asked when she called him in.

"Not yet," she said with a downward curve of her mouth. "I shudder to think of the state he'll be in."

"I was a little concerned by something you said earlier," he began and saw a tiny crease appear on her brow. "After Miles left, you told me you couldn't cope with any more."

She gave a curious hoot of laughter. "And is this why you're here, Alex, because of some silly remark?"

Her laughter rang false in his ears, convincing him she was under great strain. "If there's anything I can do?" He raised his eyebrows and held her troubled gaze.

It was a moment before she could bring herself to speak. Slipping into her shoes she admitted quietly, "Actually, it's Serena. She's upset because someone at school said Miles isn't her father."

"Am I to understand she always believed he was?"

"I don't know. It only came about when she remarked on the colour of her eyes." She hesitated before adding, "She then said she didn't care as she didn't like him, anyway."

"I see," Alex murmured, "but perhaps you could point out how Miles was happy to accept responsibility for her."

Seeing her cover her eyes he paused and heard, "But he's absolutely horrible to her."

Alex went over to perch on the arm of her chair. Placing a comforting hand on her shoulder, he could feel unhappiness wrenching at her body. "My poor Elizabeth," he murmured, "you have more troubles than any of us realised..." Hearing a noise he broke off as the sitting room door crashed back on its hinges to reveal a swaying, bleary-eyed Miles supporting himself against the door jamb.

"Where is everybody?" he slurred, lunging into the room. "We-we're supposed to be having a bloody party but I see you buggers are up to something else!"

Elizabeth's cry immediately had Alex on his feet, moving quickly to avoid Miles' fist. "Come on, Miles, be a sport," he cajoled as Miles again lurched forward. "There's nothing unprofessional going on here."

Miles came to an unsteady halt in the centre of the room, and glaring at Alex he rocked on his feet as he spluttered, "Unpro...Unprofessional, did you say? " He broke off, staggering forward to land at Elizabeth's feet when he managed to raise his head to say, "Maybe you're not, b-but she is. She's a bloody whore!"

Elizabeth's horrified gasp brought him up to his knees when he repeated, "Yes, a bloody whore!"

"Miles, why don't you and I find a comfortable seat, then you can tell me about it," Alex cajoled, urging Miles towards a chair. And as the drunken man flopped into it, he motioned for Elizabeth to leave.

Trembling from head to foot, she hurried past where Miles was slumped to hear Alex saying, "You shouldn't excite yourself, old chap. That's right, now lie back and rest."

Closing the door behind her so the children would not hear, she met Thomas coming downstairs. "Is there anything I can do," asked the elderly butler, fastening the last few buttons of his waistcoat.

"Thank goodness you're here," she said shakily, going into the kitchen. "Doctor Wilson is trying to calm him, but perhaps a strong, black coffee would help."

A few minutes later, hearing no sound from the sitting room, she went to listen at the door just as Alex emerged to report Miles was now asleep.

"Thank you, Thomas," she said when they returned to the kitchen. "You go back to bed, I'll be all right."

Thomas glanced in Alex's direction. "If you're sure, Mrs Grant..."

Alex nodded. "I'll stay a while, though you shouldn't have any trouble now." But once alone he asked, "Is this a regular occurrence?"

Taking the pan of hot milk from the stove, she admitted, "It's becoming more frequent, particularly since his mother died."

Alex pursed his lips and nodded, noticing the weary droop of her shoulders and how thin she had become. "Of course, the money. Well, I'll stay yet awhile then see you in the morning. Better not be too late in case I'm called out."

"I'd appreciate that. He usually sleeps for hours, though I doubt I can get him up to bed."

Alex gave an incredulous laugh. "I should think not! Goodness knows what your parents would say."

"I try to keep it from them and Grandmother won't hear a word against him."

Alex clicked his tongue and took the cup of coffee offered. "How he drives in this state, I don't know. He's a danger to himself and everyone else on the road."

"Before you go, Alex, there's something I must say. It's not true what Miles said, you know, that awful name. I'll admit there was an occasion when I may have been indiscreet, but it was someone I dearly loved, nothing like he suggests."

Alex drained his cup before he looked up and smiled. "I know, and I suspect it may have been more than once. Even so, you most certainly don't deserve an insult like that."

The following morning when Doctor Wilson called Miles was in bed, presenting his usual shamed expression. "For God's sake, Alex, can't you convince her I'm sorry."

Alex sighed. "I think it would sound better coming from you. She's been extremely tolerant, you know."

"I know, and it was Timothy's birthday. I really regret not being here for that," Miles went on. "I felt so damned upset when I came back to find everyone had gone."

"I don't think you were up to entertaining, old chap, and if you're not careful you'll land yourself back in hospital. Quite frankly, Miles, your body won't take much more."

"I'll admit, I felt dashed awful when I woke up," Miles confessed, "but from now on I'm going to leave the booze alone. It just doesn't agree with me."

"Good, but make sure you do, otherwise Elizabeth's patience will grow very thin," he said, taking his stethoscope from his bag. "Now, lie still, I want to check your heart."

Downstairs, Elizabeth busied herself in the kitchen. Alex's remark the evening before had brought Maurici to mind, and now she wondered about him; wondered if he had qualified or, more painful to bear, had found someone to replace her? So many years had passed, yet the familiar ache of longing was still there. Was it too late to explain why she now devoted her life almost solely to Miles? She glanced out to the garden where Timothy played, his expression the image of his father's.

* *

On the fifth of June the following year, Miles succumbed to the joyous mood of the nation. It wasn't every day there was something like this to celebrate and he considered a couple of drinks to toast the health of the new Sovereign would do no harm. He'd expected someone would open a bottle when he'd gone to the Hall with Elizabeth and the children to watch the ceremony on James' new television set but was disappointed to be offered only soft drinks or tea. Since his stay in hospital late in the summer of the previous year, when doctors had warned him of a serious deterioration in his health, he'd been scared into exercising more self control. Only at Christmas had he weakened, and he'd suffered for his indulgence throughout the month of January. After that, with the support of Elizabeth and Alex, his health improved slightly though he was often moody and difficult to please, only appearing to be in better humour when seated astride his horse. But now, with the country in high spirits over the Coronation, Miles took it as a sound enough reason to relax control.

It was when Elizabeth and Timothy were on a visit to the dentist in Malton that Miles gave in to the urge to drive in the opposite direction along the Helmsley road. It was market day in the small, bustling town with stalls set out in the square where families from outlying villages shared a weekly gossip. The public houses were doing a brisk trade and it was there Miles knew he would find at least one acquaintance who rode with him at the local hunt.

Calling at his bank, he withdrew a considerable sum of money, then crossed over to the saddler's shop opposite the church gate. For the last year Timothy had been riding, gentle trots around the field behind the house, but Miles considered it was now time to transfer the boy to a larger mount, which meant ordering a new saddle. At six years of age he looked ridiculous seated upon the small, shaggy pony. He didn't want his son to appear a sissy, he must learn to handle something at least twelve hands.

Once measurements had been agreed and the order placed, he left the shop to return to his car, a new Austin A40 he had purchased a month before. Deciding not to leave the vehicle in front of the hotel in the market square in case Alex Wilson should chance to pass by, he drove it round to the rear of the Black Swan and parked it in the yard. He still found the gear control on the steering column hard to master and had difficulty reversing into the rather tight space. Just when he thought he'd managed the manoeuvre satisfactorily he heard the harsh scrape of metal and the sound of breaking glass somewhere behind. With a curse he got out and saw the light green two-stroke on its side, the glass from its headlamp in pieces. Taking a quick glance around, he dragged the motorcycle from under the rear of his car and stood it against the wall behind the next vehicle, with the headlight facing the opposite way. Satisfied he had not been observed he kicked the broken glass out of sight and made for the rear door of the hotel.

As usual on market days, the bar was noisy and crowded, the air thick with smoke, but it wasn't long before someone raised a hand in welcome and another gave him a friendly slap on the back. Still frustrated from parking he pushed his way to the bar counter, his need for a drink increasing dramatically as each waiting moment passed.

"Am I getting that drink?" he asked shortly, his colour rising as he saw the barmaid acknowledge another customer's request. And when she coolly queried his order he snarled, "Scotch! Make it a double – and be quick about it!"

Thrusting aside the water jug she placed before him he took the glass to tilt it to his lips. Without so much as a shudder he replaced the empty glass on the bar and nodded, his expression seeming to soften as the second double measure of amber liquid drained away. This time he gave a sigh of satisfaction as he handed back his glass and a comforting glow spread through him, making him feel better than he had in weeks. It just went to show, a couple of drinks did a power of good, regardless of what Wilson had to say.

But two drinks was not enough for Miles and as time passed the atmosphere of the bar seemed to change. People were staring at him, but when he spoke they moved away. He started to shiver, yet perspiration stood on his brow and he became aware of an urgent need to relieve his bladder. Lurching from the bar as waves of nausea rose he managed to find the toilets, swaying on his feet as he attempted to direct his stream down the plain white tiles. Then, hoping to make the dreadful feeling pass, he vomited into the tiled channel by his feet. Gradually, he began to feel slightly better and even thought of returning to the bar. Perhaps first a little fresh air would help clear his head, get rid of the ache in his guts.

Making his way out to his car he saw a youth leaning on the bonnet, a look of triumph on his face. "Thought it might be yours!" the younger man sneered as Miles struggled to extract the keys from his jacket pocket. "You owe me the price of a new 'eadlamp."

"No idea what you mean," Miles returned through lips that felt strangely numb. "Kindly allow m-me to get to my car."

"You know damned well what I mean!" the youth snarled. "I know where I left that bloody bike, an' it weren't where it is now! Any road, there's scratches on your back end, same colour as my Beezer."

"Now look here..." Miles blustered, reeling against the other man. But before he could regain breath to continue, he was grabbed by the lapels of his tweed jacket and flung back against the side of his car.

"I know your soddin' kind," the youth ground out, inches from Miles' face. "You think you're better than the rest of us, but you're bloody well wrong!"

The moment his accuser released him Miles slid to the ground, unable to object, even when the other raised a booted foot to kick the glass out of each headlamp in turn.

"There, that'll learn yer!" he said, glowering at Miles. "You're not smashing up my bike an' gettin' away with it!"

"You imp-impertinent young sod." Miles slurred, "I-I've a good mind to call the police!"

"I'd thought of doin' that meself, but I knew I'd stand no chance wi' your bloody old mother-in-law being a JP."

Grasping the door handle, Miles managed to pull himself to his feet, his arm raised to shout, "Bugger off!"

Thinking he was about to be struck, the younger man ducked smartly and brought up his fist, landing a cracking blow to Miles' jaw. Miles gave a grunt, his knees buckling, he sank to the ground.

At first the youth simply gaped, then pushing his machine out of the yard he ran it down the slope until it fired.

* *

Ever since Maurici had heard news of the crowning of the English queen, her name stuck in his mind. He had arranged to take a friend to a cinema in the city the day the news reached him, but now only Elizabeth filled his thoughts. Elizabeth, his queen; memories of her making the prospect of accompanying a young lady to the cinema seem almost immoral. Already he was regretting the arrangement; he'd sought the company of someone his own age, wanted a settled life, for Jaume's sake as much as his own, but something prevented him from making permanent plans, and he sensed his mother was about to broach the subject over breakfast that morning.

"Don't worry, *mama*, my whites go to the hospital laundry, I don't expect you to wash them," he replied to her enquiry.

"If you had a wife..."

"But I haven't," he interrupted with a flicker of annoyance. "If I had, I'd still send them to a laundry."

"A doctor needs the support of a wife," Carmen said for the umpteenth time. "And my poor little grandson needs a mother to care for him."

"Jaume is almost ten years old and he's had you and aunt Elvira to dote on him daily."

"But we won't be always here, and you promised to consider it after you qualified..."

"And I did," he broke in impatiently, "but the right person never came along. Perhaps when I'm in general practice, that will be a good time to think about it."

She raised her plump arms despairingly. "The right person? Pah! You left your heart in England years ago, my boy, perhaps you should go back and retrieve it."

"I've already told you, she has commitments of her own," he responded shortly, "so there's no point in you going over that again."

The *senyora* compressed her mouth and glanced away, but not before Maurici caught the glint of her tears. "I'm sorry, *mama*, I appreciate your concern," he said, explaining more gently, "Since Elizabeth, I haven't met anyone I want to share my life with, and you wouldn't wish me to marry someone for whom I have little affection?"

She dabbed her eyes. "I know I shouldn't lecture you, a man of thirty-nine, but I pray you find true happiness in your life, a family of your own."

He rose and went to drop a kiss on her cheek. "Don't worry, when felicity smiles on me you'll be the first to know, but the consultant won't smile if I don't move. I'm on duty in half an hour!"

* *

James looked up as Molly came into the room. "Any news?" he asked, propelling his chair across the polished oak floor. "I want to know what that damned Miles was playing at!"

Molly shook her head. "She's not back from the hospital, and Alex seemed reluctant to tell me. However, I insisted and, according to him, the first Elizabeth knew of it was when the police called early this morning. Evidently, Miles had been found apparently unconscious from drink at the rear of the Black Swan. It seems they'd put him in a cell for the night, but when he showed no sign of recovering they called a doctor who got him to hospital."

"But why didn't Elizabeth let us know?"

"She'd telephoned Alex, then left for the hospital right away. It seems she didn't want to worry us."

"But dash it all, Molly, we're her parents!"

She kissed his cheek. "I know, darling, but it's not the first time, I understand. I've heard rumours, and the last time we saw Miles – Tuesday it was – he looked dreadful."

"Ah yes, said he'd suffered a bout of influenza, or something like that, but he didn't seem too bad to me."

"If you recall, we were all glued to the television, and we'd closed the curtains to keep out the light."

James suddenly looked up to ask, "What about Timothy?"

"Gladys and Thomas are at Ashdale, but I've suggested they bring him here for lunch. Thank goodness Serena is back at school, otherwise it would have been difficult."

"Yes, I'm sure. I've noticed a certain reserve in her manner when I mention her father."

Molly shook her head. "Her father? I think she knows more than we give her credit for."

"That's a fact," he agreed irritably. "If he wasn't Elizabeth's husband I wouldn't tolerate him another moment. I don't like the way he sneers at Serena, and he's so impatient with poor Tim. All he can think about is putting the boy on horseback, something bigger yet, damn it all, he's only six years old! Even your mother said Tim shouldn't be over-horsed. Perhaps you'll have a word with her; maybe she can make him see sense."

Molly pulled a wry face. "I doubt it. At the slightest criticism of Miles she immediately jumps to his defence."

"Damned unnatural!" James said on a loud breath. "I think Jane cares more for Miles than her own family."

Molly raised her brows thoughtfully. "Funny you should say that. However, I don't intend telling her what has happened this morning, not whilst she's feeling unwell."

"Perhaps we should try 'phoning again," James suggested, moving his chair towards the door. "This time I intend having a stern word with Miles as soon as he's back home."

The daily routine of the cottage hospital had just begun when Elizabeth arrived that morning. The night sister was completing the handing over of her reports which included the admission of Miles Grant, and the doctor called out to attend him was now in her office drinking tea.

On arrival, Elizabeth had been ushered into the small sitting room and asked to wait until the doctor had finished treating Miles who was drifting back to full consciousness. When she eventually entered the small, private room where he lay she saw he was attached to some kind of modern drip, and another tube protruded from under the covers at the end of the bed.

A quiet word to let him know she was there brought no response, and it was shortly after half past eight when she glanced up to see Alex Wilson, the strain melting from her face.

"Nice to see a familiar face," she whispered. "I didn't want to trouble Mummy and Daddy until he's recovered."

"That will be some time," he told her gravely. "I'm afraid, he really overdid things yesterday."

She gave a ragged sigh and dropped her gaze. "Oh God, this is too much, I can't leave him for a moment." She looked up, her blue eyes brimming with tears. "I can't go on like this, Alex, it's upsetting the children. He'll have to leave Ashdale..." She broke off, choked by harsh, desperate sobs as Alex drew her aside.

"I know," he consoled, "but that isn't the only problem. Now they tell me his heart is failing, kidneys too. Frankly, Miles hasn't long to live. Even with total abstinence he's unlikely to enjoy many more years."

Her lips quivering, she said, "Then I shouldn't have said anything about, you know, about divorce."

"Elizabeth, you must not blame yourself. I know you wouldn't desert a man in his condition." Regarding her closely he continued, "Unless you have reasons for wanting to end your marriage, other than the problems associated with Miles' unfortunate habit?"

Her lips parted, but it was a moment before she uttered a barely audible, "None," and turned away.

Chapter 27

Four weeks passed before Miles was able to resume life at Ashdale House. Gaunt and depressed, he chose to spend the early part of each day in his room, other than the week-ends when Timothy was not at school. On these occasions he would take the boy to the farm to ride horseback, Miles seated on his massive Cleveland Bay, the boy in the saddle of his Shetland pony. It didn't suit Miles to see him riding the small, shaggy coated animal but Jane had managed to persuade him to wait until Timothy was a little longer in the leg. From the day Miles arrived home, Jane visited each afternoon. Elizabeth noticed her grandmother's health was failing now she had Nicholson to drive her to Ashdale in the car.

"Don't forget, he's only allowed squash," Elizabeth reminded her on the first visit.

"Poor Miles, I'm sure a little drop wouldn't harm."

Elizabeth's eyes rolled to the ceiling. "But Alex told you how serious it is."

"Alex Wilson!" she snorted. "What does he know?"

"Grandmother, if it wasn't for him, Miles wouldn't be alive today! Now, I must go, Thomas will bring in tea."

Elizabeth found her father at his writing desk, but as she went to where he was sitting he quickly turned the sheet of paper face down on the blotter."

"Secret admirer?" she teased, stooping to kiss his cheek.

"Just sending Enric a few lines, darling, don't want to smudge it. I'll add your regards, shall I?" He pulled a chair forward, indicating she should sit beside him. "How are things at Ashdale, improving?"

She put her head to one side and shrugged. "A little, but I'm worried about Serena during the coming holidays."

"The situation between her and Miles, you mean?"

"Mm, they don't get on too well these days."

He reached for her hand. "You know she's always welcome here, but if I were you I'd explain Miles's addiction to her, she might not be so inclined to antagonise him."

She nodded. "You may be right, but it would be easier to explain to Timothy, he's the more sensitive of the two."

James smiled. "A boy after my own heart."

"Perhaps he takes after you."

"Well, he certainly doesn't take after Miles!"

Meeting his eyes, Elizabeth responded quietly, "That would be quite impossible, as I believe you already know."

* *

Fanning himself with a newspaper, Enric closed the shutters against the burning August sun. He had been pleased to receive a letter from England and slit open the envelope eagerly as he went to his favourite chair. It seemed ages since he'd received word from James so he'd written a second time, anxious in case all was not well. It took him a little time to translate it until he got the gist of James' meaning, and he re-read one part where his old colleague explained he'd delayed writing because of the difficulties Elizabeth was facing at home: 'She has so many responsibilities, caring for her sick husband after his stay in hospital, looking after the children, and running a home,' James wrote. 'Molly and I are doing our best to help, though in my situation I'm pretty useless. But we are able to look after the children which helps Elizabeth during the school holidays. Serena is fairly independent now, she'll be fourteen in October and doing extremely well at school. Timothy was six last March, how time flies! Serena has her heart set on becoming a nurse, psychiatric I believe, though not for a few years yet. Takes after Molly I expect...'

Enric rose and crossed to the bookshelf where he selected the English/Spanish dictionary which James had left behind. And for the next half hour he translated certain words so that he was better able to understand all James had to say. It warmed him to note a further invitation to visit Woodington Hall, but first he would keep another promise and contact Maurici to pass on this latest news.

* *

After a visit to Enric, Maurici was puzzled by what his friend had said. 'Elizabeth's husband was extremely ill', that he could accept, and he'd been delighted to learn of Serena's progress, but this other child, Timothy... He drew his new car to a halt at the side of the road, sifting through his troubled thoughts as he gazed abstractedly over the glittering sea; Timothy – in Catalan, Timoteu – his own second name. He closed his eyes, his thoughts going back to London and nineteen forty-six; this child had been born in March the following year, not in the summer as he had thought. Could this mean Elizabeth had been pregnant when they last met? She'd strongly denied any intimacy with her husband, he reflected, but supposing the child had been premature... He drew a ragged breath; perhaps the choice of name wasn't a coincidence. Timoteu could be his son!

* *

It was the twenty-fourth of February, Elizabeth's birthday, when Jane requested she visit her at the Hall. It was a damp and foggy morning when Miles decided it was unsuitable for riding and had taken Timothy for cricket practice in the huge barn at the farm. Playing cricket in winter seemed absurd, but Miles insisted his son needed the practice in preparation for his move to a private school. So, foregoing his mid-morning coffee, off went Miles with Timothy and his school pal racing along in front. Elizabeth sighed as she watched them go, knowing Timothy was not keen on sport, but it did Miles good to take an interest in the boy; should she deprive him of that in his remaining years? Quite unaccountably, she was struck by a thought which caused a sudden ache in her heart. Would Maurici be proud of his son? Was it right to have kept Timothy's existence from him for so long? After so many years Maurici could have re-married and Timothy may be an embarrassment to him now.

Studying her reflection in the bathroom mirror, she realised a visit to the hairdresser was well overdue but having to keep an eye on Miles left her little opportunity.

His temper was growing shorter as time went on when he would rant at anyone who happened to be near. And today, after Timothy had shown a reluctance to go, she was anxious. Only the presence of his school chum had persuaded her to agree.

Needing to throw off the weight of her cares, she chose to walk to the Hall, attributing the request as being just another of her grandmother's whims which of late had become more numerous. The topic of Serena's progress to college usually arose on these visits, Jane declaring a finishing school for girls more suitable, trying Elizabeth's patience to the limit. In fact, everything seemed to get on her nerves, she realised as she walked between the tall iron gates which had escaped confiscation during the war.

As she neared the Hall she spotted the old housekeeper, Mrs Dowkes, breaking pieces of stale bread for the ducks who constantly reiterated their squawking demands. As she waved to the woman who was standing by the bank of the river, she saw how thickly the mist lay above the waters which swirled dangerously in flood. 'February fill-dyke' her grandfather used to say when he drew her away from the water's edge; she'd repeated the same words to Serena and Timothy many times. A tap on an upstairs window brought her back to the present and looking up saw her grandmother's impatient gesture and hurried indoors, calling a greeting to her parents as she passed the morning room.

Jane was seated on the chaise-longue wearing a heather coloured twin set and tweed skirt. The room seemed stiflingly warm after the chill outside so Elizabeth unbuttoned her coat, taking the chair opposite.

"Take it off," Jane advised, "otherwise you won't feel the benefit when you leave."

"Sorry, Grandmother, I can't stay too long, I must get back to prepare lunch."

"Why can't Chapman do it? You pay her well enough."

"Gladys is not in this morning, it's her day off."

Jane clicked her tongue. "Her day off! It's impossible to find good staff these days, people don't want work."

"People are discovering better ways to earn a living."

Jane exhaled a sharp breath. "Why must you always contradict? Serena is just the same."

"Is this why you've brought me here, to speak about the domestic situation, or lack of it?"

"Don't be ridiculous, child, I could discuss that with your mother. No, I want to hear how Miles is progressing. He hasn't been to see me."

Elizabeth met her grandmother's pale gaze. "Considering the state he was in last year, he's doing well, but it's entirely up to him."

Jane reached forward to grip Elizabeth's arm. "You will take good care of him?"

Startled, Elizabeth drew back. "Of course, I'm surprised you ask."

"But there are times when you and he don't seem to get along too well. People quickly resort to separation and divorce these days and I dread to think of that happening."

Elizabeth shook her head. "He's not the easiest person to live with, but you should know me well enough to realise I wouldn't desert a sick man."

Jane reached for her huge leather handbag and drew out a small blue case. "For your birthday," she said, her emotions carefully repressed. "It belonged to my sister, but you may as well have it now. Consider it a small reward for the care you've bestowed upon Miles."

"It's lovely!" Elizabeth exclaimed when she revealed an engraved silver locket and chain, "but wouldn't you rather Mummy had it? I don't wish to appear ungrateful," she added quickly as the sharp eyes fastened on hers."

"She already has the one your father gave her, though not nearly as valuable," Jane said smugly. "Now, don't forget what I said."

"I won't," said Elizabeth, but secretly wondered which part of their conversation she wasn't to forget. Was it the locket's value, or the request that she promise to care for Miles?

Seemingly satisfied, Jane rang the bell and ordered coffee to be brought upstairs. And when a timid maid delivered the tray Jane berated her for keeping them waiting.

"Stupid creature, she knows I prefer shortbread," Jane grumbled, lifting the cloth. "Why do I tolerate such service, Molly is far too easy-going..." She paused as Molly burst into the room. "I was just saying to Elizabeth..."

"Just a moment, Mother," said Molly, her expression taut as turned to Elizabeth who had sprung to her feet. "Serena's downstairs with Timmy and the other boy. She tells me Miles came home in a terrible rage. Something about him striking Timmy's friend..."

"That girl exaggerates – far too excitable! It's her foreign blood," Jane intervened but, seeing the colour drain from

Elizabeth's face, Molly cut her short and they dashed for the stairs, Jane's shrill voice ringing in their ears.

Serena looked up as her mother descended the stairs, her expression troubled as she clung protectively to the two boys. "It was awful, Mummy," she began, "he said they didn't play properly, and when Timmy's friend said he didn't want to play anyway he hit him across the face. Turning the boy's reddened cheek in Elizabeth's direction, she cried, "Just look what he did!"

The boy's lip began to quiver and he started to cry all over again. Elizabeth swallowed. "All right, I'll see to it," she said gently, her manner belying the anguish she felt as she drew the sobbing child into her arms. And seeing the distress on Timothy's face she reached out to bring him into the curve of her other arm. "Serena, run and ask Cook if she'll make a jug of hot chocolate, darling, will you? And see if you can find a few biscuits. We'll be in the small sitting room, it's warmer there."

"Mummy, why is Daddy so cross?" Timothy asked miserably as they snuggled up together on the settee in front of the open fire. "We didn't do anything wrong, honestly..."

"It's all right, darling, I know. But you see, sometimes Daddy doesn't feel well and that makes him rather cross."

Timothy turned his wide, dark eyes in her direction to ask, "Why, Mummy? Why is he not very well?"

'My Dad says it's 'cos he's always in't pub," the other boy put in, his bluntness echoing that of his father.

"We don't really know that," she managed on a steadying breath, glancing at the child's face to see the red wheals where Miles' fingers had struck. She knew, even when any outward sign of violence had disappeared, the trauma of the incident would remain. Once they had taken refreshment she would drive the child home, explain to his parents, before going on to Ashdale to challenge Miles.

"Cheeky little devil, he was sulking," Miles blustered from half-way up the stairs.

"Even so, you had no right to chastise him. Thankfully, his mother accepted it wasn't intentional."

"Oh, for God's sake, Elizabeth," Miles snapped as he continued up, "I've had enough of the little sods," and slammed the door of his room.

Elizabeth sighed and went into the kitchen with the intention of preparing lunch. But the headache which had increased throughout the morning was becoming more than she could bear, and she began to notice the discomfort when she swallowed was getting worse. Then the shivering started and she groaned in dismay.

"Better you all keep well away from me," she told Thomas, "I believe I'm starting with 'flu," and taking a couple of aspirin she went to bed.

All through that night she tossed and turned, perspiring one moment, shivering the next. When Alex called next morning he confirmed her diagnosis and advised what to do.

"I felt dreadful last night," she said, "my temperature was over a hundred and two!"

Alex smiled. "Well, it's down a little this morning so a day or two in bed should see you over the worst."

Elizabeth groaned. "But who'll keep an eye on Miles?"

"Isn't Serena at home?"

"Yes, but she's only just recovered herself, and she had cause to go out in the fog yesterday," Elizabeth croaked and explained the reason why.

"This is too much, I'll speak to Miles before I go, also tell him you must stay in bed."

Elizabeth had insisted Thomas should continue to have his day off, knowing he had planned to visit his sister in York, and Alex had given the elderly butler a lift to the station as he set off on his rounds. Content once she heard Gladys downstairs, she took a dose of linctus and sank back more comfortably in her bed when, as a result of the wakeful night, it wasn't long before she fell into a heavy sleep.

Seeing her mother was asleep, Serena closed the bedroom door and went downstairs to find Gladys in the kitchen washing breakfast dishes in the deep white sink. "Has Timmy had breakfast?" she asked, surprised to find Gladys alone.

"I expect Thomas took him to the Hall on his way to the station, Miss Serena, and I'd 'ave come in earlier if I'd knowed your mother weren't well." With a nod towards the telephone, she suggested, "Why don't you give them a ring."

"Thanks, I'll go down there instead."

"Then you'd better wrap up well, Miss Serena. We don't want you badly again."

Wearing her warm coat and thick scarf, Serena went into the damp morning air. It had rained heavily over-night, leaving deep puddles on the road and arriving at the Hall she saw the river was overflowing its banks.

"Usually happens after a quick thaw," Molly said, beckoning her into the house. "With March winds on the way it could rise even further to flood the lawns."

Serena shuddered and went to kiss James. "Mummy's asleep, she's got 'flu, Doctor Wilson said so this morning, and it's not much fun at home."

Molly glanced at her husband, knowing Serena preferred not to be alone in the presence of Miles. "I see," she said, "so I assume Timmy has gone to play with his friend."

Serena looked from one to the other. "No, I thought he'd be here..."

Molly drew a quick breath. "I'll just check with Gladys," she said, "she won't mind going round to his friend's house to see if he's there."

Closing the sitting room door behind her, she went to the telephone in the hall, and it wasn't long before Gladys rang back to say Timmy wasn't there. "And Mister Miles 'as gone out as well," Gladys told her. Molly's heart sank.

"Will you ring us immediately Timmy returns. I don't like to think he's outdoors on a morning such as this."

Straightening her shoulders, Molly took her coat from the cloak cupboard and went back to the sitting room. James glanced up expectantly, but not wishing to show her concern in front of Serena she buttoned her coat, explaining, "I'm just going to see if Elizabeth needs anything. Should the telephone ring answer it, James, will you?"

James caught her meaningful look, his concern for Timothy deepening as he watched her go. Unsure of which direction to take, Molly toured the village in her car but saw no sign of her grandson. She knew Miles went up to the farm occasionally and wondered if he had taken Timmy there. Recalling the last time, when Miles had struck the other boy, she depressed the accelerator to drive in the direction of Grant's place.

She encountered Miles leaving the stable to go across the cobbled yard toward the house. He appeared to have been perspiring freely, and merely glanced in her direction, unwilling to acknowledge her presence. Raising her hand, she made a polite enquiry after his health.

His expression sullen, he ignored her greeting and grunted, "What brings you here?"

"Actually, I'm looking for Timmy. I thought the children might like to have lunch with me as I understand Elizabeth's not too well today."

"I expect he's buggered off home, stubborn little devil," Miles said, regarding her coldly.

"Oh dear, has he been a naughty boy?"

"He deserves a damned good hiding, ungrateful little brat! I get him a decent mount, what does he do? Cries like a baby when I put him up in the saddle...."

"I'm sure it's just beginner's nerves," Molly broke in, noticing how agitated he had become.

"Beginners nerves!" he echoed with a sneer. "He's a bloody sissy, that's what he is, and unless he pulls his socks up, he'll be the laughing stock of the school."

"There's more to life than riding!" Molly retaliated, then thought it wiser not to antagonise him.

"Stupid bitch!" she heard him hiss as he turned away, when her immediate desire was to kick her insufferable son-in-law's backside. But her concern for Timothy outweighed the indignation she felt, and hurrying back to the car she drove on to Ashdale House. On arrival, it was a relief to see Timothy's dark head snuggled against Gladys' shoulder, but at the sound of the closing door he gave a nervous start, glancing round to reveal signs of tearful distress.

Taking him in her arms she drew him close. "Whatever is the matter, darling?" she murmured, kissing his damp cheek. When he burst into a fresh flood of tears she looked to Gladys for an explanation.

"I don't know, he's done nowt but yell since he got in. I was about to call Miss Elizabeth."

"Darling you're quite safe," Molly comforted. "Tell Gran what's wrong, we'll soon put it right for you."

"Daddy says I mus-musn't tell anyone or he-he'll give me a walloping," Timothy managed, his words interspersed with loud, heart-rending sobs.

"He doesn't mean it," Molly soothed, hugging the unhappy child, "he just says these silly things when he's cross."

"But I don't want to go to the farm again, Gran," the boy cried brokenly, "don't let him make me..."

"All right, I'll have a word with Daddy," Molly promised, and tilting her head asked shrewdly, "Didn't you want to ride on the big horse today?"

His lip quivered. "It makes me frightened," he admitted on a ragged sigh. "I want my own pony..." Unable to continue, he sought the comfort of his thumb as he twirled a strand of Molly's hair round the fingers of his other hand.

"The poor kid," Gladys sympathised, "he don't like them great big 'orses. Do you, Master Timothy?"

"I think Timmy and I will go and see what Grandpa's doing, shall we, darling?" Molly suggested to escape Gladys' misplaced kindness which threatened to bring further tears. "Perhaps when my daughter's awake, you'll tell her I've taken him to the Hall. Serena is there already so we'll have lunch together and play card games this afternoon."

By the time they reached the Hall, Molly noticed Timothy was shivering slightly, his hands dreadfully cold. "I think we should ask Mrs Dowkes to run you a nice hot bath before lunch, Timmy, don't you?"

Timothy uttered a long, shuddering breath, nodding as she unfastened his coat and took off his mud-caked shoes. "Can we play Happy Families after lunch?" he asked, adding persuasively, "Grandpa likes that the best."

"I don't see why not," she agreed, smiling to herself over the irony behind his choice.

Up in the huge bathroom, pleased to observe his crying had ceased, she helped Timothy undress. But as she lifted him onto the cork-topped stool to remove his socks, she saw him wince and heard his gasp of pain as he arched his body in an effort to get down. Curious, she turned him round to discover a number of red wheals up the back of one thigh which disappeared beneath the hem of his woollen vest. She made a choking sound, but managed to control the horror she felt.

"Oh dear, I didn't mean to hurt you," she said gently. "I know, you hang on to the bath and lift your foot whilst I take off your socks." Once those were removed, she turned him away and took hold of the hem of his vest. "What do we say?" she asked with forced brightness. "We say..."

"Skin a rabbit!" he responded with the beginnings of a giggle as he lifted his arms, revealing the full extent of his suffering as she pulled off his vest.

Her shock dissolved into deep concern; a trellis of red wheals ran from the side of his thigh across his little buttocks, and an inflamed line stood out clearly on the delicate skin of his throat. Someone, and already she was convinced it was Miles, had held the boy by his collar causing a friction burn to his neck. And that same someone had continued to hold him while he inflicted the other stinging blows. She closed her eyes momentarily, fighting back the tears; seven years old, and beaten so violently because he was afraid of a horse. She wanted to cry out to everyone in the house, including her own mother – oh yes, including her – but the trusting dark eyes prevented her. Instead, she smiled and kissed his pale cheek, checking the water was not too warm and likely to sting the inflamed skin.

She bathed him very gently then, to add a little pleasure to his day, pulled him back and forth through the water on his tummy, something he always enjoyed. She would telephone Elizabeth after lunch to say Timmy could stay at the Hall, away from the risk of infection and safe from further violence until she found an opportunity to confront Miles over this extremely serious matter.

Chapter 28

Serena's anguished cry brought Molly rushing to the bedroom where Timothy had spent the night. "Gran! Have you seen what he's done to poor Timmy?"

"Ssh, dear, I know," Molly whispered casting an anxious glance in her grandson's direction.

Serena was aghast. "But you must do something!"

"Yes, leave it to me," Molly insisted with a calming gesture, and raising her voice to a cheerful level, asked, "Now, who's ready for breakfast?"

"Me!" yelled Timmy. "May I have scrambled egg?"

"Of course you may," she agreed with a smile, her eyes resting on Serena for a moment before she left the room. It will be ready by the time you are dressed."

Careful not to put pressure on the inflamed areas, Serena assisted her young brother with his dressing. Hugging him close, she whispered, "Don't worry, Timmy, I'll not let him hurt you again. Gran doesn't know what he's like," she continued as she fastened his braces, adding with a troubled sigh, "I suppose it's because she's getting old."

"But not as old as Grandma Cussons. She's really old!"

"I know that, silly," she said irritably. "But Grandma Cussons likes him so she won't listen to me."

"Do Gran and Grandpa Purcell like Daddy?" Timothy asked, his eyes fixed trustingly on his sister.

"How should I know?" she replied sulkily. "They don't tell me anything."

"But will they send us home?" he persisted, raising his arms in readiness for the next item of clothing.

"Well I'm not going back to Ashdale whatever they say," she announced, her expression rebellious as she pulled a hand-knitted grey jumper over Timothy's dark head.

"Not going home, Serena? Not ever?"

"No, and I'll ask Grandpa to bring Mummy here, too."

"When are you going to ask him?"

"Oh do hurry with your shoes, Timmy, it's time we went to breakfast. I'll ask him then."

James looked up as Molly came into the dining room. "Well, how did you find Timmy this morning?" he asked worriedly. "I couldn't sleep for thinking about the poor child."

Molly drew a steadying breath. "He appears to have got over the worst," she said, "but Serena has seen the marks on his little bottom so she's very upset."

James' mouth set in an angry line. "The cruel bastard, he should be damned well shot!"

"Ssh, darling, they'll be down any moment. Serena was already helping him to dress when I got there."

"And now, understandably, she'll hate Miles even more."

She nodded. "I've told her I'll deal with it, anything to keep her quiet until Elizabeth is fit to leave her bed."

"Oh no, I intend speaking to Grant myself," he stated firmly. "When the children are suffering because..." He fell silent, managing to bring his emotions under control as the door opened, and Timothy dashed across to give him a hug.

Swivelling his chair towards the window he pointed to the scene outside, shaking a warning finger to say, "I was just saying to your Gran, you must stay well away from the river, the water's rising fast."

Serena gave a groan and remarked dismally, "I do wish it would stop raining, we want to feed the ducks."

"Better not," James advised, "the bank is flooded and the grass is terribly slippery. Wait until it subsides."

"I'd rather Mummy didn't visit," Elizabeth said when Alex Wilson called to see her later that morning on return from his rounds. "I don't want her to risk an infection, though I'd appreciate it if you'd ask if she'll have the children for a couple more days, save me going down to the 'phone."

"Of course, and now we've got you settled I'll go and have a word with Miles. I hope he hasn't neglected you."

Elizabeth shot him a bitter smile. "I assume you're joking, Alex, I've not seen him since he left the house sometime before eleven. He was in such a truculent mood this morning I was thankful Timmy and Serena are staying at the Hall. I'd had a simply awful night so when he came pestering me to write a cheque I told him to go to the farm."

"Quite right," he agreed. "Meanwhile, I suggest you get some sleep, I'll call on you tomorrow."

Elizabeth took a second dose of the medicine Alex had prescribed then lay back on her pillows. Except for the rain pattering on the window, the house was silent. Thomas had gone to the Hall to deliver Timothy a change of clothes while Gladys did some baking in the kitchen. All was so quiet she wasn't aware she was nodding off to sleep.

Not wishing to disturb her mistress, Gladys weighed out the ingredients for her pastry as quietly as she could. Going to wash her hands at the kitchen sink her heart gave a sudden jolt when she glanced up to see Miles' face framed in the open window.

Her hand flew to her throat. "Oh, sir, you startled me! For a minute I thought you was one of them tramps we've had round the village lately."

"Stupid bitch, do I look like a bloody tramp!" he returned harshly, staggering in by the back door and knocking over a bag of flour.

"I'm sorry, sir" she said, trepidation rising when she realised his mood.

"Where's Timothy?" he demanded. "Has he had lunch?"

"Him and Miss Serena is at the Hall, sir."

"Is at the Hall!" he repeated derisively, kicking the half empty cotton flour bag further across the floor.

"Just while Mrs Grant is badly, that is."

"Badly!" he sneered, "For God's sake speak properly, woman!" The baking utensils rattled when he brought his fist down on the table and leaned forward to hiss, "It was my intention to take the boy riding this morning. He should have been here!"

Catching a strong smell of alcohol, she trembled beneath his narrowed gaze to ask, "Can I do anything, sir?"

"For a start, you can clean up this bloody lot or you'll find yourself out of a job!" With that he swung away from the kitchen, across the hall and out through the front door.

Assuming he intended to go riding at the farm, Gladys blew out her cheeks in relief and went to close the door against the cool, damp air. At the foot of the stairs she paused but, hearing no sound from above, continued back to the kitchen to clean up the mess.

James had heard the lunch bell and was manoeuvring his wheelchair round the side of the house when he first spotted Miles Grant coming down the hill. For a moment he simply watched, hatred in his eyes, but when he saw Grant's stumbling gait was leading him towards the entrance to the grounds, his immediate concern was for the children; surely, the only reason Grant would be coming here.

As Miles struggled to open the ornamental gates, James realised it gave him an ideal opportunity to waylay the man, prevent him reaching the house. He had not expected to meet Grant face to face so soon, to challenge his harsh treatment of Timothy, and this urged him forward.

Experiencing a curious surge of triumph, his strong fingers gripped the wheels to propel his chair across a corner of the lawn with the intention of confronting Miles on the drive. But the ground proved difficult, the narrow wheels barely turning as they sank into the sodden grass, increasing his frustration as he attempted to reach firmer ground.

Grunting and puffing from his efforts, he saw Grant come through the gate to wind his way along the drive, apparently oblivious to the wheelchair jerking slowly along in his direction.

"Hey, Grant!" James called and saw the man come to a swaying halt. "Stop right there, I want a word with you!"

"What in hell's name do you want with me?" Miles slurred with an obstinate thrust of his chin as he lumbered on.

"I demand an explanation for your violent treatment of Timothy," James grated, bringing Miles to a halt once more.

"I'm not obliged to explain anything to you, you Irish bastard!" Miles bellowed, leaving the drive to head towards James. "I'm not having my son grow up a sissy, he's damned well coming riding with me!"

"Don't be stupid, you're in no condition to sit on a horse!" cried James, dragging his chair forward a few more inches by sheer force.

"Stupid, am I?" Miles ranted as he lurched closer to thrust an accusing finger at James. "At least I'm not a useless bloody cripple like you!"

James' expression froze. "But I don't resort to cruelty, and your treatment of Timothy is exactly that..."

"What the hell has it got to do with you?" Miles spluttered, grabbing the arm of the wheelchair to steady himself. "He's coming with me!"

"The only way you'll take my grandson from here is over my dead body."

Miles' expression became ugly and he grabbed both handles of James' chair, swinging it round so violently it almost overturned. "That can be arranged!" he snorted, lunging forward. "I'll not have a bloody cripple tell me what to do, I'll throw you in the sodding river first!"

James felt the chair move beneath him and gasped in alarm. "For Christ's sake!" he cried making a grab for the wheels. But, incensed by his drunken state, Miles continued down towards the river bank, the locked wheels sliding over the grass, thwarting James' attempts to hold it back.

Struck by the horror of his predicament, James went rigid as Miles plunged forward, splashing over the flooded lawn towards the swirling, brown water, now just feet away. And giving a last desperate yell he let go of the wheels and reached back to grab Miles' arm.

"Let go, you bastard!" Miles bawled, tipping the chair as he tried to release himself from James' powerful grip. But James' strength was too much for him and as the wheelchair toppled completely he felt himself being dragged down into the swiftly moving water.

Fighting to hold his breath as he plunged into the dark, icy depths, James felt the chair and Miles' flailing body land on top of him. And as he struggled to free himself he was aware of the other man thrashing around above him, making it harder for him to escape the confines of his chair. With lungs almost bursting he grabbed for his air cushion as it floated by and struck out for the bank, allowing it to take him upwards between the partly submerged bushes growing there. Clinging grimly to the branches James managed to pull his head above water as he fought against the current.

The relief of feeling air on his face was almost too much as he choked and gasped for breath. His shoulder muscles burned and he felt his strength ebbing away, his waterlogged clothing dragging him down. In desperation he managed a strangled cry before the river pulled him back.

It was a moment before James realised the voice he could hear wasn't his own, and making a gasping effort to keep his head above water he hung on to the undergrowth, blinking his eyes to see a blurred figure silhouetted against the sky. Again he heard the high pitched shriek and shook away the water streaming from his hair to see Serena and Nicholson on the bank.

"Hang on, Sir!" the chauffeur shouted as James heard something strike the water nearby.

"Grandpa! Grab the rope!" he heard Serena screech and reached out, but it floated away.

Splashing along the river bank, Nicholson drew back the rope and threw it out again, directing it a little further upstream to give James a chance. And this time he managed to catch hold with one hand just as the gardener, a ladder on his shoulder, came hurrying over the grass. By now it seemed the whole household had gathered there, and soon the ladder was placed across the flooded ground, partly overhanging the bank. The gardener was making his way over the rungs while the rest put their weight on the other end, and James could hear Molly's voice encouraging him to hold on until he felt the muscular arms of his rescuer hauling him out.

Overcome by relief, he found it difficult to help himself as he was dragged over the bank, his legs trailing uselessly behind. In a kind of daze, he was aware of being lifted, of Molly wrapping a blanket round his shoulders and kissing his wet face, and somewhere in the background he heard the distressing sound of Serena's weeping. He feared where Grant had got to and raised a tired arm in appeal, but no-one seemed inclined to enlighten him as they rushed him into the house.

It took some time for the heat of the bath water to penetrate James' chilled body. Carefully moving aside his feet, the nurse added more hot water and placed a folded towel behind his head so he could lie back and wallow beneath the foam.

"These new salts soften the water," she observed, swishing her hand around to create more bubbles. "Nice and frothy – smells nice, too."

"And keeps my private bits and pieces away from your prying eyes," he shot back humorously, but she knew his manner belied the shock he suffered deep inside.

"At least you've stopped shaking, and now you're feeling warmed through the best place for you is bed!"

"And perhaps a drop of whisky will help..." he began just as Molly came back to the bathroom when immediately he saw her expression he knew all was not well.

Molly shook her head in response to his questioning look. "No word yet, I'm afraid," she said when the nurse had left, "but Thomas has gone to break the news to Elizabeth."

"And Jane, has she calmed down?"

"She's in bed. Alex gave her a sedative before he left." Molly knit her brows as she disclosed, "I've never known her be like this before, she was quite hysterical, wanted to go out and search with the men."

James dropped his gaze. "It's worrying, not knowing if he managed to get out."

Molly made a tiny snorting sound. "After what he would have done to you, I'm surprised you can show any concern. Thank the Lord, Thomas saw what was happening out there."

He looked up in surprise. "It's not like you to be bitter, darling. I'll admit I never cared for the man but, whatever my feelings, I wouldn't wish him to go this way."

She leaned over to kiss his cheek. "You're right, I should show more compassion." And continuing to gaze at him fondly, she remarked, "Thank goodness you kept up your swimming exercises, otherwise you'd never have managed to get out."

"I didn't do it entirely on my own, I have the men to thank for that and I shall ensure they are well rewarded."

"Fortunately, Serena and Thomas had gone out to call you in to lunch, they saw it happen, and she was quick to get Nicholson. You know, she's amazingly like you. You've come through this ordeal remarkably well, whereas Timmy would have been dreadfully upset."

James' expression hardened. "That drunken fool Grant had the nerve to say he's too soft." He shook his head despairingly. "I ask you, Molly, just how tough does he expect a seven year old child to be!"

"It's time to get you out, darling," she said, placing warmed towels on a chair. "I'll ring for nurse."

But when the nurse returned, Molly realised from her expression the news regarding Miles was grave. "There's a policeman downstairs, Mrs Purcell, he'd like a word with you when you have a moment. I've taken the liberty of asking Pincott to help me lift Mr Purcell from his bath, no need for you to worry."

"Then I'd better not keep him," Molly said and left the steamy bathroom to go downstairs where the local policeman waited in the hall.

"Bad news I'm afraid, madam," he said. "We recovered Mr Grant's body a short time ago, a couple of yards beyond the bridge, caught up in a tree brought down with the flood."

"Body?" Molly whispered. "He's dead?"

"I'm afraid so, madam. Doctor Wilson was on the scene when we found him and I believe he's gone to break the sad news to your daughter."

"Oh, yes, she's not well, I hope he'll bring her here to us."

"And your husband? I understand he's making a good recovery, considering what he's been through."

"He was shocked, naturally, and extremely cold," Molly replied, "but, although he may not have use of his legs, he's remarkably strong."

"I'll need to have a word with him as soon as he feels up to it, for my report, you understand. We need to get the facts down on paper."

She nodded. "Of course, I expect there will be an inquest. Once Doctor Wilson has finished with my husband you may speak to him."

"Do you happen to know if anyone was present when the er, accident occurred?" he asked, taking a notebook from his breast pocket.

"Yes, Constable, my granddaughter and Thomas actually saw them fall into the river. She'd gone to call my husband in to lunch so, as one would expect, she's extremely upset."

"Very understandable," he murmured, then surprised her by asking, "Do you know if Mr Grant had been drinking?"

Molly let out a wavering breath. "By what Thomas tells us, I believe he had. It was a problem of his, you see, he wasn't a well man."

"Don't concern yourself, madam," he said kindly, "the postmortem will tell us all we need to know."

At Ashdale, an ashen-faced, Elizabeth reached for her dressing gown and struggled out of bed. "It's my fault!" she cried, searching wildly for her slippers. "If I hadn't told him to leave this would never have happened!"

Alex uttered an exasperated sigh. "You must stop blaming yourself. He was an ailing man with little time left, and if he chose to end it this way, you're not responsible."

"But I should have known he'd go drinking," she opposed brokenly. "I could have prevented it..."

Alex strode round the bed and took her firmly by the shoulders. "How? By giving him the money he asked for? If you had it would have made things even worse! Forget your own misgivings, Elizabeth, think of your father, and Serena, how do you imagine they feel!"

As he left the bedroom, Elizabeth fell silent and stared blankly ahead, only vaguely aware of his conversation with Gladys downstairs.

Minutes later he came back, a small glass in one hand. "I keep a drop for emergencies," he said. "Now, drink it down."

It may have been the brandy, or his sudden change to a more gentle manner, she didn't quite know, but she couldn't control the sudden flood of tears as she whispered, "If only I hadn't been ill..."

"I understand," he said softly, taking the window seat nearby, "but you were expecting too much of yourself, taking responsibility for Miles. Quite frankly, no-one can have complete control over another person's life, particularly an alcoholic. Yet, you probably kept him going for more years than he would otherwise have had, but at fifty-seven he wasn't going to find it easy. It was your grandmother who clung to the belief marriage would persuade him to change."

"How wrong she was," she said, her lips quivering so much she found it difficult to speak, "but I should not have stopped trying."

"You haven't heard everything," he said, intending to ease her guilt. "You don't know about Timothy's trauma whilst you've been in bed."

"Timmy?" She raised an anxious face. "What's happened, is he all right?"

"Don't worry, he'll survive," Alex said and related details of the events which had led to the injuries Miles had inflicted on her son. "Actually, that was the basis of the argument between your father and Miles. Your father confronted him about it, which is why Miles pushed him into the river. Unfortunately, Miles was too damned drunk to prevent himself from going in as well."

"Miles would have killed Daddy," she whispered, her eyes widening as the horror of it struck home.

"Had he been sober, I doubt it would have gone that far, but the alcohol he had taken would make it difficult for him to survive. Thankfully, your father's in pretty good shape, though how he managed to find the strength to avoid being swept away, I'll never know."

Elizabeth straightened her shoulders and downed the remainder of her drink. "Would you mind driving me to the Hall, Alex?" she asked, her voice tense. "I must see Daddy and the children as I can't bear to stay in this house another moment!

Chapter 29

Maurici pushed his glass aside. "Thank you, Enric, just coffee's fine, I must get back to the surgery."

Enric called the waiter, and then turning back to Maurici said, "Hope I didn't interrupt anything?"

Maurici glanced towards the door of the restaurant and smiled. "No, she had to get back to her boutique."

"Good looking woman. Are you making plans?"

He raised his shoulders. "I've considered it, though I've become used to being single. Jaume is less dependent now, he's almost twelve..." He hesitated, "and my daughter, she will be almost sixteen."

Enric cast him a quick glance. "You've not heard anything from England?"

Maurici shook his head. "Have you?"

"Not since last year, which is unusual for James."

Absently stirring his coffee, Maurici remarked, "Strange isn't it, how the past stays in one's thoughts. Various snippets of news keep reminding me of that family, such as report on the hospital for spinal injuries in England. Places, names, a mention of Yorkshire, or Ireland, they keep cropping up." He paused in his ramblings to add, "Perhaps I should marry, maybe then I can forget the past."

Enric wasn't convinced. As they rose to leave he planned to write a letter to James immediately he arrived home.

* *

Months passed before Elizabeth felt well enough to consider selling Ashdale House. Pneumonia had followed the influenza she had been suffering at the time of Miles' death, leaving her feeling lethargic and depressed. The debilitating effect of her illness frequently reduced her to tears and it was to her father she turned whenever things got too much to bear.

Early in the following year, shortly after Jane passed away, Alex called at the Hall to see Molly. He found her looking completely exhausted, yet for the last six months he noticed Elizabeth did little else but complain.

On leaving, she accompanied him to the door when he paused on the threshold and said unusually bluntly, "Are you not aware how tired your mother is, or have you become too self-centered to notice? It will do you no harm to shoulder some of the burden, no harm at all."

Elizabeth stared at him, her cheeks turning pink. But quickly regaining her composure she exclaimed indignantly, "Self-centered? I don't know what you mean!"

"Exactly! For months she's given you support, cared for your father, your children, and her mother, all without complaint. Yet, except for your father who truly appreciates all she does, I don't recall hearing one word of gratitude from you. Think about it, Elizabeth, see if you can go back to being the sweet natured girl you once were."

"If you've quite finished, Doctor," she managed tautly, "I'll bid you good night!"

It had really shocked Elizabeth to hear Alex speak so bluntly. Perhaps he'd had a difficult day, or been called out frequently the night before. She tried to convince herself this must be the reason for his harsh words, but the more she thought about it, the more obvious it became he was right.

Lying awake that night she became aware of the faint sound of her mother weeping which pricked her conscience. Alex was right, she had taken her mother for granted. Perhaps she would make her a cup of tea, or simply offer a word of comfort, she decided and tiptoed along the landing towards the rear staircase in the direction of the vast, dark kitchen.

When the telephone rang the following morning, Alex Wilson's voice caused Elizabeth a sharp pang of guilt. "I want to offer my apologies, Elizabeth," he said. "I had no right to speak that way, I'm truly sorry."

"There's no need," she protested in a small voice. "I deserved every word."

"It was because of my concern for your mother, though I must confess I rather overdid it."

"No need, Alex, I've already told you. After you left I thought very hard about what you said, tried to see myself through your eyes and I felt terribly ashamed and realise I've a lot of making up to do."

There was a smile in his voice as he said, "You know, if you were not one of my patients, I'd invite you to dinner."

"Thank you, but that shouldn't stop you joining us here."

"Invitation accepted," he replied quickly. "But would you object if I brought a colleague along with me?"

She was surprised but managed to murmur, "Of course, he'd be most welcome."

"You don't sound too enthusiastic, but he's a charming fellow, studies psychology in Leeds..."

"It isn't that, it's just that I rarely hear you mention your friends," she broke in, adding wryly, "A further indication of my total self-absorption."

"We all love you, Elizabeth, you should know that."

Choking back tears, she said, "I hope so. Now, about this dinner, obviously we can't arrange it at present, not until after grandmother has been laid to rest. Curiously, I find it painful to think of her passing, even though we've known it was inevitable for some time."

"Naturally, I quite understand."

"You know, Alex," she continued on a thoughtful note, "she never was the same after Miles died. I couldn't believe the effect it had upon her; she just seemed to fade away."

"Perhaps it was the kindest way," he responded with sympathy, "we should be thankful."

* *

James looked at his wife across the breakfast table, setting down his knife and fork as he went on to say, "It's not only Elizabeth, the children are much happier, and I notice Timmy has gone back to playing the piano." Turning his wheelchair away from the table he gave a contented smile. "Thankfully, she appears to have got over her depression. I was beginning to think it would never end, then she seemed to change, almost overnight."

"Which is why I've decided not to mention the letter," Molly told him. "It would serve no useful purpose."

"I assume you are referring to the one concerning Miles?"

Molly nodded as she continued to sort through the bundle of papers she'd brought from her mother's room. "You know, recalling how things used to be, I can understand why my mother concealed it from us. She must have been desperate to keep her promise regarding Miles."

He sighed and gazed unseeing through the window. "Poor old Jane, God rest her soul. To have an unmarried sister pregnant in those days must have been hell, and it was forntunate the Grants wanted to adopt. I wonder if they were aware that Jane was his aunt?"

"From this letter, is appears not, and it can't have been easy for her, I agree. Yet, as a child he used to spend weeks here at the Hall." Molly's face crumpled. Covering it with her hands she exclaimed brokenly, "But to think she encouraged Elizabeth to marry him..."

"Don't distress yourself, darling, it's all in the past. We'd not have known any of this if the dear old vicar hadn't enlightened you about that registration of birth you found amongst those papers."

Molly sighed and looked at her husband. "But Miles was a relative of Elizabeth which is not a very healthy situation, however distant, so I'm thankful he couldn't father a child because of that past illness he'd had."

James reached for her hand. "I suspect he wasn't aware of it so you shouldn't torment yourself. But now we know why your mother was so fond of him, from that photograph he looked so like her twin sister."

"According to the vicar, she and mother were very close, and after she died giving birth, Miles would be a constant reminder."

"I'm sure he was, but now both Jane and Miles have passed on I feel we ought to let the matter rest."

She gave him a wavering smile. "You're right, James, I've decided to burn these old letters, so there's no point in mentioning them to Elizabeth."

Molly broke off when Pincott brought in the post. A letter from Spain lay uppermost on the pile and James slit it open with eager hands, saying, "I must bring dear old Enric up to date, it's simply ages since I wrote." He glanced up, his smile widening. "Listen to this, darling, Enric hopes to visit us this year!" With the smile still on his lips he ended dreamily, "I wonder if travelling by plane would prove too difficult for me."

* *

Fanning himself with his newspaper, Enric took a seat in the shade of the open doorway to read the morning's post. There was a reply to his enquiry about travel to England, also a written confirmation of his promotion along with a request to cover an event in the next town. But when he spotted the envelope addressed to him in James' bold handwriting he put a match to his cigar and uttered a contented sigh.

James expressed delight at the prospect of his visit. 'Just the tonic we need,' James continued after he'd apologised for not writing and explaining the reason he had been so remiss. But Enric found it difficult to understand to where exactly Elizabeth's husband had passed after his accident a year ago; had his going away to hunt been the reason for Elizabeth's depression? He then read of the death of James' mother-in-law, occurring only weeks before, and felt a wave of sympathy for Molly. But he was happy to contemplate meeting his old friends, and hoped his travel arrangements were finalised in time for him to escape the heat and humidity of Sitges in August, a month away.

As he ate a leisurely breakfast of bread and smoked ham, he read through the travel details; by rail to Paris where he could transfer to the boat-train, or by air. It would be much quicker by aeroplane, but the thought of flying sent a quiver of apprehension through his ample body. But when he recalled Maurici speaking of flying, saying how pleasant an experience it had been, he decided to telephone him for reassurance.

Being Saturday, he didn't expect to find Maurici taking surgery, particularly now he had moved his practice to a more prosperous area of town. But the only number he had was that of his parent's in Sant Adria.

It was Maurici's mother who answered his call, and more than once did she ask Enric to repeat his name. "I'm a little deaf," Carmen explained in Catalan, "my nephew usually answers the telephone these days."

"My apologies for troubling you, *senyora*," he said in a raised voice, "it is Maurici I wish to speak with. Your number is the only one I have."

"He has moved address," she said, her voice filled with pride. "He now has rooms befitting to his position."

"Of course," he murmured politely. "But can you tell me where I may contact him by telephone?"

"Not today, *senyor*, he has taken his son to visit friends in the city."

"Then would you please tell him I rang? He has my number – the name is Puig."

It was early in the evening of the same day when Maurici brought his car to a halt outside Enric's home. "It wasn't my intention to bring you out of your way," said Enric when he went out to greet his visitor.

"It isn't a problem," Maurici smiled, and turning back to his car he signalled for his son to alight. "This one nags me constantly to bring him to Sitges so I've agreed to him spending time on his own to look around."

As Jaume strolled off in the direction of the church, Enric admitted, "Actually, it was not important, only information about flying. Perhaps your mother didn't catch what I said."

Maurici's smile faded. "When I telephoned home she said you had asked me to ring, sounded important so I decided to come straight here."

"I hope it was convenient," Enric said, ushering him into the house. "You were not visiting your lady friend?"

"No, no, I'm dining with her family tomorrow," he told him as he took a seat by the small front window.

"So, does this mean you have decided to marry?"

Maurici drew in a long breath before he admitted, "I just can't bring myself to make that decision."

"Does your son not approve? He's almost a man, probably has firm views of his own."

"Quite so, but that's not the reason I'm wavering..." He broke off and rose to his feet, staring through the window in silence for a few moments before he continued. "I think you know what my trouble is, Enric. For some strange reason, I can't let go of the past."

He glanced round and managed a quick smile. "Enough of my problem, I believe you wanted to know about flying. Where do you plan to go?"

~454~

"England," replied Enric, catching the quick spark of interest in his visitor's eyes. "I hope to go next month but can't make up my mind which way to travel."

With a tentative lift of his brow, Maurici queried, "You intend to visit the Purcells?"

"Remember, when we met in that restaurant a few weeks ago, I mentioned I'd not heard from James? Well, I wrote again and received a reply only today when he reiterates his invitation for me to visit."

"Elizabeth?" Maurici queried. "And Serena, have you news of them?"

Enric raised his hand. "My dear friend, you say you can't let go of the past so you may as well read it for yourself. In fact, there's something I don't understand," he went on, smoothing out the letter to run his finger down one page. "The grandmother of Elizabeth has died, this I understand, but these words, here, they say her husband 'passed on to happier hunting grounds'..."

He glanced up to find Maurici staring at him with an incredulous expression on his face, and it was a moment before the younger man could find his voice. "It means, Elizabeth's husband is also dead," Maurici translated aloud. "He died last year."

Enric frowned. "So, this 'hunting ground', it means death?"

"*Si, si,* it appears he died after an accident," Maurici managed raggedly, closing his eyes as guilt grappled with elation to take precedence in his thoughts.

* *

There was a buzz of excitement in Woodington Hall on the day Enric was due to arrive. James and Molly had arranged for Nicholson to drive them to York station while Elizabeth stayed behind to organise the household in preparation for his stay. As it was a warm August day with a clear sky, she planned to have afternoon tea served on the lawn and coaxed her children to help with setting out the table and chairs. Serena had shown a particular interest in Enric's coming and looked forward to meeting this guest from the Catalan region of Spain. She had picked flowers to place in the guest-room at the front of the house and helped Elsie make up the bed. Timothy was concentrating on a piece of piano music he'd planned to play, the hesitant notes floating out through the open window to where Elizabeth was waiting for the arrival of the car.

"He does speak English?" Serena queried when she joined her mother.

"Yes, quite well. French too, I believe."

"Oh good!" she said, perching on the edge of the table, "I can practice my French on him. Do you think he'll mind?"

"As far as I remember, *Senyor* Puig is a very agreeable person. He was extremely kind to us when we were there."

"Does he know my father?" the girl asked suddenly.

There was a moment's awkward silence before Elizabeth replied, "He did when I was there, but it's so long ago."

"I wish you'd tell me more about him," Serena said on a petulant note. "After all, I'm almost sixteen."

Elizabeth glanced away. "Well, the subject hasn't arisen before, and it makes no difference to you now..."

"The girls at school are jealous!" Serena broke in passionately. "No-one else has a Catalan father. They want to know what he's like."

Elizabeth was startled. "Goodness me, I hadn't realised this was something you discuss with your class!"

"I expect he was very handsome," Serena remarked dreamily, "or you wouldn't have fallen in love with him."

"Darling, please, we'll talk about it some other time."

"You always say that," Serena accused, "but you must have been in love with him to have had me. In fact, one should be in love to conceive a baby, Grandma said so."

Elizabeth's eyes widened. "Did she indeed. And what other words of wisdom has she spoken?"

Turning her head to one side, Serena smiled, "Sorry, Mummy, I think I hear a car. As you always say, some other time."

Enric gazed contentedly from one to the other as he sipped tea with milk from a delicate, gilt-edged cup. "I recognise your mother immediately I leave the train," he said to Elizabeth, "she is not changing. But you..." he went on, meeting her sapphire gaze, "you have become mature."

"I think you mean old," she laughed.

"No, no, Elizabeth. In nineteen thirty-eight, you are a shy girl, but now a beautiful lady."

Elizabeth experienced a tiny glow of pleasure. "Thank you, Enric, that is sweet of you. Now, will you have another scone, or a slice of cake?"

Enric accepted a slice of the three-tiered cake spread with raspberry jam and butter icing. "Is perfect cake!" he said with a nod of approval, and met the intent, brown-eyed gaze of Timothy across the table.

At first, it came as a shock to Enric to find himself face to face with a miniature version of Maurici. Now, as the boy's gaze rested curiously upon him, he saw a sad-faced child, his expression the image of his father.

"Are you tired, old chap?" James asked a second time when Enric didn't respond. "You're welcome to rest a while. We'll meet for drinks around six. Does that suit you?"

With a quick smile, Enric pulled himself back to the present. "*Si, si,* James, I will rest, I am more tired than I am realising," he said, and hearing a faint giggle from across the table he met Serena's dark, laughing eyes. And he noticed the glance of disapproval Molly shot her as she rose and came round to his side.

"I'll show you to your room, Enric, and we'll look forward to seeing you later when I hope you will give us news of Sitges. I'm sure many changes have taken place since we were there."

Enric was finding his first visit to England very enjoyable and spent many hours of each day with James. Sometimes they would organise an outing in the car, Nicholson driving, with Molly or the children going along. But Elizabeth avoided spending too much time with their guest, nervous of the questions he may ask, and she was pottering about in the vegetable garden one afternoon when Alex Wilson called by.

"I saw the car go past but you weren't with them," he remarked as she pulled off her gardening gloves and went to join him on the seat.

"Not enough room," she said, brushing back a strand of damp hair. "Anyway, it's too warm for picnics just now."

"But not too warm for working in the garden?"

"Hardly working, I'm only picking beans for dinner," she said with a reproving glance. "We don't have so many staff these days."

He smiled. "Point taken, though I'd have thought you could have managed one day out while Mr Puig is here. He's a pleasant chap, most interesting, particularly when he spoke of that incident in thirty-eight when he almost died."

Elizabeth merely nodded and averted her head.

"Yes, he was damned lucky there was a doctor to hand," Alex continued. "Heat-stroke can be difficult to deal with in those conditions."

Her expression was cold when she turned to him. "For goodness sake, Alex, I don't wish to discuss it!"

"Touched a sensitive spot, have I?" he pursued gently. "I could tell by your expression you recognised one face on the photographs Enric brought out after dinner the other night. Remember? the ones with the young doctor, an English Brigader, and the ambulance driver."

She jumped to her feet and cried, "I know damned well what you're getting at but it belongs in the past!"

"Are you denying Serena the right to know her father? Is this why she has begged me to ask Enric to help because you, her own mother, won't even listen!"

Elizabeth lifted a dejected face to his. "But he may be married, may not have mentioned he has a child. I've no intention of disrupting his life."

"At least you could tell her who he is, explain that his marital status is unknown to you, she's old enough to understand. It's preferable to allowing her to believe he is some anonymous Spaniard whom you won't even discuss."

"Catalan, actually," she corrected him with a lift of her head. "He's Catalan."

"Don't prevaricate, Elizabeth. Whatever he is, he also may wish to know her. Have you considered that?"

"I can't take the risk. Anyway, he'll have changed as have we all. One can't go back."

"Frightened of rejection, is that what bothers you? So you load your fears upon your poor innocent daughter."

She eyed him coldly. "Alex, I respect you as a doctor, but I won't allow you to act as my psychiatrist!"

"I don't need to be a psychiatrist to know that both your children share the same father, a man you still care about," he said as he watched her walk away.

He sighed and shook his head, perplexed as always by the emotions that stood between women and men.

* *

As Enric's visit drew to an end, James called Elizabeth to his room. "Do consider Enric's invitation, darling," he said, indicating she sit on the bed. "The children can't possibly travel such a distance without you."

Elizabeth uttered a weary sigh. "First the children nag me, then Alex, and now you. I'm beginning to wish Enric had stayed away."

"If I didn't require special transport, I'd take them myself," he said, a note of pain in his voice, "whereas, there's nothing to hold you back."

Regretting her sharpness, she dropped her eyes. "Sorry, it's just..." She paused, her throat aching, and felt his hand take hers.

"Is it Sitges?" he asked softly, drawing her down beside him. "Would there be too many painful memories?"

Surprised by his perceptiveness she could only nod as hot tears spilled over. She turned into the curve of his arm to whisper miserably, "I gave up my chance of happiness when I made the decision to stand by Miles."

She brushed her wet cheek against the sleeve of his pyjamas to continue, "I couldn't bear to be rejected now."

"You forget, Elizabeth, there's also the children's happiness to consider. His children," he reminded her softly. "But that is something only you can decide.

Chapter 30

On Friday evening, Serena gathered together the last few items she would need for her journey. As she took her passport and tickets to slide them into the pocket of her mother's old travel bag which she had found in the attic, she encountered something already inside, and withdrew an envelope which she discovered contained a few papers and her mother's passport. With an interested gaze she opened the passport and saw the date of issue. January, nineteen thirty-eight, when her mother had been eighteen, just one year older than herself.

A small sigh escaped her as she gazed at the photograph inside the first page of the young woman who looked not unlike herself, her oval face framed by dark, shoulder length hair. Only the eyes were different; her mother's were lighter – in reality, the colour of sapphires – whereas her own were a dark brown. Serena thought she detected an expression of anticipation on her mother's face. Elizabeth Purcell, as she then was named, would also have been preparing for a journey to Barcelona when this photograph was taken.

Another photograph fell from between the pages of the passport; a sepia picture of her mother, dressed in clothes which were fashionable at the time, standing beside a drinking fountain on a tree-lined avenue with tall buildings in the background. And on the reverse, faintly written, 'Canaletes Fountain, Barcelona, February, 1938'. Smiling, she turned to meet the gaze of her mother...

"I expected you to be in bed," Elizabeth reproached then spotted the photograph in her daughter's hand. "Where on earth did you find this?"

"In your old passport. It was taken before I was born!"

Elizabeth stared at the faded photograph, closing her eyes as her thoughts travelled back. "I'll keep this if you don't mind, darling. Now, do hurry, I have my own packing still to do."

* *

"You will visit me soon?" Enric reminded James and Molly the following morning as they said their final farewell.

"You can be sure of it, old friend," said James, his face alight with enthusiasm as they escorted Enric to the waiting car where Elizabeth and the children were already seated.

"Safe journey!" Molly called as Nicholson pulled away.

The children waved and Elizabeth turned to look through the rear window until her parents faded from view. Then, facing ahead, she fought back the lump which had risen in her throat, wavering between excitement and apprehension over what memories their destination may evoke. Even yet, she could recall her last conversation with Maurici when he'd telephoned Ashdale House. She'd been desperate to explain the reason she must deny herself the freedom she so desired, convince him her loyalty to her husband was based on compassion, not love. But Maurici had sounded both hurt and angry; "If that is your wish, your final word," he had said stiffly, the memory bringing a stab of pain to her now.

"Mummy! *Senyor* Puig is speaking to you," Serena whispered, bringing Elizabeth out of her pensive mood.

She managed a smile. "I do apologise. You were saying?"

"You are sad to leave your parents?" he repeated, observing her with concern.

"It's a new experience as I've not travelled any distance from Woodington for years."

"What time shall we be there, Mummy?" Timothy piped up.

"Shush, Timmy!" Serena cast him a warning glance.

Elizabeth gave them an indulgent smile. "Don't you think the journey itself is exciting?" she asked as they travelled towards York. "I told you of things to look for on the way."

Reminded of this they settled happily, their noses twitching to the smell of cocoa drifting through the car's open window as it neared Rowntree's factory. And when they drove into the walled city before turning in the direction of the station, Enric's glance lingered on York Minster which he had visited with Molly and James the week before.

Finally, after covering the lengthy journey south they transferred from the train to travel out to the airport, Elizabeth concealing the apprehension she shared with Enric about flying.

"For me it is easier this time," he whispered once they were airborne, and went on to point out certain landmarks as they flew overhead.

"Look, Mummy, snow!" cried Timothy after Enric had drawn his attention to the range of mountains below.

"We're passing over the Pyrenees," Serena told him, welcoming the opportunity to air her knowledge. "That is where Grandpa had his accident, somewhere down there."

Enric and Elizabeth exchanged glances, when he murmured, "I also thought about James when I am flying to England."

She nodded, a tight little smile on her lips, memories from seventeen years ago filtering back to when Serena had been but a speck of life within her. Her thoughts flitted to the amethyst ring in her handbag, the one Maurici had given her in London. Reflecting again on their last, brief telephone conversation, she glanced across to her daughter. 'Take care of Serena and bring her to me when you can,' he had said, his voice a broken whisper.

"We are soon to land," Enric leaned over to say, and she looked up to see excitement on the faces of her children, feeling a tremor of emotion as her heart increased its beat.

The drive to Sitges along the winding coast road was almost as she remembered it; below them, a sparkling blue sea lapping tiny golden beaches, as it was all those years ago. And when at last Enric pointed ahead to where the church stood out beneath a cloudless sky, she found it difficult to contain her tears as she took in the familiar scene.

Immediately they drew to a halt Timothy's eyes widened as he spotted the almost deserted beach, and he looked round hopefully as they alighted from the car. "Soon," Elizabeth promised, "after I've unpacked."

"I'll take him," Serena offered, "give you some peace."

"Very well, darling, but don't let him go too far."

"Mummy, don't fuss!" she objected, taking her brother's hand, and as they strolled off across the sand it suddenly occurred to Elizabeth just how grown up her daughter was.

Inside the house she looked around her, marvelling at how little it had changed, as if the intervening years had been swept away. "I always loved this house," she said, her eyes shining. "It's wonderful to see it again."

Not knowing he would have three guests on his return, Enric's mind was in a whirl and he decided Rosa must be called in.

"Everything looks spotless, just need to make up the beds," Elizabeth pointed out. "If you remember, we did it once before."

He grinned. "And you sleep in the same room, but Timothy and I will share the room of your parents. For Serena, maybe a bed in my study, *si*?"

"That will be fine, Enric, I'll call the children, Serena can help."

"Please, a moment," Enric said, his expression serious, "I wish to speak with you alone."

She looked up and noticed he appeared a trifle uneasy. "What is it, is something wrong?"

"No, but in England Serena is pleading with me..." He paused and spread his hands in a helpless gesture. "She wishes to know her father."

Elizabeth's expression froze. "Oh no! I'm sorry, she shouldn't have asked you."

"But why not? I think it is very natural for her."

"Well, for many reasons – he could have a wife, she may not know about Serena – we could be an embarrassment."

Enric sent her a speculative glance. "For the moment, no wife."

She frowned. "For the moment?"

"Maybe soon..."

"Then we mustn't complicate his plans," she rushed in, struggling to keep the disappointment from her voice.

The children went to bed later than was usual after they had all dined out in a local restaurant. Elizabeth, also sleepy, chose to retire at the same time. She'd found the invading memories troubled her, and with her thoughts unresolved she slipped into bed.

Throughout the night she was restless, waking frequently for no reason other than the disturbing content of her thoughts. In the early morning she fell into a dream-filled sleep, taking her back to the hospital in Barcelona where she saw rows of beds draped in white sheets. There was a burst of distant gunfire, then Maurici's voice, harsh and bitter, demanding she raise the sheets for him to inspect the bodies beneath as he accompanied her along the line. In the first bed lay Serena, her complexion like marble, her brown eyes open as she pleaded with Elizabeth to lift her out. It was when she began to draw back the sheet the gunfire started again, this time closer and more terrifying than before. She cried out for Maurici, over and over again, until she felt his hand on her shoulder, pulling her away as he called her name..."Elizabeth!"

Then she heard, "Elizabeth!" again, and the hand on her shoulder, gently shaking her awake when she heard, "You have dreams?"

Struggling to gather her thoughts she opened her eyes to find Enric bending over her, his expression anxious. "Forgive me for coming to the room," he said, "but you are screaming, I am worried..."

He broke off when she gave a startled cry as another burst of noise like gunfire came in through the open window. But he merely shook his head and smiled as he said, "It is only the fireworks of the children, I am surprised they don't wake you before?"

Elizabeth uttered a long groan of relief and sank back on her pillows. "Fireworks!" she gasped. "Only fireworks! Oh, Enric, I've had the most awful dream..."

Over breakfast Elizabeth related her dream to Enric while the children had their rolls and coffee outside. "It was most upsetting, a real nightmare!" she said with a slow shake of her head. "But tell me, why are the children letting off fireworks this morning?"

"It is the festival of our saint," he told her. "But it is surprising me that you are back with the war after so many years. This is something you think about, *si?*"

"Perhaps," she admitted softly, "though I wasn't aware of it until now. But when I do reflect upon it, foremost in my mind is the gunfire, and the bombing in Barcelona, and all those injured people in the hospital, many already dead." She shuddered as a mental picture returned; the bloodstained face of Maurici when he arrived in the ward and her fear when the hostile plane flew over as they lay in the ditch...

"But it is not the city you are remembering. We are not hearing the guns any more... only fireworks in the mornings." He smiled. "Now the city has flowers and gardens, the buildings repaired. Maybe we have a little time in Barcelona, it will stop the bad memories."

She looked doubtful. "I'm not sure, but Daddy did ask for photographs. He wants to see the hotel where we stayed and the hospital where Mummy and I worked – views of the city – you know the kind of thing. And Sitges, of course."

"Of course," Enric laughed, "and I will take my camera and send him a picture of the old Press Office."

She gave a sudden smile. "He'd like that as he's collecting material to illustrate his story about the war, and I know you will take much better pictures that I."

"We will go together," he said and saw her smile fade. "I had many photographs but the best destroyed when Nationalist troops break into the office. Here I have pictures of you and your parents outside this house. You like to see?"

While Enric went to his study she began to clear away the breakfast dishes before settling down to look through the photographs he brought out. These were not the usual family snapshots, but more professional, larger and clearer than those he had taken to England, and she laughed as she saw how she had looked more than seventeen years ago. She giggled over the dresses she and her mother were wearing at the time, the angle her father wore his Trilby, and looking so handsome, but it saddened her to see him standing tall and straight.

"Is a pity James is not on the feet now," Enric remarked, "but thanks to God, he is alive."

"God, and my mother," Elizabeth included softly, and seeing him pause at the next photograph, she reached over to ask, "Is that another of Daddy?" But immediately she saw who was pictured there the pain of longing pierced her once again.

"It was taken near the fightings when I was ill with the heat problems," he explained, noting the quiver of her lip. Her eyes fastened on the enlarged picture of Maurici taken at the field hospital, an ambulance in the background. "He is saving my life, Elizabeth, without him I am dead."

Only the tiny movement of her head indicated she had heard, her eyes dwelt still on Maurici's face as the ache of longing clutched her heart.

"You would like to meet him, maybe?" Enric's soft voice penetrated her sadness.

"I'd like to, but I haven't the courage," she responded quietly.

Enric gave an understanding nod, but felt sure he detected a false note in her voice when she rushed on to add, "After so many years he'll have made a new life for himself, and so must I, it will be easier that way."

"For you, Elizabeth, yes, but for the children, how easy for them is this life?"

"I wouldn't prevent him seeing them, he's their father, though he doesn't know about Timothy. But we may be an embarrassment, particularly to his future wife."

Enric held her gaze as he told her, "He and his son, Jaume, they visit me in Sitges not many weeks ago. Would you like that I invite Maurici here again, to this house?"

Wordlessly she looked at him, then gathered her composure to say, "I'd be too nervous, but he did once say he would like to see Serena and I'd be grateful if you can organise a meeting for them. She's spoken of little else, whereas Timmy isn't aware of who his father is." She uttered a small sigh. "It's cowardly of me, I know, but I couldn't bear it if he rejected me, he no longer cared..."

Enric's tiny satisfied smile went unnoticed. "So perhaps it is good if I show photographs to Serena, yes?" he suggested and called her indoors.

Serena giggled over some photographs, but became serious when she saw her grandfather on his feet, and when Enric related the story of how his life had been saved by this certain young medical student, she looked at her mother, a question in her eyes.

"Yes, he is your father," Elizabeth said a trifle stiffly. "Enric tells me he's a fully qualified doctor now."

"He looks more like Timmy than me, his hair grows just the same way," she observed to Elizabeth's astonishment, then looked up, her dark eyes accusing. "But part of his index finger is missing, you never told me that!"

"Oh really, Serena, what difference does it make?"

"But he's my father, I want to know everything about him, and if you won't tell me I shall find out for myself!"

Fortunately for Enric, who'd had little opportunity to make a private call, Maurici telephoned the next morning. "Ah, you are back from your travels! How did you enjoy England?"

"Very much, and it didn't rain as I expected."

"And the flight? You weren't too nervous, I hope."

"No, no, my friend, it was a thrilling experience."

There was a short pause before Maurici asked, "And the Purcell family, they are well?"

"*Si, si,* all very well," Enric assured him in Catalan.

"Elizabeth, and Serena, you saw them also?"

"Yes, and the boy," Enric replied, lowering his voice.

"I can't hear you too well, is there something amiss?" Maurici asked and went on to enquire, "Are you ill from the journey? I could call..."

"No, no, not ill," he responded quickly. "I was about to ring you. I have visitors, the three you just mentioned."

"No! Not Elizabeth! Elizabeth... here?" he heard Maurici gasp.

"*Si,* and the children, they travel here with me."

"She wishes to meet me?" Maurici asked, then held his breath.

"The girl, yes, she asks all the time, but Elizabeth is very nervous, you must be patient with her," he explained, going on to relate what she'd said.

"Then, what am I to do?" Maurici responded hollowly. "I also must know that she still cares and wants to see me without her feeling obligated because of the children."

"I understand, my friend, but after so many years she is convinced you have changed, you might reject her now."

"Ah, I see," said Maurici, "then I must convince her. Perhaps you will do me a favour..."

* *

"I suggest we go to Barcelona today," Enric announced over breakfast the next day.

"I haven't finished showing them around Sitges," Elizabeth objected laughingly.

"But you must, we can take the photographs for James, then I will have time for developing before you leave."

"Oh, I'd forgotten the photographs. So, if you insist, we'll go with you."

"I've got a tan, see," Serena said, displaying the golden tint on her arms as they hurried to get ready for the journey..

"You're lucky," Elizabeth smiled. "I usually burn."

"I expect it's because I'm half Catalan," Serena pointed out, and shot her a curious glance as she remarked, "I notice Timmy doesn't burn, either."

"Come along, I expect Enric is waiting," Elizabeth broke in hastily and bustled them out to the car.

But Serena hung back. "Can we meet my father today?"

"Enric will arrange it," Elizabeth responded shortly. "You can't expect to do everything in one day."

"But don't you want to see him?" she pressed, causing her mother to glance away.

Enric smiled to himself as they all climbed into his car.

"I'm glad you persuaded me to come," Elizabeth said as they left the hotel where she and her parents had once stayed. "Of course, it looks quite different now, I can hardly believe we were here during the bombing."

Enric smiled. "I told you, the signs of war have disappeared. And now I will take photographs for James before we drive to the hospital."

Even though it had been almost rebuilt, their visit to the hospital brought back many memories, and as they sipped a cool drink in a nearby café, Elizabeth thought over the weeks she had spent there, some happy, others sad. She learned that Sister Teresa had retired to a convent, and although the ward arrangements had been modernised somewhat, the atmosphere of tranquillity she once knew remained.

"I'm hungry," Timothy announced shuffling restlessly on his chair. "When are we going to have lunch?"

"Just one more place to visit," Elizabeth said, flushing prettily as she drew the old snapshot out of her bag.

"Mummy's going to look at the fountain again," Serena laughed. "No, it doesn't have water spraying out," she told her brother as he craned his neck to see.

"Then I don't want to see it," he protested, flopping back in his chair, "I'm tired."

"I have the suggestion," Enric said, glancing at his watch for what seemed the umpteenth time this morning. "I must take the photograph of my office. Why not come with me, children, let your mother go to the fountain alone?"

"I don't expect you to act as nanny," Elizabeth laughed, and Timothy's hungry now."

"Please," he insisted. "We will lunch in the restaurant near the office after I take photographs. You join us, *si*?"

"If you're sure," she said uncertainly. "I'd like to see if anything has changed since this old photograph was taken."

Going towards Plaça de Catalunya, Elizabeth quickened her pace. To see the Canaletes fountain before joining the others for lunch gave her little time. Crossing the busy square to enter the tree-lined avenue, she soon reached the fountain, posing in exactly the same place as she had on the photograph.

Closing her eyes behind the dark lens of her sun-glasses, she recalled the last time she had been standing there. Believing she heard the repeat of gunfire, she was quickly relieved to realise it was the backfiring of a car. And the heart-rending screams she remembered were now replaced by the boisterous shrieks of happy children, and the sound of hooves rattling over the setts were not those of a runaway horse but mounted policemen riding by. The bedraggled figure crouching on the pavement was not someone dying from a bullet wound, but a sightless beggar who mumbled a response when she placed a coin in his hand.

There was something strangely comforting about the new city sounds; the chattering of people as they strolled by, tourists mingling with the throng, pausing to browse at the book stalls, or selecting a bunch of flowers, each lifting her out of the past. Yet, deep inside, she longed to go back in time, to recapture her meeting with Maurici, feeling strangely compelled to return to the places she had known years ago and continued down the busy tree-lined avenue.

The jeweller's shop where she had first sought cover now displayed entirely different wares, and the hotel opposite where the horse had fallen whilst she had sheltered from the gunfire, was no longer boarded up and closed. Crossing the wide avenue, she paused in the shade of the busy entrance and leant against the spotless woodwork, her thoughts dwelling on the man she truly loved. She clutched the handle of her bag, as if she were holding the barrel of a gun, and pictured his face as she'd seen it when she had opened her eyes to him that day. She could picture him clearly yet, and however hard she tried to recall how it had then been, there was no smell of cordite in the air, no dust and torn posters swirling round her feet.

She lingered a moment, her head lowered, eyes misty behind the dark lens of her sunglasses, trying to recapture the atmosphere of more than seventeen years ago. The sound of a Catalan greeting came back to her. "*Bon dia, senyoreta!*" And a familiar voice asked, "S'ha perdut?" just as she remembered... and for a heart-stopping moment she felt warm hands take hers, part of one finger missing.

"Maurici!" she gasped. "Oh, Maurici, I can't believe it!"

"Elizabeth," he said brokenly, his dark eyes glittering, "you are not lost, you came back."

Drawing her towards him he kissed her, and for a few precious moments they simply gazed at each other in wonderment until her sob of emotion broke the spell.

"I can't believe you're really here," she gasped. "After all these years... the same place."

He looked down on her and smiled. "And you remembered," he said huskily. "I had been hoping you would come here."

She stared up at him in amazement. "How could you know?"

She broke off as he raised her fingers to his lips before he murmured, "I was sure, if you still loved me, you would come here to recapture the memories because they mean something special to you."

"Oh they do, they really do," she responded breathlessly. "But what brought you here, how did you know?"

"I knew you were in Barcelona, so I came here hoping to find you," he said simply. "I love you, Elizabeth, and this time I will not let you go."

"The children are with me," she told him. "They are with Enric..."

"Children?" he queried in mock surprise, holding her at arm's length. But a smile flickered on his mouth as he said, "You mean, Serena, and Timoteu?"

"You knew?" she whispered, looking up anxiously as she explained, "I wanted to arrange a meeting for them, but I didn't know your situation, what your reaction would be."

"He smiled. "My reaction is one of pleasure, Elizabeth. I understand our son also looks like me."

"Enric must have told you..." she began, then glanced at her watch. "Oh, I promised to join them for lunch. They'll wonder where I am."

"Merely a ruse on Enric's part," he smiled. "Don't worry, he will take them back. Meanwhile, you and I have a lot to discuss before Jaume comes home at five. Then I will drive you both to Sitges and meet the rest of my family."

"I must tell you all that has happened since we met in London in forty-seven."

He took her hand. "*Bé*, I know a quiet little restaurant not far from here."

They had gone only a short distance when he paused to ask, "But before we speak of anything else, I must know, Elizabeth, will you be my wife?"

Displaying the amethyst ring on her finger, she nodded, "Yes, Maurici. I love you still."

He smiled. "On our wedding day there will be a great celebration, just as I once promised."

"And fireworks in the morning," she murmured, all sad memories fading. Her eyes were shining as she implored, "Darling Maurici, tell me this is really happening, not just another dream."

Gazing down on her he uttered a tiny groan, his eyes growing dark with emotion as he said almost fiercely, "Elizabeth, believe me, this is not a dream." Then, with a sensual movement of his lips, he added a whispered, "I want you so much," as they continued on their way.

**